YO-DTB-705

The
War
was
lost
but
still
they
fought
on—

★ From all sides ragged rebels swarmed into San Antonio to join up with General Joe Shelby, whose famous Iron Brigade was bound for Mexico to wage new war on the Union from there.

★ On the heels of the recruits came Southerners of every stripe—profiteers, adventurers, ruined aristocrats, political exiles—all lured by a heady new dream of establishing a new Confederacy south of the border.

★ What lay ahead for them all was incredible danger, hardship and betrayal in a primitive land. Could this new life, so utterly different from what they all envisioned, burn away their bitterness, bring them peace at last?

# WEST OF APPOMATTOX
was originally published
by Appleton-Century-Crofts.

*Are there paperbound books you want but cannot find at your retail stores?*

You can get any title that is in print in these famous series: POCKET BOOK EDITIONS • CARDINAL EDITIONS • PERMABOOK EDITIONS THE POCKET LIBRARY • WASHINGTON SQUARE PRESS • ALL SAINTS PRESS Simply enclose retail price plus 10¢ per book for mailing and handling costs. Not responsible for orders containing cash. Please send check or money order to.....Mail Service Dept.
Pocket Books, Inc.
1 West 39th Street
New York 18, N. Y.

*Free catalogue sent on request*

# HARLEY DUNCAN WEST OF APPOMATTOX

A PERMABOOK EDITION published by POCKET BOOKS, INC. • NEW YORK

*West of Appomattox*

Appleton-Century-Crofts edition published October, 1961

A *Permabook* edition
1st printing.......................June, 1963

All names, characters, and events, other than historical personages and situations, are fictional. Any resemblance which may seem to exist to real persons is purely coincidental.

This *Permabook** edition includes every word contained in the original, higher-priced edition. It is printed from brand-new plates made from completely reset, clear, easy-to-read type. *Permabook* editions are published by Pocket Books, Inc., and are printed and distributed in the U.S.A. by Affiliated Publishers, a division of Pocket Books, Inc., 630 Fifth Avenue, New York 20, N.Y. *Trademarks of Pocket Books, Inc., 630 Fifth Avenue, New York 20, N.Y., in the United States and other countries.

Copyright, ©, 1961, by Harley Duncan. All rights reserved. This *Permabook* edition is published by arrangement with Appleton-Century-Crofts, Inc.
*Printed in the U.S.A.*

The author is indebted to the staff of the Arcadia (California) Public Library for its aid in locating and obtaining research material.

# WEST OF
# APPOMATTOX

# 1

THE YELLOW TEXAS PRAIRIE, for all its hidden dangers, was an old friend to Dan Kilbourne. Long before the first rumblings of a war some people thought had finally stopped two months ago at Appomattox Court House, he had come to know the endless, sometimes malicious tricks the vast land could play with the aid of sun and shadow.

But the silent wagons semicircled about the small stand of cottonwoods and willows were real. Now he could make out, in mottled shadows, the "CSA" markings on rough canvas covers. He rode closer, uncomfortably aware that the blue of his uniform stood out stark and shiny against the sere grass, a prime target for a whistling minnie ball.

He pulled up behind the rear wagon, listened, heard nothing but faint wooden creaks caused by the warming air.

A man could take little for granted in this country, but it seemed a fair bet that he was alone. More than likely, he reasoned, the five vehicles had simply been pillaged and abandoned when some stray rider had brought word that two weeks ago Kirby Smith had surrendered the last of the three great Confederate armies. The troops had taken the mules and whatever else was loose, and started the long trek to Shreveport to add their arms to Smith's sword; or maybe they had gone instead to join the Missouri brigade which formed the core of those who intended to fight on.

Dan began to poke into the rear wagon. He was a tall man, two inches over six feet and appearing taller because of his gauntness. At twenty-eight the strength of his wide shoulders and big, hard hands was rightly mirrored in his taut angular face. Deepset black eyes, burning now with a fever that came intermittently, scanned the contents of the wagon from beneath solid black brows.

Nothing. Only empty boxes, thoroughly ransacked of the tinned foodstuffs they had contained. Supplies against the coming hard times? Or supplies for a fighting army?

He rode on down the line, remembering the words of the old teamster who had shared his campfire yesterday morning.

"Most of the Rebs are stragglin' in to give up, right enough," the old-timer had admitted. "But some are swarmin' together like yaller jackets and wavin' their guns like tommyhawks. This feller Shelby's the ringleader—him an' part of his Missouri outfit. They're figgerin' on doin' some fast recruitin'—afore Texas gets occupied—an' then goin' to Mexico. Say they'll fight on from there, however best they can."

Glad of an audience, he had talked on about Confederate detachments threatening to waylay the oncoming Yankees, running roughshod over their own people in the meantime. But Dan had heard little beyond the news of an army that refused to surrender. He had thought of little else since.

The third vehicle he searched contained the uniforms he was seeking, but most were rags. Old clothes had been traded for new, and only the old were left. The one coat he could have squeezed into was ripped down the back from collar to hem.

He rode on, easing himself around in his saddle. The half-healed wound in his side acted up spasmodically as though to remind him of the cause of his fever. Now it was pushing hot claws out across his belly.

The heat vanished as quickly as it had come. He slacked Cromwell's reins and began to study the sign as they went along.

2

The trampled grass showed that several days ago more than two dozen mules had left the camp ground, heading east. Yesterday a shod horse had ridden a course paralleling the wagons. This morning two unshod ponies had been here.

This last caused him to look up, but he saw no slashed or torn canvas tops to bespeak Indian mischief, and the undisturbed burble of a mockingbird claimed that no enemy lurked in the trees. He went on, stopping twice more to poke aside loose canvas flaps.

One of the remaining vehicles had contained rifles and ammunition, as evidenced by the labels on four gaping, emptied boxes. The last vehicle, like the first, had held several cartons of food. It still contained a scattering of crumpled messware. Dan loosened his hold on the endgate and guided the sorrel back to the third wagon.

Another look convinced him. He took the coat with the split back, folded it, and stuffed it into his saddlebag. When he camped tonight he could sew up this rip with something—a thong if he could find nothing else. His spirits rose and he was surprised to find himself humming "The Bonnie Blue Flag." The sounds issued harshly from his dry throat; except for a few words to the old teamster and an occasional word to his horse, he hadn't spoken aloud in over a week.

Still humming he turned and rode toward the remnants of charred sticks that appeared to have been kindled last night over the ashes left by the soldiers.

He saw then the dead Comanche lying behind the nearest tree. He stopped humming in midbar. The Indian still clutched a rifle barrel. The weapon's walnut butt was freshly stained red; it had clubbed a man before the bullet tore into the painted chest.

The unshod pony tracks said there had been two Indians; the paint suggested that more could not be far away. A pair of Indians might not hesitate to ride into disputed territory—now that the outlying forts had not been properly manned for four years—but two didn't make a war party.

In the sultry stillness a trickle of sweat stung its way into the wound. Dan let it go unchecked as his eyes probed and poked into every shadow.

A spot of color appeared through the grass and his revolver leaped out to cover it. He guided the sorrel closer and found the second Indian. The buck's hand still stretched toward the horse pistol he had fought to recover as the life poured from a severed vein in his neck.

If the fever had not been burning in him, Dan might have ridden a circle around the camp area before this. He started one now and quickly came to a sign that was easy enough for trained eyes to read.

Two people had stayed here last night. One, a man inclined toward heaviness, had arrived on a big horse, with a loaded pack mule in tow. The other, a boy to judge by the size of the booted feet, had come along later in a buggy pulled by a smaller horse. This morning, after the man had been clubbed, the boy had tried to lift his body into the buggy, but being unable to do so had constructed a travois and rolled him into it.

Now the wounded man was being bumped and jostled across the prairie at the tail end of a strange procession. For the horse which pulled the travois was following the led mule, which in turn was following the buggy.

Dan stared in the direction the travois had taken, sitting stock-still to let his vision grow accustomed to the vast distances. At last he detected movement—several specks threading quickly around the crest of a moundlike hill far to the east. The rest of the war party, if his guess were right.

His eyes swung back toward the scuffed clearing where the travois had been assembled as he searched for something he had only half-seen before. They stopped as he spotted it—a small brown comb that had been pressed into the ground by a heavy, stomping hoof. The comb was

4

curved in a manner that suggested the driver of the buggy might have been a girl.

He examined the footprints and was certain.

He slid his revolver back into its holster, wondering if she knew that she was guiding the buggy directly toward the Indians.

The strands of loose hair that scraped at Jane Morgen's eyes were a lashing torment. She saw each blow of the hatchet through a pale brown waving blur. But she continued to hack and chop at the buggy's sideboard with a desperation born of remembering the awful terror that lived in the Warrick girl's eyes because she had seen her parents slowly and mercilessly cut to death by Comanches.

Her own father lay crumpled on the ground far behind the buggy. One leg of the travois had broken, spilling him from the thin bedroll quilt. He was still unconscious, and blood still trickled from the swollen purple wound on his scalp.

The hatchet fell again and again, but half the blows were badly aimed. Stinging sweat poured into her eyes and she wiped at them with aching shoulders. The lump in her throat grew bigger as she castigated herself. If she hadn't goaded the horse the instant she saw the Indians, the travois might never have broken.

The Indians had looked no bigger than coyotes then, but now she could tell when one waved his arms.

Chips flew and the top of the sideboard splintered into unusable fragments. She tried to get a grip on herself. Unless she took her time she could tear the entire buggy apart bit by bit and never get a brace big enough to hold. Why couldn't she stop trembling?

She tried to take courage from the things she had done already today. She had killed a man. She had taken a close look at him to make certain he was dead, had looked also at the one her father had shot during the first shock of the unexpected attack. She had reloaded the heavy pistol and found the strength to drag her father's heavy body to the buggy. Then, discovering that she couldn't lift him, she had cut branches and built the travois. Fear had given her the strength to do these things instead of sapping her energy as it was doing now.

She swung again, two-handed, and the wood split into a section big enough to brace the travois. She grabbed it, running rough splinters into her slim, bleeding hands. She shortened it with a few quick, uneven blows and hurried back to the travois.

She paused for a moment to straighten Wil Morgen's head, to listen for his stertorous breathing. He was still the same. She made up her mind not to look toward the Indians again. To keep herself from hurrying too frantically, she would pretend that they were not there.

She used a bandanna to tie the brace in one place and her belt to bind it higher up. Her hair streaked again into her eyes. She had long since lost the hat which, along with her brother's old levis, she had hoped would make her look like a boy as she pursued her father from the settlement. Now the sun beat down and her head ached until she could hardly think.

She finished tying the brace and shoved her hands beneath her father's wet armpits. She pulled hard, but this morning's strength had burned out; his body refused to budge. She pulled again and he moved a bare inch, then settled into a shallow depression with a finality that exhausted her.

Now she couldn't keep from looking up. There were five of the Indians, so close that she could see bare skin glistening.

She hurried almost blindly back to the buggy, got the pistol, her father's rifle and a small canteen. If only Wil could come to long enough to talk to her!

At his side again she poured water into his eyes and splashed it into his mouth until he nearly strangled. "Daddy? Wil—please!"

He coughed weakly, but his eyes remained closed. She capped the canteen and let it slip from raw fingers as she sank down beside him. It was no use. She readied the rifle and the pistol and waited mutely.

The Indians rode toward her with the unhurried calm that grew out of certainty. Her mind rebelled at their coming and she began a frantic search for some past turning that would cause her not to be here.

It was only a week since she and Wil had returned from Galveston to the weed-grown farm that had turned wild during four years of war. A day later her brother Bill had come back, one-handed and bitter and newly discharged from Johnston's army. With him was the stoop-shouldered giant, Cogan, whose life he had saved during the war. The family was together again, home to stay, Wil had promised.

But it was a time of roiling restlessness—after defeat and before occupation—and none of them felt any kinship with the predominantly pro-Union German immigrants in the settlement. High feelings were rampant and shortly Bill and Cogan had angrily set off to join General Shelby who, rumor said, was not going to surrender. The next day Wil had received word from San Antonio that Reed Marman wanted him to guide a wagon train of Southern refugees to Mexico, and had set out as quickly as he could arrange it. Jane, left with the Marcus family, followed four hours later, foolish as it was to travel without escort in this country. If she had to live with strangers, it would not be with someone who criticized her father and brother and expected her to listen in silence!

She wiped her brow with a damp sleeve. It was too late to change anything, but she could take some small comfort in the fact, that, by following Wil, she had at least prolonged his life, even if she couldn't save it.

The five silent Indians were almost within range now and she grimly decided that she would not consider taking her own life or Wil's. She would get hold of herself, fight

7

as long as she had a breath. Hands that were raw and bleeding and shaking would have to become steady and unfeeling. Eyes that ached and burned from the heat and the glare would have to sight coolly down a hot steel barrel and align iron sights on a bare painted chest as they had done once before this morning.

Low thuds sounded behind her and she screamed and turned, raising the rifle. She had all but pulled the trigger when she saw, with complete disbelief, the tall soldier in the blue uniform. Intense black eyes burned at her from beneath the bill of his blue forage cap.

She stared, unable to speak. All morning she had hoped to stumble into the party of Mexicans her father was to meet somewhere this side of San Antonio. But the sight of a Federal soldier was more than her mind could believe.

A rifle came with him as he swung down from his slick stock saddle. He touched the bill of his cap by way of greeting, looked gravely at her father and said, "This Sharps will reach. Maybe I'd better lower the odds some before they get any closer."

As he knelt down and shifted to get comfortable, the Indians fanned out. They stopped at the signal of a raised rifle and argued impatiently while the lead Indian peered intently at the buggy.

The upraised rifle came down like a shot. Sharp yells split the air and the ponies surged forward. The soldier's gun spoke and the lead Indian slumped forward. His weapon slipped from his fingers and he veered aside, but the other four galloped on.

As the soldier reloaded he said, "Pick out one and hold your fire until he's right on top of you. Shoot when you can't miss." In spite of the uniform his accent was Texan. She knew a brief, irrational sense of relief.

The soldier's gun came up again, but he waited with a stoic patience that bolstered her own shaky hands. She gathered all her courage and concentrated on a single Comanche as he had suggested.

Chilling whoops knifed through the thunder of ground-shaking hoofbeats. Rifles cracked and bullets cut through the high grass. Her frightened horse pulled the buggy forward several feet. The tied pack mule tried to bolt, dragging the buggy sideways. She cried out, but held her nerve. The Indian she was watching was almost upon them. She waited, filled with some unreasoning assurance that his death would bring safety.

She shrank as the pony loomed big, as flying hoofs threatened to chop her to pieces. Lathered hair glistened as the horse swerved left and the Indian made a flying leap from its back. She pulled the trigger and he landed convulsively at her feet. The shock was so great that she expected a word of congratulation as she turned toward the soldier.

The confusion that met her eyes brought her to her feet. The bluecoat and one of the Indians were spinning in a mad, grappling dance. A second Comanche, shot in the leg, was crawling away, but one was still mounted. He had ridden past and was whirling his horse to charge back.

She dropped the empty rifle and scooped up the pistol. Holding it in both hands she fired and missed.

At the same instant the soldier managed to break his attacker's hold and fling him aside. The soldier's revolver leaped up, fired two rapid shots, and the mounted buck slid heavily from his pony.

The lone unwounded Comanche was bent low in erratic flight through the tall grass.

She suddenly remembered the one who had been hit in the leg. He was gone—had somehow caught a pony, crawled onto its back, and was moving away at a stiff, ludicrous trot.

The prairie began to rise and fall in long, uneven waves of hot yellow, causing her head to sway slowly to match its uncertain rhythm. The waves grew smaller; the earth, still hot and yellow, settled to a familiar shimmering. She breathed deeply, turned and knelt beside her father to make sure he had not been further hurt.

He was untouched and the purple bruise on his scalp had stopped bleeding. If only his breathing weren't so hoarse! She began to dab gently at the wound until hard fingers touched her shoulder. She flinched and stared up into a gaunt face, into dark eyes that burned feverishly.

"Ma'am, we'd better get him into that buggy and strike out." His brittle words were urgent. "We've got more visitors coming, though they might be Mexicans this time."

She said, "Mexicans?" and brightened. "Thank God! My father was supposed to meet some Mexicans. But I didn't know where." She looked up at him and in the heat he seemed shadowy and indistinct. She shuddered for fear he would disappear and she would find that the Indians were still swooping down on her and the fight had not yet begun.

He took her elbow and helped her to her feet, seeming to stagger as he did so.

She felt a quick concern.

"I'm all right, ma'am," he said hastily. He looked out across the prairie. "Especially now. Those are Mexicans, right enough."

He bent over her father, carefully turning the swollen head to one side. "Well," he said finally, "he'd be better off in bed, but I'd say he'll be good enough in a few days." He spilled water from the canteen onto the bruise and allowed a trickle to seep between the puffed lips. "We'll give him more in a minute or two." He pushed himself up and stood so that his shadow protected Wil's face. "I'll shade him until you can cover his head."

She hurried to the buggy and dragged a dress from her small trunk, furious with herself because she hadn't done it before. Why, he had practically been broiling all this time just because she was thoughtless! She came back and made a sort of bonnet that shut out the sun without interfering with his breathing.

She stood up wearily and found the soldier looking at her with faint amusement.

"I'm Dan Kilbourne," he said. "When I first saw your tracks, back at the wagons, I thought you were a boy."

She managed a weak smile. "I'm Jane Morgen, and this is my father, Wilhelm—Wil. He was hit . . . there . . . this morning. By another Comanche."

Dan nodded as he found his cap and put it on. "You'd better get something on your head, too," he suggested.

She stood looking at him. "We'd . . . be dead if you hadn't helped us." She looked toward one of the dead Indians and shuddered. "Maybe we—that is, if we could do something for you—"

He seemed to study her carefully before he turned in the direction of the approaching Mexicans. He did some figuring. "They'll be here in less than ten minutes. If you're up to it, there is something you can do in the meantime—provided you've got a sewing kit. It's important, or I wouldn't ask."

She said wonderingly, "Yes, I've got needles and three or four kinds of thread."

He walked over to his grazing horse, ran his hand into a saddlebag, and pulled out a badly crumpled gray coat. He brought it back to her and held it out. "If you could sew up this seam in back, I'd appreciate it. I intended to do it myself, but I got short on time."

She looked up at him with disbelief; it must be some kind of joke. But she met the same stoic gaze, the same flat mouth and deepset, burning black eyes she had seen while he waited for the Indians.

"Why—why, of course." She wished it weren't so hot and humid. Everything might make more sense then. She took the coat and he followed close behind her as she wearily walked toward the buggy.

"If you can work on the ground I'll try to fix your dad a place in here." His hand waved loosely at the buggy.

"Thank you," she said fervently. She opened the small

11

trunk, rummaged through it and got out a sewing kit. As an afterthought she found a bonnet and slipped it on.

She climbed down and settled herself up against a thin wheel, facing away from the Indians. She examined the scratchy gray wool. She would have to work carefully; the material was so worn in some places that the thread might tear through. She wondered if he'd gotten it from one of the wagons where they'd—had the trouble this morning.

As she began to sew she couldn't help wondering why he hadn't given some explanation. She knew Buchanan's Secretary of War had seen to it that Southern arsenals were bursting with war materiel, including uniforms, before the fighting had started. Blue had virtually been standard in Southern armies for a long time. But if he were outfitted like this because gray was scarce, why hadn't he explained? It wouldn't make sense anyway, after four years.

She looked up at him as he wielded the hatchet on the buggy seat. He had shed his coat and she gasped at the raw puckered wound that seemed to lean against one of the suspenders plastered to his bare torso.

She grew ashamed. She had no right to ask any explanations. He hadn't questioned her; he had simply ridden up and helped.

She continued to sew, looking up at him from time to time as the hatchet pounded metal. The sweat was pouring down his back in little rivulets; the light blue trousers were soaked where they hugged his narrow waist.

The buggy seat gave with a splintering crash just as she bit off the thread. He turned toward her, panting, and she held up the coat.

"I'm finished, but I'm afraid it won't last long. The material is rotten."

He took it and put the hatchet down. "It'll do," he said. "Thanks." He picked up the blue coat, looked around him, and walked toward an eroded mound of dirt up against a bush. The mound marked an abandoned, half-filled badger's burrow. He stuffed the blue coat into the hole, then reluctantly added his cap. His boot soles scraped up loose soil and kicked it after them as his arms struggled into the gray sleeves.

When he came back he said lightly, "I'm indebted to you." His hand was unsteady, but then he must be exhausted. She marveled at the things he had done; another man with a jagged wound like Dan Kilbourne's would have been in a sick bed.

She again silenced the questions that came to her lips. He must have noticed, for she was sure he was amused as he busied himself dismantling the travois and bringing the quilt to the buggy. The sun was hot enough to boil blood and her body was caked with dirt and grit. She wondered how he managed to keep going.

"We were on our way to San Antonio," she volunteered. "Are you—do you know this part of the country?"

He paused beside the buggy. "Yes, my father's ranch—my ranch," he corrected himself, "is about fifty miles from here." He seemed about to say more, but changed his mind and set back to work as one of the loose Indian ponies trotted up, nickering at the oncoming Mexicans.

There were six of them, all in uniform. They were riding at a fast walk now, but the horses were heavily lathered; most of the last several miles had been covered at a dead run.

The lead soldier was a slight man, dark complexioned and no taller than she. He looked more Indian than Spanish. He waved to her while he was still fifty yards away.

"Lieutenant Esteban!" Though she had met him only once, he was an old friend of Wil's, was, in fact, here because Wil wanted to arrange through him to get Juarez' protection for the wagon train he was taking to Mexico. She ran to meet him.

His eyes were sharp and took in everything at a glance as he reined up. "Your father?" he asked at once.

13

"He's hurt, but Mr. Kilbourne, the . . . soldier there . . . says he'll be all right."

The lieutenant spoke rapidly in soft Spanish and two of his men dismounted to go to Wil. The officer looked toward Dan.

"You travel with only one escort?" he asked sternly.

"With none. If he hadn't come along we'd be dead."

Dan was walking up to them now and she introduced him to the lieutenant. As they shook hands she said, "Will you—be able to stay with us, Lieutenant? Please?"

"Of course, Señorita. We will escort you from here." Esteban spoke to another of his men, who climbed down with a canteen and started for the buggy where his fellow soldiers were already struggling to lift Wil's unconscious body.

The lieutenant's attention returned to Dan. "I have known many soldiers in both your armies. It is a strange uniform you wear."

Dan grinned. "Not too strange. You can find it listed in the Confederate book. But I'd say yours was a little bit unusual in this country."

Esteban's face grew solemn. "Yes, you are right." He sighed. "It would seem," he said sorrowfully, "that no country could be more broken than yours. In the North the President lies dead of an assassin's bullet and the Congress does not respect his successor. In the South entire cities are without order, as your Southern officials flee Federal vengeance.

"But my country fares worse. An Austrian emperor sits on a Mexican throne raised by French bayonets. Because of this many of us have taken refuge. But we will go back."

"If what I've heard about General Shelby is true," Dan said, "I might be with you. I'm hoping to join his army when we get to San Antonio."

Esteban did not answer until the silence had grown heavy. "I have heard that General Shelby is a powerful

14

man and a fearless leader," he said at last. "And I have heard that he refuses to surrender. Beyond that—*quién sabe?*"

"Meaning what?" Dan asked.

"Perhaps he will not come to Mexico. Or if he does, he might fight for the French. Or for himself. One cannot tell the future!"

"Whatever he does will be for the South," Dan said. "It would have to be. He's all of the Confederacy that's left."

"It may be that you are right."

"But I thought—" Jane's eyes darted to the badger mound, back to Dan's face. "I thought you had a ranch nearby."

He nodded. "It doesn't change anything."

"Señorita," Esteban said softly, "with your permission we must start. It is still many miles to San Antonio."

Gratefully, Jane agreed, and began trudging back to the buggy. Each step she took was more exhausting than the last, but the very pain of walking served to remind her that if Dan Kilbourne hadn't come along she would now be lying dead, staring skyward with sightless eyes like the Indians they were leaving. It was something she must never forget.

# 2

LIEUTENANT MANUEL ESTEBAN possessed a rude store of frontier medical knowledge and a large core of common sense; by late afternoon Wil Morgen was sitting up in the swaying buggy. He was stiff, his slightly rotund face had acquired a fresh burn over its deep, prairie-weathered tan, and his head required frequent holding, but otherwise he seemed none the worse for this morning's fight.

Dan, riding point with a Mexican corporal, didn't hear what Jane told him but his gratitude was expressed in terms that were embarrassing.

Dan tried to shrug away the voluble praise, but Wil was insistent. "You ever need anything, you just call on the Morgens, y'hear?" His inflection was predominantly Southern, but he was German-born, and traces of his mother tongue were sprinkled through his words.

"Now, Daddy, let him alone," Jane said softly.

She was so slight of build that Dan wondered at the strength she had shown this morning. In spite of the rounded bosom pushing at her shirt, she was a trifle slim for most men's tastes, he decided, though not what any man in his right mind would call skinny. Her face was slim as well; high cheekbones and a narrow straight nose gave her a patrician look that was softened by her gently rounded chin. She handled the buggy horse with quiet composure, but her blue eyes reflected the heat and exhaustion that had nearly overtaken her. Dan grinned. He could understand the senseless stubbornness that made her refuse to let someone else drive; he might have done the same thing.

Esteban was up ahead now. From the peak of a nearby hill he waved for them to stop, then came back at a slow trot. "San Antonio is but nine miles to the east," he said. "It will be an easy journey in the morning."

"Then I'll be leaving you," Dan said. "I'd like to be sure I don't miss Shelby."

"That is your right, Señor," Esteban agreed readily. "But our friends the Morgens must have rest and tomorrow there will still be danger for them."

"Meaning?"

"My men and I—we cannot escort them into the city. We are foreign soldiers, and who knows what might be reported of us to that Yankee soldier Sheridan? That is a man I do not want looking for me!"

"Then I guess I'd better wait."

Esteban smiled at his disappointment. "Can one night mean so much?"

"If he wants to go on," Jane protested, "it wouldn't be right to keep him, and I'm sure we'll be safe now."

"I'm sorry," Dan apologized. "I didn't mean for it to sound the way it did. I'll be glad to wait."

Stars were twinkling in the deep black sky and a moon as orange as the campfire hung low on the horizon when the last of the beans and tortillas had been scraped from tin plates.

Esteban posted his sentries and one by one the rest of the Mexican soldiers wrapped themselves in serapes and stretched out on the warm, hard ground. Their snores soon softened the scratchy serenade of the katydids.

Dan and the Morgens remained at the campfire to drink a last cup of bitter, strong coffee.

Wil blew steam from his tin cup. "Jane thinks I'm too old to go chasing off to a new land," he complained. "But Mexico is not new to me. I ran wagon trains the length and breadth of it before and during the war."

"It won't be the same," Jane patiently pointed out. "We're going there to live, to become Mexicans."

"Not in the true sense," Wil argued. "As Reed Marman puts it—he's the one behind everything—we're going there to form the core of the new South."

"But why?" Dan asked. "There's plenty of open land in Texas."

"Texas will be occupied soon, and the Yankees will take their vengeance. A colony in Mexico is the only chance some people will have to build again."

"Maybe that depends on what they try to build."

"I can tell you exactly what they want," Wil said. "They want the South—like it was before the war. It's not as impossible as it sounds, either. The people we're taking will not be dreamers. They'll be practical men—judges, senators, high-ranking Confederate officers—people who know how to get things done. Some will be going because

17

they can't stand to see things changed, as they're bound to change in this country; I'll admit that. Some will even be going because they just can't stand the thought of living under Yankee rule. But most of 'em have no choice; it's that or a Yankee prison. Maybe worse than prison."

"Are you one of those?" Dan asked.

"No, I don't guess so," Wil said, "though I did haul lots of supplies for the South. That might be enough. There's no way to tell till the Yankees get here."

"The uncertainty is the worst of it," Jane said. "Not just for us. For everybody. We have only a few days left, and nobody knows what will happen." Her eyes swept over Dan's Confederate coat and tension crept into her voice. "We only know that after four years of fighting we can't hope for anything very pleasant."

"Well," Wil said, "it's a time for people to decide things. This is where we are after four years; we can throw up our hands, or we can try to set things right, each in his own way."

Dan nodded. "If Shelby's army is real, and not just talk, my way is with him," he said firmly. "Right or wrong."

"And mine's the colony, right or wrong," Wil replied. "Texas is the gathering place for all those who are running —their last refuge in this country. The next jump is Mexico, and some will have to take it. I'm going to help all I can."

The shadows alternately hid and highlighted the purple bruise on his head. He touched it and groaned.

"If Jane hadn't already shot dot Indian, I'd go after him right now." He was worn out and his words were growing more gutteral.

"We'd better fix you a place in the buggy," Dan said.

Wil nodded, grimacing as his head moved. Jane and Dan each took one of his arms and helped him up, then Jane began to rummage through her trunk for cotton petticoats to make his bed softer. The faint smell of carnation floated out to Dan.

"I wish you wouldn't join Shelby," Wil said. "I wish you'd come with us instead. I'd think you'd be tired of wearing a uniform."

"Maybe I am a little." Dan boosted him up. "I wouldn't join up with any other outfit."

Jane looked at him peculiarly. "It . . . seems strange. . . ."

"I suppose. But these are strange times."

"You're right," Wil said. He was breathing heavily from exertion. "A war . . . cuts people loose. When it's over we . . . run in all directions . . . looking for a fresh start."

"I'd say this war wasn't over," Dan answered. "Not till Shelby surrenders, or is taken." He helped Wil lie flat, then braced himself as exhaustion nearly overtook him. "Wil, sleep well. Miss Jane, good night. I'll see you both in the morning. Before that if you need me for anything."

He turned and made his slow way to his own bedroll. He wearily shook it out and spread it on a bare spot of ground. He sank down to his knees and rolled onto it with a motion that sent his brain spinning. The stars overhead, hot needles of searing light, jabbed at him and the burning pain in his side reached out across his belly. He lay unmoving, satisfied to pay for the luxury of stretching out.

The pain in his side lessened. The night cooled and the fever began to leave him. He must have dropped off suddenly, into the soundest sleep he had known in a week. He did not consciously stir until he awoke at the first feeble hint of daylight and sat up, gripping his pistol.

He couldn't make out any sounds that didn't belong with the night, but something had snapped him wide awake. He tucked in his shirt and heaved himself up to stand on slippery, dew-wet grass. A short look around convinced him that he must have been dreaming, or that whatever he had heard was only a remembrance from the past. He wet his face with a few drops of water from his canteen and then walked toward the nearby hill, nodding at the Mexican sentry as he passed. His silhouette would make a perfect target, he thought; he must stop before he reached the top. He smiled ruefully. Target for what? Indians seldom attacked at night, and he had no reason to believe that soldiers lay hidden out here in nervous readiness to fire at shadows.

He sat down and closed his eyes, but a dark mood had fallen on him. He saw racing battle flags and puffs of wind-whipped white smoke. He heard the reports of heavy guns and the roll of drums. Men scurried everywhere and screamed as the horses ran them down and tore their flesh.

Jane came up behind him to wrench his mind from the past. She had changed the levis and the dirty crumpled shirt for a full-skirted riding habit. Her hair, unbound now, cascaded down her back and gleamed softly in the pale moonlight.

"If I shut my eyes I see the Indians," she explained. She sat down near him.

"We're a nightmarish lot," Dan said.

She pulled up three long blades of Johnson grass and began plaiting them. He stretched out beside her and propped his cheek on his fist, feeling the itchy growth of whiskers. He watched the green braid grow under her nimble fingers. She was comfortable to be with, but she was building her courage to say something. Raw hands would never have been so busy if she weren't. He waited.

"You saved my life," she said finally.

"We've already talked about that. You did me a favor, too."

"Yes, I just . . . wanted you to know that I won't forget that you didn't have to take the risk. What I mean is, I'll never . . . say anything I shouldn't."

"I'm grateful. And I'm sorry for the burden I've put on you." He cocked an ear to listen. "Do you hear something? Beyond the hill? I'd better call Esteban." He leaned down and put his ear to the ground. The steady chopping sounds of hard hoofs rolled through the earth.

He took her hand and pulled her up with him and they ran down the slope toward camp. It was light enough now

20

to see that the sentries had also heard. The soldiers were up and catching their horses.

Dan ran to where his sorrel was staked. A cavalry soldier was as lost without his horse as a cowboy, he thought. And he was part cowboy, part cavalryman.

As he tightened the cinch around the wind-puffed belly and knotted his latigo, Esteban rode up alongside him. Dan swung into his saddle and whirled the sorrel. They touched spurs to lean flanks and raced together toward the hill, closely followed by the Mexican corporal.

Near the peak they dismounted and Esteban signaled to keep low; it would be light east of the hill. They hugged the ground, elbowing their way up the last few feet until they could see over the highest ridge.

Below them, in full panoply of battle array, a gray-clad regiment of cavalry rode at a rapid trot toward San Antonio. A scarlet flag, crossed with star-studded blue, flew proudly from the booted scabbard of the first horseman. Behind the flag-bearer rode a short, bearded officer with a black plume waving from his hat. Then, by fours —booted and spurred and armed to the teeth—the only unsurrendered arm of the Confederacy came on.

The soldiers must have been weary from the night's ride, but they sat in their saddles with pride and assurance. And well they might have, Dan knew; for the Missouri cavalry had more than once stormed its way through grape and cannister and musket fire, and its soldiers had more than once stood their ground dismounted, sometimes in dense foliage where the powder smoke hung so heavy that a man had to take it on trust that his companions were still with him.

Behind the main body of soldiers came the cannon and the wagons to testify that this was no band of hastily organized militia, but an army of trained professional soldiers.

"It is a sight," Esteban breathed.

"A sight," Dan agreed. "Not just a rumor passed on from camp to camp; it's there and it's real."

The emotion in his voice caused Lieutenant Esteban to turn his head toward Dan and stare.

When they came onto one of the rutted wagon roads that led into San Antonio, Manuel Esteban threw up his arm to halt his detachment.

He said goodbye to the Morgens first. "I will see you both in Mexico," he promised. He shook hands with Dan. "And you, Dan—if we meet again one hopes that we are on the same side!"

He saluted them all, waving away their thanks.

Jane said goodbye again, but it was useless to try to express all the gratitude she felt. She began to wind a pale blue stock around her neck as she looked at the town ahead. From here it seemed to be no more than a collection of stark adobe and stone buildings set apart by littered dirt streets; but it was civilization and a woman had to look feminine if she could. She finished tying the knot and urged the buggy horse forward.

Wil Morgen had also changed clothes this morning and had donned a wide-brimmed hat which he constantly readjusted as the buggy lurched across ruts and potholes.

"Careful, girl!" he groaned.

"I am being careful, Daddy," she assured him. She tried to keep all her attention on the horse, but it was hard not to stare at Dan from time to time. She wished she didn't know about the uniform. Whatever it might mean, he was pretending to be something he was not.

The buggy wound its way into the crowded town. She guided it onto Commerce Street and was surprised to see that gray-uniformed soldiers stood watch on corner after corner.

They didn't look like the men she'd seen straggling through Galveston last week. Those had been ashamed and angry; defeat was stamped on them, and they hid it behind a bitter belligerence. But these were Shelby's men; they had a purpose, and it showed. She was a little proud of them, and at the same time worried. An army with no country to fight for could become a weapon for one man's ambition, or it could disintegrate and wreck the land for a hundred miles around.

Certainly these things were not really possible, she hastily reassured herself. It was far more likely that Shelby's army would help people like Reed Marman start their colonies, thereby bringing new hope to political exiles. And while she was not enthusiastic about Marman's, or any other colony, it was the only hope she had that her father might at last settle down; that Bill would have a home to come back to.

Yes, she thought, these soldiers could do a lot that was good, and she wished Dan were not planning some deception against them.

She stopped the buggy horse by the hitchrail in front of the Menger Hotel and let Dan lift her down as Wil, groaning all the while, heaved himself up and jumped heavily onto the ground.

"*Verdammt* redskin!" he muttered.

He recovered as three or four young Negroes came tumbling out of the hotel, vying with each other for the luggage.

"Here, you!" he said to one of them. "Take these animals over to Ritter's Livery Stable and have them rubbed down good. Take his horse, too." He pointed to Dan's sorrel.

"Thanks, anyway." Dan held onto the reins. "I won't be staying here."

"If it's money," Wil said anxiously, "I've still got a little left. What I've got, you've got."

"It isn't that. It just looks to me like the entire upper echelon of the army is quartering here. I can see four generals and three colonels without even straining my eyes."

"Are you afraid of them?" Jane asked.

"Of course I am," Dan said easily. "I'm a private."

23

"Where will you be staying then?" Wil asked. "How will we find you?"

"I don't know yet where I'll be. But I'll call on you in a day or two, after we're all settled. If I may."

"If you may!" Wil roared. "We'll be mad as hell if you don't! Why not have dinner with us tonight? Jane, ask him."

"We'd be pleased if you'd eat with us," Jane said.

He smiled at her serious formality. "I wish I could," he answered. "But there are some things I need to do this evening."

Wil put his hand on Dan's arm. "You'll think over joining our wagon train, won't you?"

"No. Thanks anyway, but I'll be going with Shelby if he'll have me."

"Dan," Jane said uneasily, "you—what will you do with your ranch?"

The pleasure went out of him and he looked older. "I'll have to decide today what is to become of it." Compassion welled up in her as she realized for the first time how much the ranch meant to him.

"Maybe you could just go back to it and forget Shelby," she blurted out.

He seemed to have dismissed his feelings as quickly as they had come. "No. It isn't likely."

"Well," Wil said emphatically, "I haven't given up on you yet." His expression grew defensive as he thought of something. "In the meantime I'll ask you to do me one more favor. You know my son Bill's here in town to join Shelby. Him and Cogan. If you run into 'em—Cogan's big, awfully big, and Bill's shorter than you, and fair—will you tell them we're here at the Menger?"

"Of course. I'll be glad to." He eased the reins over the sorrel's neck and pulled himself up.

"Then," Jane said, "we'll see you soon. And somehow, someday, Dan, we'll thank you." She felt a genuine regret

24

that he had other plans for this evening; but they had made enough demands on his time already, she thought.

The buggy lurched from behind her and she took Wil's arm. The day was growing hotter and he was beginning to seem weak again.

He would be anxious to see Reed Marman right away, but she would make him rest first. If he wanted the job badly enough to go off and leave her with the Marcuses, then she would have to make sure that Marman didn't take one look at him and decide not to hire him.

Talk in the Menger was of whiskey and women and gun fights; of war and peace and the imminent approach of Sheridan's Yankees; of cattle and cotton and shipping; of a new life in Mexico for fleeing Confederates; of General Jo Shelby's unsurrendered army; of the overabundance of worthless Confederate bonds and the lamentable shortage of hard United States dollars.

The bar, visible through the door of the gigantic patio, was swollen with ex-army officers, ex-mayors, ex-judges, ex-senators, ex-governors. All were running before the Federals; some would surely want to travel to Mexico with the wagon train led by Wilhelm Morgen. But the way he felt now, Wil was not even sure he could manage his own wagon, much less a train.

Luck smiled and adjoining rooms were available. Wil left a message with the clerk for Marman, and then managed somehow to get all the way upstairs and onto his bed before he collapsed.

He deserved to be left here, lying hurt and alone, he thought. He had never been a particularly good husband or father. But of all the things he had ever done, leaving Jane with Mrs. Marcus was one of the worst.

She came in and wet a cloth in the wash basin, then brought it to him and put it on his pounding forehead. "Dad," she said quietly, "we both know this trip is going to be too much for you. If you'd give it up, we wouldn't have to go back to the farm. We could settle in Galveston again. It might take us a while to get started, but at least we'd still be in this country. Maybe that doesn't matter to you, but—"

"Of course it matters," he said heavily. "It's just that . . . I've got a job that needs doing."

His head throbbed, but not enough to keep him from squirming because he had given an excuse instead of an honest answer. He had always made excuses for moving on, he thought; there was a devil inside him, and it drove him mercilessly and without regard for his family. He resolved to fight it—this minute—here.

"Jane, I . . . wasn't quite honest. I'm going because I've got to go, because I can't stay still. But I'm leaving you in Galveston . . . where you know people, where you can live a decent life. You've got no call to go along."

She shook her head. "Rest, now. I'm going."

"No. Jane, your mother followed me—from Hanover to Pennsylvania to Galveston. There I had a good business, a nice family, everything a man could want. But I was in Mexico hauling supplies for General Taylor when she died. Then you kids followed me—to the farm when I started the immigrant settlement, and back to Galveston when I got tired of it. And I left you both so I could haul supplies through Mexico for the South. Jane, I'd . . . wind up leaving you in Mexico. I know it. And I can't let it happen."

"I'm being driven to go, the same as you," she answered soberly. "But for different reasons. It's time we all had a home; Bill needs it and I need it and so do you. I think this time we'll have it."

"You've got no call to believe in me," he protested.

"For my own sake, and yours and Bill's, I've got to believe. I really do think it's time you settled. And if it turns out that you can't make the trip without my help, then you might realize it for yourself."

"It would be a hard life—along the way, and after we

26

get there. You'd miss all the fun a young woman is supposed to have."

"If we built a home, stayed in one place, it would be worth it."

Wil sighed heavily. "Well, I've got to admit, with my head hurt like it is, I could use help. Maybe more than I'd like to admit." He had wrestled with the devil and lost, but at least Jane had her own reasons for going. And maybe he would settle when they got there. A man could never tell, and he could give himself the benefit of the doubt till the time came to decide. Anyway, it was for a good cause; they both realized that.

"You know," he said, his relief evident, "I've been wondering. Reed Marman is no man to settle down. He's a blockade runner, a smuggler, a man who lives on action. I can't see him as a colonist." He sighed. "But I did hear he was broke now, and anyway I shouldn't judge other people. Let me sit up, baby. He'll be here any minute, and I don't want to look sick."

"All right," she said, almost absently. There was a slight pucker between her eyebrows and she added hesitantly, "I guess while we're waiting I'm going to do some sewing. The women in the lobby all seemed to have their dresses cut lower in front than mine. I don't want to look like a— like a country bumpkin."

Wil grinned. "The problems women have! I'm glad I'm a man."


Marman arrived hatless, evidently having just come from another part of the hotel. He bowed and said pleasantly, "Miss Morgen? I was told that you were with your father. I'm Reed Marman."

Jane smiled and opened the door wider. "Won't you come in?"

She was pleasantly surprised by his tall fairness, the immaculate, beautifully cut gray broadcloth suit, the white ruffled shirt and the blue cravat that matched his eyes. Wil had said he was bold and ruthless and cold, with the rage of the devil in his heart. She was suddenly unsure of Wil's judgment.

Her father was up to greet him. "Ach, Reed! I didn't think we'd ever meet again!"

Marman shifted his briefcase so he could shake hands. "You didn't tell me you had so beautiful a daughter." It was a nice compliment, but spoken without feeling.

"I thought you were supposed to know everything," Wil answered.

Reed smiled and put an end to the pleasantries. "I've got something here I know you'll want to see." He opened the briefcase with a flourish and pulled out a multicolored poster. He handed it to Wil, saying, "Miss Morgen, I'd like you to read it, too."

Wil sank onto the bed and she came and stood behind him. The poster was on white paper, printed in red and blue and festooned with the crossed stars and bars of the Confederate battle flag. It read:

### ATTENTION
### SOLDIERS and CITIZENS of
The Confederate States of America

*Arrangements have been made and all necessary permissions obtained to establish a Confederate Colony in a beautiful fertile Valley, wooded and watered, in the Mexican State of Tlaxcala.*

*A land grant has been made to me personally by*
*A Representative of*
### MAXIMILIAN, EMPEROR OF MEXICO
*Approval of this undertaking has been expressed by*
### BENITO JUAREZ, MEXICO'S exiled PRESIDENT.
*The initial colony will consist of thirty carefully selected families.*
*Safe transport to this Stream-Fed Valley will be assured by the careful management of*
### WIL MORGEN

*who for the past twenty years has safely conducted thousands of wagons through the most remote parts of Mexico.*
*For Further Details, Contact*
*REED MARMAN*
*Menger Hotel*

In spite of all her misgivings about the whole undertaking, Jane felt a spark of enthusiasm.

Wil sat looking at the poster, then put it on the bed beside him. "Sit a minute, Reed," he invited. "Jane, bring some *schnapps,* please."

She felt an impatience at Wil's studied delay, but poured liquor from the decanter on the bureau and brought the two glasses across the room.

Wil took his and sipped at once. "Reed," he said, "you've always bragged that you didn't do anything for nothing. Now I'm curious to know why you're so anxious to start this colony."

Marman waited till Jane settled herself with a rustle of petticoats next to Wil. "Would you accept the fact that I'm sorry for these people? That I want to help them?"

"No, I wouldn't."

Reed laughed, saluted Jane with his glass and sipped lightly. "I'm going to start a revolution," he said.

"What?"

"An agricultural revolution," he explained. "The peons still farm like they did when Cortez landed. I'll sell them plows and harvesting machines—for just enough to make them appreciate what they've bought—and I'll show them how to harvest two—maybe three—crops a year. With the French army all through Mexico, I can get contracts to supply the troops. I'll get rich and the Mexicans will make money, too."

"That sounds good," Wil said, weighing it carefully. "For one thing it would make the people around us friendly. It's the best protection we could have."

"I'm glad you like the idea, Wil," Marman answered

soberly, "because it will mean some extra work for you. I'll have to do it big. I'll have sixteen wagons in all."

"Sixteen? With thirty, maybe forty wagons for the settlers? It will be too much. You'll have to leave some for the next trip."

"No," Marman said insistently. "Sixteen extra wagons and every one of them goes."

Just as stubbornly, Wil said, "Most of the people with us won't be used to the hardships. Sixteen more wagons would finish us off. We'll leave some."

"And miss a whole growing season? No! Anyway, I already have the machinery; I borrowed money and bought out a small factory to get it, and we both know that Sheridan won't respect the property of a known blockade runner if I leave part of it behind. And he'll be here almost any day—sometime next week at the latest."

"He's right, Dad." Jane knew she shouldn't have interfered, but she couldn't give him an excuse to turn right around and make another trip. He gave her a dour look and she got up and walked to the chair that held the dress she was working on. Firmly resolving to hold her tongue until they were finished, she sat and began carefully cutting the neckline.

"Hmmm," Wil muttered. "It's too much and you know it."

"Your load won't be any bigger," Marman argued. "I have a man coming to see me in a few minutes—someone I knew during the war. He'll manage my wagons and my teamsters."

"Then you'll be after me to keep up; you'll run the rest of us ragged."

Marman abruptly changed his strategy and cast an appealing glance at Jane. "Miss Jane, this is the way it's got to be. Maybe I'll need more help from you."

She blushed and wished again that she hadn't spoken out. For one thing, he was bound to notice where she had cut into the dress and know what a vain, frivolous female she was.

"Your dress is beautiful," he added. "And that reminds me—I'm having dinner tonight with Senator Todd and his daughter, who'll be traveling with us. I'm counting on you two to join us."

"I don't know," Wil said. "I had a little accident yesterday and my head still hurts some. It's up to Jane, I guess."

Marman turned on the full charm of his Viking fairness. "I would like to see you in that dress, Miss Jane."

She found that she was flattered. She had not been without beaus during the last few years, but both in Galveston and on the farm they had mostly been gangling youths lacking Marman's polish and grooming.

She nodded to her father. "We do have to eat, and it would be nice to meet Miss Todd."

Marman turned back to Wil. "Then all we have to settle now is the business of the wagons. Will you take them—no more argument?"

"I don't know."

"Miss Jane? You didn't say whether you'd help me."

She said gravely, "Daddy, I really think you should. Let's make one trip and be done with it."

"I couldn't manage."

"Even if I helped all I could?"

Wil looked with sympathy at his daughter. "You just don't know, baby. You'll have work enough already. But maybe if Reed hired somebody to help me out—"

"You have someone in mind?" Marman asked cautiously.

"I do," Wil said. "Dan Kilbourne."

"I don't think I know him."

"He's a cavalry soldier. Tall and strong as a rock."

"He saved our lives on the prairie yesterday," Jane said. "He has a nasty wound in his side, and yet he came out of his way to fight an Indian war party for us; he didn't even know who we were. But," she added emphatically, "he wouldn't take the job. He's joining Shelby."

31

"He just might change his mind," Wil said, and Jane didn't bother to answer. He knew as well as she did that Dan was, for some reason, giving up his ranch to serve with Shelby; but Wil attached little importance to owning property. He had left the farm behind as easily as if it were an old shoe.

"How about your son?" Marman asked curiously. "Wouldn't you rather have him?"

Wil sighed tiredly. "No. Bill can't . . . hold his temper any more."

Marman nodded and stood up. "Kilbourne it is, then, if you can get him. But, Miss Jane," he added, turning to her deferentially, "I'll depend on you to see that your father doesn't change his mind, whether Kilbourne comes with us or not."

She was just as anxious to make only one trip as Marman was, no matter how much work it meant for her. She was sure that once they got to Mexico, if her father didn't have an excuse to come right back, he would finally settle down; more honestly, she was convinced that at least there was a chance, and it was Bill she was thinking of most of all. If he had a decent home to come to, maybe he wouldn't follow in his father's footsteps. Maybe he'd even . . . go back to being like he was before the war.

"I'll . . . talk to him," she promised.

He seemed to share a secret with her as he moved toward the door. "I hope you succeed, but we can't let this whole expedition depend on him. Please remember that."

When he closed the door Marman was tempted to linger a moment to see if the Morgens spoke again about the extra wagons. Instead he shrugged and started for his own room. It was enough for now to know that Jane was on his side. He couldn't guess her reasons, but he was certain he could keep her from changing her mind. He would court her, if necessary.

In his room he waited an impatient fifteen minutes for

the knock to sound at his door, then delayed answering when it finally came. He was deeply disturbed at having to trust his caller as he had never before trusted any man. He had known Major Quillian, lately of Longstreet's command, since the early days of the war; knew him as a good leader unburdened by moral scruples. But these characteristics, while they tended to make him suitable, were certainly no basis for trust.

Time was short, he reminded himself. He composed his face and opened the door. "Come in, Major." He held out his hand.

"I take it your plans have matured," Raney Quillian answered dryly, shaking hands. He was a small, quick, well-educated man, with a flair for fancy dress. Today he wore a black hat, flat-crowned and ornamented, with a drawstring hanging loose under his chin. IIis string tie was embroidered in a silver pattern that matched his embossed silver belt buckle. The pattern was repeated in the stitching on his fancy boots.

But he was unshaven, and his pants and shirt were not particularly clean. The last several weeks had not treated him well, which was something Marman had been bearing in mind since meeting him again at the Menger bar last week.

"My plans are almost in order," he agreed. "Close enough to merit a drink, anyway." He motioned Quillian to one of the two armchairs he had arranged near the window, alongside a table which bore a decanter of whiskey and two glasses. He poured the liquor, then settled himself in the other chair.

Quillian bolted his drink as though he hadn't had one in a long time and held out his glass for a refill. Marman gave it to him and settled back, watching closely. He had been looking for the right man since the day after Johnston surrendered, had talked to and discarded half a dozen others already. Today, with time running out, he still must not make a mistake.

He saw that the second drink satisfied Quillian's devouring thirst and as he poured the third for him and watched him sip it with obvious enjoyment he relaxed; he had been afraid that alcohol might have become a weakness.

"You said you had a job for me," Quillian reminded.

Marman was pleased. Anxiety was a sign he had been waiting for.

"It's a hard job, Major, and it's dangerous. But the pay is good."

"Money is one of the two things I need," Quillian admitted readily, staring in open envy at the luxurious room and Marman's impeccable gray broadcloth.

"And the other?" Marman asked.

Quillian's eyes glistened. "Tall beautiful women—or short beautiful women."

Marman experienced a quick distaste at his crudity, but kept his thoughts to himself. He knew that plenty of men were like Quillian—sex was an overriding hunger that sapped their ambitions. His own craving came fiercely, but sporadically; once it was satisfied he could forget it for a time.

His silence seemed to make Quillian ill at ease. The little major said quickly, shifting his eyes, "Let's forget the women and talk about money."

Marman still hated to say the words. He poured himself another drink. "You know I was a blockade runner during the war."

Quillian nodded. "I heard you got rich, but not rich enough. At the last minute you put your profits into a few shiploads of cotton, and a little Yankee gunboat sent your whole fleet to the bottom. You ended up like the rest of us." He seemed pleased.

"I don't intend to remain like the rest of you," Marman said coldly. His pressure on the whiskey glass increased. "The last merchandise I brought from Europe included a large number of fine rifles. The guns are still here in San Antonio, in a warehouse, and the man who paid me for them has left the state. So has everybody else who gives a damn, which means they don't belong to anybody, and won't till the Yankees take them."

With some disgust, Quillian said, "Guns are a dime a dozen in Texas. They're laying all over the plains and they're stacked in the cities."

"I had about decided to hire you," Marman said. "But you don't give me much credit; maybe I shouldn't tell you the rest of it."

Quillian looked surprised. He considered for a moment, his eyes dropping to his soiled pants. "Go ahead," he said reluctantly.

"The guns are to be sold in Mexico, not Texas."

"Then I still don't understand. The French have all they need, and Juarez won't have long to wait. The Yankees will give him guns—free—so he can drive Maximilian out."

"That much is correct—but there are more than two sides in Mexico. While Juarez and Maximilian fight for the center of government there will be a few others—smaller men, but equally enterprising—who'll gain control of some of the states. I know one such man, not far from Mexico City. He's ambitious and smart and he's got an army of guerrillas—with just about one ancient muzzle-loader for every twenty of his so-called soldiers. He wants to buy and has the money, but the guns have got to be delivered to him —and I have no ships."

"I see." Quillian did some hasty figuring. "And the overland haul means cutting through what troops Juarez has, going through cities controlled by the French army, fighting your way past other guerrillas, and then if you're lucky the bandit pays you, you deliver the guns, and he promptly uses them to kill us all and get his money back."

"I've thought of those things and a few more that haven't occurred to you."

"All right," Quillian said sullenly, "I'm still listening."

"Then first of all you're to hire teamsters who'll mind their own business and obey orders. We're going to Mexico

35

as part of a colony, with a land grant from Maximilian, and Juarez' approval. The extra wagons are supposed to be hauling machinery, so we can count on protection from both the French and the Mexicans. A man named Wil Morgen knows the way and has contacts that also will be a help."

"And if someone finds out about the guns?"

"They mustn't. The colonists would panic, and with good reason. Mexico is infested with bands of guerrillas and *bandidos* who'd risk anything for a haul like ours. We'll be torn apart if they even suspect."

Quillian took a big breath. "And what will I get for all this?"

"Fifteen per cent, and you'll earn it. To start, while I'm organizing and selecting colonists, you will hire your men, collect the wagons, unload the warehouse, and camp outside of town until the rest of us meet you. And I'm sure you realize that every guerrilla in Mexico will know about the guns if you don't play straight with me."

Quillian brushed the threat aside. "How will we make certain that we get paid and get out alive?"

"The money will be delivered in Mexico City to someone I can trust. We'll turn over the guns, but leave the ammunition several hours behind us. By the time they're set up, we'll be gone." He was pleased as Quillian's skepticism began to give way to admiration.

"And what will happen to the colonists?"

Marman shrugged. "If they get safely through the guerrillas, they have the land grant. And that reminds me. Morgen wants a man named Kilbourne to help him. But I don't want Kilbourne with us for two reasons—I may have to control Morgen through his daughter and Kilbourne would be sure to interfere. Also he might snoop. I want you to make sure that he doesn't come along. He has a wound in his side, according to Jane Morgen, and you can probably hurt him easily enough. But I don't want you to kill him, and I don't want you to take any chances that

36

might bring an investigation from Shelby. We mustn't call attention to ourselves."

"Where would I find Kilbourne?"

Setting his pattern of authority for the future, Marman said, "Look for him. He came here to join Shelby."

"All right," Quillian agreed, "I'm working. Give me another drink and some money, and I'll be on my way."

# 3

AFTER LEAVING THE MORGENS Dan had stopped at a narrow Mexican restaurant for several tacos and a bottle of cool beer. A few doors down he had bought some socks and underwear; now he was once again riding the sorrel down rock-strewn streets long familiar to him, as familiar as the smells of garbage, rank vegetables, sweaty stock and horse manure that cloyed the air and clung to the buildings.

The town was choked with cowboys, farmers, Confederates, and hundreds of motley individuals who could not be identified by their trappings. Some of these, no doubt, were adventurers and opportunists, bummers, or downright outlaws. A few, he judged, were bound to be natives, but they were so accustomed to mingling with strangers that it was impossible to single them out. As far back as Dan could remember—and long before that—San Antonio had been a constant host to noisy crowds of people who wanted to buy, sell, trade or simply make contact with a vestige of civilization. His own first gun, bought with his own money, had been purchased in a store not three blocks from Military Plaza. He still remembered the wonder of it; remembered, too, that it had caused him to become overly confident, to stray too far from the ranch and get himself cornered by Kiowas. His dad's blooded stallion, intended to become the forebear of a hardy, swift breed of ranch horses, had caught an arrow in its neck that afternoon, and Dan had worked for a year without wages to pay for it. Here among the familiar sights and smells that had brought back the incident he was reminded also of the relief he had felt when at last the debt was called even.

Dan continued to thread his way between wary-eyed pedestrians, squeaking covered wagons and rumbling two-wheeled carts until he reached a hotel that apparently had no name. Its façade simply said HOTEL—ROOMS. A small sign advertised HOT WATER BATHS.

A middle-aged man was fitting new boards on the front steps. "No rooms less'n you share," he said before Dan had even dismounted.

"In that case, I'm looking for two soldiers—Bill Morgen and Mike Cogan."

"Got no sojers stayin' here."

At the next three hotels he got the same answers. At the fourth, a soft-spoken Negro asked, "What dose men look like?"

"Morgen is about medium-sized and fair. Cogan's supposed to be the biggest man in these parts."

"What you want to see dem men about?"

"Morgen's father's in town. Wants to talk to him."

The Negro grinned, a soul-satisfying, white-toothed grin. "Didn't seem to me like that little man had no earthly papa. Thought maybe he call the Devil daddy. Dat ain't the names they give me, but you'll find 'em upstairs. First door to the right of the landing." He turned and took a key from the honeycomb behind him. "Guess I could give you a room by yo'self at dat. Dat is, if yo're willin' to pay fo' two?" he added anxiously.

Dan picked up his haversack and held out his hand for the key.

"Two dollahs, payable now. And seventy-five cents extry for the bath."

Dan shifted his load, dug, and slid the hard money out onto the counter.

The Negro said, " 'Bout dem men, suh. Was I you, I'd be powahful careful. Dey seem mean to me."

"All right, Uncle." Dan took the key and headed for the stairs. "And I'll have that bath right away," he called back.

"Yes, suh! Fix it mahself, suh. Right now!"

The soldier who answered Dan's knock towered over him. At first glance his face seemed to consist of big teeth in a mouth that remained partially open, and big, soulful brown eyes. Though first lieutenant's bars were attached to his collar, his sleeves showed clearly that he had recently been a sergeant. Past him, Dan could see a thick, shorter man standing at the window, his head uptilted as the contents of the bottle in his hand gurgled steadily down his throat. He was a sergeant, and even against the light, Dan saw unfaded spots on his collar where, presumably, bars had recently been.

"What the hell do you want?" the sergeant yelled. "I told that nigger we didn't want to be disturbed!"

"He's a little touchy when he's drinkin'," the lieutenant explained.

"Touchy when he's drinkin'," the sergeant mimicked. His twang contrasted sharply with the lieutenant's soft drawl. He finished the bottle and threw it across the room where it splintered with a loud crash.

The lieutenant winced. "Ouah last bottle," he said sourly. "What did you want?"

"I'm looking for two men. Morgen and Cogan."

"Nope." The lieutenant held out his hand. "Randolph," he said. "Archibald Francis Randolph. You can call me Frank."

"He can't call you Frank, God damn it!" the sergeant roared. "You're a lieutenant! He'll call you sir!"

Frank Randolph grinned. "We held elections last week. Before that he had my job and I had his. Cain't seem to get used to the change."

The sergeant suddenly focused his eyes on Dan. He came to the doorway, grabbing Randolph's arm to keep from falling. His blond moustache helped emphasize the dark scowl on his big blunt face. "Those Yankee pants are near new! Where the hell did you get 'em?"

"Now, Alex, you've got no call—"

"Where did you get 'em?" the sergeant demanded again. "If you found a cache someplace—"

"I didn't," Dan said pleasantly. "But it's none of your business where I got them."

Randolph again took on the role of peacemaker. "Maybe he got those like I got my butternuts. For two years the only uniform I could find to fit me came out of a Yankee ars'nal. Then I ran into this big rich drunken south'n boy." He dismissed the whole incident. "You'd better be introduced. This is Alex Walcott."

"Sergeant Walcott, by God!"

"Dan Kilbourne. Private."

"Who'd you fight with?"

"Terry's Rangers."

"His outfit was good enough," Walcott admitted grudgingly.

"Who'd you fight with?" Dan asked.

"Shelby!"

"He was good enough, too. If things work out, I'll be with him tomorrow."

"Well," Randolph said, "we wanted to rest for a while, but come in anyway. We're supposed to be talkin' enlistments."

"Supposed to be, balls!" Walcott growled. "We are. The same as a dozen others. Come in and sign up."

"Do you know yet what Shelby intends to do? All I've heard are rumors."

"We'll recruit here, then go to Mexico," Randolph said positively. "After that, who knows? Maybe fight for Juarez for a time, though our end purpose is to continue the war. To build up our side again."

"Come on, dammit," Walcott said insistently.

Dan held back. "No, I'll wait till morning. I've got some things to do first. But I will sign—tomorrow."

"We may need you tonight." Walcott argued. "We've taken over the job of policing the town, and our men are tired."

"If you've got to have me, I'll be here after I've tended to my business. Meanwhile, maybe you could tell me if there's a mail service to Houston."

"Not much of one," Randolph said. "The best way to mail a letter is to leave it at the lobby of the Menger with one Yankee dollar. The stage'll pick it up in the mornin'."

Dan could hear clumping on the stairs. The old Negro hove into sight carrying two buckets of steaming water.

"Then I'll see you later. If you'll excuse me—"

Walcott's big blond moustache seemed to curl downward from his annoyance. It straightened just as suddenly and his eyes shone.

"You got any money?"

"A little," Dan said cautiously.

"Enough for a couple of bottles of tequila?"

"Yes."

"In that case," Walcott said craftily, "I've got a couple of extry uniforms here. I could sell you an outfit, hat included. Your coat," he added, "wouldn't pass muster on a scarecrow."

"You aren't supposed—"

Walcott moved surprisingly fast for a heavy stocky man. "You hush up!" He pawed through a large knapsack and pulled out a wadded gray uniform. "Sell you this right here—for enough to buy two bottles of tequila. Slouch hat thrown in. But it'll have to be in Yankee or Mex money. Ours is no good unless there's a pistol behind it."

Dan took out two loose bills. Walcott grabbed the money, inspected it, and handed him the uniform. "Yankee dollars," he said, and his voice seemed choked between contempt and reverence. He thrust the bills into his

41

pocket. "See you when we run out of liquor!" He shut the door solidly.

Randolph's immediate protests filtered into the hall. "You know we're supposed to give those uniforms to anyone who was too ragged—"

Walcott didn't let him finish. "Uncle!" he roared. "Now where in hell is that nigger? Uncle! Uncle!"

The white-haired Negro was just finished filling Dan's bath. "Comin', Sahgeant," he was saying softly. "Comin'."

Dan soaked till the water cooled, then shaved. Last of all he began to dress his wound. It was raw and sore, but he figured he could just about forget it in a week or so.

He finished the dressing and put on his uniform. It fit well enough and he was briefly pleased that Walcott had given him a slouch hat instead of the little forage cap; it made a lot better sense if they were going south.

He put the cap aside and lit the coal oil lamp. This was the moment he had come to dread during the last several days. It was time to dispose of the ranch, and far more than his own hurt was involved. His father, dead these two years, was not the kind to express disappointment in his own daughter, but Charlotte's dislike of the ranch into which he had poured his life had caused him a deal of unhappiness. He had, in fact, bought her the cotton lands near Houston so that the ranch would belong solely to Dan, who would properly appreciate it.

In spite of this, Dan decided, he would understand. The old man had always held just payment of debt above all other values.

Dan slid the table next to the bed and dug pencil and paper from his haversack. He had already considered and rejected the alternatives, including hiring someone to get the ranch back in shape and run it in his absence. The future was too uncertain for such notions. He thought for a time, and then began to write:

42

*Dear Sis: Hope you and Gene and the kids are well and happy. About a year ago I ran into a soldier who had met you and he said that the war hadn't disrupted things too much in Houston, and that you and Gene were building a new home, and Gene was doing very well. I'm glad. I hope Gene got my letter thanking him for taking care of the probate and such after Dad died.*

*However, now that everything is over, I won't be going back to the ranch after all. I know you were never particularly fond of it, but I'd like for you to keep it for the kids. It's a fine outfit, and doesn't deserve to be neglected like it has been, and will be if I keep it.*

*The enclosed paper should be legal enough but if you have any trouble, have Judge Henry write it out properly and send it to me to sign. I'll be with Shelby's army, probably in Mexico. As soon as I have an address, I'll send it on.*

*My best to all of you.*

> *Dan*

Taking another sheet of paper he wrote:

*To all whom it may concern:*
*I am herewith signing over to my sister, Charlotte Kilbourne Duval, to have from this day forward, the Kilbourne Ranch (registered brand K) which was left to me in the will of my father, William Rexford Kilbourne.*

He signed his name: *Daniel Hayes Kilbourne, Shelby's Army, San Antonio, Texas, June 15, 1865.*

He folded the two sheets together, carefully addressed the envelope, and thrust the paper into his pocket. The act was as final as if the ranch had vanished before his eyes. He stood up, got his hat and kicked the haversack under the bed. Now nothing in the room showed that he had ever been here except a tubful of dirty water and three damp towels. The ranch would also be like this; after a few years his imprint would amount to no more than a passing whisper.

He blew out the lamp and started downstairs, checking, as had become his habit, the three hundred dollars in United States currency that he carried in his waistband. The money seemed of little consequence this minute, but it was enough to remind him that he was more fortunate than most of the soldiers he would serve with. More fortunate than a lot of people in the torn South.

Dan found the Menger unbelievably crowded. Its noisy patrons were blocking the doorway to the courtyard and spilling out into the dark street so that he had to squirm and squeeze to wedge his way through.

The patio was lit by lamps suspended from the walls. In this emergency, tables had been shoved outside until the outermost customers found themselves staring through overhanging citrus branches. The door to the bar was equally jammed, but Dan decided to go and have a drink after his letter was deposited in the lobby.

He began to push gently through the close-packed crowd. The humid air carried the smells of liquor and perfume and cigar smoke, and scrubbed but sweating men. The combination formed a peculiarly civilized odor, one that Dan had not enjoyed for more years than he cared to think about.

He was startled as huge, heavy fingers clamped onto his arm. He looked up at a stoop-shouldered giant of a soldier.

"You Kilbourne?" the soldier asked. His nose was cocked severely to one side and his breath whistled through his one open nostril. "If you are, the Morgens want you to join 'em." His squinting eyes said he hoped he got an argument, and the broken nose and the puffed scars on his face indicated that he had already been obliged more than once.

44

But he had the cocksureness of a man who didn't often come out second best.

"You must be Mike Cogan," Dan grinned. "I was going to look for you and Bill tomorrow. Where'd they find you?"

"We dropped by for a drink," Cogan said. "Have you met Bill before? You know about him?"

"Know what?"

"He lost his right hand during the war. Saving my neck. He's sensitive about it, so don't try to shake." He motioned with his big head. "Come on. You tag after me now."

"Show me where," Dan said. "I've got a letter to leave in the lobby, then I'll be over."

Cogan frowned. "It wouldn't be too polite to ~~~ ~~~ waiting. Not when Miss Jane saw you and sent ~~~ for you."

He was so determined that Dan smiled. "No, I don't guess it would. I'll mail it later."

"Then tag after me, like I said." Cogan elbowed his way around and shouldered across the patio, clearing a wide path that left people muttering and cursing in his wake. Dan trailed after him.

Jane and Wil Morgen were sharing a table with three other people—a freckled young man in a gray uniform, an older man with the distinguished mien Dan had learned to associate with politicians, and the most beautiful woman he had ever seen. A single glance told him that she had nearly perfect features, set off by lustrous dark hair and brows and complemented by black Creole eyes and a creamy complexion. He swung his gaze to Wil with some reluctance.

Wil looked a little sour, possibly because the bruise on his head still bothered him, but his portly face lit up as he spotted Dan. "This is the man I've been telling you about," he said heartily. The two other men stood up with him as he announced with some reverence, "Dan Kilbourne."

45

The beautiful woman interrupted his introductions. "We've been hearin' all about you." She spoke with admiration, but Dan thought he detected amusement as well.

"We can't say enough," Wil assured her. He continued, "This is Miss Mavis and her father, Senator Russell Todd. And this is my son Bill. You've met Mike Cogan, of course."

Dan shook hands with the gray-haired Senator, but Cogan stood aloof and Bill sat down sullenly, his right hand seemingly in his pocket. Dan, remembering, quickly dropped his own hand.

"Won't you join us, Mr. Kilbourne?" Jane asked coolly. He thought for a moment that she was piqued because he was here after refusing her invitation. But then, as her fingers touched the front of her dress, he suddenly understood that she needed to be formal and withdrawn to bolster her own assurance. The shell-pink, low-necked gown contrasted cruelly with the sunburn that covered her face and dipped halfway down to the cleft of her breasts. By comparison with Mavis Todd's mature beauty and uniform coloring she must have felt like a hoydenish schoolgirl.

"I'm grateful for the invitation," Dan said, moving closer to her.

Mavis Todd subtly indicated the chair between her and Jane, across from where he had intended to sit. He hesitated, then went around.

"We'ah all goin' to Mexico together, Mr. Kilbourne," Mavis said in her soft drawl as he seated himself. "After what we've heard, we'd be delighted to have you join us. Wouldn't we, Jane dear?"

Jane said quietly, "Yes, we've told him that."

"We're going to be quite insistent, Mr. Kilbourne," the graying Senator put in. "Aren't we, Mavis?" He seemed to need her assurance.

A commotion with a waiter took place behind them then, and several raised voices prevented conversation for a moment.

One steely voice said, "We're no less Southrons today than we were last month, or six months ago. As such we're entitled to the same courtesies we've always gotten, and we're quite prepared to convince anyone who disagrees."

Somebody said, "Hear! Hear!" and Dan smiled a little. The Southerners who had gathered in San Antonio, whether they were here to join Shelby or to form their colonies deep in Mexico, might fully share the South's defeat, but they would be the last to admit it.

The smile dropped away as he suddenly realized that Mavis Todd's attention was centered on him obviously and fully; he squirmed a little at the unexpectedness of it, glanced at Bill Morgen and saw his deep resentment. He could not understand what was happening, unless Mavis deliberately wanted to make Bill jealous and was thoroughly succeeding.

Bill, he judged, was about twenty-two, only a year or so younger than Jane. Mavis, in spite of her smooth skin, was probably a good few years older, possibly slightly older than Dan; but her beauty was enough to make any man ambitious.

The noise subsided and Bill said firmly, "We were talking about Galveston."

Cogan, who stood over him as watchful as a mother hen, seemed to approve of his statement, but Wil said abruptly, "That was before Mr. Kilbourne got here."

Mavis, observing the blow to Bill's pride, spoke softly. "We will get back to it, but I do think we should sound out Mr. Kilbourne first."

Russell Todd nodded instant agreement. "Yes, I think the important thing now is to explain to him about the objectives of our colony. We're going to need men like him."

"I appreciate the thought," Dan answered, as Mavis began gracefully to pour coffee for him. "But I've already made arrangements to join General Shelby."

"But you haven't actually joined, have you?" Mavis asked.

"Not yet." Dan found himself admiring her beauty again. Everything about her compelled attention, including the jade earrings and necklace and the white taffeta dinner dress that plunged downward to reveal the tops of smooth breasts.

He took his coffee, thanked her, and lifted his cup toward Jane. As Charlotte Kilbourne Duval's brother, he couldn't keep from realizing that she was being whipped by superior forces and needed all the assurance she could get. She was pretty enough in her own right, but the flaming sunburn and the pink dress had completely unnerved her before Mavis.

"Jane," he said, "I'll drink to your health. We went through a lot together."

Jane stiffly acknowledged the toast, touching her own cup with tense fingers.

"I'll join you in that," Mavis said.

"So will I," Wil cut in.

"And I'll drink to Lieutenant Esteban," Bill said.

Because of the emphasis he put on his words, another uncomfortable silence followed, until Dan said, "It's a worthwhile toast. I'll vouch that we were glad to see the lieutenant."

As they drank the coffee a petty triumph showed in Bill's eyes. Dan couldn't decide if his antagonism stemmed primarily from the loss of his hand or from Mavis' lost attention; it was probably both, he thought, and he was also a little jealous because Dan had happened along on the prairie yesterday afternoon. He wouldn't have wanted anything to happen to Wil or Jane, but he resented not being the center of conversation.

Bill turned away from the table to talk to some passing colonel, and Jane said softly, "Dan—I'm sorry for the way Bill is acting. It's partly because . . . everyone has asked you to go along with us. But no one except me has asked him. I can't make Wil believe that such things are important."

48

"What's that?" Wil asked, but then Bill was turning back to the table.

"The Yankees are in Galveston," he announced. "In force. They'll be here in whatever time it takes to make the march."

Mavis did not seem alarmed by the news, but her father said worriedly, "I do hope Marman works fast. We're all depending on him."

"He'll be on schedule," Wil assured him. "Dan, I wish you could meet him. Maybe you can, later. He said he'd try to get back here."

Dan was ready to nod agreement when he suddenly discovered that Lieutenant Randolph who, as he put it, was supposed to be taking enlistments, had come up to the table and was standing at Cogan's elbow.

"I'm sorry to interrupt," Randolph said with a courtly bow, "but these two men"—he indicated Cogan and Bill—"signed up with us this afternoon, according to the colonel I just talked to, and now I need them."

"Bill!" Jane said. "You've already joined up? You didn't tell us!"

With some satisfaction, Bill said, "We're telling you now."

Randolph was pointing loosely at Dan. "We can use you, too, if you're still of a mind to sign up. You see, we're shorthanded now, more so than we will be in a day or two, and we not only have got to earn the little bit of money the merchants are payin' us; we've got to show the world that we stand for law and order, that we're a real army, and not freebooters."

"All right," Dan said. "I'll come with you."

"Oh, but—I thought you hadn't decided yet," Mavis protested.

The sultry look on her beautiful creamy face virtually melted Randolph. "I wouldn't blame him if he stayed here. But perhaps, by servin' now, he could be free another evenin'."

49

Wil said urgently, "Dan, can you put it off? Marman and Jane and I have some plans we'd like you to consider."

"Wil, I'm sorry. But serving with Shelby is as important to me as the wagon train is to you."

"But it won't hurt to wait a day, will it?"

Bill and Cogan were arguing with Randolph now, not listening to him. Dan said quietly, "I'm needed now, and I guess I'll feel better about it if I pay my way in. I've got to belong; I can't just tag along. But I will try to see you both before we leave—or before you do."

"Dan," Jane said earnestly, "I apologize again for the way things were tonight."

"It was only a passing thing and of no importance," he assured her. "But I am sorry the evening was so short. Miss Mavis, I'll say goodbye to you."

She nodded gravely. "Jane told me a great deal about you. I hope we'll see you again. We'll welcome you any time." She plainly meant it and Dan was pleased, though still a little mystified by the amount of attention she had given him.

"We really must go," Randolph said insistently. "It's almost time for patrol and I'm afraid it's pretty important work. The job of cleanin' up the town is far from bein' finished."

Bill shot Dan a last sullen look, then began to have his own troubles as Jane and Wil both tried to speak to him at once.

Dan excused himself and moved over to Randolph. "Lieutenant, I still haven't mailed that letter. I'll catch up to you."

He began to move again through a crowd that had suddenly been stirred anew by the recently received word that the Yankees had reached Galveston.

He was caught up in the excitement of their talk, and all remembrance of his unpleasantness with Bill Morgen, even of his attraction to Mavis Todd's beauty, was washed away by his own mounting excitement.

Starting tonight he was a part of General Joseph O. Shelby's unsurrendered Confederate army, and who knew what the future might bring?

# 4

THE MOON HAD RISEN; the four men walked toward Market Street in the company of long thin shadows that bent sharply upward and sprang flat again each time they passed a building. The soft light gleamed over Lieutenant Randolph's big teeth as he chuckled.

"Don't y'all get the idea I went after you pers'nally. I was reportin' to Colonel Slayback, who was dinin' with the General, and I just happened to see you."

The tone was friendly enough; it was his way of getting better acquainted. But Bill Morgen took offense.

"You sound like those bars on your collar are beginning to get heavy. We heard you were only a sergeant last week."

"And a private for a couple of years before that," Randolph said equably. "How about you?"

Morgen muttered something and Cogan's fingers twisted as though he wanted to ball them into fists. They shuffled along silently then until Dan said, "Does anybody know how long we'll stay in town?"

"Nope," Randolph answered cheerfully. "The Yankees aren't a million miles behind us, but it'll take several days to build our army—God and Phil Sheridan willin'—and we'll try to stick it out. Meanwhile, as I've said, the merchants are payin' us a little somethin' to patrol the town.

51

We could be worse off; we did the same thing in two or three other towns and didn't get paid."

They turned the corner and joined a stream of men hurrying toward a well-lit, two-story adobe building.

"That's headquarters," Randolph said. "Most of the soldiers rushin' up to it only joined us today, just like you. The rest of us were twelve hours in the saddle yesterday and didn't any more than have our blankets warm when a deputation of merchants came out to beg us to come on into the city. So we saddled up again and rode all night and a third of the outfit was on duty today. They did a fine job, too. In case you hadn't heard, three of San Antonio's biggest troublemakers were caught, tried and executed. I bring this up so you'll know we're serious about what we're doin'."

As they reached the building Sergeant Walcott stepped into the doorway and stood silhouetted, holding aloft a small wooden box. Like Randolph, he seemed to have sobered in time for duty. "All right," he yelled, "all you gabbledy turkeys come over here and get your feathers!"

Randolph chuckled again. "The feathers were Colonel Slayback's idea—stolen straight from the plume General Shelby wears in his cap. With the town so full of uniforms we've got to have identification."

The men crowded up to the doorway, then flinched back as Walcott's bellow blasted the foremost soldier. "You will, too, wear this God-damned feather! You want to get shot by your friends?"

A musical voice, slightly thickened with whiskey sang out: "*Stick a feather in his hat/And call him Yankee Doodle!*"

Shouts of laughter followed, and a few rebel yells.

"You'll be called worse than that, damn it," Walcott threatened, "if you don't put this feather in your hat!"

"Lay 'im out, Sarge!"

"It don't go like that anyways! It's—*Stick a feather in his hat/And call him Macaroni!*"

"All right, Macaroni," Walcott snapped. "Take this!"

The slim, middle-aged man in front of him disgustedly took the feather, stuck it in his battered slouch hat and postured. The others laughed good-naturedly, with a feeling of camaraderie that had not existed seconds before. Dan smiled as Walcott gave him his feather and paired him with "Macaroni."

Randolph assigned them to the northwest end of town, amiably agreed to pick up Dan's haversack from the hotel, and bade them a pleasant good evening.

As the lieutenant turned to the next pair of soldiers, Dan's companion said, "Name's Maehler."

They began to move off. "Leastwise it used to be," he went on. "Got an idea it'll be Macaroni for a couple o' days—after which it'll be Pop."

Dan grinned. "And I've got an idea this isn't the first outfit you ever joined."

"Not by three wars it ain't! I wasn't more'n a snot-nosed kid when I fit for Texas independence, but by the time the Mexkin War busted loose they figgered me fer a vet'ran and give me a bunch o' recruits to train. We didn't do so bad neither," he added reflectively, "when ol' Santy Anny come at us at Buena Vista. I didn't get your name, by the way."

"Dan Kilbourne."

"You seen your share of fightin'?"

"Enough, I guess. The war, and before that a few Indian and outlaw fights."

"You'll see more, sure as hell," Maehler promised.

"Why'd you join up?"

"Personal reasons. I'll stay with the Confederacy as long as any part of it is left. And you?"

"Just for the hell of it. Didn't have nothin' to do today."

They crossed the bridge and headed northeast. Starlight and moonlight bathed the town in a bright glow that seemed to wash away the day's dirt and debris. The daytime crowds had thinned now, to a few stragglers traveling down the center of the streets toward home or wagon,

53

to the drunks staggering from one saloon to another, and to the ladies of the night who tried to prey on both other groups. These last were numerous, insistent, and poor losers. Dan and Maehler were accosted and then railed at on four occasions in the few minutes it took to reach their post.

In this area shrill noise and shriller yells poured periodically from several squat buildings to create swift dust devils of sound that swept along the street.

"Well, now," Maehler said as they halted, "we might as well push into the first saloon and see what happens. You with me?"

"With you," Dan said and followed him across the threshold of the nearest building.

Because uniforms were so plentiful in the town they attracted no particular attention as they moved down the aisle between the tables and went up to the bar. The bartender came to them and Maehler said, "Everything quiet enough?"

The pale barkeep looked at the feathers. "Quiet enough tonight," he said. "Hell last night, but word's got around that you fellers are playin' for keeps. I'll be sorry when you leave and the Yankees take over."

A drunk staggered in between them. "Look at that!" he said in wonderment. "They're not soldiers. They're turkeys! Stinkin' ol' Tom turkeys!" His tongue and his Adam's apple quivered as he gave a quick, short gobble.

The drunk was about Maehler's size, half a head shorter than Dan. He was young, heavily weathered and a little dirty, apparently a farm hand who hadn't bothered to clean up much before coming to town. Two or three of the customers immediately began to egg him on, and he reached out with a clumsy hand to grab Maehler's shirtfront.

Dan stiffened, not because of the drunk, but because he hoped Maehler wouldn't turn out to be the kind who'd

54

jump at the chance to beat a helpless man. It took a while to learn what was inside a man.

Maehler said roughly, "You wanna fight? You hell bent on it?"

"Fight," the drunk said. "I'll bust your jaw for you, you damned turkey!" He swung a looping right at Maehler's face.

Maehler pulled loose from the other hand and ducked. The right missed and Maehler spun the drunk around, caught him by the collar and the seat of the pants and propelled him across the room toward an empty chair. He spun him again and plopped him into the chair.

The outraged drunk immediately started to rise, but Maehler spread his palm outward and said, "Now! Now! You whupped me once fair and square! Ain't that enough? What the hell you wanna do? Kill me?"

The perplexed farmer hesitated, blinking as he tried to figure.

"You give me another chance," Maehler said, "in a week or so, or maybe a month, when I've got well."

Laughter was beginning to fill the room, but Maehler was enjoying the show even more than his audience.

He waved a pointing finger around the room. "The rest of you, now, you let that be a lesson!" he shouted. "Don't go pickin' on this here farmer!"

The farmer was still trying to figure things out as Maehler turned and came back to the bar, digging at a tooth with a fingernail.

"This is what it's gonna be like tonight," he said philosophically. "By tomorrow night some of the tough ones'll have their nerve back and come out of their holes. But tonight it'll be like this."

They spoke another minute to the bartender and then Maehler bowed all around and they went out.

As they hit the street and turned left, Dan grinned. "You said you fought in three wars," he reminded.

"Not countin' little ones, like helpin' to drive ol' General Woll out of this here town in '42," Maehler agreed.

"Then I'd be curious to know what you did between wars. You could have been an actor with some medicine show."

Maehler laughed. "I did ever'thing but. I went to Californy and didn't find no gold. Shipped out on a clipper to Chiny and found me a pretty little slant-eye that 'most made me want to stay. Did stay in Hawaii damn near a year, but couldn't stand them New England preachers. Then I come home an' busted broncs. To tell the truth, I wasn't sorry to get back to soldierin' when the war come along."

They reached an alley and Maehler said, "Not that I want a war . . ." and broke off in surprise as an avalanche of men hit them from the dark shadows.

Dan was spun around by a hard shoulder that rammed into his chest. Powerful fingers grabbed his gun arm and hung onto it. A mass of solid muscle charged into his legs and swept them from under him. As he tumbled forward he heard Maehler give a sharp yell that was chopped off in the middle.

Dan landed head first in sharp gravel, shook away the blinding shock, and rolled himself onto his right side. But no amount of struggling could free the arm that was now twisted behind him.

He reached his left hand over his shoulder and bony knees plunged down into his exposed ribs. Air whooshed out between his teeth but he managed to catch a hank of hair and twist. At the same time he rocked upward to butt the man on top of him.

A blow on the back of his neck gave him a dizzy momentum; teeth cracked and the assailant above him flew backwards with a strangled groan. He crawled aside, making room for another dark bulk.

Dan's arm was twisted harder and a boot dug into his ribs. He grunted and pawed out with his free hand. His fingers numbed as the hand was kicked aside. He tried to dig for his pistol and heavy boot leather caught his elbow. Dead fingers tried and failed to close on the pistol butt. Knuckles beat the base of his neck and boot heels shot blinding pains into his belly. Another such stomp would put him in limbo, helpless as a baby.

Dan hunched his shoulder upward and caught a chin. Feeling came back into part of his hand as he tried to tug free. He looped two fingers around the pistol butt and pulled. Moonlight shone on a polished boot as it swung back for another kick. The gun came free, swung in an arc. The steel barrel whacked through thin leather to catch an oncoming shinbone.

A scream pierced Dan's ears. The attacker twisted and flopped onto the ground like a bird with a broken wing. Dan lashed behind him with the gun. The sight raked across flesh, gouging deep. His right arm was suddenly freed. He tried to reach back over his shoulder and encircle a neck with it. A blow sent it forward again. Boot soles pushed against his back like steel springs suddenly released. Dan was flung forward to land full length. A gun roared somewhere as he hit the dirt.

His lungs tried hard to suck breath back into his body. Blood pounded in his ears with a roar that was like the thunder of stampeding buffalo. Consciousness came close, receded like a mirage, came again as the night air pushed into his chest. He struggled up, began to fumble for his pistol as his attackers darted back into the alley. His fingers closed on the weapon and he started in pursuit.

He stopped abruptly, remembering Maehler. He turned, heard running feet far down the street, saw that the old soldier was alone. He had struggled up by himself and was staggering toward the corner of a building, his hand stretched out to give him support. His breath came in groans as Dan moved to him. They both stood gasping for several seconds, guns still ready, until finally Maehler flashed a grin.

"I reckon . . . there's one won't . . . ride a horse for a while. I bit his ear, then . . . got my gun and . . . shot him in the cheek of the ass."

Dan found the strength to laugh. "I've got a mark on one, too. I'll be looking for a man who has to walk with one boot off."

"What the hell happened?" Maehler wondered. "I even forgot what I was talkin' about. Must be gettin' feeble-minded."

Dan laughed again, partly because the tension had slipped away so fast. He had learned a lot of things about Maehler this night, he decided. The old-timer was good for a grin under the blackest of circumstances, and there was no meanness in him. On the other hand, he was ready and willing to fight and knew a trick or two to help himself over the rough spots.

"What you figger they were after?" Maehler asked.

"I don't know. Maybe nothing. Maybe they don't like Shelby."

Maehler pushed himself from the wall. "Well, like I said, tonight the town'll be quiet enough, but tomorrow night there'll be hell to pay." He sighed. "You ready to move on?"

"Ready, I guess." Dan was suddenly discovering that his side had grown sticky.

As they started again to move down the street, his fingers pressed around the tender edges of the jagged cut. He realized now that it was hurting like blazes, that he had failed to notice because his whole rib cage and both arms and his head ached from the blows he had taken. He cursed silently, hoping he wouldn't have to fight any more for a few days. One good lick exactly on top of the wound and he would be back in bed again.

Meantime he would make out all right, he thought. He was like a man who had headaches all the time, and thus could stand them better than the man who only had one once in a while.

At daylight, when the morning stage rolled past them, beginning its long trip to Houston, Maehler was saying, "I was only a jump or two ahead of the Yankees when I come here." He laughed. "Wouldn't we look for a crack in the ground if a whole passel of 'em rode up right now?"

He stopped his speculations when he saw the way Dan was watching the stage. Dan felt his curiosity and turned away, and then they saw Walcott riding up, followed by a dozen mounted troopers.

"Sherm! Featherly! Fall out and take over!" he bellowed. The reverberations sang through the street and a curious householder put out a nightcapped head to see what was going on.

The sergeant peered at Dan and Maehler and a broad smile split his face. "Well, if it ain't Macaroni! Anybody take you for a Yankee?"

Maehler compressed his lips and nodded. "I reckon," he said sorrowfully. "Somebody sure as hell poked me a time or two, but at least we didn't have no trouble after that. How come these men are mounted and we had to use shank's mare?" he demanded.

"That's the army for you," Walcott said. He reined his horse around. "Report to camp now—just north of town. You'll find it easy enough." He gestured the troops forward and they clattered after him.

Sherm and Featherly hitched their horses and strolled over. One was fair and the other dark, but otherwise they were as alike as two sand fleas—young, with downy faces and skinny frames, yet carrying themselves with the easy assurance of veterans.

The dark one tilted a shapeless forage cap with his forefinger. "Featherly," he announced. "And this here's Whitey Sherm. Why'd the Sarge call you Macaroni?"

"Because he stuck a feather in his hat," Dan explained.

"Oh." Featherly looked blank.

"You can use our horses to get yours," Sherm offered.

59

"Good," Maehler nodded. "There's nothin' I hate worse'n walkin'."

Dan said, "Thanks," and thought how strange it was to have served this night with an outfit he had never seen except from a distance. But he had served, was as much a part of the Brigade now as any man in it.

The Iron Brigade was quartered north of San Antonio on a sloping hill that butted up against a dense growth of post oak, elm and hickory. Wood was abundant, water was plentiful and the flat grassy land at the foot of the hill provided forage and served as a drill field.

And drill there was in this man's army. A man drilled and he fetched wood and water and kept his camp clean and took his turn patrolling the city. The rest of the time he readied enormous stockpiles of equipment for the long trip south. For this was no raggle-taggle army; tons of supplies destined for other theaters of war but kept from them by the complete deterioration of Confederate supply lines, had been abandoned all through Texas. From these dumps Shelby had obtained cannon and sidearms, uniforms, ammunition, rifles, muskets and tents. Enough to keep a large detail of soldiers steadily uncrating and handing out and setting up and sometimes crating again. But three days brought in almost three hundred recruits—if the stream of veterans could be called recruits—to lighten the load. Thursday night Dan was in bed before midnight.

At dawn on Friday Maehler, who had pulled headquarters watch during the night, came tearing into the tent, searched frantically in his bedroll, dragged out a bottle of whiskey and took a long pull.

"I have just heard the goldangdest story in all this wicked world!" He took another long pull at the bottle.

It was still a few minutes till reveille, but curiosity opened Dan's eyes.

Maehler handed him the bottle. "Help yourself," he invited. "You'll need it."

Dan grimaced. "Not this early!" He braced himself on one elbow and propped his head in his hand. "Sheridan here?"

"Worse! I just heerd tell that Abe Lincoln give Shelby permission to take troops into Mexico, recruitin' from bluebellies same as us Rebs. Wanted us to drive ol' Maximilian right off his throne. I reckon it's true, too. I picked it up from Bob Post, who got it from Major Edwards' orderly!"

Dan fell back on his bedroll and tucked the thin blanket around his shoulders. "I'd expect a recruit to fall for a rumor like that," he said with mock derision. "But an old soldier like you should figure that Lincoln was killed on April fourteenth, Johnston surrendered a month later, and Kirby Smith not till two weeks after that. How could Lincoln know about Shelby's army?"

Maehler capped the bottle. "I recollect hearin' that Kirby Smith talked to the Mexkins in February. Saw the end comin' and went so far as to give 'em cannon to hold fer him." He rolled out his bedroll and crawled into it, boots and all. "What do you think of that?"

The high clear notes of reveille sounded over the compound. Dan wormed from his blankets and began to struggle into his boots. "First of all, I think this is Shelby's army—not Smith's. And second, I think you shouldn't spread rumors. They always sound like gospel coming from an old man."

"Old man!" Maehler began to express his indignation as Dan filled a small can from the water bucket, picked up his shaving kit and collected some dry kindling. "Hell," he snorted, "a man don't reach his prime till maybe fifty!"

Dan left him talking and went out to start his morning cook fire. Men like Maehler made the best soldiers, he thought; they were content to live from day to day because they didn't have any ties.

He realized then that the same thing would apply to him. He didn't have any ties either, and couldn't think about making any. Knowing that as he did, it was strange that he would even consider Maehler in a different light from himself. He supposed it was because he had come to think of Jane and Wil as being close to him, almost as if they were his family. That was strange too, since he hadn't known them long, but he had taken a solid liking to them both. He was sorry he hadn't found the time to call on them.

After breakfast Dan had to help issue equipment to a detachment of twenty-five men who had arrived in a body during the night. They were ragged and ill-equipped for the most part, having traveled the back trails to avoid the Yankees they knew were on the way, but they were cheerful enough. As one put it, they were glad to be back in the army.

"How're the women around here?" another asked.

"Beautiful," Dan grinned. "Like all Texas women."

It was a little thing, but enough to set him thinking about Jane again. He decided on the spot that he would visit her and Wil this very night if he could arrange it. There couldn't be much time left now.

When he had finished passing out the supplies he fed and watered the sorrel, then started for headquarters tent to see if he could arrange for an evening off. He smiled as a small Negro trotted purposefully ahead of him, carrying a letter to the tent. Somebody had a pretty invitation.

The boy was there ahead of him by a full minute, long enough for Walcott to stick his head out and start to bellow. He stopped short, seeing Dan.

"You came running fast enough. You must know this boy."

Surprised, Dan took the perfumed letter he handed over.

"French perfume," Walcott said. "The only way to fight a war."

Dan, pleased but flustered, said, "Am I on duty tonight?"

"Midnight patrol," Walcott answered.

"In that case, tell me where and I'll meet my partner in town." He suddenly found himself warming to the thought of a pleasant dinner with pleasant company. It might be a long time before the chance came again.

Walcott, smirking, gave him his directions. "But don't you forget to be there," he warned.

"Don't worry," Dan assured him. "Her father will see that I don't."

He left Walcott still smirking and began to make his way to his own tent, opening the letter as he went along. He took the narrow scented paper from the envelope, unfolded it, and slowly came to a stop. It said, *I'd be pleased if you could take me to dinner this evening. Mavis Todd.*

Dan looked up. The boy who had delivered the message had already scampered. He would have to find another way to decline her invitation; he could do it, he decided, without giving offense because their acquaintance was short and the notice she had given him was even shorter. Maybe he could simply leave a note with the hotel clerk when he went to see Jane and Wil.

He resumed his walk, spotted Maehler, his partner for the night, chopping firewood, and pulled up again, remembering the comparison he had made earlier between himself and the old soldier. They were both without ties, and both lacked the right to make any. Spending an entire evening with Jane suddenly did not seem right. He had a strong notion that the better he got to know her, the better he would like her, and it would be totally unfair to Jane to court her, which is what an evening with her would amount to.

In the same circumstances he would not be courting Mavis; he would be paying court to her. It was a thing she no doubt expected, and had long since grown accustomed to.

If he wanted to be completely fair to Jane, he decided,

he would visit her and Wil, but only for a little while. If he spent an evening out, it would have to be with Mavis.

He went on, was ducking into the tent when Maehler's greeting of several seconds ago penetrated his consciousness.

Jane answered his knock and her blue eyes beamed with instant pleasure. "Dan, how nice to see you! If you hadn't come we were going to ride out to the camp tomorrow."

"You can anyway." Dan smiled his own pleasure, noting as he did so that her sunburn had dimmed now to an even tan that blended nicely with her pale brown dress.

As he went inside, Wil boomed, "Come in, Dan, come in!" He was lying on the bed, a wet cloth across his forehead. He raised himself up on an elbow and made a face. "Excuse me for not getting up. That Indian must have had iron muscles and Jane's making it her mission in life to coddle me. Besides, I worked all day."

Dan shook hands. "I'm sorry you're not feeling better."

"So am I," Wil said ruefully. "Jane, pour us a drink like a good girl. Dan, sit and tell us what you've been doing."

"We've been working, patrolling, building our army," Dan said. "Drilling our fair share. I expect you've heard all of it from Bill and a dozen others. But I haven't had much news of the colony; I've been too tied up."

"Well, we've got our problems," Wil replied. "But nothing we can't whip one way or another. I heard something this afternoon that might make things easier."

"I want to know all of it," Dan said. He took a chair and leaned back, watching Jane pour the liquor. She was neat and economical in her gestures—pleasant to watch as she crossed the room.

He took his glass and lifted it. "*Salud y pesetas!*"

"*Prosit!*" Wil saluted back. He smacked his lips and said, "Jane, please don't go back to that infernal sewing!" She was obviously hovering about the white fabric because she was nervous, but she obediently left it and came over to perch beside Wil. "Dan," he went on, "have you seen Marman's signs around town?"

Dan nodded affirmatively and Wil pushed the cloth off his forehead and swung his legs onto the floor. "Thirty families. That means thirty, maybe forty wagons. All the colonists are picked now. No kids, and the men are all middle-aged soldiers or politicians, like Russell Todd."

"Well," Dan said gently, "outfitting to immigrate takes money. Most of the young men haven't seen hard money in years."

"I expected it to be like this," Wil agreed. "And I'm not too surprised that most of 'em are bringing Negroes with them, mostly house niggers who only know how to fetch and serve. But one thing I wasn't ready for. Reed is bringing sixteen extra wagons of his own, loaded with farm tools. Not that we can't take it in our stride," he added quickly. "It'll mean extra work, is all."

"Wil—why not take your son with you? Shelby would discharge him, and it might be the very thing he needs."

"Ach! I love Bill, but he's a child. Less than a child. He looks for glory, not work."

Jane shot Wil a look, evidently starting to defend Bill, but she must have realized that there was little she could say. The silence she left hung heavy in the room; the oppressive heat underlined and overlaid it. Dan uncomfortably looked out the window at the small dusty town caught in a twilight that was especially meaningful because San Antonio was waiting for the end of one government and the beginning of another. He could sense the nervousness everywhere, could feel it strongly in this room, though Wil seemed determined not to let it show.

"We've got things in our favor," Wil said. "I don't look for the kind of trouble you might think. Juarez knows me—Esteban came personally to tell me we could cross their lines. And Marman has permission from Maximilian and the French commander. Maybe we won't even be troubled too much by guerrillas; I know a lot of their leaders. But we will have a job on our hands. Dan, now I'll tell you what I heard this afternoon. There's a strong rumor that Shelby is not going anywhere. He was just going to pass through this town, as he did Houston and Austin. But he's been here five days now. Some think he's losing his nerve."

"From what I've heard, he could lose a lot and still have plenty," Dan smiled.

"S'pose he does back out? What will you do?"

"I don't know. I don't believe I'll have to think about it."

"Well," Wil said, "if he does, I want you to know you're still welcome with us. Think about it, anyway. In fact, I'd like for you to meet Marman while you're here. He sent for me a little while ago, and I guess I'd better see what he wants. Why don't you come along?"

"Thanks anyway, but I have to go somewhere." He said it without enthusiasm, yet knew that he really did want to go out with Mavis now. Maybe an evening with a beautiful woman for whom he had no particular feeling would put his thoughts back in order.

"I'll be back in a little while," Wil said, rising.

"I've really got to go, too." Dan stood up.

"At least stay a minute," Jane said softly.

Wil was picking up his wide-brimmed hat. Before Dan could answer he was saying, "Well, I don't mind telling you I hope Shelby busts up. And I think he will. I'll see you either way in a day or so. Thanks for stopping by." His hand lingered on the doorknob but he thought better of arguing further and went on out into the corridor. The door closed and his footsteps stomped away.

"Why doesn't he hire someone—anyone?" Dan asked.

Jane came to her feet. "He's going to. But the only ones who will go are . . . adventurers. Men looking for excitement. He can't find anybody who is really interested in the colony or the wagon train." For some unaccountable reason

66

her lips trembled. "Dan, I've wondered what you decided to do about your ranch."

"I gave it to my sister."

"Oh. Then if something happens to Shelby, you could still go back to it."

He slowly shook his head. "No, it's given. It will belong to my nephews and my niece now."

She seemed to gird herself, and her eyes dropped. He was aware again of the gentle odor of carnation which enveloped her.

"Dan, on the plains, when the Indians were dead and we were alone except for my father . . . I was almost afraid of you."

"Why?"

"You were in a blue uniform, and all through the South there were stories about men in blue. Do you understand what I'm saying?"

He nodded soberly.

Her lips parted. "What I'm trying to say is . . . I know you'll stay with Shelby if he keeps his army, but if he doesn't, and you were to come with us, I wouldn't be afraid of you . . . any more."

"Jane—please don't." He was shocked and his stomach sickened at the double realization that she liked him more than he ever should have permitted, that Wil's need for him must be far greater than he had realized. There was a sickness, too, because Jane, lacking the subtleties of women who were accustomed to flirting, had not been artful and evasive; the meaning of the words she had spoken could not be skillfully changed to save face.

He said roughly, "Jane, nothing will happen to Shelby, and I must stay with him. Your colony might be a new Confederacy, but he's all that's left of the old one. I owe that Confederacy more than I can ever repay, but I must try to repay it."

"Then—your blue uniform—you really were a Yankee?"

"Yes, I served with the North," he nodded. "And that

makes me as responsible as the next man for what has happened. I'm as responsible as anybody else for these few days—this midsummer night's dream when everybody must frantically choose a course for the future because the past is about to catch up with them."

Her eyes looked past him. "I . . . almost threatened you with the blue uniform. But I couldn't."

He bent forward and kissed her warm lips. "I thank you for that," he said, "and I'll wish you well. You and Wil both. And I want you to know that I could wish that things were different. But they're not, for us or for anyone in the South."

It was not the kind of farewell speech he had wanted to make; but neither had he intended to feel like this.


After lingering over a drink at the crowded bar, Dan made his way upstairs again. The door to the Todds' suite was slightly ajar, and as he raised his hand to rap he heard Bill Morgen's voice inside.

"—I've even reserved a table."

Mavis' drawl was almost sharp. "I'm sorry, but you shouldn't take so much for granted. . . . Now Bill, that's enough of that!"

There was a low scuffling sound, a sharp slap. The unhurried tattoo of Mavis' footsteps came closer and the door pulled inward. Dan looked beyond her and saw Bill, without Cogan for once, standing in sullen anger.

The slight frown between Mavis' eyes smoothed out. "You're just in time, Mr. Kilbourne. Mr. Morgen was just leavin'."

Dan said politely, "I'm sorry I'm a little late."

Bill came over to the door and bowed slightly to Mavis. "I'll call another time," he said woodenly. He shot Dan a dark look and moved past him without speaking.

When he was out of hearing Mavis said, "I don't know what came over him. He's really a nice boy, I know." She was classically beautiful and classically dressed in a low-cut cream silk gown that matched her complexion. Her hair was arranged in Spanish fashion, its gleaming black covered by a lace mantilla so old that it, too, was the color of cream. Her heavy gold earrings matched an intricate necklace and a pair of wide bracelets.

She seemed pleased at his unintended stare. "I didn't think—after we met the other night—that I would have to invite you to dinner." She smiled to take all rebuke from the words as she picked up a short jacket that matched her dress. She came out into the corridor and he helped her into it, his rough hands scraping the silken mantilla. He lightened his touch as he felt warm flesh through the fabric.

"I know a nice Mexican restaurant not far from here," he said, easing the door closed.

"Then let's try it," she said, pleased. "Just for once I'd like to forget about this awful war. Maybe that's a good place to start."


The restaurant was softly lit with individual candles on each table. The sharp smell of spices was in the air. A guitarist lightly strummed his mellow instrument, lifting his voice from time to time in muted song. It was a place to gather memories for some future campfire.

Mavis smiled at Dan across the table. "It was forward of me to invite you to dinner."

"Was it?" Dan matched her smile. "I'm afraid I don't know much about etiquette."

Her laugh was as mellow as the smooth chords of the guitar. "You're easy to talk to. Maybe I recognized that the other night, when we met. Or maybe I invited you only because you didn't ask me."

"Does there have to be a reason?"

"Always," she said with mock seriousness. "There's a reason for everything that happens, and I always have to know what it is." She cocked her head, appearing to study his features. "You're not nearly as good-looking as Reed Marman. The skin is tight on your face, and your eyes are set too deep, and your brows are so black you seem to be scowling sometimes when you don't mean to. So it can't be looks. Maybe it's because of the way Wil Morgen described your fighting off the Indians."

Dan tried to hide his embarrassment. "When you get to know him better, as you no doubt will on your trip, then you'll realize that he likes to exaggerate."

She frowned. "I wish I weren't going."

"But you must . . . because of your father?"

"Yes. He used to be a United States senator, but he walked out and seceded with his state. Then he became a Confederate senator, and I'm afraid that's too much for the North to forgive."

"Lincoln promised malice toward none."

"Lincoln is dead and the witch hunt is growing. A few days ago a troop ship jammed with Yankees from the Andersonville prison blew up in the Mississippi and they didn't even look for defective boilers, or blame the firemen. They just said it was diehard Southerners, another crime to be paid for. And you know about the indictment they drew up after Lincoln was killed. It wasn't limited to his assassins; it named Jefferson Davis and *others unknown*—which could mean just about anybody who ever held office in the South."

The waiter brought them huge dishes of guacamole and hot crisp tostadas. Mavis placed one small bite on her pink tongue and worried it for a moment before she swallowed.

"We were going to forget the war," she reminded.

"Yes. But it seems there's little else to talk about these days."

She smiled, a little wistfully. "A long time ago men used to spend entire evenin's payin' pretty compliments to the ladies they were with, and making light, charming conversation about nothing at all. But I do admit we had less on our minds in those days." She sighed. "It seems an eternity since we lived for fancy balls and parties and fashionable clothes—for rides through a country so beautiful it could

70

bring tears. Just imagine—I was to have married the . . . young man on the plantation next to ours, and all of both places—two fine homes and acres and acres of forest and cotton lands—would have belonged to us. And now, here I am reduced to two wagons and a little proud that I've got them."

"And the man you were engaged to?"

"Killed at the very beginnin' of the war." She hesitated. "I think of him often, but I do intend to marry someone else; if I find the right person, that is. I'm afraid I want far too much."

"Well, it's a little late for those compliments," Dan grinned, "but I've got a notion you'll get everything you want."

She shook her head and said, half-seriously, "It won't be easy. Besides a loving husband, I want money, property, influence, position—whatever else you can name. I know I won't meet anybody who can give me those things, mind you; not any more. But one day I'll find someone strong enough to get them. With my help, that is." She laughed a little. "I'm only talkin' in fun, of course. I'm sure when I fall in love I won't care what the man is like, or what he'll be able to give us."

Their plates arrived. She began to eat with relish and Dan, trying to guard against four years of campfire manners, pitched into his own food. He liked Mavis' company, he thought; besides being beautiful and intelligent, she had an easy ability to share her feelings by dint of minute facial expressions and gestures. And she was blessed with an ability to be warm and friendly without allowing the least presumption.

The meal was seasoned as he liked it, and he enjoyed every morsel. When he had finished he watched her gracefully eat the last bite on her own plate. She touched the napkin to her lips and raised her eyes; they studied each other soberly for several seconds.

"Dan," she said finally, "when I sent my note I was think-

71

ing that soon I wouldn't be able to select the company I keep, that because time was so short I was privileged to choose myself an escort. It not only was forward of me; it turns out I wasn't being very fair."

"I don't have any complaint." He smiled.

"But you will have, because I was dishonest. I just couldn't bring myself to warn you how short the evenin' would be, because I didn't want to miss it. But now I can't put it off any longer. I'm dyin' at bein' so rude, but I'll have to ask you to take me back to the hotel. If there were any way I could make it up to you, I would. I want you to know that."

"But why, then?"

"Because I have so much packing to do, and we have so little time."

He was surprised. "Do you know when you're leaving?"

"Sunday morning."

Frowning, he said, "I just saw Wil Morgen and he didn't mention it."

"He didn't know, but he does by now. Reed had already sent for him when we got the news. About an hour ago."

"Well, then," he said slowly, "since it's our last evening, it seems a shame to make it so short."

She said, "Our only evenin', really. And I am sorry. But I honestly have things to do."

"Well, short or not, I've still enjoyed it." Dan dug out several bills and put them by his plate. "Maybe I can change your mind when we get back to the hotel patio." He got up and made his way around the table to slide back her chair.

"I hope you don't think I wanted it to happen like this," Mavis said. "I just can't help myself."

"If I'm making a fuss," Dan answered as she rose, "it's because I'm sorry you're leaving."

They threaded their way out of the restaurant and he took her arm for the short walk to the hotel. The moon glowed brightly, seeming to frame her face in light. "I'm sure I can still hear the guitars," she said. "They must have made an impression."

"The hotel has an orchestra," he reminded.

"If time weren't so short—"

"Time is always short—whenever there is any time."

"Then we must all learn to act quickly," she smiled.

Dan lapsed into a thoughtful silence. He had made all the proper overtures—out of politeness, out of his own need for company, even because Mavis was genuinely pleasant to be with. But news of the wagon train's imminent departure had caused a mood to fall upon him; it would be a measure of relief not to have to make the conversation she wanted.

The patio was as crowded as it had been Monday night. Their progress through it was further slowed as Mavis paused often to speak a word or two in response to the many greetings she received.

When at last they reached the stairs, she said for Dan's ears only, "I'm sorry to have to say it, but most of these people are only talkers. They'll be here blustering and threatening to do big things when Sheridan comes, and they won't understand how they happened to be caught in spite of all their plans." She slowly shook her head. "The only exception is Reed Marman. He's a man with few likable qualities, but he does get things done."

"Shelby will not leave San Antonio far behind him," Dan said confidently.

They came to the door of her suite. "I'm afraid your man Shelby is one of the talkers," she said. "He thinks he can do with a thousand men what Lee couldn't do with half a million! Why, some of his officers actually think Louis Napoleon might recognize his army, when he refused to recognize the South all during the war. It doesn't seem probable, does it?"

"That part of it doesn't, no."

She laughed. "Every man has his dream, I suppose. Well,

I'll say good night, Dan, and goodbye as well. We're not apt to see each other again."

She stood on tiptoe and put both arms around his neck. His hands slid onto her back and their lips met. The fire that burned through him was so swift and sudden that it was unlike anything else he had ever known. She shuddered and pulled free from his tightening grasp. She managed another little laugh, but her voice was shaky.

"Perhaps it's just as well we haven't known each other too long. Goodbye, Dan. I'll always remember you."

She was inside and the door was closed and he had not yet found his voice. He stood staring at the solid panel. She had come into his life and gone out again, he thought, with the swiftness of a hummingbird, but in that brief interval she had stirringly reminded him of her womanhood.

Since he was not the type of Southern gentleman she had been engaged and had none of the qualifications she claimed to want in a husband, he couldn't figure why she had gone to the trouble.

The buzzing talk in the bar flowed endlessly, but it traveled in circles. Dan heard it all several times, then took an hour's walk to clear his head for duty.

As he drew up to the corner where he was to meet Maehler, dark scudding clouds began to roll in to hide the waning moon. He thrust both hands into his pockets and leaned up against a warehouse, tuning his ears for Maehler's coming. The streets were deserted and quiet. In the daytime this district bustled with life, but it was a transient life that disappeared with nightfall.

He felt a thud through his leaning shoulder, then heard a muffled sound. He listened closely and knew it for a groan of pain. Something crashed inside the warehouse and the noise trailed away like dying thunder.

There were no windows on this side of the building, and the big loading door was locked and bolted. Long strides carried him around the corner and he stumbled onto a boardwalk; the uneven planking impeded him.

He came to two windows. One was wide open, and yet the sounds coming through it were muted. He vaulted up and twisted his body, plummeting onto a wooden floor. In the darkness he could see nothing. The short match he struck showed only a small office that held a paper-strewn desk.

He lit another and saw a closed door. He pushed a chair aside and wrenched the door open, and the volume of noise swelled. The warehouse, he saw, was jammed with boxes that were scattered in loose piles reaching almost to the rafters. He could find no way of reaching the scuffling sounds.

He wasted precious seconds going back into the office. He wrenched a hanging kerosene lamp from its hook and hoped there was fuel in it; somebody was taking a harsh beating while he fumbled.

The lamp caught on the first match, and he hurried back into the vast room. Now, in the increased light, he found a narrow corridor threading through the boxes. He held the lamp in front of him and began to twist and weave his way through.

A clearing opened before him and the unsteady light flickered over a soldier struggling with three civilians. Only the stygian blackness could have kept the one from being overwhelmed; in the struggle only he would have known that anyone he hit was an enemy.

Dan looked hurriedly for a place to drop the lamp. He found a jutting box corner, set it down and waded in just as the man in gray landed a roundhouse punch that took one of the ruffians out of the fight.

The other two began frantically looking for a way to escape, but Dan was in front of them. One whipped up a pistol and Dan's gun barrel parted his hair. The second desperately tore into the other soldier and wrestled him to

75

the floor. His thumbs sought a windpipe and the soldier, already worn out, could not fight him off.

Dan grabbed the attacker's shoulders, yanked him to his feet and sent him full-length with a blow from the pistol butt. The man groaned and rolled over, pushing himself up to his knees, but saw Dan's pistol and remained on the floor.

Dan looked toward the man in gray and understood why Maehler had been late. The old soldier, out of wind, grunted and shakily pulled himself to a sitting position. "Almost gave you up," he croaked. "Heard sound in here—"

"Rest a minute," Dan said. "That was quite a little fracas you were having."

"A beauty," Maehler gasped. He rubbed his throat and held the waist of his pants open until his breath came slower, then managed to wobble onto his feet. "You . . . saved my bacon fer sure."

"Forget it," Dan said.

Maehler continued rubbing his throat. "Don't know what they were doin'; stealin', I guess." He went on disgustedly, "Only an old fool like me woulda rushed in here with no light. I deserved ever'thing I got." He pointed at the man on his knees. "Up," he said, "you got a cell waitin'."

Dan began to drag one of the others to his feet.

"Might be," Maehler said hopefully, "we can spend this patrol bummin' around headquarters. I wouldn't mind, tired as I am." He shook his head. "Don't think I'll ever forget how you come in after me, 'cause I won't. If it's ever the other way around I'll come runnin' too, you can bet."

"Forget it," Dan repeated. For some reason he was a little disturbed by Maehler's words. He wished people wouldn't keep making such promises. Some superstitious streak said that one day things might try to even out.

# 5

Friday night's patrol earned a day's rest for Dan and Maehler both, but Sunday morning again found Dan on duty in the town. This time he had asked for it, in lieu of other chores, and since it didn't seem like too much of a favor Sergeant Walcott had grinned and granted it to him.

A talk with Lieutenant Randolph had further gotten him assigned to the vicinity of Military Plaza where Marman's colonists were assembling. His duty companion was a bearded young man named Peal; the beard, Dan suspected, was a token that although Peal had served for eight months in the army and hadn't fired a shot, he was a man for all that.

Dan tarried, watching the wagons, and the impatient Peal sought to hurry him. "Hell," he said disgustedly, "haven't you ever seen a wagon train before this?"

"A few," Dan answered, and reluctantly moved along. There was activity aplenty, and Wil Morgen was very much in evidence, moving from wagon to wagon, giving each family a short lecture, waving his arms like an animated puppet. He glimpsed Jane as well, but she also was on the move. Of the Todds, he saw only Russell, and that during the brief minute he listened to Wil's directions. Wil was gradually getting the wagons—thirty-seven, he counted —lined up in the shape of an enormous horseshoe. Marman's vehicles, Dan supposed, would fall in later somewhere along the road.

"Chrissake," Paul said, "you comin' or not?"

"Coming," Dan said. They swung along the edge of the buildings, making their way toward Laredo Street. Peal, shorter than Dan, had brownish hair and eyes and a reddish face. He paused, and made a show of lighting a stogie. When he had puffed out several big clouds of smoke he pointed with the still-flaming match.

"That's the General riding yonder," he said importantly. "There was a party just left for Mexico—a few governors and the like—and General Shelby went to see them off. That's Colonel Elliott with him, and Major Edwards." He paled suddenly, as they turned and rode directly toward him. He looked about for something to do with the cigar, and finally stomped its coal and put the rest in his pocket. To explain his discomfiture, he muttered, "How the hell can a man salute a general and smoke a cigar at the same time? It's not fit."

The three officers rode slowly along the street, seemingly unaware of the patrol until Dan and Peal both saluted. Shelby returned the salute and reined up. Elliott and Edwards, flanking him, followed suit. The scarred Elliott reminded Dan of a cavalry saber and Edwards also commanded attention; the heat of his passion showed clearly in virtually every report that Shelby had filed during the war, and now he was keeping a careful, if somewhat biased, chronicle of the new Iron Brigade. But it was Shelby himself who caught a man's eye. His broad forehead, full nose, and thick golden moustache and beard were made more severe by the downward dip of brows that overhung his uncompromising eyes. Dan mentally withdrew his observation about Peal's beard.

Colonel Shelby—the General—smiled pleasantly enough, but Dan knew that his eyes were not missing any detail of appearance or manner. "You men are both new to me," he said. "I trust, now that you've joined the Brigade, you find everything satisfactory?"

"Yes, sir!" Peal responded promptly.

Dan's own hesitation had been but the merest fraction

of a second, and yet Shelby caught it. The smile left his face and his brows drew together. "If you have a complaint, speak it."

"Not a complaint, sir," Dan said. "A . . . concern. There is a rumor about that this army will never leave San Antonio."

"And do you believe it?"

"No, sir."

The smile came back. "Then I would advise you to maintain confidence in your own judgment." He saluted and moved off and his two officers followed; Edwards was also smiling, but Elliott had not changed the grim set of his features.

"Chrissake," Peal said, when they were out of earshot, "you got a nerve." He dug out his cigar, flicked off some of the burnt tobacco, and relit it. He puffed out smoke and flung away the match. "We better get started. Shouldn't take more'n twenty minutes to make our rounds."

Dan agreed, thinking that the General should drop around more often; he had a good effect on Peal.

But the effect was short-lived. A little later Peal managed to kill a full ten minutes examining a fancy saddle in one of the stores. He inquired the price several times and examined every last stitch and carving, though it was obvious to Dan and the storekeeper both that he was only making talk. Chances were good that he couldn't have bought a toe fender.

As Peal reluctantly tore himself away from the saddle, Dan heard the rumble of the wagons beginning to move out. He hurried now, in spite of Peal's protests, and managed to complete the circle and reach the old Cathedral while two-thirds of the vehicles still remained in the Plaza. A gathering crowd was shouting its advice and good wishes; the settlers were waving back, and several yelled their approval of Peal and Dan. Dan guessed it gave them courage to see that at least somebody was still wearing gray.

His attention was distracted by a lone rider galloping

out of the Plaza. He was small in stature, quick in his movements, and he wore a black outfit with matching patches of embroidery. He stared at Dan for only a second, but with such hatred as Dan had never seen before. Then he stuck the spurs to his horse and raced onward.

Peal whistled. "Who the hell was that?"

"I don't know." Dan was as puzzled as Peal.

"Whoever he was, you better not ever let him get behind you."

The man was soon forgotten as wagon after wagon went by—mule-drawn and shipshape, for most were newly made for the army, and had been used little if at all. The big wheels ground past and middle-aged people sat on the rocking wooden seats with all the cheer soldiers felt after orders had been g____ ____o strike camp. It was too early yet for the complaint___ ___start rolling in.

Dan search__ ___for Jane, stubbornly disregarding Peal's renewed impatience. At length he spotted her close to the rear of the train, sitting sidesaddle on a beautiful bay gelding. Her blue riding habit was topped by a flat-crowned white hat with a fairly broad brim that was upturned on each side by a tight blue ribbon. Her face, with its nicely rounded chin, seemed composed enough, but her blue eyes were watchful as she constantly took stock of the wagons. Dan began to worry that she had seen him, but did not wish to speak. He called to her.

Her face lit with pleasure at once and she reined over toward him.

Dan said, "Peal, will you excuse me for a minute? What I want to say is private."

Peal took offense, but nevertheless managed a grin. "I wondered what the hell you were looking for," he said. He moved off a few steps.

Jane brought with her a sense of neatness and orderliness, Dan thought. She held out her hand and Dan reached up and took it.

"I'm glad I had a chance to see you," he said. "I wanted to be sure everything was right between us."

"We're fine," Jane acknowledged, though her face reddened.

"If so many people weren't around," Dan said, "I'd kiss you goodbye."

She smiled. "You've been a good friend to us, Dan. You always will be." The smile faded. "I've got to tell you—Bill doesn't like you very much. He's jealous, I think; he's changed so much I hardly know him. I wish . . . something could be done to straighten him up."

"If there's anything I can do, I will," Dan promised. "And you know I hope you have a wonderful trip, and find everything you want."

"Thank you." She glanced after the wagons. "I'll have to catch up. It would be . . . funny, wouldn't it . . . if you stayed and then Shelby broke up?" Her eyes traveled over his face as if to fix it in her mind. "Goodbye, Dan. God bless you." She whirled the horse and raced it down the street to regain her place in the train. Dan watched the skirt of her blue habit flare up to trail behind her slight figure.

Peal came back beside him and said again, "I wondered what the hell you were looking for."

Dan, inclined to snap, kept quiet. They moved off, walking alongside the wagons for a time, then cutting right into another street. Gradually the noise began to lessen.

"They sure make a racket," Peal said.

Because Peal was quick to take affront, Dan ordinarily would have let the remark pass for what it was—an attempt to strike up a conversation to wipe away the loneliness. But now he was in no mood to listen to picayune criticisms.

"I guess you can stand it for a few minutes," he said, "if they can live with it day in and day out."

Peal shut up and they continued their round in antagonistic silence.

After the last wagon was out of the town, and the last

whisper of their going had faded to nothing, Walcott rode up to them. He cast a supercilious eye down at Dan. "You see what you wanted to see?" he inquired.

"I made out well enough."

"I had a funny idea you might run out on us," Walcott said. "I got a look at that senator's daughter the other night."

Peal's spirits bounced up. "If she was the one I saw, I wouldn't blame him."

"I'm glad you both take so much interest," Dan said.

Walcott brushed a thumb across his blond moustache, as though flicking away a fly. "I've handled men enough to know when I see one weakening. What would you do right now if I told you Shelby was going to disband to-morrow?"

"Why, I guess maybe I'd go after the wagons."

"Then I'll have to disappoint you. We got the word a few minutes ago. The Yankees will arrive on Thursday, but we won't be here to say hello. We're pulling out Wednesday morning."

After the effect of the initial announcement had worn off Dan said, "The wagons are headed for Eagle Pass, and from there to Monterrey. It seems likely we might run into them."

Walcott laughed. "They've got too much start on us. They'll be through Eagle Pass before we get there. We might or might not head toward Monterrey, but even if we do they'll be sticking to the wagon roads and we won't. I'd say you'd seen the last of them."

"Maybe we ought to stay here till Thursday and get us a Yankee or two," Peal said.

"Wednesday morning," Walcott stated flatly, and rode on to make his rounds.

A bugle call rang out sharply and pridefully, and the men who responded to its clear, sharp stacatto were as proud as its highest note. Excitement swept through the cavalry-trained horses as well. They high-stepped into a column of fours without urging, prancing nervously as a mounted rider dashed down the lines for a hasty inspection.

A few shrill, high-spirited yells rang out, but were quickly suppressed by those who were conscious of their large audience. Citizens of San Antonio had turned out in a great body to witness this historic moment—the departure of the last remaining Confederate army.

A breeze stirred the guidons and whipped commands all along the line. It was ten o'clock, exactly the time set for departure. The sun was bright, but not yet insufferably hot. Dan Kilbourne did not believe in omens, but it was still a matter for thought that not one horse had gone unexpectedly lame at the last minute; nor had a single wagon been crippled by a broken wheel or axle to cause a detail to remain behind. The army was ready to move.

The commands came and horses wheeled and pranced off. Wagons creaked into motion. Horse-drawn cannon lurched forward. Up ahead the line had already begun to stretch out as Colonel Joseph O. Shelby set the pace.

With him rode General Kirby Smith, who once before had been to Mexico, as a captain in the Mexican War. Even though Smith had surrendered the Army of the Trans-Mississippi after promising not to do so, Shelby had graciously offered the General his command; but Smith did not intend to remain with the expedition.

With Shelby, too, rode General "Prince" Magruder, who had driven the Yankees from Galveston in '63, and Governor Reynolds of Missouri, and a host of others—government officials three months ago, now just plain men in search of a home.

They rode off and behind them were a few spotty cheers from the citizens of San Antonio, though these soon subsided into a deep silence. Dan thought he could decipher the feelings behind the silence. During San Antonio's turbulent hundred-and-fifty-year history, many armies had come and gone. Today one was leaving; an era was drawing to a close. But before this week was ended another would come, this time clothed in blue. The citizens would again be carried in a new and uncertain direction before the shifting wind.

The first night out men were inclined to lie in their blankets and look at the stars and examine their souls. San Antonio was still nearby, so close that the leaving of it did not seem complete, and for some reason its nearness soberly emphasized the growing chasm that separated the old life from the new.

It was not until the afternoon of the second day when, as the distance behind them increased and the terrain changed to chapparal-infested flatlands, the parting seemed final. Loneliness spilled over then and timid feelers were extended in a search for comrades. Under that night's full moon, men suddenly needed to reminisce and speculate and hope, and so remained grouped about their cooking fires until flames gave way to simmering coals and even these began to die and grow cold.

Dan was messing with Maehler, Sherm, Featherly and Peal. Maehler was by far the oldest of the group and his graying hair, thin on top but hanging long on the back of his neck, lent a certain authority to his words when he stuck to his subject and didn't get caught up in some wild, improbable tale concocted for amusement.

The bearded Peal couldn't stand to be left out of things. He butted into everything that was said whenever it was possible to do so without emphasizing his own lack of combat experience. Sherm, the blond youngster, and Featherly, his look-alike dark companion, were calmer of nature, but their skinny frames were so filled with assurance that it shone through their big eyes. Sherm, the more talkative of the two, pressed Dan for a résumé of his war experiences.

"I started with the Eighth Texas Cavalry," Dan said. "Terry's Rangers, we were called. I sort of cut my teeth in the woods at Shiloh. Later we fought other places in Tennessee, and some in Kentucky. Near the last, some of the outfit wound up facing Sherman."

"You ever hit?" Maehler asked.

"A couple of times." Dan grinned. By Maehler, if a man hadn't been hit he sure as hell hadn't been in the thick of it.

But Sherm and Featherly neither one felt that way. Since both had fought through some of the thickest battles and neither had been wounded, getting hit to their way of thinking was something that happened more often than not when a man kept his head in his butt. Sherm, his twang rumbling from deep within his thin chest, said as much.

"Hell," he added, "it ain't always the case, but we seen it happen time and ag'in. There was two kinds that took it the worst. Them that got excited and stood up when they shoulda took cover, and them that had been through so much they got careless."

Maehler took stolid exception. "Them that keeps down in a hole and don't pop up till it's over won't never git hurt, I reckon. We carried some like that on our back, all through the war."

Sherm protested, but Dan put a quick stop to the argument. "There'll still be time to settle some of these things. Maybe sooner than we think."

Peal sneered. "You one of those that can't stand an argument?"

"He's right," Maehler said. "Tonight we'd do better to quit yappin' like a lot of kiotes and get some shut-eye."

"We haven't figured yet what everybody thinks this outfit will do," Peal objected.

Featherly spoke up, his teeth gleaming from his narrow, sun-darkened face. "I've thought on it. But nobody can figger it. Not till we hit the Rio Grande."

"One thing we do know," Peal said, grinning. "We know why everybody joined up. For women and gold."

"Some for that," Featherly agreed. "Some for excitement

and adventure, some because they hate the Yankees, some because they want to go on killing—some because they think they might still win the war."

Peal took offense at Featherly's disagreement and got up to ready his blankets. The rest of the camp had already begun to settle, and Dan got up as well. He was standing when firing broke out at a point about a mile to the rear of the camp.

The revolver fire crashed with outraged fury. The blasts joined one another like rumbling thunder, sweeping on and on in a rolling, earth-shaking barrage. The night was ripped asunder and an army popped from its blankets, fumbling for guns and boots.

The thunder suddenly broke off as though it had been sliced with an ax. Sentries yelled wary questions, and then several more distant guns exploded. The silence which fell after that was final.

Officers began running through the camp shouting orders. Lieutenant Randolph stormed up to Dan's fire in his stockinged feet.

"You men! Saddle up!" His arm described a swift arc to include all five of them, and then he hobbled on in a hasty search for others who were still fully dressed and armed.

As they made for the horses with flying legs Maehler and Peal bumped into each other, cursed, and ran on. Dan was first to reach the horses, first to catch up his own mount, but his companions, with the exception of Peal, were not far behind. Peal had stumbled and fallen and skinned himself, and wanted the world to know he blamed it on Maehler.

Once again, when Dan was saddled and bridled and up, the others, excepting Peal, were not far behind him. The four kept their horses spinning in tight circles while Peal fumbled, cursed, and fumbled some more.

He was still not ready when they were joined by a major and seven more men, and received the order to race forward. But shortly afterward Dan heard him bringing up the rear, pleading loudly for everybody to wait up.

In the light of the full moon the road shone like a winding river; the illusion was instantly branded a lie when fine, swirling dust, barely settled in the wake of today's churning march, began to puff upwards in powdery, choking clouds. Peal was getting the worst of it, and Dan could not help but find humor in the thought.

Shadowy bushes moved by in waves as the sorrel stretched out, trying to pass the other horses. Dan held him in tight check and tried to see through the haze in front of him. It was a blind charge into the unknown. The major pulled his gun and the soldiers followed his example. Steady, surging minutes passed, and then they spotted someone on the road ahead, slowed, made out their own Captain Williams and several of his men. Another few seconds and they could see that Williams was not now in trouble. The major shouted and they were recognized. They halted roughly and Dan swung down with the others.

When the onrushing column of dust had begun to move past them he stared with shock at the mass death Williams and his men had dealt out. In a small ravine, huddled tightly together, were roughly two dozen men who had sought to ambush Williams—for the sake of the mules he had with him, he said. But Williams' advance scout had spotted the ambushers and it was they who had been caught. Half had been killed before they had even been able to return Williams' fire.

In spite of this, four of the Brigade's soldiers were dead, and a fifth lay dying.

Dan caught a movement to his left and found it hard to believe his own eyes. Peal was stealthily sneaking his revolver from its holster, apparently with the intention of shooting into one of the dead bodies in the ravine. Maehler saw it too, and they both reached out to grab Peal's arm.

Peal struggled angrily. "One moved!" he snarled. "One moved, I tell you. That one with the hat half over his eyes!"

Maehler yelled suddenly. One of the group was moving —not the one Peal had pointed at, but another at the far end of the huddled mass. The moonlight passed over a gun barrel as it swung upward. Dan's gun came out and the hammer arced back as the revolver below pointed directly up at him.

But another of the soldiers had been watching and had spotted the movement earlier. He fired and the gun discharged from the ditch to shower Dan's boots with dirt. It fell then from a lifeless hand.

Dan felt a sickness in his stomach as he slowly put away his gun. He had just begun to realize that the outfit had lost no mules today, that the animals therefore were sure to be stolen property, that the dead men in the ravine had without a doubt been trying to recover their own stock.

He knew all the arguments that would support the act of stealing. Even the killing could be justified easily enough. An army, in order to live, had to take from the land, and had to fight when the taking was resisted. But somehow he had thought—had wished—that this army would be different.

It wouldn't be. The war was barely over, not over at all as far as the Brigade was concerned. This was no dress parade, and there would be no mock battles where smiling dead men stood up to end the sham.

After the bugle had started them up for the new day the soldiers fetched wood and water and talked with pride of the new Iron Brigade. The why and wherefores of last night's fight were unknown and not really important. The facts were that a detail, made up of both old and new men, had been attacked, and had overcome great odds. To be sure, five men were dead, but that was the way of the life they had chosen. They would be missed by some, but so many comrades had been lost to most of them in the past several years that even a man's friends did not dwell long on the surface of his memory.

A detail had been assigned to dig graves, and by the first peep of sun breakfast was done, the morning chores were finished, and the army was assembled for the joint funerals.

The first funerals of the new Iron Brigade. It awed some of them, but some were impatient to have it over and done with. Nevertheless they stood respectfully while the sweet, wailing notes of taps sounded over the Texas plain, leaving echoes that hovered in the hot still air until the crashing rifles took over.

Then the reverberations of the final volley died away and the bugle lashed out again, sending men to their horses and wagons. Last night's battle was finished and duly recorded. The markers over the dead were only a milestone, a reminder that a long and unknown road was yet to be traveled.

Mesquites—big trees and stunted, finger-thick seedlings —abounded along the high road to Eagle Pass, but there were grassy clearings, too, greener now than usual because recent rains had left sheets of water standing in creek beds that were usually dry. Color was lent to the whole scene by a scattering of yellow flowers sprouting from spiny prickly pear.

Less than twenty years ago this road had seen the flow of hundreds of forty-niners, as they cut across northern Mexico toward California, avoiding the Comanches and the inevitable water shortages they would be bound to encounter on the *Llano Estacado*. More lately it had been used by stages, and by heavily guarded wagons freighting cotton on the first leg of the long, roundabout trip to Europe.

The abundance of game all along the way seemed normal enough to Dan, but to many of the soldiers it was unbelievable. As the shadows of afternoon lengthened, one produced a fowling piece and got permission to ride out of column toward a clump of trees that marked a waterhole. He came back shortly with more than fifty doves—the result of two shots fired.

Maehler was one of several detailed to go out after bigger game. He took Peal with him. After some of the others returned with deer, he and Peal came in with the major portion of a reasonably young longhorn cow lashed to a mule's back.

"Peal shot it," Maehler said. Peal looked surprised and then preened himself a little bit. "Mistook it for an old doe," Maehler went on, and Peal immediately began angry denials. Maehler had shot it, deliberately, and in preference to a big buck he could have shot instead.

They camped that night alongside a steep-banked creek with only a trickle of water running between its series of deeper waterholes. Dan was whittling shavings for his fire when he got a visit that set him back on his heels.

From the first day he had joined Shelby a worry had nagged the back of his mind that he would run into somebody who knew him. Now the man was suddenly standing in front of him. The name immediately came to Dan—Mason. Larney Mason. Before the war he had been a cowhand, but the first bugle call had set him scurrying to join Terry's Rangers.

"Thought I saw you," Mason said. He held out his hand and Dan stood up and shook it. "What the hell ever happened to you?" Mason asked.

"You see me," Dan smiled. "All roads go around in circles."

"I reckon so," Mason said. He was a blunt-looking, heavily tanned and weathered man, with wide, square jaws and craggy eyebrows. "Thought you had a ranch," he said curiously. "I'm surprised you didn't go back to it when the war was finished."

"I'm just as surprised to see you here," Dan answered.

"Yeah, well, I like soldierin' better'n cow-chasin', it looks like."

"When we get to a town," Dan said, "I'll buy you a drink."

"I'll take you up on that. Might buy a round or two myself."

"Yeah," Dan said. "Meantime, I guess I'd better kindle this fire."

"Sure," Mason said, "I've got chores, too. See you around, and don't forget that drink."

He smiled, half-saluted and started away, and Dan squatted back down with relief. Mason didn't seem to be the kind to think about things too much, and he had never really known him well. Maybe a drink or two would be the end of it.

He began to light the fire and then trouble came from a totally unexpected quarter, in the persons of Bill Morgen and Mike Cogan. By way of greeting, Bill spoke to Cogan rather than to Dan.

"Maybe he won't need such a big fire after he divvies up a little bit." When Dan looked up Bill was grinning, with an arrogant twist to his lips.

"Hello, Bill—Cogan." The fire began to blaze and Dan stood up. "It's good to see you both."

"Maybe he won't think so," Bill went on to Cogan, "when he finds out what we're here for."

Maehler came back from fetching water and Dan introduced him, but all three managed no more than a curt nod. Maehler plainly didn't like the tone of what he had heard, and Bill and Cogan just as plainly didn't like being interrupted. They were further annoyed as Peal came up and stood, gawking.

Bill spoke directly to Dan now. "We heard one of your outfit killed a cow."

"Me," Maehler said.

"We don't care who," Bill snapped. "All we care is, we know Kilbourne here, and we're damned if we're going to eat neck meat off a buck while he gets fat off the back-strap of a cow. We figure we're old friends of his, so he'll divvy up with us."

Pots and pans had begun to rattle and water to sizzle at

the other little fires around them. Now the closest rattling stopped and the steam hissed out starkly as the men strained to hear.

"We've divvied up already," Dan said. "What's left is enough for supper and breakfast for the five of us."

"We figure then that maybe you'll trade some of your share for neck meat."

Sherm and Featherly came from behind Maehler and dumped a few sticks of wood near the fire. They looked at Morgen and Cogan and then went to stand beside Maehler in a slouchy fashion that made them look more formidable and deadly than if they had doubled their fists.

"The rest of you," Morgen said, "are not in this. We just figured an old friend would want to share his backstrap."

"I might have," Dan said, "if you'd come and asked me, instead of putting on a big show."

Cogan bristled. "You watch how you talk to Bill."

"Then you'd best take Bill back to his own campfire until he grows up."

Cogan advanced several steps. "You'll apologize for that damn fast or I'll bust your head wide open."

In spite of trying hard to keep civil and calm, Dan's eyes narrowed and his voice grated hard. "Before this goes any further, you'd better understand two things. The first is, you won't get what you came after, so you might as well go back to your own fire. The second is, I don't want to fight you. Maybe sometime, but not today."

Cogan's breath whistled loudly through his twisted nose. The puffed scars stood out and his eyes fairly danced. "It's gone past what you want to do."

"He's so scared his teeth are clicking," Morgen said.

Cogan moved forward. "I'll fix that. He won't have any teeth."

Several men gasped as Dan's gun flashed out. Cogan halted, staring in disbelief.

"I said I didn't want to fight," Dan reminded. "Not today. It might spoil some plans I've had for a long time."

"Hell," Cogan snorted, "you won't use that pistol. You've got to fight."

"I don't want to use it," Dan agreed, "but I will. You came over here and started something and today's not the day for me to handle it. Not your way." He slipped the pistol back into its holster. "If I pull it again I'll use it," he promised.

Cogan started to take another step forward, then looked into Dan's eyes and held back. "He'd do it, by God," he said incredulously. "He'd shoot me to keep from fightin'."

"Well, we've got him tagged," Morgen said with satisfaction, "and so has everybody else. We can go back and eat our neck meat and it won't be so bad after all. It'll taste better than his backstrap does tonight, I'll bet."

Cogan's breath still whistled loudly, but he relaxed. "I'll catch you without that pistol," he said. "When I do, that'll be the day." His hands were clenching and unclenching as he turned away. Morgen gave Dan another arrogant smile and went after him, leaving Dan standing in a silence thick enough to cut.

Finally, Maehler said, "It'll be all over camp before you can snap your fingers. There's a time when it's better to get hell beat out of you than to back down."

Dan nodded. "I know that. But like I said, today's not the time. Maybe in another week or two. I've given up too much to be with this army to let it get spoiled with one punch in the belly."

"I don't know what you mean by that," Maehler said, "but you gave up plenty more just now." He moved over to the fire and set the water down on the coals. Sherm and Featherly also busied themselves readying supper, but Peal remained to stare.

"You sure as hell had me fooled," he breathed. "I had you figured for a pure hellion, but you don't have enough guts to wad a shotgun. I might even take you on myself one of these days."

Dan continued to hold his temper in check. There was

no sense in taking out his anger and his feeling of helplessness on Peal. "I'll keep that in mind," he said.

At noon on the fourth day a picket charged up from the rear to announce that they'd see fighting in Texas after all. And this was no harum-scarum raid like they had run into the first night out. An army of Yankees was on their heels, and the Yankees outnumbered them three to one.

The Iron Brigade halted, tucked in its wagons, and readied its cannon. Excitement was rampant, but there were misgivings, too.

"It don't seem right," Sherm said. "Fightin' three thousand Yankees won't help us any." He was standing beside his horse, checking his equipment as he said it. "The thing is, we figured on buildin' a big army around this little one. An army that could rock the whole Union back on its heels."

But Peal, who had never fired a shot before, was delighted at this chance. "You didn't want to fight, you shouldn't have come along!" He checked the load in his rifle for the tenth time.

Maehler was in no way worried, but he was disappointed. "Me, I don't feel as strong as Sherm does about buildin' a big army. I'm willin' to keep things like they are. But I'm tired fightin' for somebody else's reasons. I'd like to think there was a jug o' whiskey, or a few gold pesos or maybe a woman on the other end of a fight."

"You look like a lover," Peal sneered.

"When I got money," Maehler said, "I'm a lover."

"There goes a messenger back to the Yankees!" Sherm poked Dan, who sat quietly in the sparse shade of a greasewood bush. "You ain't said much. But I'll bet if I knew what you were thinkin' about this minute, I'd know if you've really got the stomach for a fight. A lot of people think not since the other evenin'."

"What do these same people think about you?"

"Why, I reckon they don't think much, one way or another. You ducked a fight, I didn't. I didn't have to. If you got nothin' to hide," he persisted, "s'pose you tell me what you're thinkin'."

"I'm thinking that it doesn't make much difference if we fight or don't fight. I'll be doing what I set out to do."

Peal had his paper cartridge out again.

"Time you get into it," Maehler said, "that ca'tridge will be plumb wore out."

Peal put it back in the gun. "The thing I don't understand is, I heard one of the civilians talking. He as much as said that the Yankees were glad we were going to Mexico to join Juarez. They want us to help drive out the French."

"S'pose we don't join Juarez?" Featherly rarely talked, but he thought about things a lot. "S'pose we join ol' Maximilian? That'd stick in their craw plenty."

"That's foolish talk," Peal said.

"It may be foolish, but there's lots of it. Think what a time we'd have."

"While it lasted, maybe," Sherm agreed. "But it's only talk anyway. This is Shelby's outfit, and him and Kirby Smith have been figurin' for a long time on joinin' up with Juarez. So that settles it."

The five men were not far from the road. For a time a line of battle had started to form on either side of them, but sometime back all preparations had suddenly halted. Now a buzz swept over the Brigade as the messenger returned.

Word came to them swiftly, as word always travels swiftly in an army. Shelby had announced that he intended to move on a few more miles today. But he would wait an extra day at his next camp, giving the Federals plenty of time to attack if they wished to do so.

"What the hell?" Peal demanded angrily. "If we're not going to fight, why the hell don't we throw down our guns?"

Others grumbled as well, but the column untwisted itself, drew together and resumed its march.

That night Dan drew sentry duty, along with a few caustic words from Walcott. "I hear you're not much for a fight," he said cuttingly. "Well, I'll tell you this. There's a certain kind of man we want in this outfit, and a certain kind we God damn well don't want. Maybe we're all wrong about you. I hope so. But until we find out I've got a special little job for you. Whenever we pull out of here, if we're both still alive, you ride as far as Eagle Pass up at the head of the column, with me. I need a messenger boy, and you just about fit the description."

Nothing Dan could do or say would have changed Walcott's mind, so he kept his mouth shut and went on duty.

As he made his rounds that night, an unusual thing happened. One of the other sentries, after regulations were duly observed, admitted a small party of women into the camp to see Colonel Shelby. Word soon spread that they were settlers, wives of Confederate soldiers who had not yet returned from Louisiana, and they were appealing for help because their settlement had been ransacked by a considerable group of outlaws, many of whom were Mexican or Confederate deserters to judge by their uniforms. It seemed a strange time to ask this army for help, and yet it was not so strange.

The next day, unexpectedly, camp was struck. While some of the soldiers proudly said the Federals had been afraid, others thought that they considered a fight useless, since the army was leaving the country anyway. Still others claimed that Shelby had reminded the opposing colonel of an agreement between Lincoln and Kirby Smith, made months ago.

Whatever the reason, the Federals turned away, and after the first few minutes of speculation a demoralization set in that was almost as bad as defeat. It seemed suddenly that here was an army that didn't belong to any government, and nobody gave a damn about its existence. It was an army of lost souls, doomed to wander in hell forever without succor or friendship, even without enmity. And who knew how long forever was, or how far hell extended?

Some part of the lost morale was regained when a detail of two hundred men, under Colonel Slayback, was sent to dispatch the outlaws who had robbed the women—reminding Dan that an army might do terrible things, but it also did things that were worthy.

The column got under way and farther along the road Slayback rejoined it, his harsh work accomplished without the loss of a man.

The road to Eagle Pass—the stepping-off place—had now been cleared of all obstacles, and Dan Kilbourne found himself riding up ahead as Sergeant Walcott's private messenger.

# 6

THE IRON BRIGADE, in a column of fours, marched quietly, solemnly, toward the bank of the muddy river. At the water's edge it turned left without command, moving slowly past a few wide-eyed villagers who stared at grim faces and did not speak or wave.

From Fort Duncan—a collection of small, dilapidated sandstone and adobe buildings downriver from the column —a rider dashed forth to meet them. He galloped flashily through thin brush and sawed on his reins when he reached Sergeant Walcott and Dan. His horse pranced and reared and he waved a salute.

"Sergeant—Corporal Foster! I'm to report to your commanding officer for Lieutenant Chapton. He sends his compliments."

Sergeant Walcott stopped his horse. In a voice that was deep and choked with emotion he said, "You go back to your lieutenant and tell him we'll see him in about an hour. Till then he's restricted to his post, along with every other man in his outfit. You tell him that if one man breaks that restriction, I'll kill him myself before this day is over. Now, git!"

Emotions played over the corporal's face as it changed colors. He was ready to argue in spite of Walcott's stony grimness. But then he glanced at the oncoming column. It moved toward him with a slowness, a solemnity, that spoke of death.

"I'll tell him," he said. He swung his horse around and spurred it toward the fort.

The column came on, to a place where the riverbank sloped gently into the water and Colonel Shelby and his principal officers moved out. The heads of the column passed, and then stopped, unbidden. They wheeled right to face the river, and the maneuver was repeated all down the line.

A drum began to roll softly, and Shelby alone dismounted. He went to stand beside the flag-bearer and stretched out his arms, and the flag was gently lowered into them. Tears slid down a thousand pairs of cheeks as he removed the plume from his hat and began reverently to wrap the flag around it. Several of his officers got down and walked silently over to him, placing their hands on the cloth.

No man could tell what they saw in its depths. Perhaps they saw the flag waving in front of them again, as they relived the Iron Brigade's three most terrible battles, fought in the space of a single week: Westport, where thick powder smoke still clung to raw nostrils after nightfall, helping to blot out the smell of the three hundred dead they had to bury; Mine Creek, where there had been no time for burials; Newtonia, where torn but stubborn bodies fought on while their life's blood poured out onto the hard prairie.

Perhaps they saw in it as well the long, straggling

march back to Arkansas that came afterward, and felt the scars on their souls grow raw again as they remembered the terrible toll levied against exhausted, starving men by smallpox. They could take a grim pride in that fight; not one man who still lived had been abandoned.

These things they must have seen, and under them the fading memories of a homeland in Missouri. But now, for a time, the past must be set aside. Now a new flag would have to be served until this one could be restored in all its glory.

The drumbeats stopped and Colonel Elliott faced the Brigade. His command rang along the line.

"Regiment, attensh—hut!"

The soldiers stiffened and the drum began again, softly. Two of the officers took the flag, weighted it, and held it down to the water's level. They loosed it and it slipped from view into the sluggish, muddy waters.

The ceremony was over and Elliott could not find his voice. The men waited, knowing that they must ride on, that the artillery must be moved up to face the town across the river. They waited, and then understood because their throats were also full.

Without command they turned, and the wheels of the cannon began to grind forward.

Drill took place as if this were a routine early afternoon on the San Antonio parade ground. But partly today it was a show of strength to impress the Mexicans across the river. A deputation had gone across this morning, and now Shelby was there.

When the men fell out, hot and perspiring and still on call, there was not even a shady place to rest. Dan squatted down cowboy fashion and wished for a big hat, but he had spent too many years in this type of heat to be more than passingly annoyed by it.

Maehler sat beside him and rolled a cigarette, something he did three or four times a day. "They's some hot argyments goin' on," he observed. "Featherly was right. They's more talk about joinin' Maximilian than you'd think."

Sherm and Featherly led their horses up, and behind them came Peal, cursing the heat and cursing the waiting, when it would be just as easy to cross over and look the Mexicans square in the eye.

"You're too hell-fired anxious," the bony Sherm said.

All over the flatland around them soldiers had dismounted and were trying to sit in the thin shadows cast by horses, or to crowd up into scratchy bushes.

Featherly squatted down beside Dan. "You thought any more about who we'd join up with?"

"No." Dan considered for a minute. "I joined up with Shelby. From here on out I'll follow along and do my damndest."

A ruckus flared up just to the west of them. Two men tore into each other and rolled on the ground, clubbing and swearing. Skin was rubbed off, a few bruises picked up, and sweaty bodies became covered with mud in the few seconds it took to pull them apart.

Maehler grinned. "I'll bet they ain't even very mad. It's just that they ain't used to the heat."

The five of them settled and Sherm pointed across the river. "What you reckon they're talkin' about over there?"

"Why," Maehler said, "I reckon Shelby's settin' down the way it'll be when we lead the Mexkins after the Frogs."

"We're gonna vote," Featherly said. "I heard it. We're gonna vote to see if we fight with Maximilian or Juarez."

Dan had been saying all along that it didn't matter one way or another, but now he found that it wasn't true. "We just lost a fight," he pointed out. "If we joined up with Maximilian we'd be apt to lose another one. So I think if it comes to a vote we'll join Juarez."

Peal said disgustedly, "Why'd you come along with this outfit anyway? Just so's you could find somebody you could whip?"

"Shelby represents a lot," Dan said. "Maybe we'd be foolish to throw it away."

"Maybe there's things you don't know," Sherm argued. "You join up with an emperor, you've got somethin'. He snaps his fingers, if he's a mind to, and you've got beautiful women and gold and fine horses and fancy uniforms to wear and fine places to live. What the hell can a president give you? Nothin'!"

"Well, I've got no love for the Mexes," Maehler said. "I've fought 'em enough. Maybe I'd like to try it again."

"You see that bunch over there?" Peal asked. He pointed to a group of about fifteen men who had left the detachment at Fort Duncan to join Shelby after their commander had announced his intention to surrender to any Union officer who would take over the fort. "They could give you reasons why we should join up with the French," he went on. "Ol' Juarez let a whole outfit of Yankee troops march right across Mexico so they could sneak up and stab us in the back. You ask them."

The weathered Maehler cursed the last quarter-inch of his cigarette for being so hot, and spit it out. "If they're all so hell-fired mad at everybody," he said, "then how come that lieutenant intends to hold the fort here until the Yankees come?"

"He feels a responsibility," Sherm said. His blondish face split into a grin. "That's somethin' you wouldn't understand."

They were arguing about it when Dan looked across the field and saw Bill Morgen and Cogan. He stiffened in spite of himself. Since the other evening, half the outfit wouldn't pass the time of day with him. Excepting Maehler, even the little group here, men who for the most part found it as hard to mix as he did, fenced off their friendship when it came right down to it.

He saw Walcott standing half across the field, his thick shoulders as straight under this broiling sun as they were during drill. He didn't blame Walcott for making him messenger; the sergeant was so much a military man that it was hard to blame him for anything he did in the line of duty. But he couldn't help wishing that he hadn't been lowered further in the eyes of the men.

He touched his side. It was still tender, but it wouldn't be apt to bust open now. Even so, he couldn't deliberately start something with Cogan just to salve his own pride.

Maehler caught his minute of self-examination and misinterpreted it. "When we cut across the wagon road I thought about you," he said. "I figure they went through here about two days ago."

"Yes, it looked like two days ago." In spite of himself Dan thought about Jane a lot. He could remember all her little gestures, the way she carried herself, the way her slim body moved when she walked; he remembered the blue eyes and the gently rounded chin and the soft warmth of her lips on the night he had kissed her. It was hard to see her with the wagons, except as he had seen her in San Antonio, yet he could place her on the ranch easily enough, could follow her through her womanly chores as though he had seen her perform each one of them a thousand times. He could see the more intimate side of life with her as well, with tenderness and fierceness, even with lust, perhaps, but it was a shining lust.

To be honest, he thought about Mavis sometimes, too. But he thought of her only in terms of beauty and a fiery passion that could melt a man's bones; even the images of her caressing movements, of her pink gums and tongue, of her blue-black hair, were enough to arouse him. But these flashing glimpses, whenever they came to mind, were quickly shut away because they caused a discomfort that could not be satisfied.

Peal yelled, "They're back in the boats! They're back in the boats!"

Maehler's hand slowly slid down his holster as he loosed the butt of the gun at his hip. "Hell," he snorted, "the way you said it, I thought the Mexkins was attackin'."

"Maybe they will," Sherm said. "You don't know what they talked about over there."

Instead of a formation it was, "Gather around, boys, and listen close. You, there! Get that swaybacked horse to hell out of here. He cain't vote! The rest of you, now, huddle in closer an' squat!

"Now, keep your lips buttoned, boys. The General here —the Colonel, that is—wants to tell you about his talk with the Mexkin Governor."

Shelby stepped to the center of the ring and there was a strained, eager silence. He was a short man, but sometimes he could stand as tall as any mountain. He not only knew how to lead men up a shot-torn hillside, Dan thought; he knew how to get their attention when things were still.

Quietly, he said, "Well, we've won a mighty battle for the Confederacy!"

He waited to let that sink in good before he went ⌐. If somebody had so much as spit between his teeth the sound could have started a riot.

"Governor Biesca," he went on, "is with us. In spite of all we've heard about the Mexican troops here being so well trained—most of that grew from the fact that they used to entertain the families at Fort Duncan with their fancy drill—all the Governor has now are irregulars. And he can't march against the French unless he has regular army reinforcements. That's us, boys, and ten thousand, even twenty thousand more like us. Once we've settled and grown to size, our first task will be to drive the French from Monterrey. For our efforts we'll receive the military governorship of three Mexican states—and those states will be the great gathering place."

Talk swept over the outfit, then. Many, like Peal, simply couldn't keep their mouths shut any longer.

Peal was torn between disappointment and pride. "Hell," he said, "that could mean we wouldn't fight for another year."

The noise subsided, and Shelby went on. "Now in spite of all we've been offered, there seem to be some who disagree. Colonel Elliott wants to tell you how he feels."

Colonel Elliott, taller than Shelby, fully as grim in battle and with a reputation for thinking things through, got up and smiled—something he did only on special occasions.

"I haven't disagreed with General Shelby too many times in the past," he said.

A little cheer went up.

"But I do now," he continued soberly, when it was quieter. "Let it be understood that if General Shelby chooses to give orders, I will follow where he leads. But ours is not like any other army we know about. We are not settlers, looking for a place to roost. We do not want to spend the rest of our lives organizing while we wither and grow old and lose our spirit. But that is not my main argument. The main thing, as I see it, is that the Federals are bound to try to drive the French out of Mexico. If we're with Juarez, we're also with the Federals, and all our plans are dead."

It was a sobering thought, and Colonel Alonzo Slayback stood up to give emphasis to it.

"What Colonel Elliott says is true. If it's a roost we want, we've got it. We can even do plenty of fighting, if that's all we care about. Indians are thick on both sides of the river—Lipan Apaches and Comanches, each one meaner than a one-eyed yard dog and tougher than whang leather. And we could fight Mexicans every time they changed presidents or dictators. We could fight the Feds once in a while, too. But who the hell would want to join up with us if we throw away our original plan? Hell, who would even stick with us?"

Shelby argued. "With three Confederate states in the palms of our hands, hordes of Southerners could escape the crushing heels of the Yankees and come to us. We would be the first wave of a tide that would pour into Mexico, and then sweep back to destroy the Federals. We would not join the Yankees in a fight against the French; we would fight the French ourselves, and grow stronger with every battle."

Shelby became less oratorical and went on to describe in detail the opportunities they held, emphasizing the arms already in their possession, their possibilities for recruitment, the doors that had magically opened to them. All they had to do was show a small amount of patience.

When he was finished, Elliott, his face showing a sadness, rose again. "We must serve one flag or another," he stated, "and the French have been our friends throughout the war. Our life with them would be of a kind we can understand and appreciate. They can offer us a splendor, a ceremony, a brightness that all of us want. And we can serve our own purposes as well with them as we can with anyone. Would we join the Mexicans instead, then, because the odds are better? Will an army of Southerners favor the odds because one war has been lost and they fear to lose another?"

A sense of fairness placed Shelby at a loss. "I have tried to show you the kind of things we could have on the one side," he said. "Several—" he smiled, "several of us have tried to point out what we might expect from the French. Let us put an end to it then, and vote, and I will accept the verdict that we all render. Try to do what you think is best."

Sherm whispered frantically, "What about them cannon and things Kirby Smith was supposed to have give to the Mexicans?"

Triumphantly, Peal said, "To the Mexicans, yes. To General Mejia, who serves the French. I found that out. Anyway they're in Matamoros, and Sheridan's right across the river."

The vote was taken then.

Shelby voted to support Juarez. A voice vote by the rest was so overwhelmingly in favor of Maximilian that Dan's opposing shout was lost in the wind.

105

If the Devil himself had appeared magically in front of Governor Biesca, he would politely have asked him to sit so they could discuss their differences. And now that he was here, perhaps Biesca had something the Devil wanted? Or perhaps it was the other way around? Never mind. Surely a bargain could be made.

This was the attitude with which the Governor received the news that Shelby's army had refused his grand offer, choosing instead to support Maximilian.

Very well, then, the most direct route to the interior of Mexico was rough. If Shelby intended to make much time, surely he would not want to drag those heavy cannon behind him? Those wagons?

It was a point that Shelby himself had already thought of, and his army needed money. He agreed to sell the guns and much of his equipment. If the armament appeared deep in Mexico to be used against him at some later date, why then he would take it back.

A bargain was struck. Ironically, in addition to the hard cash which was to be raised at once by a levy against the merchants, much Juarez script was to be included. If Maximilian stayed in power the script would most certainly be worthless. But probably it would not be worth much even if Juarez won back Mexico.

Shelby was then invited to move his army across the river. Biesca could not stop him anyway, and would it not be fair to let the men have a good time before they moved on? And would it not be fair to give the merchants a chance to get back at least a part of their money?

The army struggled across that very afternoon. Guns and money changed hands, and except for pickets the soldiers were turned loose to race for the *cantinas*.

The sun was low when Dan headed along the dirt street for an evening of solemn drinking with Maehler.

"Mind you," Maehler said, "I don't promise not to be no bearcat after I've had a few. And I don't promise not to chase no skirts, either. I don't want you to be misled just because I don't bull all the time about women and whiskey, like some do. I've trained myself not to think about either one too much, less'n I'm right where they are."

Dan was tired, not more than half-dry from the crossing, and as thirsty as the next man. "I feel a little bit like being a bearcat myself," he admitted. "But I'll say once again that you're not making yourself very popular by drinking with me."

Maehler snorted. "I still don't know the straight of why you didn't re-bust Cogan's nose, but I told you back in that warehouse in San Antonio that I'd come runnin' if you ever needed me. I still mean it, an' I sure don't count this."

The *cantina* they entered was quiet, but a thick, dark bartender went into quick action as they came in. He greeted them profusely, leaving them only for the interval it took to rap frantically on the back wall.

A rear door opened as a girl almost immediately answered his summons, straightening her hair as she crossed the room to take their orders. She was shapely and pretty, and the way she preened herself left no doubt that she would be interested in making extra money.

"Hot damn!" Maehler said. "Think what I'll feel like after I've had a few!"

But their orders of tequila with lemon had no more than been delivered when several more of the Brigade came inside, and the girl's attention turned to the other soldiers.

One of those who entered was Sergeant Walcott. He left the group he was with and came to Dan's table. "How's my messenger?" he asked condescendingly.

"Fine enough," Dan said.

Walcott pulled a chair around and straddled it. "You beat me," he said. "I've picked at you for two or three days. I've been as rough on you as I'd be on a Yankee bounty jumper. And you haven't blinked an eye."

"I thought it was your nature," Dan smiled. "I didn't know you were trying to rile me."

Walcott laughed. "It's my nature, but I don't expect a

man to take everything lying down. Maybe you're doing it because you're afraid. I just hope not."

"It all goes back to Cogan," Maehler said. "But maybe they's things you don't know. I can tell you for damn sure that Dan ain't afraid."

"Maybe," Walcott admitted, "but I can tell you this. If Cogan had rubbed me like he did Kilbourne, I'd have butted him in the belly before he took two steps. I don't pull a gun on a man who wants to fist fight."

"Then you want me to fight Cogan," Dan said. "I'd think you'd be trying to keep peace in your little army."

Walcott shook his head. "If you were little, I'd run Cogan off myself. But you're big enough to stand a chance, and I don't want somebody in this army who might hightail it when trouble comes. So I'll be blunt about it. Days have gone by and you haven't done anything. But you won't get many more days. Either you'll fight Cogan, or you'll fight me, or you'll get out of this man's army and head back across the river. If you want to leave us, now would be the best time, before we get deep—"

A heavy rifle and pistol barrage in the street chopped off his words. He looked at Dan and Maehler incredulously. "What the hell?"

"Just some celebration," Maehler guessed.

Nevertheless they scrambled up from the table and rushed for the door, jamming their way through with the others.

Shadows had begun to fall across the street from the sinking sun, but sunlight was still bright on the heads and shoulders of gray-clad men pouring from other *cantinas*. They stood blinking at the brightness, many of them half-drunk and only half-curious until the bugle sounded to stir them wide awake. There was a general rush, then, toward the Plaza where the first shots had sounded.

Many of the outfit had ridden their horses into the main part of town. These and the men from the nearest *can-*

*tinas* were first to arrive, and as Dan, Walcott and Maehler rushed to join them the shooting began again.

A fierce, intense battle took place at deadly, point-blank range. Smoke burgeoned out to obscure the fighters, then drifted upwards in the hot stillness to show dead men sprawled and dying men kicking. The Mexicans had apparently been caught by surprise, for the number of their fallen was so much greater than the Brigade's that it seemed unbelievable.

The remaining Mexicans were fleeing as Dan and his companions arrived. A soldier knelt to take aim at a broad back, but Walcott rushed over to kick the rifle aside.

"The fightin's over," he said grimly. "Now let's find out what the hell this is all about."

A wind-reddened soldier pointed to one of the dead Brigade privates. "This here soldier and a couple of his friends—that one lying there and that one with his arm chopped off—told the Mexicans we stole their horses back in Texas. Said they only joined up to get 'em back. Claimed they could prove their ownership by the brands. The Mexicans backed 'em up."

Walcott looked down at the dead soldier. "I hope to God they were wrong," he said fervently.

"What the hell do you mean by that?"

"The God-damned horses in this outfit had to come from some place! Some had and some took. It's always the way!"

The soldier's lip twisted. "Maybe you'd like to be stretched out where he is."

"Maybe you'd like to put me there, you son of a bitch!"

A shooting might have taken place but drums at the Mexican fort began to beat a furious crescendo.

"Get your horses," Walcott ordered grimly. "It'll be a full-scale battle now."

Dan and Maehler raced along behind him and dozens more were at their heels as they made for the temporary compound where the horses were kept. Some who were already mounted screamed that they would block all escape and burn the town, and raced first of all toward the boats that were tied along the edge of the river. Others made for the cannon that had been sold, and some for the money that had been paid for the guns.

It took time to catch up the animals and fling saddles onto their backs. No trouble had been expected and after the exhausting crossing many had carelessly put their equipment aside. Several officers poured into the compound and their hasty orders rang out as they organized into two main groups. Through it all Walcott's raging voice whipped, spurred, prodded, cursed, by its force alone lashing the troopers into frantic action.

Dan mounted his sorrel and moved out of the throng to lessen the milling; others began to do the same and gradually the two groups came to order. The smaller of these charged to reinforce those who had gone for the cannon. The main body, at the command from a colonel, dashed for the Plaza.

The Mexicans had arrived and were kneeling across the Plaza to meet the charge. In front of Dan an officer's sword flashed up and down and Dan fired with the others. Mexican muskets answered and beside him, as the charges blasted, Dan heard an anguished cry. He looked at the stricken expression on Sherm's face and thought the lanky young veteran had finally been hit. Maehler would respect him more now. It was a foolish thought and made worse the thing that Dan saw next. It was not Sherm who had been hit, but Featherly. And he was not wounded, but dead.

The charge slowed as others toppled from their saddles. Dan twisted sideways, far too late to dodge the ball that brushed his shirt sleeve. He lifted his gun again, fired, saw a Mexican soldier press his neck and crumple. He flipped the hammer back, held his fire as the Mexican Governor ran for the center of the Plaza. The Mexicans took this for a command to charge and jumped up, speeding forward to mix with their mounted opponents. Someone would surely have shot Biesca, even though he was unarmed, if Shelby had not suddenly joined him, waving both arms.

Lieutenant Randolph rode between the Mexicans and Shelby, trying to protect his commanding officer with outstretched hands. Several Mexicans formed a cordon around Biesca. One of these dropped, struggled up, and resumed his place.

Shots continued to spit, but Walcott's voice blasted into them. "God damn it, hold your fire! The General says hold your fire!"

The explosions gave way to the nervous shuffle and snorts of excited horses, to the rattle of cavalry gear, and Biesca was able to get word through to his soldiers. They must go to their barracks at once. They must not fire another shot, on pain of death.

He drew back in dismay as a Brigade detail swept up, dragging the cannon behind them. It was another crucial moment, but now Shelby was in full control again. He silenced them, and in the quietness his words, spoken softly, still swept out to all.

"What has happened," he said, "was a misunderstanding that could easily have been settled with words. No guns were required."

Biesca gave more orders in Spanish, then translated the gist for Shelby. "My men will return to their barracks," he said sadly, "but first they must collect their dead."

Dan looked at the carnage around him and strove hard to overcome the feelings that rebelled in him. He had seen mass death many times now, had even shot men before this. Would he ever grow used to it so he could kill easily and without afterthought, as some seemed able to do?

A captain appointed a detail to gather up the Brigade dead and wounded and a colonel gave curt orders for the rest of the men to put up their horses. "Then you can go back to your *cantinas*," he said grimly.

"I'll damn well do that," Walcott said softly. "My guts ache for a drink."

They rode back to the compound slowly, filled with the depression brought on by the knowledge that death on both sides had been needless.

"I just hope to hell," Walcott said, "that those soldiers weren't trying to get back horses that really belonged to them."

Walcott stayed with Dan and Maehler as they returned to the *cantina*. Others joined them, pulling the tables together. Tomorrow Dan might again be down on everybody's list, but tonight he was only one man, too small to think about.

They were ordering drinks as Sherm came in. Dan got up and said, "Sherm, would you join us?"

Sherm gave him a look of hatred and headed for the bar alone.

"Tonight," Maehler explained, "he hates you and everybody else who's alive."

Dan slid slowly back into his chair, sharing the hurt with Sherm. The others, too, could feel it. He could see it in their eyes.

Peal came in to break the silence. "I got me one," he said proudly. "Shot him through the collarbone, and then right through the belly while he was tryin' to pick his gun up." He dragged over a chair and sat down at the deathly still table and began to tell about it in greater detail. The dark bartender brought the drinks on a wide tray. The girl had disappeared and the bartender himself was now making no effort to win the approval of these foreign soldiers. He placed the drinks in a tight circle in the center of the table to let each man reach for his own. He seemed in no hurry to attend a new group coming in the doorway.

One of the latest arrivals was Lieutenant Randolph, and he spoke briefly to the men at the table. "Drink up," he said soberly. "In the mornin' we're headin' for Monterrey. We couldn't stay heah another day, not after what happened."

The bartender answered him—in good English, though

his words were sibilant. "Perhaps you will not reach Monterrey."

"What do you mean by that?" Walcott asked.

The bartender's little smile contained triumph. "You have sold your cannon to the Juaristas, and the French will not love you for it. And the Juaristas will not love you for what happened today. Perhaps they will wait for you somewhere along the road. It is my hope."

Peal growled at him, but Walcott said, "Shut up and drink! One more word out of you and you won't be riding out with us. You'll be floating downriver till Sheridan's Yankees pull your body out."

# 7

As THE LIGHT in the east turned from cool gray to warm orange the Iron Brigade crawled onto the sloping high road and began to stretch out, in a long column of fours, toward the nearest promontory, which lay west and south.

The sun pushed up to stand full and white-hot on the horizon. It began its early morning task of burning away the haze and the men paused for a backward look across the Rio Grande.

There, beyond the narrow ribbon of water, was Texas, green and golden in the shimmering heat of the new month of July. Fort Duncan stood out, small but clear. As Shelby's men sat their horses in an alien land, the Stars and Bars came fluttering up the flagpole, stood out for a moment bold and free, then slowly collapsed to hang dispirited in the still hot morning.

Every hat came off; again tears ran unchecked down veterans' cheeks.

If the omens had been good when they left San Antonio,

thought Dan, they didn't bear thinking of here. In all the vast land over which that flag had floated proudly four years ago, likely Fort Duncan was the only post where it was raised this morning; and of all the myriad forces that had followed it, today there was only the Iron Brigade—and its flag lay under stones in the river that marked the end of their homeland.

Commands rang out; hats were replaced; the Brigade turned its back on Appomattox, on the West itself, and marched southward.

Hard hoofs struck sparks off the rocky road. The shuffle of horses, and their occasional snorts, the sounds made by leather and armament and accouterments, became one monotonous, wearying noise. Men had their own thoughts and were buried in them.

On the second day, after the noon mess, Dan and Walcott galloped down the road ahead of the column. The country was rock-strewn and desolate, covered with thorny mesquite, ground-hugging cactus, and dead yellow grass.

Farther along the mesquite gave way to dry cornfields and they could see a small village with flat-topped roofs and one steeple nestled low on the horizon. As they looked toward it, a cloud of buzzards rose awkwardly into the air, then settled heavily in the wake of a lone horseman who reeled in his saddle as he galloped toward them.

Walcott had sent Maehler ahead on scout duty before the noon fires were out. As he pulled up to them they could see that his lined face was gray, the wrinkles etched deeper into his skin.

"What the hell's the matter?" Walcott demanded.

"The buzzards," Maehler managed, then choked, leaned over his horse and was sick.

Walcott motioned at Dan and put spurs to his horse.

"Wait!" Maehler called feebly, following them.

They were close to the village when Dan recognized

the sweet, cloying battlefield odor of death that accounted for the buzzards.

Then they came onto the little village street. From every doorway spilled the dead. Men, women and children lay in the agonizing postures of torture. From door lintels bodies hung over charred ashes, tongues and eyes protruding in the attitudes of slow strangulation.

Walcott began muttering, "Oh, my God! Oh, my God!" It was part curse and part prayer.

Maehler came up the road toward them, shamefaced, his mouth set grimly.

Dan had trouble with his stomach; compared with this a battlefield was a clean and decent place. He forced himself to look for a sign. There had been at least twenty-five horses; they had come from the south and had returned there.

Walcott looked at the tracks. "It ha to be guerrillas or Indians," he said shortly. "Either one could mean an ambush up ahead. We'll have to take a look."

They galloped out of the village with the smell of death clinging to nostrils and throats, refusing to be left behind. In seconds the rustling of wide wings announced that the vultures they had scared away were returning to their feast. Dan leaned over his horse and retched miserably. Walcott angrily bit off a mouthful of tobacco and began to chew viciously. Maehler drew his pistol and checked the loadings.

They reached a point where the marauders had turned abruptly into the mesquite toward a small grove of cottonwood trees. Walcott, in the lead, slowed. Once again the grim smell of death clogged Dan's nostrils and once again a cloud of buzzards swept awkwardly toward the sky.

They rode close enough to see that every tree held its dead fruit. About twenty roughly dressed men were hanging from the stoutest limbs, their broken necks forcing their heads into an attitude of prayer. The village had been avenged.

Walcott cleared his throat and spit tobacco juice with no force. "We've got word that an army of Juaristas will be waiting for us at the Sabinas River. I'd say it was one of their detachments who strung up these bastards. If so— figure it for yourself. This is something they won't get over in a day or two."

"They'll be black-mean mad," Maehler agreed.

"Go tell Shelby what he's coming to," Walcott ordered Dan. "Maehler, get up ahead and keep your eyes open." He spun his horse, turning away from them. He had held onto his insides far longer than either of them, but now his cud of tobacco had suddenly become too much for his queasy stomach.

Going back, Dan circled the village; but he had to ride through it again with the Brigade. The long column galloped past the awful carnage grimly, helplessly. They could neither avenge the dead nor bury them; the Juaristas had done the first and their imminence kept them from doing the second. Until the Sabinas was crossed, vigilance must not be relaxed even for a second.

Camp that night was pitched on a low promontory rising from sandy, parched land. It was the eve of the Fourth of July and the feelings of the Southerners toward the day were ambiguous; the Revolutionary leader had been a Southerner and Southerners had won those last battles which led to Cornwallis' surrender at Yorktown. But it was hard to think of celebrating a holiday the North held so dear, a day which had seen Lee's defeat at Gettysburg and the capitulation of Vicksburg.

Dan, Maehler and Sherm messed quietly as Peal fussed over the coffee pot. Sherm had the look of a bespectacled man one sees for the first time without his glasses; he looked naked and vulnerable without Featherly, and he kept drawing in his breath as though he were starting to say something to him, then glancing over his shoulder at the empty place.

116

"Happened to just about ever'body else I knowed," he explained miserably. "Just didn't think after four years it'd happen to us."

"You boys grow up together?" Maehler asked sympathetically.

Sherm nodded. "His folks lived over on the next farm. Lots o' kids in both families. But me and him hit it off right away. Reckon we was about four when we met. Like as not he'd stay at my place, or I'd be at his till our folks didn't know which belonged where. We was fifteen when the Yankees come through and burned the harvest back in '62. We knowed the families'd be hungry that winter and figgered they'd be best off with two less mouths to feed. So we took off that night." He stared at the cook fire, but no one interrupted him, and when he looked up his eyes were angry. "Fought in a dozen big battles," he said fiercely, "and more little ones than I can rightly remember. Then he goes and gets hisself killed in a fight like that!" He got up and walked away from the fire to stare miserably into the distance.

It was a restless bivouac. The night was breathlessly hot, and July Fourth dawned sullen with hazy humidity. Smoke from the cook fires hovered straight over the flames, then curled outwards to settle in men's eyes.

Peal was grumbling as usual this morning. As the only bearded man in the mess, it fell to him to grind the morning coffee while Dan, Sherm and Maehler ran razors over windburned faces.

"I never had a mess before where ever'body but me shaved," he grumbled. "How come none of you grew beards?"

Sherm wasn't paying any attention. Maehler grunted, "Tried it once. Too many places for bugs to hide."

"What about you, Kilbourne?"

Dan made a long path across his chin and wiped the blade, considering. "Guess I never had the patience to go past the itching stage," he said finally.

"Humph," Peal grumbled. "Maybe it does itch for a week. Look at all the time I've saved ever since!"

"If we don't make it across that river this afternoon," Maehler said, "you explain to ol' Saint Pete that you've got some time comin'. Maybe he'll put you back on this earth for a little while."

"Why wouldn't I make it across the river?" Peal demanded.

Maehler shut up and waved the subject away. Shelby didn't want his army keyed up too far in advance. Except for the scouts and the top ranking officers, the men had not yet been told.

In early afternoon Shelby called a halt and began a consultation with his officers. The reason for the meeting became known to his whole Brigade almost instantly, and the prospect of a fight helped dispel some of the scorching heat.

Decisions were reached calmly but quickly. Captain Williams was immediately sent ahead with a special scouting detail, and a smaller volunteer detail, under Elliott, was selected to make the initial charge across the river—provided Williams verified that ambushers lay in wait for them.

The plan of battle completed, the soldiers again swung up into blistering-hot saddles; some grumbled as they got under way because they had not been included in the volunteer detail, but they gave the matter a second, sober thought when—virtually at the river's edge—they got Williams' report.

War was war and the Juaristas had to get men where they could find them; the army across the river included four hundred Lipan Apaches. If a man went down his scalp would be off before he could rise again.

Maehler said to Dan, "Unless that river's slowed down some in twenty years, this ain't goin' to be no easy crossin'."

118

Dan patted the sorrel. "Oliver Cromwell Kilbourne has done some fancy swimming before this." The sorrel bobbed its head in a satisfied snort, and Dan wondered why he had thought of the full name. Years ago his mother had named her horse Oliver Cromwell Kilbourne, and Dan, though not often given to such fancy, had named the sorrel the same on the day he had bought the animal, and had hardly remembered all of it again until today.

Maehler grunted. "I ain't worried too much about the horses. It's the men that cain't swim troubles me."

They studied the river, a frothy, rock-studded torrent which downstream suddenly dropped several feet to a new level. The banks were of steep shale and the rocks in midstream were like stone spears. The opposite bank was wooded.

Shelby called up his volunteers. There were no suitable places to cross the river, few places where any kind of crossing could be made. The first detail could try to fight its way across and get a hold; if it couldn't do that, maybe it could empty enough of the concealed guns so that the others could make it.

"It kind of puts me in mind of Zack Taylor durin' the Mexkin War," Maehler observed. "I reckon the only command he ever learned was 'Charge.' But I'll admit he won his share of battles, and I cain't think of nothin' better than what Shelby's doin'."

Shelby gave the signal.

Eleven horses slid down the steep banks into the rushing water. Shrill yells sounded from the forest across the river and were answered by the Brigade bugle. Shots—too many and yet not enough—spit up water in the faces of the horses. The main column waited for the hundreds of hidden rifles to empty—accepted that the hope was a failure, and plunged into the river.

Amazingly, the advance detail—"the forlorn hope" Shelby had called it—reached the opposite bank untouched.

119

But then horses fell dead beneath them and bullets tore into struggling bodies.

The lead horses in the main column were in midstream when a mighty volley spoke from the trees. Men toppled, and men and horses alike, hit and bleeding, were swept downriver toward the jagged rocks below the waterfall.

Dan crouched down as the sorrel hit the water, sank low, and struggled to the foaming surface. As the animal struck out strongly for the opposite bank the sporadic revolver fire increased to a higher pitch to show that a few more of Shelby's men had gained the other side. The dull cracks of the defending muskets were continuous.

Next to Dan the water roiled as Sherm's horse was hit. The animal screamed once and the water turned red as torn lungs spewed blood. Sherm kicked free of the stirrups, and floated for an instant. Then a look of angry incredulity crossed his face as his arms flapped uselessly and the current began rushing him downstream.

Dan pulled on the reins, but the sorrel would turn only a little. Sherm was ten feet away now, half-submerged.

Dan kicked free and plunged into the icy river. Four hard strokes brought him up to Sherm. He grabbed the boy's shoulders and tried to side-stroke toward the bank. The uniform coat impeded him, and his boots, filled with the icy water, dragged him downward.

Sherm struggled and they both sank. Dan's mouth filled with water as he fought his way to the surface and he came up choking.

Sherm fought loose. "You son of a bitch!" he screamed. "You son of a bitch! Let me go! Let me go!"

Dan treaded water as Sherm sputtered and coughed, flailing his arms wildly. His own arms grew heavy from the weight of the soaked gray wool and his booted feet felt numb and swollen. He forced strength into his right arm and his left hand again grabbed Sherm's coat. He jumped high in the water and let gravity aid him as his fist struck the base of Sherm's jaw. The boy stiffened, sank a little, then his unconscious body bobbed to the surface. Dan grabbed him under the shoulders and began to fight his way across the current to the far shore.

Bullets thudded around him as he pulled Sherm up the shale on the opposite side. He slapped the cold, boyish cheeks until Sherm groaned and struggled to sit up. The angle of the bank kept the bullets from hitting them here, but Sherm's angry eyes said he didn't care one way or another. He pulled out his bowie knife and clawed his way up the bank, cursing.

Dan saw his sorrel just inside the thicket a few yards upriver. He started splashing toward him, continuing to hug the shale bank.

Men were still crossing. As Dan looked toward them, a horse threw up its head and died. The bearded lieutenant in the saddle tried to kick free from the stirrups as the horse began swiftly floating downstream. The look of horror on his face told Dan that he was caught.

He plunged back into the icy stream, trying to shed his coat. His arms, heavy with fatigue, tangled in the sleeves. He struggled, broke free, and swam toward the officer with a strength he didn't know he had. The man had gotten one leg over the saddle, but this had only caused his other leg to twist the wrong way. His struggles tightened the hold of his stirrup.

Dan was on the wrong side of the horse. He tried swimming in front of it and the dead weight of the animal forced him downstream. He swam back and tried to get out his bowie knife. His fingers were stiff and the wet leather of the scabbard clung like iron; Dan tasted water again as he sank beneath the river.

He fought his way up and tore the knife out. He caught the soaked leather of the stirrup and sawed desperately as the rushing sound of the waterfall came closer.

It came free and the force of its parting spun Dan around. The lieutenant was floating half-submerged, his mouth and nose under water.

Dan caught him, got his left hand under an armpit and fought his way toward the shore. Juarista muskets spewed a hail of bullets around them.

Dan's arms felt torpid and slow, his legs leaden and stiff. He churned on, with no thought but to reach shore before the falls clutched him.

His feet sank, hit the rocky bottom of the river. He tried to stand upright. He stumbled and barely missed losing his hold on the lieutenant. He dragged him onward, held him upright against a perpendicular bank and gasped.

After a minute he began laboriously climbing the rough bank, pulling the lieutenant after him. As he crawled onto crushed grass, he turned the officer onto his stomach, his movements slow and onerous.

He let the man's head fall over the bank, and with his right hand pressed his back.

Water rushed out the lieutenant's mouth. He choked. Coughed. Dan kept up the pressure by the force of his mind; he had no feeling in his arm at all.

The lieutenant stirred, sat up and retched, the tears streaming down his cheeks, his nose and mouth still running driblets of water. He tried to speak, but at first no sounds came. Then he was able to croak, "Thanks."

Dan nodded, too exhausted to move.

The sounds of battle upstream had reached a crescendo. Rifle and revolver shots were beginning to drown out the musket fire. Rebel yells could be heard above all the sounds, but the pall of smoke that covered the thicket hid everything.

A Juarista suddenly burst out of the thicket behind them. His eyes swept the two sprawling men and told him that here were two easy victims. He raised his bayoneted musket and came toward them.

Dan struggled onto his feet. He felt in his belt for his knife, but it was somewhere at the bottom of the river. There was no point in going for his Colt; though holstered it had been in the water too long.

The lieutenant, with slow, nightmarish motions, pawed at his bowie, but he hadn't the strength to pull it out. Dan leaned over him and got it. He pushed himself straight and stood waiting for the Mexican to come.

The nightmare continued. The lieutenant lay exhausted, unable to help, while the Mexican advanced with the slow deliberate steps of an executioner. The knife in Dan's hand dragged his deadened arm down against his trousers.

Then a wild mass of Mexicans burst from the thicket followed by a milling troop of horsemen keening the high shrill Rebel yell. They were slashing with sabers and firing with pistols, standing high in their stirrups and bending down to cut and gash and kill.

The Mexicans were in full retreat. Singly and in groups they came bursting out of the thicket trying to run. Shelby's men waving their sabers, shrilling their cry, came tearing after them.

Dan felt his fatigue leave him. As a riderless horse came by, he coaxed it to a stop and managed to mount. He dragged a rifle out of the saddle scabbard. He turned the horse with his knees and joined the chase.

Up ahead, one Mexican had stopped running, had turned and was bracing himself against a mesquite, was aiming his musket at Shelby himself. Dan forced the rifle up and pulled the trigger. The shot rang out in the company of a dozen others.

The Mexican fell, riddled.

The Juaristas were disappearing; many had fallen and the rest were vanishing into the thickets. The firing slowed, stopped. The din trailed away like the dying ring of a monstrous brass bell. Realization came slowly, but with a great relief. The battle was over. The Iron Brigade had struck the first blow for Maximilian and they hoped he'd be pleased.

But a score of men lay dead on the high ground, and the rocks below the waterfall would yield more crushed and battered bodies. The wounded were everywhere.

Word went out that they would camp at the Sabinas for a few days, while the lightly wounded recovered, while rigs were made for those unable to travel without help.

# 8

THE NEXT DAYS were spent nursing the wounded, fattening and caring for the horses, and standing so much picket duty that those who had been untouched in battle became hollow-eyed and worn and began wishing for at least a minor wound. Although the ill-organized Juarista forces were scattered, some few had remained behind to snipe at pickets, and to attempt periodically to frighten away the horses.

Late in the afternoon of the third day, Dan, Sherm, Maehler and Peal, all to stand picket duty that night, were squatting at their small fire eating an early supper when Morgen and Cogan again paid Dan a visit. Dan was facing the rushing river, listening to its sound, and did not hear either of the men until Morgen gently tugged at his shoulders, spilling him backwards.

"Thought I'd pay the hero a visit," Morgen smirked. "Thought it might be catching." Cogan stood challenging Dan to say or do anything about being dumped.

Dan set down his tin plate and started to get up, thinking that now would have to be the time to tangle with Cogan. But before he was fully on his feet Sherm reacted with such speed and such intensity that it left them all astonished.

He flung his plate to the ground and bounded up, screaming. "You sons of bitches, if I want my supper spoilt I'll do it myself!" He whipped out his gun and fired between Morgen's feet and put another quick slug not more than an inch from Cogan's right boot. As Cogan and Morgen both danced to one side he fired again, barely missing Cogan's head. Both men ran for cover, churning over the ground as fast as their legs would carry them.

An alarm went out over the camp and at least fifty soldiers came running, waving their guns. "Get out of here, all of you!" Sherm screamed. The hammer of his revolver went back again and they looked into his mad eyes and scattered.

Peal gulped, tried to swallow, and couldn't. Dan and Maehler both stood unmoving, but Sherm squatted down, picked up his plate, and went on eating as if nothing had happened. The rest of them sat down uneasily then; for the last several days it had been impossible to say anything while they ate without arousing Sherm. But only now had they realized the full extent of his madness.

Two days passed with no more outbursts from him but Dan and Maehler were grateful when they got orders to move. Each passing moment seemed to tighten Sherm's raw nerves. Dan suggested to Walcott that he be assigned to helping the sorest wounded on and off their horses, in the hope that it would help him to settle, and Walcott agreed.

"And while we're talking," the beefy sergeant said, "I might as well tell you that you'll still be a scout, but I've got a new messenger—Bill Morgen."

The troops broke camp an hour after daybreak, giving Dan and Maehler a chance to move well ahead. Maehler was quick to react to the rustle of a bush or even the unexpected sounds of a bird bursting into song. His horse seemed as nervous as he was, as often as not shying from the wind itself.

"I cain't figger it," Maehler said dolefully. "I ain't never been one to hold back when there was danger of dyin'. Maybe it's because these Juaristas have got some right on their side and I know it. Me, I've been hell on Mexkins a time or two when they come up into Texas. But I ain't usually this spooky."

The words were barely spoken when a musket ball cut across Dan's shirtfront and spun Maehler's slouch hat. After a split second's surprise they jerked their horses around together, touched spurs to ribs, and raced left toward a splotch of smoke on the side of a rocky, low hill. As the smoke thinned they saw a furtive figure duck back into a narrow cleft.

They charged onto the higher ground at a dead run, guns cocked and ready, but the ambusher had disappeared. Dan spun his horse and plunged into the cleft and Maehler guided his struggling mount up over the hill. They stopped at the same time and Maehler shouted down to him, but Dan was far enough through the hill to see with his own eyes. A lone man, not uniformed, was astride a mule heading for the brush. Maehler snapped a shot at him, but the range was already long for a hand gun and by the time he could drag out his rifle the Mexican had disappeared.

Dan got his horse turned in the narrow passageway and Maehler let his slide downward. They met again at the bottom of the incline and Dan grinned. "Maybe you're spooky for the same reason I am," he said.

Later that day Maehler re-enacted the spinning of his hat for Williams, and the fair-bearded Shelby himself laughed at his antics. But he said soberly to Dan, "I'm afraid it will get worse instead of better. We don't know what to expect from the French, but the Juaristas will continue to cause all the trouble they can; and now we've got word that a band of guerrillas is set to waylay us."

"The man who told us," Williams explained, "lost his sister to one of the guerrillas, and this was the only way he knew to get even. Or maybe," he reflected, "he made it up to get even with us for something."

The army traveled onward, tortuously climbing upward into rough mountains, into frigid air and cold showers. Snipers took their toll all along the way. Most of the men,

126

in spite of their nervousness, in spite of sudden death-deal-ing shots from ambush, began to discount the possibility of a really large scale guerrilla attack; the sniping by itself would be enough to drive them crazy if it continued.

But the band of guerrillas was a reality. On a dark night shortly after the Brigade had settled in its blankets, thick musket fire broke the quiet of the camp. Leaden balls beat into tinware and scattered the dying coals. As the tense soldiers sprang up, armed and ready but unable to see the enemy, a second round of flames blasted into the night.

"There's nothin' to do but run into their teeth," Maehler said grimly. He snapped a shot and charged toward the loudest commotion.

Dan surged after him. A thorn lanced into his foot but he ran on in his stockinged feet until he pulled even with Maehler. Sherm passed them both, jostling Dan, and Peal caught up with them. "Why the hell don't they come out in the open?" Peal protested.

A musket ball brushed the hair above Dan's ear and he didn't answer. The terrain rose sharply in front of him and he fired back at a thick, dark bulk. A man grunted and he fired again.

Yells pierced the night all around him. Dan charged on, shooting until his hammer clicked over a spent cylinder. He tried the gun again, gripped it tightly for a club, and began climbing over sharp rocks. The guerrillas backed uphill, crumbling under the counterattack. The Brigade was a solid wave, growing thicker now, merciless as it struck back.

The firing became less frequent as guns all along the line emptied and could not be reloaded. Those armed with sabers continued to press. The guerrillas made it to the top of the hill and began pouring down the other side. Their attack had been ambitious, but apparently they had been prepared for a rout instead of a grim and deadly counterattack.

Somebody shouted orders to halt the blind chase. It

sounded like Elliott's voice and Dan complied. Just then a dark figure sprang at him from his right. Dan caught the gleam of a blade as it sliced toward him.

He ducked under the flashing weapon and swung his revolver in a looping overhead blow that cracked solidly against a skull. The man was only stunned and Dan made ready to swing again. But his eyes had grown so used to the dark now that he was able to make out a silhouette. His attacker was Peal.

Peal fumbled to recover his knife and Dan said curtly, "Hold it! It's me, Dan."

"Oh, God," Peal said. "You split my head wide open!"

"I'm sorry—but you tried to cut mine off. Here. Grab my arm and I'll help you back to camp."

Someone had lit a lantern now and was holding it aloft so all could survey the damage. The dead were everywhere, but most were guerrillas.

Peal groaned. "Someday I'll break . . . your God-damned head," he threatened.

Dan half-dragged him back into the camp and got him settled in his blankets. By striking matches he could tell that the lick had been a good one, but Peal's skull didn't appear to be broken. "It's not too bad after all," Dan comforted.

"God damn this army," Peal said. "All we do is get shot at from every bush in the daytime and shot at in our blankets at night. Hell, this ain't what we all wanted."

"We've had our share of funerals," Maehler conceded from behind Dan, "but we'll be back on the flatlands pretty quick now, and then we'll sail into Monterrey without another hitch."

Back of him Sherm's desperate, hard voice grated out, "Then maybe we'll go a round or two with the French, and I don't give a damn if we do."

Peal groaned again and felt his head. "God damn it, Dan, you'll pay for this. You mark my words. You'll pay."

"In another day or two the lump'll be gone and you'll forget it," Dan said.

True to Maehler's predictions they crossed the flatlands without a hitch, although more than once the scouts saw little groups of uniformed Frenchmen riding far to their right or left, marking carefully every step the Brigade took.

Monterrey was a sight to behold, Dan thought, and Maehler was doubly enthusiastic. As they approached the city he said, "We didn't come quite this far before, not on the first day. We camped just back of us—by them springs. But some of us rid in to see how close we could git without bein' hit. I was younger an' maybe a little bit more foolish in them days. The Mexkin cannon was puffin' out balls so big they looked like tumbleweeds comin' at us."

Approaching from the northeast they could see a bridge crossing a small river ahead of them; above the bridge towered a fort that would withstand a lot of charging.

"I'd hate to try to run under that fort," Maehler grunted, "but I'll say this—it looks to me like gall might pay off with the French. The Mexkins was shootin' at us afore we got this close."

Orders to halt were passed along and the men had barely stopped when pickets were posted. An unofficial messenger from the city—in Confederate uniform and therefore possibly sent by one of the generals who had left San Antonio ahead of Shelby—arrived in time to be the first man challenged.

Whatever password he gave got him to Shelby at once, and Dan and the other scouts stood near enough to hear what he said.

Ill at ease in the presence of a general, the tall soldier alternately straightened to attention and slumped, the latter in tune with feet that insisted on shuffling.

"This here Marshal Jeanningros," he said. "You've heard

about him, I reckon, sir. He executes a man quicker'n you can bat your eye. Why, he heard you sold cannon to the Juaristas, an' he says he'll stretch ever' neck in the outfit. Means it, too, I reckon."

Shelby was a man who often acted on impulse, or in the throes of emotion. Today he stroked his beard while the men waited, then smiled in a way that made his teeth look sharp and called several of his officers together.

"Boys," Old Jo said, "we hear this Marshal Jeanningros is quite an executioner. But I'd say he knows a thing or two about us, as well. If executions are what he admires, he might know what we did to a few guerrillas back in Missouri, and what we did to a few outlaws in Houston and Austin and San Antonio. What we might do to him, too, if he makes us fight and we win. So we'll write out a letter for M Marshal Jeanningros."

Shelby's letter, translated into French by Governor Reynolds, was a two-edged communiqué. On the one hand it expressed a hope for peace and strove to obtain sympathy for this strange army that had traveled deep into a foreign land to serve Maximilian. On the other hand it threatened immediate attack if this bid for peace were not found acceptable.

The communiqué was dispatched at once under a flag of truce, and the camp settled back for an uneasy wait.

Dan was as anxious to know the outcome as any man in the outfit, perhaps doubly so after the first few minutes. Over near the city, beyond the bridge and to the left, he had seen a long line of wagons; what he hoped didn't seem likely, but figuring it out in terms of time, it didn't seem too improbable either. The delays Shelby had suffered would easily have given Morgen's wagons time to get here ahead of them.

His impatience grew until it became razor-sharp; not only was he concerned with the question of Jeanningros' intentions, but if the wagons were those of the Marman expedition, would everything be settled in time for him to see Jane and Wil?

Word came back while the afternoon was still young. Jeanningros was a man greatly impressed by boldness; he would see Shelby and his staff; the men had permission to enter the city as long as they bore nothing but sidearms.

Dan rode into the city alone, though so many of his fellow countrymen were riding or walking the narrow streets that it seemed he had more company here than he'd had back in San Antonio.

Despite his impatience he couldn't help noticing the beauty all around him. The streets were clean and cobbled; the buildings, joined together to present a solid front for a whole block at a time, were neat and freshly white-washed, standing out strongly against the backdrop of the dark, towering mountains. The trees were big and old and the grass in the Great Plaza unbelievably green.

The omnipresent beggars importuned him, and street vendors tried hawking their wares under the very nose of his horse. Otherwise he went unnoticed. The occasional French patrols gave him no more than a passing glance and the Southerners who thronged the city seemed bored even with each other.

He rode through another Plaza, a great outdoor vegetable market, permeated with a thousand odors, over which the sweet biting smell of pepper stood out.

Along the edge of the street he saw a slight Mexican, dressed in the typical white cottons and multicolored serape of a peon, and reined up in the surprise of recognition. The man was Lieutenant Esteban, who had aided him and the Morgens back on the Texas prairie. Half a block behind him was a four-man patrol of French Zouaves. Dan could not tell if they were following Esteban or merely traveling in the same direction.

He dismounted and was fumbling with his stirrup as

Esteban passed. "Are the French after you, Lieutenant?" Dan asked.

"I do not know," Esteban said rapidly. "It is possible they wish to know where I go."

"Keep going, then," Dan said as quickly. "I'll try to hold them up."

As though satisfied now with his stirrup, Dan led his horse up to the French corporal and touched his hat. "Pardon me, Corporal. There is a wagon train somewhere to my left. Can you tell me the shortest way to get there?"

The corporal looked impatient. "*Je ne parle pas anglais,*" he snapped, and tried to pass.

Dan politely barred his way and repeated his question more loudly.

"*Je te dis que je ne parle pas anglais!*" the corporal shouted just as loudly.

"Spanish, then?" Dan asked, and repeated his question in that language.

"*Ni espagnol!*"

The three other Zouaves were grinning broadly as their corporal let go a string of quick, staccato French. From the reddened face of the youngest of them Dan deduced he was being sworn at. When the corporal finished, Dan stepped back and saluted. "Thank you for your courtesy, Corporal," he said soberly and mounted.

The Zouaves hurried on down the street, but looking back Dan could see no sign of Esteban. He grinned. Esteban was his friend, and the fight between the French and Mexicans was no personal war as far as Dan was concerned. Anyway, the French had not yet accepted Shelby's services. He rode on, wondering what the little Mexican was doing in Monterrey. Did it have something to do with the wagons—or with Shelby?

Wil Morgen's impatience had built steadily since the minute he had seen Shelby's troops approaching Monterrey. Now he was trying, without much success, to calm himself by stretching a new maguey rope. One end of the rope was securely tied to a wagon and he was rocking against the other end, which was looped around his buttocks.

He heard hoofbeats and slacked off; he looked up, saw a gray-clad rider who could have been anyone. He squinted, knew for sure that it was Dan, and threw the rope aside, waving vigorously.

"Dan! By damn, I'm glad to see you!"

Dan jumped easily to the ground and wrung the hand Wil held out. "It's good to see you, Wil. I never thought your wagons would get here before we did."

Wil grinned. "Marman's been pushing us like the Devil was at his heels! But we're making out. You've got to remember that these people are all headed for home, even if they've never been there before." The grin slowly gave way to worry. "Dan, is Bill all right? We heard you had a run in with the Juaristas at the Sabinas."

"He looked healthy enough when I saw him yesterday," Dan replied awkwardly. "Likely he'll be here soon." He hitched the sorrel to a nearby bush. "How is Jane?"

"You can see for yourself," Wil answered, pleased. He kicked the rope from underfoot and led Dan across the wagon-studded field, making a trumpet of his hand. "Jane!" he called. "Jane!"

A few curious people popped their heads out and gaped and Wil dismissed them with a wave of his hand, wishing they were in town with the teamsters and the other colonists. Not all of the teamsters, he corrected quickly. At least four always remained to keep a tight guard on Marman's part of the train.

Jane's face showed at the rear of a wagon and she started to speak, then saw Dan. Her cheeks suddenly flamed and her eyes began to dance. "Dan! Dan Kilbourne! I didn't hear you ride up!"

Wil looked at her with fatherly amusement; for a girl who hadn't heard a man ride up, she was looking all-fired prim and pretty. Come to think of it now, he hadn't laid

133

eyes on her since he'd pointed out to her the gray-uniformed cavalrymen coming up over the horizon this morning. And that pale blue dress she was wearing hadn't just come out of a trunk.

Dan was looking up at her uncomfortably, as if he'd never seen her before, and Wil couldn't help trying to speed things up. If they were to get married it would solve every problem he had in the world. He would have help to replace the shiftless hired hand who had quit yesterday, and he could stop worrying about Jane's future.

"Come on down from there, girl," he said, "and spread out a blanket so we can talk."

She reached back inside, got a colorful Navajo blanket and let Dan help her down. There was a womanly quality about her that made Wil proud and he snatched a glance at Dan to see if he recognized it.

Dan was plainly not one to court in public. He spread the blanket under a well-leafed oak, helped Jane sit down and settled himself a good distance away from her without seeming to notice her charm. Wil thought for a moment that he ought to invent an errand for himself in Monterrey, then decided that that might look too obvious. He lowered himself with a sigh.

After a silence that dragged, he said heavily, "The army agrees with you, Dan. You look a lot healthier than you did in Santone."

"Thanks. My side is well now and I guess it shows. You're slimmer than you were."

"I wouldn't mind that," Jane said quietly, "if he weren't also tired."

"It hasn't been bad!" Wil protested "You've helped plenty. And that shiftless Kennily was some help, though I'm just as glad he quit."

"Kennily is the man Dad hired in San Antonio," Jane explained.

"What made him quit?" Dan asked politely.

"He had wages coming, didn't figure he needed to work

134

any more till they were spent." Wil squirmed a little, decided to change the subject. As one who disliked routine himself, and hoped that Dan had grown tired of Shelby and might now come with the train, it was better not to speak of such things.

"Dan," he said. "I've got some pretty sad-looking horses down at the picket line. Help me decide if they ought to be replaced—or if you think they're good for the trip. Prices are sky-high here, and I'm afraid I'm leaning over backward trying to say they'll do."

"I'll be glad to, Wil. Jane—will you come with us?"

"We'll want you to stay for dinner," she protested, "and I'd better get started with it."

Wil smiled with satisfaction. When Marman came calling for her tonight he would find that she was already occupied with somebody else. He hoped it would offend Reed to the point where he wouldn't court her any more. Seeing to it that Jane got herself a fine husband was one thing, but he didn't want her marrying the likes of Marman.

Dan was saying, "Let's eat out, instead."

Jane nodded a flustered agreement, and Wil's spirits soared. Jane could talk all she wanted to about Dan's strong ties with Shelby. Sure he had left his ranch to join the Missouri General, but that didn't mean anything. Sometimes a man got restless and had to move on, and he had to give excuses because women didn't understand such things.

He would not ask Dan to join them, he decided. All he had to do was let things work themselves out.

In the ornate lobby of the Hotel Americano, where Mavis Todd and her father were staying while the wagons were in Monterrey, Mavis paced restlessly, trying to hold on to the frayed edges of her temper. It was more than an hour since she had sent Peter to Shelby's camp to ask Bill Morgen to come to see her, and he wasn't back yet.

To add to her discomfort, the afternoon was hot and the

black broadcloth riding habit she wore was far too warm for Monterrey. Nevertheless it was the most becoming thing she had for riding and she well knew how the velvet collar and the white stock highlighted her lustrous complexion.

She looked at the little watch that hung at her lapel. From the time she had first learned of the Iron Brigade's arrival this morning, she had felt that things were going to work out just as she wanted. Yesterday, because she had no escort for herself, she had been irritated that Reed had asked Jane to dine with him tonight and then hear the Italian opera company that was touring Mexico. Now the very thought of their date filled her with pleasure.

The lobby door opened and Bill Morgen, trailed by his friend Cogan, came inside and looked around.

She stepped out from behind the potted palm and remembered to hold out her left hand. Bill's sullen mouth turned up in an arrogant smile, and she smothered a sigh as she held her other hand out to Cogan. "I'm glad you could come. Both of you."

Cogan grunted. Bill's eyes glistened and he tried to put his arm around her shoulder. "You didn't have to send for me, Mavis," he said roughly. "I was planning to look you up as soon as they turned us loose."

"Were you?" she asked, ducking from under his arm. "I'm flattered that you thought of me. But right now there's somethin' I'm dyin' to tell you. Will you both come and sit?"

She looked about, grateful that it was siesta time, and glad that the Southerners staying here had so wholeheartedly adopted the Mexican custom. The lobby was virtually empty.

She led them to a small couch half-hidden behind potted palms, and sat in a facing chair. She waited while Cogan's towering form folded down.

"Now then," she said, leaning forward and flashing her

brightest smile on Bill, "first of all you must promise never, *never* to tell anyone I told you. Will you do that?"

Bill nodded, but Cogan grunted, "What's this all about?"

Bill dug his elbow into Cogan's side. "It doesn't matter!" he snapped. "Mavis knows she can depend on us."

"Thank you, Bill. I do know that." She hesitated a moment. "Sometimes . . . I think people don't pay enough attention to a man's instincts. You never did like Dan Kilbourne, did you?"

"What's he got to do with this?" Bill asked sullenly.

"Everything. You see, the day I met your sister—it was the very day after Dan saved her from the Indians—she told me all about him. She was more than half in love with him, and she couldn't think about anything else."

"I still don't see—"

"Well, then wait!" Mavis snapped. She quickly smiled again. "When she was telling me about the first moment she saw him, she said she couldn't believe her eyes because of his blue—pants. 'Pants' was what she said, but she stumbled and got confused and hurried on, and when I mentioned his uniform again she blushed and couldn't meet my eye. She thought she passed it off well enough, but she didn't. The truth leaped out at me. She couldn't believe her eyes because he was wearing a Yankee uniform!"

"But—" Bill said incredulously, "how can you be sure?"

"I am sure," she said firmly. "If you could have seen how she looked and acted, you'd be sure, too."

"Then why didn't you tell somebody?" Cogan demanded.

She lowered her eyes. "I'm ashamed to say it, but—I'm a lone woman. Worse than a lone woman—I have my father to think about. It occurred to me that instead of comin' to Mexico, I could hide my father on Dan's ranch, even use his Yankee discharge papers for protection, if necessary." She knew her words carried the ring of truth, because she was speaking the truth. If Dan had fallen for

137

her, as she had hoped he would, they might be on his ranch this minute, and she would already have begun to rebuild a life for herself. But yesterday's failure could not keep her from trying again today. Only this time, instead of his ranch, she needed his services.

"I just couldn't go through with it," she went on. "I still won't say anything if you want to let it go because your sister is in love with him."

Cogan clenched his big hands and stood up. "He's right here in Monterrey. Let's find him."

Bill half-rose and Mavis gently pushed him back onto the couch. "I know you men are both so much smarter than I am, but it seems to me he just might go for his gun if you say anything here in town—and maybe both of you would get killed, and he'd still be with Shelby. Of course you know best, but I think tomorrow morning, back at camp, would be the best time, don't you? The other soldiers wouldn't let him fight with guns then, would they? Why, they'd probably just put him out of the army." Her big eyes were wide with innocence as she seemed to wait breathlessly for their answer.

"She's right, Mike! We'll tell it around camp and then see how much of a hero he is!"

"I don't care what anybody else thinks." Cogan flexed his fingers. "When I get through with him he won't be very good to look at."

Mavis flinched. She thought of protesting, but she knew it would be useless. "You'll never tell anybody who told you, will you now?" she asked appealingly. "You promised."

"You know we won't," Bill assured her.

Mavis glanced at her watch. "My goodness!" She stood up and began backing toward the door. "I promised Daddy I'd meet him at three o'clock and here it is almost three-thirty. You'll come and see me before the troops leave, won't you, Bill?"

"Let me go with you now," he demanded.

"Oh, I couldn't! Peter's outside and Daddy would have

a regular fit!" She kept backing. "But I'll see you soon," she promised.

He was sullen and angry, a nasty little boy once again, and deserving of the very kind of treatment he was getting. She opened the door behind her and almost ran to where Peter was holding the blue mare. He helped her mount and she had the reins out of his hands before her feet were firm in the stirrups, and was streaking toward the wagon train.

Dan, Jane and Wil were again seated on the spread-out blanket when Mavis rode into camp. Dan was more relaxed than he could remember being since the start of the war.

After his first glance at Mavis he saw the quick chagrin on Wil's face, and then on Jane's. He wondered at it as he jackknifed up to help Mavis dismount.

She made herself heavy and slid down the length of his body. He grinned, but backed away a little because he couldn't keep from feeling the effect of her touch.

"Dan," she chided, "I thought you'd come to the hotel before this. That is, I thought you'd at least want to say hello." She smiled. "But Jane seems to capture all the men I know, and I can't say I blame any of them. Jane, dear, I just saw Reed. He said to tell you he has the tickets for the opera. He'll call for you about five."

It was Dan's turn to feel distress now. He should have expected that a girl as pretty as Jane would have suitors.

Jane's lips compressed and she looked coldly up at Mavis. "I'll have to tell Reed that I can't go. Dan is taking me to dinner."

"My," Mavis laughed, "you do want to keep all the men on your string. Oh, well, I suppose Reed will forgive you."

Dan said reluctantly, "I wouldn't want to interfere with plans you have already made. I should have known—"

"You won't be interfering," Jane said positively.

Wil seemed pleased. "I'll let Reed take me to the opera." He smiled happily. "Or maybe he'd rather go with you, Mavis."

Eyes gleaming, Mavis answered his smile. "I'd much rather go with Dan. Of course, if he insists on spending his time with someone more popular—but knowin' him, I'm positive he wouldn't break up someone else's romance just for the sake of an evening, and it will only be for an evening, since we're leaving tomorrow."

"It's nice of you to look out for Reed's interests," Wil said pleasantly.

Mavis smiled and took Dan's arm. "I wasn't. I was only thinking of the embarrassing position Jane is in. But then, if she doesn't mind, why should I? We'll say no more about it. Dan, tell me all about yourself—what you've been doing—every little thing. It seems forever since our evening in San Antonio, doesn't it? But I do remember it."

"Well, I—a lot has happened, I guess." Jane, from the moment Mavis had mentioned their evening together, had been staring at him, pink with embarrassment, and he fully shared her discomfiture. Even though he recognized that Mavis was deliberately trying to move between them, the fact remained that Jane was having to break another date to go out with him. Supposing that she wanted to do it —and it was possible that she didn't, was only going out with him because she felt an obligation to him—she still might be sorry in days to come. He was not acquainted with Marman, but Wil had certainly seemed to think highly of him.

"Jane," he said, "I'm not sure you should break your date this evening. I don't know when I would see you again, and it doesn't seem right."

She looked at him for another moment, then shifted her gaze to Mavis. "Maybe . . . maybe I shouldn't," she agreed. "It's . . . nice of you to understand."

Wil said indignantly, "Nonsense, girl!" but she quickly said, "Daddy, please!" and he shut up.

140

"I've embarrassed everyone," Mavis said, "and I'm sorry for it. But perhaps we'll all forget it while Dan tells us about his trip."

Quick darkness fell as Mavis led Dan into the small restaurant she had chosen for them. She was singing beneath her breath; Dan had nearly balked at coming out with her because of the unpleasantness she had caused, but she was sure he was over his mood now. While they saw parts of Monterrey he had gradually loosened up. For the last hour or so, as he told her about the expedition, he had even reached a point where her nearness sometimes broke his chain of thought.

She wished she could have changed her riding habit before dinner for something much more feminine and attractive. But that would have taken too much time. She didn't want to leave him alone for a minute now.

The ride had given them appetites and they ate ravenously, while a three-piece string ensemble played softly in the background. As they finished their coffee, she said wistfully, "Riding boots don't make very good dancing shoes, and I've never danced in a public place but—things are so different now, aren't they?"

"Shall we try it, then?" He moved back her chair and took her hand.

He was a much better dancer than she had expected, not at all stiff or self-conscious. The big hand in the small of her back was strong and sure and he moved gracefully. She allowed herself to be drawn a little closer and for a brief second pushed her breasts against his chest. She moved back then, as if the whole thing had been an accident, but soon moved in close again, as though she couldn't help herself. He was affected by it; she could feel a slight tension in him now. Possibly he could feel it in her, too. She had not permitted herself to be awakened for so long that now it was hard to control.

She really could love Dan, she decided. Maybe she did.

Once he was hers, he just might turn out to be everything she had ever dreamed about. But first he had to be hers—so completely hers that he was willing to take chances for her.

In time with the gentle rhythm of the music she brushed her fingertips along the shaggy hair on the back of his neck. He was big and strong and lean and hard-muscled, and he had a mind that was capable of doing great things if he were pointed in the right direction, she decided. A thing that would have to be changed—a little thing—was his reticence. Except for rare bursts of gallantry the spareness of his hard body was matched by his spareness with words.

They danced three waltzes and she truly enjoyed each step, but she couldn't allow herself to forget that much still remained to be done tonight. She had accomplished all that she would ever accomplish on the dance floor, she decided.

"Dan," she whispered, "I'm enjoying every minute of this, and I hate to do the same thing every time I'm with you, but I never see you except when I'm about to go away. And I do have some things that must be packed. We're leaving awfully early."

"I guess I hoped you wouldn't think about it," Dan said. He led her back to the table and helped her with her jacket. "It's been a long time since my last dance. Someday," he added reflectively, "maybe all of the things we used to do will become normal again."

"They might," she smiled, "but I'm afraid we can't depend on it. Things are the way they are and you have to accept that, or you're lost."

Riding back to her hotel he argued about it some. "Things change. We all know that by now. We've seen it happen—we still see it all around us. Isn't it better to plan and hope for 'someday' than to ignore it?"

"No, it's better to ignore it, because if you're caught up in planning for the future you're not doing anything about now. And now is always the important time. . . . You

142

haven't told me how you like your life, this minute. Is the army all you expected it to be?"

"I'm not sure I really expected anything. Joining the Brigade was something I needed to do, and I did it, and while I can't say I might not enjoy myself more doing something else, it's not bad at all. As you were saying a few minutes back, it's the way things are. Maybe I didn't have as much to argue about as I thought."

They reached the hotel and turned their horses over to the ever present attendant. As they went inside she brushed lightly against him and just as quickly moved beyond his reach.

At her door she turned and smiled gaily. "I've enjoyed seeing you, and I do hope we meet again sometime."

He bent forward slightly, as though he might kiss her. "You make sometime sound like never."

She placed a fingertip over his lips. "I'd like to kiss you," she said frankly, "but I still remember the last time. We were almost carried away."

"Yes, I remember it, too. I guess I've been thinking about it a little."

"Then we'll have to shake hands and say good night like two strangers. We are, almost, though it doesn't seem that way."

"No, it doesn't. Maybe it's because whenever I think of you I can see you so clearly—all in colors. Shining black eyes and shiny white teeth and pink gums and a red tongue, and a complexion like milk." His hand had begun to put so much pressure on hers that it hurt.

She withdrew it and touched her tongue to her lower lip. "I remember you well, too, and I know now that we had better say good night."

He would not push himself at her like any other man might have. "Good night, then," he said, "and I wish all the best for you, always."

He let her inside and had started to close the door when

143

she said, "Dan, wait. There's a trunk lid that sticks. Would you mind opening it before you go?"

"I'd be glad to try," he grinned. He came into the room and she pointed to the trunk.

He tried the clasp, failed, and pried harder. It popped open with a sharp, metallic snap.

"There, now," Mavis said, "I couldn't very well fail to kiss you after that, could I?" She moved to him and tilted her head.

His lips came down on hers, gently at first, and then more demanding. Her hands slid up and began to play along the back of his neck. His strong fingertips found the small of her neck and she trembled inside. It was no game now; she was almost completely carried away. But he pulled back.

If he began to think now about the right and wrong of it, she would be bound to lose. She tugged his head down again and the red tongue he had spoken of began to play against his lips. She felt him tremble, and was lost herself, but again he drew back. Damn his moral, stuffy soul to hell!

In spite of harsh breathing, his words were firm enough. "The war has done many things to all of us. We're all trapped by it—maybe more so here than in Texas or the rest of the South. But a Southern lady must still be treated as a lady; if she isn't, then we have lost yet another thing that was once important."

"Why," she said furiously, "you—you don't even like me! You're only flirting when I thought—why, you're not even attracted to me!" Her mouth trembled with the indignation of being spurned, and it was not altogether an act.

He stood rock firm, fighting her, until she caressed his face to weaken his resolve. Then his mouth slowly descended again. This time he, too, was carried away, and she knew it. She could no longer think about it logically, as his hands became demanding, searching, remolding warm, white flesh.

Suddenly he lifted her high in his arms and carried her to the bed. Her hands played over his neck. Her eyes swept over his face, looked upward into her own brain. In the dim past she had known the man she was engaged to marry, but that faint memory was suddenly overpowered and washed away.

Sober thought brought an awe at the wonder of what had happened. She was fulfilled and she gloried in it, but more important, she had succeeded. If Dan had thought of her sometimes in the past, he would be able to think of nothing else now. And his sense of moral responsibility would drive him to her.

She saw the serious set of his face as his arms slid into coat sleeves, and had to hide the triumph.

He came close, not touching her, and said, "Good night, Mavis." He seemed to want to say more, but couldn't find the words.

Her own voice was serious, a little shaky, as she said softly, "Good night, Dan," and watched him move for the door.

He stopped there, but once again could only say, "Good night."

# 9

DAN AWAKENED at daylight to find Peal's grinning face hovering over him. Peal was not talking and yet a gabble and muttering assailed his sleep-dulled ears. He sat up to take stock.

A crowd of soldiers encircled him; expectant eyes stared down at him with the curious fascination of children who had never seen a horned toad before.

"You're in for it, Yankee boy," Peal said. "Cogan's on his way here right now to tear you apart and send you back to Yankeeland in pieces."

Dan pulled on his boots, hardly believing what was happening. He stood up, saw that the crowd was growing by the second. Cogan was sure enough coming, pushing his way through. Morgen was at his heels.

As they moved into the clearing Morgen stepped in front. "Well, you want to tell everybody how come a Yankee to be in our outfit?" he demanded.

"Who said I was a Yankee?" Dan asked sharply, but he knew as he said it that he was only stalling for time in an effort to collect his thoughts. Only one person had seen him in the blue uniform, and that was Jane. He couldn't imagine why she had told Bill, after she had kept his secret this long. Certainly it wasn't because he had spent the evening with Mavis instead of her; it just wasn't like her.

Cogan gently pushed Bill Morgen aside. "I'm the one says you're a Yankee," he announced. "You figure to call me a liar?" A silence fell over the crowd until the whistling of Cogan's crooked nose loomed loud, like the shrill call of a curlew.

Cogan was willing to go through the formalities of picking a quarrel, Dan thought, but it would only be a waste of time.

"Yes," he said, "I'm calling you a liar."

Somebody gasped—a pleased gasp—and a muttering swelled up. Cogan's eyes flashed and he began his advance across the sandy ground, kicking up little spurts of dust as his big feet hit small mounds of grass and dead weeds.

Dan spread his heels and dug in, looking quickly at the men around him. Maehler was not here, nor Sherm, but there were plenty he recognized. Their eyes were lit up now in anticipation of the fight, not caring about the reasons for the time being, though they would be quick enough to remember when it was over.

146

The sleep was still in his eyes. He rubbed them and then Cogan kicked out with a thick, booted foot.

Dan twisted and the heavy shoe lashed alongside his leg, taking hide. He swung a quick left at Cogan's mouth.

The giant had been in too many battles to get caught that easily. He clutched the left with a rough palm, and pulled. The puffed scars stood out purple from exertion and his eyes glinted as he jabbed a hard fist into Dan's belly. Dan doubled forward and a left bounced his head back up. Lights danced but he dodged the long right that followed.

Dan took a step backward and got hold of himself. He had thought more than once about fighting Cogan, but had not tried to make any plans. If the man had a weakness he had not been able to discover it by looking. He would have to find it the hard way. He sidestepped a charge and his fist landed solidly on Cogan's hairy temple. The big man was caught off balance; he plunged headlong into the dirt.

He got up slowly, his dirt-spattered face an ugly red from the humiliation of going down. The preliminaries were over now, Dan thought. Cogan was ready to settle down to the steady business of wrecking his body. It was his last chance to take stock and he studied Cogan hard. He was strong, he was fast, he was heavy, he was experienced. The only thing left was to do the unexpected. Cogan was still six feet away. Dan lowered his head and charged.

Cogan grunted as Dan's head rammed into his belly. He almost withstood the charge, wavering before he toppled backwards. Going down he caught both of Dan's upper arms and flung him on. Spinning about, he dived after him, not bothering to rise.

Dan had made it to his knees but Cogan's weight smashed him down again. Cogan's powerful hands bit into his arm and twisted; a solid skull butted his cheek.

At this close range Dan was unable to swing. He arched his shoulder around and chopped with an elbow. Cogan's

147

lips split and blood spurted out. Dan pushed the bloody chin backwards and scrambled loose.

As he reached his feet again, a swimming vision of Jane's face appeared before him, and he saw her lips moving to tell about his blue uniform. The shock and disbelief transfixed him and Cogan caught him with a high right. A jarring hook to the ribs followed. Another hit in the same spot. A grunt of pain tore from Dan's lips. Cogan knew about his side, was aiming for it.

He would try to make it Cogan's undoing, not his. It hurt to be hit there, but the side was well now, solidly scarred over.

They traded blows and from the sheer force of Cogan's weight Dan was forced to back up. He hit the massed onlookers and felt himself shoved forward. Cogan tried to catch him in a bear hug and failing brought up a knee. It hit the inside of Dan's leg, bringing a flash of pain.

Dan whirled around, pushing Cogan into the crowd. As they shoved him back, Dan bent low and his fist met a hard belly. Cogan grunted but hit Dan with a right that made his ears ring.

They slugged again and Dan was matching each bruising blow, but forced to give ground. For the first time the yells of the crowd came to his roaring ears. Maehler had come from somewhere and was shouting encouragement.

"In the Adam's apple! In the Adam's apple, Dan!" He was shouting it over and over again, while Bill Morgen cheered Cogan, reminding him of Dan's side.

The next blow was aimed for the side and Dan was ready. He swiveled away and put all his strength into a blow at Cogan's jaw. It landed, hurting Dan all the way up to his shoulder. Cogan floundered, but did not go down. He made again for Dan's side and again Dan hit him hard. He staggered and Dan pressed into him. His savage attack caused the giant to stumble, sent him floundering to the ground.

Amazingly, he took his time getting up; and each passing second brought a noticeable measure of recovery.

Dan tore into him, began to pound over and over at the big man's head, taking hard punishment as he gave it out. His arms grew weary and his strength diminished. Somehow he would have to finish it soon. Cogan would cripple him for life if the chance came. He shouldn't be concerning himself with how it had all come about but he couldn't shut the betrayal from his mind.

Cogan feinted for his side and sidestepped as Dan swung. A chopping right sent Dan face first into the dirt and Cogan dived onto his back with both knees. His back wanted to double up and pains shot through his chest. He tried to roll over but the strength was gone from him. A blow at the base of his skull numbed him and made his body quiver involuntarily.

He heard Bill Morgen's voice, shrilly triumphant. "Boys, you're about to see now whether Kilbourne's a Yankee or Cogan's a liar!"

Another blow almost broke his head. He shielded his neck with a big hand but still couldn't roll. His jarred brain could not hold a coherent thought but an impression came through. Morgen was right. If he won Cogan was a liar. If he lost Dan Kilbourne was a Yankee and Shelby's outfit wasn't taking Yankees.

His raised wrist caught the next blow and then lifted to grasp Cogan's neck. He pulled the giant's head down beside his and forced the whistling nose into the dirt. Cogan struggled and kneed but Dan held on. Cogan panicked and tried to pry himself loose. Dan got his hand on top of Cogan's neck and held on. Cogan caught a handful of rib flesh and twisted.

The flesh seemed to squash into jelly and Dan's grasp weakened. Cogan pulled free but now Dan was able to roll away from him. He got up, caught another blow, and staggered into the crowd.

Instead of pressing the attack Cogan stood for a moment,

head tilted back to aid his breathing. His mouth was open, gasping in the blood that had trickled down from his lip to smear his whole lower face. Dan knew then where Cogan's weakness lay. He had used it once already when he had shut off the air supply from the crooked nose. But he mustn't fall into a trap, as Cogan had done attacking Dan's side.

Dan shoved forward, striking first at Cogan's belly. Hands came down and his right hit the crooked nose. Then crashing knuckles brought streaks of light into his own brain and sent him reeling backwards. He came on again, then backed. Force Cogan to move. Make the breath come hard.

Cogan came after him. Dan struck and nimble-footed away, avoiding two more looping blows.

"He's gettin' yellow," Morgen shrieked, but Maehler's voice was delighted.

"Stay with 'im, Dan! He's poundin' air! Whooeee! He's whistlin' like a lost steamboat!"

Everybody was excited now and Dan heard more shouts of encouragement. "Keep away from 'im, Dan! Then move in and let 'im have it! Pound that ugly nose, Dan!" Dan listened and bone-jarring knuckles hit his cheek a hammer blow.

After that he shut out the voices and concentrated on Cogan. Keep him moving. Don't let him tilt his head back. Strike when he wants to breathe. Dance away when he bores in.

Cogan was beginning to reel, but Dan was careful not to put him down. He struck and moved back. Suddenly he realized that his own breath came and went in sobbing jerks. His own face was dripping blood. His chest burned and pounded. His arms were weak. But Cogan was a liar or Dan was a Yankee; it had to be one way or the other. He struck and moved back.

Cogan clutched at him. Dan butted, flattening the crooked nose. Cogan sagged and Dan supported him, then moved back. Cogan tried to pause for breath and Dan moved in swinging. Cogan's knees buckled and he sagged to the ground.

For a moment Dan stood, unable to react. His swelling head wouldn't let him think. But he knew that in another few seconds Cogan would get up; he would be stronger, back where he was minutes ago. Dan dived on top of him, struggling, wrestling, twisting until Cogan's nose was forced into the dirt. The giant flapped his arms and tried to swivel his head. Dan held on, putting all his weight on the scarred head. Cogan began to beat the ground. His struggles grew weaker and he moaned. His body shook as all his strength went into the moving of his head. All of Dan's strength worked against him. Cogan was a liar or Kilbourne was a Yankee. And a Yankee couldn't stay with Shelby. They were locked until Cogan moaned from the corner of his mouth, "Enough! Enough!"

Dan's fiery brain did not fully understand. He held on till Maehler's voice pounded in his ear. "Come on, you fellers! Help tear this Johnny Reb loose, afore he kills 'im!" He still tried to struggle, but weakness overcame him and he felt himself lifted to his feet. They supported him while his chest continued to heave and the blood threatened to beat its way through his ears. Fire still burned in his lungs and the words he wanted to speak stuck in his throat.

"Morgen," Maehler yelled, "you get that liar to hell away from our camp afore I git mad and turn Dan loose ag'in!" His voice became more soothing. "You just come along now, Dan. We'll git you back to your bedroll and doctor some life back into you. Aye God, a feller wouldn't know who won just by lookin', but you got more friends now than if you'd lost. More bones, too, I reckon."

Dan found it next to impossible to rest. In spite of Maehler's curses and protestations men kept crowding around to express their admiration for the way he had handled Cogan, and in the crowding kicked loose dirt onto his bedding and fine dust into his eyes.

"You've got to get to hell out of here!" Maehler yelled. "Hell, this man'll swell up and bust if I don't finish doctorin' 'im!"

That was about the truth, Dan thought. His cheeks were puffed until his eyes were half-closed and his swollen upper lip made it almost impossible to talk. But those were little miseries. His back felt as if it would break if a broom-straw were placed on it and his tired lungs still threatened him with a cough if he so much as breathed hard. There was skin missing here and there, too, to sting and add to the general over-all achiness. But still he tried to answer the men. What they might think was important to him, and he had to find out if they would brush away the thought that he'd served with the Federals, or get it into their jaws and hang on.

Finally one man said, "As far as I'm concerned, Cogan is a liar. You proved that right enough. But we'd all feel easier if you'd come right out and tell us one thing—whether you fought with us or with the Yankees."

Dan said, "If I have to go into it again, I will."

Maehler began wiping his lips with a damp cloth, at the same time saying, "I've stood about enough o' this. I'm gonna be madder'n Sherm if you ain't gone from here in about one second!"

Reluctantly the man left, but his eyes were still asking questions that would have to be answered. It seemed to Dan then that they had all looked like that. When the wet rag was out of the way and he could talk again, he said, "What I did—whipping Cogan—wasn't enough, was it? They still want to know how the idea got started."

Maehler didn't meet his eyes. "You'll have to say some-thin'," he agreed. "There's too many here that was brought up on the old story that where there's smoke there's fire."

"What if I said I did fight with the Federals?"

"Why, to me it wouldn't make no difference. To some o'

152

them it likely wouldn't, neither, 'specially now that you whipped Cogan. About the rest, I dunno. There's a powerful lot of hate stored up against the North."

"Well, I guess whatever happens will come to pass," Dan said, "whether I worry about it or not." The rest of the outfit, those who were not in town, seemed to be settling in their own camp areas now, and Dan decided it would be best if he put his mind to something else. Forget about the aches, forget about the fight, and forget about what had brought it on, if he were able.

"How did Shelby make out with Jeanningros?" he asked.

"Why, I don't reckon they settled anythin'. They just had a sort of visit, the way I heard it. Shelby's goin' back there this afternoon, to stay most of the night ag'in, I reckon."

That left only Jane and Mavis to think about. The one had betrayed him in a way that hurt worse than all the bruises on his body, and he had done a great wrong to the other. A man took women, if they were willing, whenever he had the need for them, but there was a kind of woman to make love to, and a kind to save for marriage. Last night he had walked over the line. Even so, that wrong was not so great as the one that had come back to face him now.

He wondered where Peal had gone, and looked around; he saw Walcott instead, striding purposefully toward him.

Walcott pulled up and hooked his thumbs under his belt in back. He grinned. "I guess I heard wrong. I heard you won."

"Maybe it depends on how you keep tally," Dan said. He flinched as Maehler rubbed a raw place.

"Well, the fact that you fought was something. You know how I feel about Yankees, and if you're one you're no different to me than all the rest. But I've got a damn sight more respect for a Yankee with guts than a Reb with a weak belly." The soldier in him turned his face rigid and serious. "I'm here to bring you an order from Colonel Slay-

153

back. He wants to see you right now. In headquarters tent."

"I don't suppose you'll tell me why?"

"He'll tell you," Walcott said. "All I'll do is give you a warning. He's a fair man, but he can be hard. If I were you I'd talk straight to him."

Slayback's desk inside the tent was an upended box, his chair a box on its side. Adhering to procedure Dan reported first to Sergeant Ramsdale who sat nearby at his own box furniture.

"Yes, he wants to see you," Ramsdale said. "Man, that fight must have been all they said it was."

Dan moved over and saluted the colonel. "Private Kilbourne, sir." The salute was returned and he dropped his hand.

Colonel Slayback was not really hard-looking, but he could adjust his eyes to a depth that seemed to probe a man's insides. He looked at Dan that way now and said, "Your fight must have been a good one. What was the reason for it?"

"There were several reasons, I guess. Part of it was due to an earlier trouble I had with Cogan."

"What was the reason given this morning?" Slayback persisted.

"I was accused of being a Yankee."

"You're a fine soldier," Slayback said, "Yankee or Johnny Reb. I'm aware that you pulled two men out of the Sabinas, exposing yourself to gunfire all the way. One of those men, incidentally—Lieutenant Carter—was killed in Monterrey last night after he'd had a little too much to drink. But back to today's problem. I want a solid answer. Did you at any time, for any reason, serve with the Federals?"

"Yes, sir." They were words Dan hated to speak, but it was bad enough to live a lie. To speak one on top of it was a thing he could not have done.

"Stand at ease and tell me about it."

154

Dan spread his feet and reached into his pocket. He pulled out a sheepskin wallet and drew from it a folded piece of paper. He spread the paper open, rubbed the wrinkles, and handed it to Slayback.

Knowing the words from memory Dan could follow them from the movements of Slayback's eyes.

*TO ALL WHOM IT MAY CONCERN: KNOW YE, that Daniel Hayes Kilbourne, a private of Captain John Lewis Company . . . enrolled on the fifteenth day of November One thousand eight hundred and sixty-three to serve one year or during the war, is hereby DISCHARGED from the service of the United States this twenty-fifth day of May, 1865, at Socorro, New Mexico Territory, by reason of being mustered out. . . .*

*Said Daniel Hayes Kilbourne was born in Bexar County, in the State of Texas, is twenty-eight years of age, six feet two inches high . . . and by occupation, when enrolled, a prisoner of war.*

*Given at Socorro, New Mexico Territory this twenty-fifth day of May, 1865.*

When Slayback's eyes came up, Dan said, "I was captured near Vicksburg a week or so before it surrendered. My horse was killed and I went down with him. When I woke up I was in a Yankee hospital with a sore head and a broken ankle. I was lucky at that. The surgeon was too busy to amputate."

Slayback nodded with sober understanding. "I can see how it came about." He sighed. "You pose a problem for this army. If you hadn't saved those two men at the Sabinas, if you hadn't won your fight this morning, I could dismiss you and you would soon be forgotten. But unfortunately you've gained a lot of support for yourself. I say unfortunately because you've caused a split in our ranks. We have your supporters on the one hand—and on the other those who are not yet ready to forgive a Yankee

155

anything. Particularly they are not ready to forgive a Southerner who went over to the North—for any reason at all."

He thought about it for a time.

"We cannot let feelings run wild in this outfit because of one man," he said finally. "We must bring it all out into the open, to clear the air. I will have to try you—to convene a court-martial. If the members of the court find you not guilty, then you can stay in. If they find you guilty, then you will be dismissed and, I hope, forgotten. Would it really make a lot of difference to you?"

"A lot," Dan said. "I'll explain that at the trial."

"Then I will appoint a six-man court and a trial counsel. You can defend yourself, or get someone to do it for you. The court will convene at three o'clock, in front of headquarters tent. It will have to be in the open because everybody in camp will want to attend."

"What will the charges be?"

Slayback rubbed his forehead. "I could charge you with a wartime offense—aiding the enemy, I suppose. Or I could charge that your enlistment with us was fraudulent, since you deliberately withheld from us a part of your background. I think that will be it—that you enlisted fraudulently. As I have explained, it is the attitude of the men, and not how or why you came to be with us, that really concerns us. You are dismissed now, to go and make your plans. And because of your record with the Brigade, I wish you luck."

Dan said his thanks, took his discharge, saluted and walked out of the tent, his mind awhirl. First he would talk to Maehler, he thought, and tell him everything. But who, in this whole outfit, would be willing to defend him?

Two hours before the trial a soldier-lawyer came to Dan, offering to defend him for a hundred dollars. He was a slim, sallow-faced man with a steely handshake and a cold eye.

"The prosecutor—trial counsel—is sure to be a lawyer," he pointed out. "I will be aware of any tricks he might try to pull, I will know how to appeal to the men, and I have two immediate advantages. I will not become involved emotionally, because I know you only by sight. Whatever I say will not be held against me personally, because I am a lawyer and not a friend."

It made good sense and Dan was ready to hire him until Maehler intervened.

Maehler's disappointment and his hurt were each thick enough to cut.

"I said I'd come runnin'," he reminded, "an' now's my chance to prove it. It's true I'm not a lawyer, but these men don't give a damn about gabbledygook. They want a show, somebody to cheer for and somebody to yell at. To my mind whoever puts on the best show will win. I ain't tryin' to insist, mind you."

Maehler's words made sense, too. The six-man court would not be composed of lawyers and judges, and maybe they wouldn't want what he called gabbledygook. Besides, how many others in this outfit really gave a damn besides Maehler?

At three o'clock everybody who was not in Monterrey was assembled in front of headquarters. Lieutenant Templar had been appointed to preside. His court consisted of two officers, Captain Melber and Lieutenant Marius, and three enlisted men—Sergeant Jamison, Corporal Sewell and Private Peal. Colonel Slayback's two boxes were set up for Lieutenant Templar, several more were placed on their sides for the rest of the court, and one extra was up-ended in the middle for witnesses.

Maehler had said, "Don't you worry none about Peal. He'll vote the way the wind blows, an' that's just the kind of man I'm after."

Now it was too late for misgivings. Lieutenant Templar was pounding on the box in front of him with a pistol butt.

As the hammer blows drew quiet, he said, "Will the prisoner please step forward."

Maehler jumped up. "I object to that there word prisoner! Hell, this ain't no criminal we're tryin'. It's a man that's fought with us!"

The lieutenant cut short a few cheers. "All right, will the accused please step forward?"

Dan, sitting in the dirt like the men around him, got up and went to face the lieutenant, brushing himself off, narrowing his eyes against the glaring sun. The lieutenant was hardly more than a dark silhouette against the brightness.

"Daniel Hayes Kilbourne," Templar announced, "you're accused of joining this army under false pretenses—fraudulent enlistment. To be exact, you're accused of having served with the Federals, when you led us to believe that you were a Southerner through and through. Now this Brigade is composed mostly of men new to it, but the old outfit is still here, too, and the Brigade has its honor to uphold, and some might not think it's honorable for a Yankee to claim he's one of us. That's what we're here to decide."

"Object!" Maehler yelled. "That ain't what we're here to decide. We're here to decide if he enlisted fraudulently or not!"

Lieutenant Templar grimaced, pounded his box desk, and said, "All right. The accused may be seated unless the court counsel wishes to call him. Please remember—we must get this trial over with as quickly as possible because other duties are being neglected while this court is in session."

A tall, thin man, emaciated and wrinkled, got up and said, "If the court will swear in the witness, I'll call him at once."

Dan took the oath, his heart pounding as he looked at the counsel. The skinny soldier's name was Wilton Enders and everybody in the outfit knew his story. An ex-lawyer from Louisiana, he had held a hatred for the North so bitter that it had led him to stump his state making inflammatory speeches before the war had started. Later, he had fought and then been captured. After two and a half stubborn, starving, fiery years in a Union prison camp, during which time he had been beaten often for inciting the other prisoners, he had escaped, only to find that the war was virtually over. This frustration, if anything, had increased his passion against the North.

Dan sat on the witness box and the wrinkled old man, hump-shouldered and bent, fixed him with hot blue eyes. He spoke as if a frog had lodged permanently in his throat, but his voice carried well.

"I understand, from hearsay, that you joined up to fight for your country as soon as the war started. Is that correct?"

"Yes, that is correct."

"It's a point in your favor," Enders conceded. "What outfit did you serve with?"

"Terry's Texas Rangers—the Eighth Texas Cavalry."

"Where did you fight?"

"Shiloh. All through Tennessee and Kentucky. Vicksburg, finally.

"And what happened at Vicksburg?"

"My horse fell. It knocked me out and broke my ankle, and I was captured."

"When Vicksburg fell every man there—thirty thousand of them—got released on parole. Most loved their country so much they came back and fought again. What did you do?"

"I wasn't paroled. I was captured about a week too early and sent north all the way to Illinois."

"You were put in prison?"

"Yes."

"And how long were you there?"

"About four months."

"Then the Yankees turned you loose?"

"Not exactly. I was sent to New Mexico Territory to help protect settlers from the Indians."

"You were sent there? How could they send a Southern prisoner of war anywhere to protect anybody?"

"I volunteered to go, because the settlers needed protection and I wasn't any good to anybody in a prison camp."

"You volunteered to go, but you won't say it, will you? You won't say that you had to take an oath to serve with the Yankees, just as you had already taken an oath to serve the Confederacy?"

"I took an oath, but I didn't take one to fight the South."

"But you did take an oath to serve with the Yankees?"

"Yes."

"When you joined up with this outfit, did you tell anybody that you had served with them?"

"No."

"Then I have no further questions for the moment. I know you'll try to give explanations and justify what you've done, and I'm as anxious to hear a good story as the next man. So I'll listen along with everybody else. But I want the court to remember this—he did serve with the Yankees, and he didn't own up to it when he joined this army. No matter what the reasons are—and I'm sure he'll think of some good ones—he's still guilty by his own admission."

He walked, stoop-shouldered and sagging, back to the circle of squatting soldiers. He spun around and settled for all the world like a big dog. He had made his point and it was Maehler's turn.

Maehler took his precious time getting up and when he did finally make it he walked out into the circle, picked at his teeth a few seconds, and then spit. "Grape seed," he explained. "Now I can git down to business. First, though, I got to tell you; this one soldier whispered to me a while ago that his reason for wantin' to kick Dan Kilbourne out of camp—provided he lied, o' course—was plain and simple. He said this outfit was so chock full o' liars already that there wasn't room for another'n." Laughter came quick enough and he waited, with perfect timing, until it had died down. "I reckon there's one that ain't here, though. I ain't seen Cogan since they drug 'im off." Mock alarm crossed his face. "By dang, I reckon I thought of somethin'. Is there any one of you fellers thinks he can whip Cogan in a day or two, when he gets well ag'in? Raise your hand if you do, and I'll try to fix it." He looked out across the whole outfit, but no hands were raised.

"Well, then, there's somethin' I want you to think about. I know Dan Kilbourne can whip 'im. I seen it. An' if you call him a Yankee you're sayin' a Yankee can do what no other man in our outfit can do. I'll be blessed if I want to think that."

For the first time he regarded Dan. "This is too serious for me to go on like that, but I want you to remember them things. Now, Dan, s'pose you tell us. Did you ever try to break out of this Yankee prison camp?"

"Yes, I tried to escape."

"What happened?"

"I was caught and put in solitary confinement for two weeks—on bread and water."

"The way I heard it, prisoners never did get too much better'n that."

"The food was bad," Dan agreed. "Especially after word got to them that our Southern prison camps were not feeding captured Yankees."

"All right. What made you decide to go to New Mexico and fight Indians?"

"They told us how the Indians were rising, killing the settlers, burning their homes. I knew something about that, from before the war."

"Do you figger you did the right thing?"

"No. But I didn't realize it at the time."

"When did you realize it?"

"When we rode up to the fort and an equal number of Yankee soldiers rode out—to fight the South, I guess."

"Did you try to run away from New Mexico?"

"No. It was too late for that. By then nobody else was there to protect the settlers, and somebody had to do it."

"When did you git discharged?"

"The last week in May."

"You had a wound at the time. Is that right?"

"Yes. An Apache lance tore up my side some."

"How come a sick man to git discharged?"

"Lee and Johnston had both surrendered, and the post commander figured the rest of it would be over soon enough. He was already beginning to get reinforcements. He either had to doctor me till I was well or discharge me, and he hated Southerners as much as Enders hates Yankees, so he let me go."

"Why did you join up with Shelby?"

"Because, to my own way of thinking, I owed a great debt, and General Shelby held out the only chance I would ever have to pay it. I figured this army was all of the South that was left, that I needed to be a part of it for as long as it existed."

"Now I'm damned if that sounds like somethin' a Yankee would think about!" Maehler said emphatically. "An' if he ain't a Yankee, then we're glad to have him. We ought to be glad anyway. You seen 'im pull men out of the Sabinas, with bullets thicker'n buzzards on a dead buffalo. Now the rest of you out there ain't decidin' this, I know. Jest these six men here. Officers and men, I reckon I better say. But the rest of you elected the officers and I reckon you can still let 'em know your mind. So if you figger you want to let 'em know right now that Dan Kilbourne is all right —the only Johnny Reb in the outfit that can whip Cogan, and cain't hold a candle to half of you when it comes to downright lyin' and tall tales—then you just yell a little bit."

Cheers immediately began to sweep up to the skies until they joined together to become a solid roar. Lieutenant Templar pounded violently for order, but soon gave up and sat in helpless silence. When the cheers diminished and

162

grew ragged, good-natured yells at Dan and Maehler took their place. But all of the noise began to subside when the frail, broken old man stood up to fix his fiery countenance on Dan.

He walked forward slowly, seeming more stooped than before. He waved a violent forefinger. "I spent two and one-half years in a Yankee prison!" His hoarseness threatened to sweep his words away and he paused to get control of himself. "For breakfast I was beaten," he went on. "And again for dinner and again for supper! Why? Because I was a Southerner! A true Southerner, who wouldn't knuckle under whenever the Yankees said squat. During that time men starved because there was nobody there strong enough to feed or nurse them. They had to depend on men like you for that—but you turned tail and looked out for yourself and let them wither. By God, if you think I'm skinny, you should have seen some of them—with nothing left alive but their eyes! Now figure—all of you—what kind of a man would leave his fellow soldiers to starve! I'll tell you what kind. The same kind who, to save his own skin, would spy for the Yankees—spy on the men he eats with!" His voice lowered to a husky whisper.

"Now I don't say he's a spy. Maybe he's not. But he used deceit and trickery to get into this outfit. He's deceived you since the day he joined up in San Antonio."

He spun on Dan. "Were you wearin' your Yankee uniform when you enlisted in this outfit?"

"No. When I swore in, I had already served a night on patrol. My uniform was Confederate."

"Did you have a Yankee saddle on your horse? Yankee cavalry spurs?"

"No. I had an outfit that I bought in New Mexico. My horse and saddle gear had to be turned in when I was discharged."

"Then there was nothing that would really identify you as a Yankee?"

"My pants were blue when I rode into town. Beyond that, nothing."

Enders turned back to his court. "I'm going to give him the benefit of the doubt! There is doubt, lots of it, but I'm going to give him the benefit and say he's no spy. I'll give him further benefit of that same doubt and say he didn't mean to leave his fellow soldiers to starve. I'll even say maybe he wouldn't do it to you. But I for one want men around me I can trust. And I don't trust Dan Kilbourne after all the things he's done, and neither can you. Even if we could learn to live with Yankees—we couldn't live with turncoats!

"Now there's just one other little thing I want to say. I can sit down and the so-called defense counsel can get up here and do a jig for you and maybe strum his banjo a little bit—but he can do that whether Dan Kilbourne is here or back in Texas! And I say, for the safety of the whole outfit, that we owe it to each other not to take a chance on a man who admits he served with the Yankees almost as long as he served with the Confederates!" He looked at the six members of the court. "It's your responsibility. The rest of the men can laugh and yell, but if he leads this whole outfit to ruin, it will be on your conscience, not theirs!"

He was exhausted from the effort and it seemingly took the greater part of his strength to get back to his place at the edge of the circle.

Everybody was sober and serious now and Maehler stood up and looked into their faces and Dan saw uncertainty cross his wrinkled features. If he did the wrong thing now —if he put on a show that rubbed everybody wrong—Dan was done and it was plain that he knew it.

On the other hand, Dan knew that everything had been said now. All that remained was to try to arouse emotion in the men, as Enders had done. Only it had to be turned in the other direction.

Maehler desperately wanted to do what was right, but he

164

was so afraid of making a mistake that he was nearly paralyzed. He stalked out with the kind of shuffle a blackface minstrel might use. He worked his mouth a time or two and scratched his head. He started to speak, but the words stuck. He tried again. "Now this here is ridiculous. He's sayin' all you fellers out there have got no say in the matter."

"The lawyer is correct," Lieutenant Templar said. "The decision rests solely with the court."

Maehler looked helplessly at all six members of the court. "I was intendin' to call a man—Larney Mason—to testify that Dan here was a good soldier while he was with Terry's Rangers. But I don't need to do it now. Wilton Enders won't even argue about that part of it. An' the rest of you know what a good soldier he's been with our outfit. Now all you've got to say is 'not guilty' and he can keep on bein' a good soldier—one we should be proud to have in our outfit."

He looked out at the crowd, back at the court. Dan could almost read his thoughts. Suppose he danced a jig, as Enders had put it, and in doing so stirred more anger in men who were already thoroughly aroused. Wasn't it better to leave things the way they were? He was not risking himself. He was risking a friend.

"Dan is my friend," Maehler said, and his voice broke. He tried to speak again, couldn't, and shuffled back to his seat, knowing he had failed, but not sure why.

Lieutenant Templar rapped the box a few times and addressed his court. "Each of you has been given a slip of paper. Write 'guilty' or 'not guilty' on it and pass it forward. I ask you to remember this. The prisoner is being tried for fraudulent enlistment. But the thing we're really deciding is whether or not we want him in our army."

Dan looked at Peal, but could make out nothing from his face. He wrote on his paper, the same as the others, and all slips were passed to Templar. He shuffled them and then read them.

"Guilty, guilty, not guilty, not guilty, guilty—guilty. The

prisoner is guilty by a vote of four to two, and may hereby be considered not to be a part of the Iron Brigade."

Dan was almost in a state of shock and Maehler seemed like a ruined man. He came toward where Dan still sat on the box, but Peal got there first.

"I'd like to shake your hand," Peal said, "to show there's no hard feelings. The only reason I voted against you was for the good of the outfit."

Dan looked into his eyes and saw the smugness. Peal had never again mentioned the blow on his head, but now he was even for it.

Maehler hit the grinning, bearded face with all his might and Peal went down squealing. But Maehler was grabbed at once and held. He struggled and said, "I'm sorry, Dan. God, I'm sorry."

"I thank you for all you did," Dan said. "It was a big job."

Lieutenant Templar moved to stand in front of him. "I want you to know that I feel nothing personal either," he announced. "But some of the men will. You can hear the muttering and talking now, and it could grow into something. You'd be doing whatever friends you might have a big favor if you'd get your horse and gear and get out of camp as soon as possible."

Dan stood up, staggered by what had happened. "I've got to see General Shelby. Or Colonel Slayback or Colonel Elliott. I've got to see somebody."

"They're with Marshal Jeanningros now. If you get to see them at all it will be tomorrow. And I'll have to ask you again to get out of camp as soon as possible."

"Dan," Maehler called, "I'll still do what I can. God knows I will."

Dan nodded and spoke to Templar. "All right, then. I'll leave now and spend the night in town, and do whatever I can tomorrow. But I've got to get back in. I've told you why."

He looked at Wilton Enders and saw his triumphant smile. But he couldn't hold rancor against the old man. Enders' feelings ran as deep as his own, and maybe most of the outfit couldn't appreciate how deep that was.

# 10

DAN WOKE in the morning with the same feeling at the pit of his stomach that he'd felt every day from the time he left Rock Island prison camp till he joined Shelby at San Antonio. Only for the few weeks he had served in the Iron Brigade had the feeling left him; now it was worse than ever, for an obligation to Mavis had been added to it, and the hurt Jane had dealt him by her betrayal was deep and bitter.

He opened his eyes and looked around the shabby hotel room; it was the second time since '61 that he'd had the privacy of a room to himself and the first time didn't bear thinking of. He moved slightly and his bruised and aching muscles protested. Every bone in his body felt battered. He hoped the hotel ran to a hot bath and someone who could mend and clean his uniform.

There must be some way he could get back into the outfit; maybe when Shelby heard his story and realized the depth of his feelings, he would overrule the court.

He pushed back the covers of the sheetless bed. It was still comparatively cool; it couldn't be much after dawn. It might help if he could get to Shelby before the General had his own report of the trial.

The fat Indian wife of the hotel proprietor spoke neither Spanish nor English, but eventually Dan made her understand what he wanted. She puffed into his room with a small tin bathtub, and her two *niñas* followed, each with a bucket of steaming water. Before Dan could get them to tell their mother about mending his uniform, they disappeared, giggling. And *la patrona*, laughing and casting sly glances at the tall white man who wore nothing but his underwear and seemed to want her to do something with the gray suit in his hand, finally went off with it and brought back the complete set of her husband's Sunday cottons. When she at last realized that that wasn't what he wanted, she took the cottons away and brought a bright-colored serape.

In desperation Dan wrapped the serape around him and went looking for the two little girls. By the time it was all straightened out, his shaving water was cold and the bath tepid. Still, it helped soothe the bruises on his body.

*La patrona* came waddling back just as he started to climb out of the tub. He grabbed a towel while she cheerfully poured forth a torrent of Indian and held his uniform over her arm. She circled the tub, her fat face expressing joy at seeing so fine a man, her long black braids jouncing on her breasts at every step. Dan felt like an utter fool, turning in the tub, the towel draped in front of him.

She finally put the uniform on the bed and after only two backward glances, left the room, closing the door softly behind her.

In his exasperation Dan had momentarily forgotten his problems. Now he smiled ruefully at himself as he stepped into the neatly mended pants; women, whether young and pretty or middle-aged and fat, complicated everything and added hours to the minutes you planned for something.

He looked at his watch as he paid his bill. The Indian woman's eyes watched him from under incredibly long lashes and her jovial white-toothed smile told him that they shared a secret; his watch told him that thanks to the delay he had no time for breakfast, not even coffee. Well, he couldn't have gotten them down anyway until things were settled with Shelby.

He might just as well have had the coffee and breakfast; arriving back at camp he found that he had missed Shelby by ten minutes.

The picket who told him added, "They should've waited to hold that trial till the General was here anyhow. I'd feel better about it did he have his say-so in it."

"Thanks," Dan said.

"Ain't nothin' to thank me for," the picket shrugged. "I seen you at the Sabinas. Fer's I'm concerned, you already been proved trusty. Whyn't you go on up to the General's tent and wait fer him?"

"Thanks," Dan said again. "I guess I will."

Lieutenant Randolph, the O.D., was in Shelby's tent writing a letter. "Oh, it's you," he said looking up. "The ex-Yankee." But his tone was not unfriendly. He sighed and put down his pencil. "You'd have been off if you'd told me back in Santone where those blue pants came from."

"Would you have accepted me then?"

"I don't know," Randolph said honestly. He got up and stood by the tent flap. "My brother was one of those who died at Rock Island, but it seems like it was always the big strong ones who died and the little skinny ones like Enders who pulled through. Maybe nursin' had nothin' to do with it." He paused, reflecting solemnly. "I don't guess I'd really want to argue the rights and wrongs of anything that happens in a war. I was one of those paroled at Vicksburg, and I went back to fight without bein' exchanged."

"I'd like to be able to tell Shelby that others will think as you do—that there won't be a lot of trouble if I come back in."

"You couldn't—not honestly," Randolph said. "Enders isn't one to let a thing like this die easily. Neither are some of the others."

"Shelby must know about it by now," Dan said. "Has he said anything?"

"Not to my knowledge. Major Edwards drew up a fancy piece of paper, but I don't know that Shelby read it too carefully. He was with Jeanningros till late last night and you know how early he took off this mornin'. He's tryin' to get permission to march to the Pacific and recruit from there. Thinks he might get troops from California. Frankly, I'm expectin' orders to pull out any minute."

At Dan's grim look, Randolph added, "I'll speak to him if I get a chance. So will a few others. Maehler, for one, has been here every half hour since last night."

"I'd rather talk to him myself."

"Take a seat and wait," Randolph invited. "I doubt if he'll be here much before noon, but you're apt to see a pretty steady procession of your friends."

"I couldn't settle," Dan said apologetically, "and I don't much feel like rehashing everything with a lot of people."

Randolph nodded sympathetically. "I'll send you a message if he gets back here before you do. Where'll you be?"

"Vallejo's *Cantina* on the Main Plaza."

"Well, as they say here—go with God. I really will see what I can do."

Dan saluted. "Thanks for everything."

He left the tent grateful for Randolph's attitude and for the persistent efforts of Maehler and the others, but with the heavy weight of his dismissal clouding his senses, shutting away the hot, busy, noisy, noisome streets. He found himself at the Main Plaza before he quite realized he had left the camp ground. He shook his head slightly to clear it; until he'd seen Shelby he had no right to feel discouraged.

Passing the Cathedral he saw huddled on the steps a small Mexican in the ubiquitous white cottons, colored serape and wide brimmed sombrero. As Dan approached a beggar's whine assailed him.

*"Limosna, por amor de Dios!"*

170

Dan started automatically to feel in his pocket for change when the beggar pushed back his sombrero, indolently got to his feet and winked.

"You are looking for a *cantina,* señor?" asked Esteban.

"I am now," Dan said.

"Be so good, then, as to follow me."

He walked north, away from the Cathedral, leading Dan through several back streets into a poor section, going boldly past contingents of French soldiers who were swaggering loudly all through the town.

They arrived at last in a little street filled with shrieking, half-naked children and bordered by the dark shapes of their mothers, who sat in doorways talking in torrential spurts as they pounded corn on *metates* or shaped tortillas with a steady pit-pat sound. The few men around sat propped against adobe walls, seemingly asleep under the sombreros pulled down over their faces. As Esteban approached each made a surreptitious sign. Esteban let Dan catch up to him.

"*Buenos días,* Dan," he said. "I have been watching for you."

"I'm surprised to see you, Manuel. The way you move around, I thought you'd be gone by now."

Esteban shrugged. "We were waiting to see which way Shelby would go," he said honestly. "It is no longer enough that we fight Frenchmen, Austrians and each other. Now we must fight *norteamericanos* as well."

Manuel led the way into a small adobe *cantina.* It was cool and dark, sparsely furnished with half a dozen tables and a well-polished bar. Two men sat at separate tables drinking beer.

The proprietor was short and fat and swarthy with heavy black eyebrows, a drooping moustache and a white-toothed smile so wide it almost split his face. "Hola! Señor *Teniente,* you are welcome." His finger wagged at his two other customers. "We are all friends here."

"This is my friend, Señor Kilbourne," Esteban announced. He turned to Dan. "Carmelito is a smuggler and a bandit, but a friend of Juarez, so we forgive him much."

Carmelito smiled modestly. "My house is yours. Señor Kilbourne. The good *teniente* knows a man must live."

"Hah!" Esteban mocked. "If you had only one wife and family the *cantina* would feed you."

"Señor *Teniente!*" Carmelito said with horror, "do not let the good Father hear you. He would have me saying so much penance I would have time for nothing else!"

Esteban shook his head severely, but his eyes were twinkling. "That one," he said to Dan. "He has a wife and family back in his village and another one here. He thinks it is a secret—but in truth, the two women often compare notes."

"You will be the death of me, *Teniente*," Carmelito cried. "Sit over there and eat and I will try to forget you are here." He poured two cups of thick black coffee and handed them to Dan and Esteban.

They took the cups and went to a corner table in back. As they settled, Esteban said, "Though I am glad you will not be fighting against Juarez, I am sorry for your troubles."

"How did you know about that?" Dan asked curiously.

"I wish I could say I had the second sight. But the truth is, in every *cantina* Shelby's men are talking about it."

Dan said nothing.

Esteban added, "But this is something they are not talking about. Shelby has received permission from Jeanningros to turn west, proceed to the Pacific and from there recruit other *norteamericanos* to fight for Maximilian. It is said that for this purpose he will even take those who fought for the North."

The revelation brought little encouragement as Dan remembered that Enders, despite his deep hatred for Yankees, had implied that he might learn to live with them—but not with turncoats. "What time will they leave?" he asked.

"At noon."

"Are you sure?" Dan pulled out his watch.

"Sí," Esteban said complacently. "One of my men has been present at their meetings."

Dan pushed back his chair. "I'll have to get right back to camp."

"If you think to see Shelby there," Esteban said gently, "I am sorry. He has sent word already to break up camp. But he will lunch with Jeanningros and join the troops only when they are riding out of town."

Dan was dismayed. "I'll try to see him at French headquarters then."

"You will not be able to, I am afraid. Jeanningros is very well guarded. You will not get near him."

"I'll try anyway," Dan said stubbornly.

Esteban's brown eyes studied him. "I think perhaps you must. But when you are finished, you will find me here."

Dan pushed through the door into the hot busy street. He jostled through the polite, good-natured crowds, breaking into a run whenever space was clear enough to do so. The battering he'd taken from Cogan didn't slow him down, but every muscle cried out in protest and the sweat, running into his bruises, stung like wasps.

French headquarters was set so far back beyond iron gates that even a shout would have gone unnoticed by anyone in the magnificent building. The fence, inside and out, was as heavily guarded as Esteban had indicated; the grinning guards spoke neither English nor Spanish, and Dan knew not a word of French. He could stay here and shout and gesture till doomsday and never get closer than he was this minute. Possibly he would even be picked up as a nuisance and locked away somewhere unless he moved on.

He could hear the Brigade assembling just outside of town, could hear the short, shrill commands of the bugle. He started to run toward the sounds, then slowed down and stopped. His horse and all his gear were still at the livery stable, and there might also be a message for him at Vallejo's. He turned back and once again pushed his way through the streets.

He got his horse first, since it was on his way, then went to the *cantina*. He hitched the sorrel and patted its shoulder, wondering at his own delay, then realizing that it stemmed from a fear that Randolph had sent no message. But the bartender did have a note for him.

He tore it open, mentally calculating the time it would take to catch up with the Brigade. Randolph had written: *Don't despair. Shelby won't get back here before we leave, but I'll try again when we bivouac tonight. I'll get a message to you somehow.*

Dan slowly folded the paper and thrust it into his pocket. "Whiskey, please," he said to the bartender.

He took the glass over to a table and sat staring out onto the Plaza. The whiskey burned its way into his stomach and made him lightheaded. He didn't remember when he had eaten last; probably not since that meal with Mavis —was it only the night before last? What kind of person was he anyway, that he'd hardly thought of her since then? What kind of person was he who, when he did think of her watched her glittering beauty shimmer like ripples in a still pool until she became Jane, who had betrayed him?

He got up and quickly paid his bill. Jane was over and done with, but his mind refused to continue ignoring Mavis, not because of the unexpected passion in her perfect body, but because of the sober seriousness of her face as he had said good night. A man's conscience was a powerful thing; it could wreck his body, torment his mind, destroy his soul.

And yet it could not be allowed to pull in two directions at once. Mavis must at least share the responsibility for that night, while the blame for turning his back on his fellow soldiers lay squarely with him, and was a far greater thing. He must therefore put Mavis from his thoughts until he knew if Shelby would have him back.

The crowds outside had thinned; most of the Mexicans

were sensibly taking their siestas, leaving the streets to the *norteamericanos* and the French soldiers of Maximilian.

Dan mounted and rode toward the *cantina* where Esteban had said he would wait for him; time would hang heavy until he heard from Randolph and right this minute he was not overly fond of his own company.

Esteban did not seem to have moved since Dan left him. He motioned to the chair next to his and made no reference to Dan's useless trip.

Dan told him about Randolph's note and Esteban nodded sympathetically. "I will send a young man—his name is José—to follow the troops. He will bring the note from the lieutenant."

"I'd appreciate that."

"It is nothing. But—why is this so important to you, my friend?"

"Because men depended on me and I let them down. Because sometimes, in my mind, I see a soldier in a blue uniform shoot down a soldier in gray, and I know that I caused it to come about. That's only a part of it, I guess."

"I . . . heard some things in a *cantina*, but not all."

Dan had been talking more to himself than to Esteban, but now he explained how he had left the prison and joined the Union forces in New Mexico, still serving in his gray uniform in the beginning, living in a virtual stockade when he was off-duty, but gradually molding into his new life until he wore blue and lived with the others.

"I couldn't leave the settlers," he finished, "—not until reinforcements came. But they did come finally and I was discharged. A few days later I heard about Shelby and saw a chance to fight again for the South, to . . . level off the past. I felt—still feel—a strong need to do that."

"Shelby fights Juaristas to keep Maximilian on the throne. How does this help the South?"

"Look, Manuel, we fight Juaristas, that much is true. But that's only a small part of it. The big part is, the Confederacy is not dead as long as this army exists. Our bugles might not blow over the Southland, but they blow here. We've got our guns and sabers and we're still alive, and that means that the Confederacy lives. It was—is my country. I let it down once and I can't forget it. As long as one particle of it is left, I'm bound to serve it."

"But the future of the Brigade remains uncertain. If it dies, crumbles, what then?"

"Then I'll have done all I can to make up for the past. But if it dies and I'm not in it—things will be like they were."

Carmelito brought over two bottles of beer. "You will eat also, señores?"

Esteban looked at Dan, who nodded.

"Fix us a good dinner, Carmelito, but first bring some tortillas and guacamole for the beer."

"Sí. And some little peppers?"

"No little peppers! And do not put them in the guacamole!"

"No, Señor *Teniente*," Carmelito said sadly. "But it is plain that you do not understand the soul of the guacamole!" He went away muttering.

Manuel sighed. "Dan, my friend, I think that your mind will never rest, that you will not . . . like yourself . . . until you can be with the Brigade once more. Tell me, how did they know that you had been with the Federals?"

"Jane told her brother. And Cogan."

"I do not believe it!" Esteban said, shocked. "How did she even know such a thing?"

"I still had on a blue uniform when I met her on the prairie."

"And she knew how important this was to you?"

"She had a strong idea. All I can figure is that Wil needs help so badly that she figured she had to do it—that I would come to the wagons if I had to leave Shelby."

"Maybe. But it does not sound like a thing she would do."

Carmelito brought a heaping dish of guacamole and two

176

plates of tostaditas. "Your friend looks too serious, Señor *Teniente*. Perhaps you will invite him to our little fiesta tonight."

"I wouldn't be good company," Dan said apologetically.

"Carmelito is right. You should come. Who can be sad at a fiesta?"

Dan pointed at his bruised face. "I'd rather rest, so I can be ready to ride out tomorrow, if I get the word."

"Then you will be my guest. I have a room upstairs. But, Dan—do not hope too much."

The lilt of the music and the beat of the castanets, the stomping feet and the carefree laughter only deepened Dan's dark mood. He tossed most of the night, falling into a sound sleep only after Esteban came in with the dawn.

When he started wide awake it was broad daylight and the heat was seeping in even behind the adobe walls of the *cantina*. Esteban was snoring on the other bed, a beatific smile turning up the corners of his mouth. Dan marveled that this man, an army officer deep in the territory of his enemy and obviously spying, could have such peace of mind.

His own mind was churning, and though he knew it was far too early to expect José, he dressed and went to the stables.

Esteban found him there two hours later, sitting on the rail of the corral, watching a vaquero break a wild horse. He climbed up beside him. "You have done this work?" he asked.

Dan nodded. "I broke my first horse when I was thirteen; I rode one of her mares during the first part of the war."

"I think you would still like to be a rancher, no?"

"Yes. I will be, sometime."

They watched in silence as the vaquero went methodically about his work. The wild horse was getting tired, soon she would be dispirited, then she could be bridled and saddled and taught to carry a man.

177

Noon came and passed, and the hot, sunny afternoon became intolerably long. No messenger arrived, and Dan thought of a thousand excuses. The messenger had been killed, or at the very least his horse had gone lame. Randolph had not spoken to Shelby, had forgotten him as soon as the outfit had lost sight of the city. The Brigade had marched into another Juarista trap.

No, Esteban would have told him this by now, wouldn't have volunteered to send a messenger.

Then Shelby had heard Randolph's plea, had rejected it, and Randolph hated to send the message.

Just after sundown José came clattering into the stable, his triumphant face announcing that he had accomplished what he set out to do. Esteban took Randolph's note from him and gave it to Dan.

*I'm sorry*, it read. *I guess Shelby just has too much on his mind right now. I would say that your only chance is to wait until we reach the coast and start recruiting and then get some friend of Shelby's—a general, maybe, if you know one—to speak for you. General Shelby will do almost anything for a friend.*

Esteban said softly, "I truly wish that I could help."

"How did you know?" Dan asked dully.

Esteban shrugged. "Your shoulders droop and the light has gone from your eyes."

Dan handed him the note, consciously straightening his shoulders.

Esteban read it and raised his eyes. "And will you do as he suggests?"

"No. I can't follow them like a stray dog hoping for a bone. And it would do me no good to go to the west coast of Mexico. Who would be there to speak for me? I doubt if anyone will go there except the Brigade itself." He considered. "No, there are two things I can do now—go back to Texas or go to the wagons."

"And which will it be?"

"The wagons. Exactly as Jane wanted me to, I guess,

178

though not for the reason she might think. I'll leave at daylight."

"The day after tomorrow I go to a small place called Engracia. You may ride with my little band. We will catch the wagons by noon of the third day." As Dan's mouth began to tighten he said, "You must wait. All over the roads of Mexico there are little white crosses to mark where travelers have been slain because they foolishly traveled alone."

"I've ridden through Apache and Comanche country," Dan said.

"I could order my men to keep you from leaving."

"Here in Monterrey—in spite of the French garrison?" Esteban grunted contemptuously. "They hold only the surface."

"Then I'll have to wait," Dan agreed reluctantly.

He began to consider how it would be. He knew he could never love Mavis as he might have loved Jane. But they could build some kind of life together. It was up to him to see that they did.


Dan and Esteban left Monterrey a few minutes after eight o'clock in the morning. The city was crowded with peons bringing produce to market, with wives and daughters coming out to buy. Dan had expected an earlier start, then realized that empty streets would have made them conspicuous to the French sentries.

Until they reached the outskirts of the town, only young José accompanied them. But as they rode further down the southbound road, they were joined by others, singly and in pairs, until the detachment numbered thirty men.

Esteban, Dan noted, had been right about the crosses. They marched neatly along the road, each with its pile of rocks to show that a prayer had been said for the dead. It was curious that he had not noticed them especially on the road from Piedras Negras; probably he had simply thought of them as roadside shrines.

The hard ride did not leave much time for such reflections. Dan judged that Esteban was on a tight schedule. Dinner was tortillas and jerky, eaten without stopping, and supper was more of the same. They made up for their late start by continuing to ride far into the night.

Occasionally they saw fires deep in the brush and from time to time shots echoed and were answered. Presumably these were a signal of some sort, but Esteban paid them no heed, possibly feeling that his force was too large to be molested—or big enough to take care of trouble if it came.

They made a dry camp that first night and got under way before daylight the next morning. On the second day they rode more easily, dismounting from time to time to walk the tired horses. The nightmare of the past week began to wear thin from the sheer exhaustion which came from carrying it. Dan tried to think what he would say to Mavis, to Jane and all the others who would have questions.

He owed explanations to no one except Mavis, he decided, and he owed her more than one. Was it better to tell her that he did not truly love her, that love would have to grow? Or was it better to live a lie that might make her far happier? Such things were beyond his experience.

On one occasion when they were leading the horses, Esteban slowed to walk alongside him.

"Dan, amigo," he said, "look behind you, at my men. Two days ago they were in great danger. Tomorrow, who knows? But look at them, as they tell their stories and laugh. Today is everything, and today is good. Can you not be like this?"

Dan glanced behind him at the cheerful, chattering Mexican soldiers and smiled. "I'll have to learn."

"You think often of the past?"

"Often, yes."

"But not always?"

"No, not always, though I suppose it drives me from the back of my mind." On impulse, in an effort to explain, he told Esteban of the time when he had foolishly allowed himself to be cornered by Kiowas, and had ended by working a year without wages to pay for the fine stallion they had killed. "For that year I was under a cloud," he concluded. "But on the day my Dad called the debt paid because I had earned enough to buy another stallion it was like . . . being born again."

"But the work you did—it could not bring back the stallion that was dead."

"No, nothing could do that. But at least I knew that I had done everything a mortal man could do to make things even."

"And this time—you have made your confession, but you have not paid your penance?"

Dan shrugged helplessly. "Maybe it's something like that, maybe not. But I wasn't thinking of these things when you let me catch up to you. I was thinking of Shelby, wondering what he was doing, wondering about the future of the Brigade. Maybe wondering a little about my own future, too, I guess."

"And because of what happened, Jane will not play a part in this?"

"No, I intend to marry someone else—Mavis Todd. We will have a good life together if I do my part."

"She is a most beautiful girl," Esteban agreed. "In some ways more attractive than Jane, perhaps."

He gave the signal to mount and the little band prepared to increase its pace.

At dusk on the third day one of the scouts rode back to report that the wagon train was camped at a shallow creek about three-quarters of a mile along the road, and Esteban sent José ahead to announce their coming.

"And now, my friend," Manuel said to Dan, "we are here and you are no longer a soldier, even though you still wear a uniform."

"It will take some getting used to," Dan acknowledged.

"Ah," Manuel said, "I will be glad when the day comes for me as well—if it comes. But my country ferments like green wine. No president goes unchallenged—not even Juarez. I think I shall spend the rest of my life fighting."

"Why do you do it?"

He shrugged. "I am not sure. I will think about it."

"You know . . . if you ever need anything and I have it . . ."

"I know," Manuel said.

They came in sight of the train, with its small cook fires springing up inside the circle of wagons. José and another horseman—Wil Morgen, they saw—were coming down the road to meet them.

Wil waved and spurred his horse. "Dan! Welcome! Manuel! It's good to see you! I was afraid after you saw us through to Monterrey you might have gone back to Texas. But I'm glad you didn't. We'll have a fiesta!" He wrung Esteban's hand and punched Dan lightly on the arm. "Jane will be glad to see you. Did Shelby break up after all? Where's Bill?" He waved at the soldiers and swung his horse around to ride between Manuel and Dan.

Dan had momentarily forgotten that the wagons had left before either the fight with Cogan or the trial. He said without warmth, "Shelby has gone on to the west coast with the Brigade—they're recruiting there. As far as I know Bill is still with them."

Wil waited to hear what had happened, realized that Dan intended to say no more, and lightly punched his arm again. "Well, I'm glad to see you! The old man's getting thin and tired." He led them into the circle of wagons, calling out, "Jane! Jane! Look who's here."

She came out of her wagon wearing a shabby gray riding skirt and a short-sleeved plaid shirtwaist. Her hair had been tied back of her ears with a blue ribbon and there was a smoky smudge across her forehead.

She saw Dan and ran to him with her face alight and both hands outstretched. "Dan Kilbourne! I was afraid I'd never see you again!"

Dan bent over his horse, took one of her hands, shook it and said formally, "Miss Jane."

Esteban looked from one to the other, and his eyebrows crept up. Bewilderment clouded Jane's eyes and color came into her cheeks. Wil forced a laugh which trailed off dismally. To cover his surprise and confusion he turned to Esteban.

"You'll stay the night, won't you?" he asked.

Manuel shook his head. "No, we only stopped to deliver this one. We can travel another five or ten miles yet. But I shall see you again soon." He reached out and wrung Dan's hand. "*Vaya con Dios*, Dan!"

"*Hasta la vista*, Manuel. And thanks for everything."

Esteban said goodbye to Wil and Jane, passed a few moments with several of the colonists who were grateful for his help in the past, and waved his men on. As the detachment began to trot away some of the curious settlers crowded up to Dan and he got down to join them.

Wil pointed to him. "Folks," he said shouting above the sounds of the departing horses, "some of you know Dan Kilbourne and you've all heard me talk about him. If you haven't met him, introduce yourselves—he'll be helping us manage from now on."

Dan found his hand being shaken by several of the men. If they wondered why he had come, they didn't ask now. He saw Jane back out of the circle and go toward her wagon. He didn't really want to hurt her, but she might as well know from the start they couldn't continue to be friends.

Russell Todd was one of the last to come up to him. "We're glad to see you, Kilbourne. For one thing, we've all hated to see Jane working so hard; but most of us don't know how to help."

"I haven't seen Miss Mavis, Senator."

Todd answered with a heavy levity. "When that Mexican boy came to say you were coming, she decided to fix up a little. I suppose she's still at it."

183

"Do you think she would mind if I interrupted to say hello?"

"No. No, of course not. That's her wagon over there." He pointed.

Dan stepped over a pile of harness and made his way to a vehicle showing the bright edges of flowered chintz curtains. He rapped lightly on the endgate and Mavis looked out.

"Dan! I'm so glad to see you! I'd be storying if I said I hadn't heard you were here." She was warm enough, yet holding herself back.

"I came because of you," he said gravely. "I . . . came to ask you to marry me."

"Why—" She seemed delighted, surprised, relieved, happy—all of the things a man could hope for if he were in love. She slid downward into his arms and he helped her to the ground. "I think I'll kiss you—right in front of everybody," she said, and pulled his head down to hers.

Her lips were soft and sweet. He was a fool if he ever let himself forget how lucky he was.

A smallish man strutted from around the wagon and interrupted them. "Name's Quillian," he announced. "Lately a Major in Longstreet's division. I work for Marman now."

Dan looked at his fancy Mexican costume, studied his face. "I'm sure I've seen you." Recognition came. "You stopped and stared at me as the wagons were leaving San Antonio."

"I remember. I mistook you for someone else—a man I served with. When I realized my mistake I was ashamed and rode on."

Mavis tightened her arm around Dan. "If you'd like to get out of uniform, maybe some of Daddy's things would fit you." She was obviously comparing his butternuts with Quillian's embroidered outfit.

"Thanks," Dan said, "but I'll wait till I can buy my own."

"Well, never mind." She smiled brightly, centering her

conversation on Dan as though Quillian had been dismissed. "Peter is fixing supper for us—something very special—so don't be lured by someone else."

"I wouldn't mind eating with you," Quillian said promptly. "Marman's meals leave a lot to be desired."

Mavis flashed him a quick look. "I'm sure we'd be glad to have you some other time," she said. "But tonight's supper is private." She tugged at Dan's arm. "You could come into the wagon and clean up. It's really quite civilized inside."

"Thanks, but I'll have to talk to Wil first."

She gave him a quick smile. "Well, don't be long."

"I'll come with you," Quillian said. "Marman's there already."

His presence kept Dan from giving Mavis more than a smile as they parted. Quillian in turn grinned at him, a saucy, knowing grin.

Darkness was beginning to descend and many of the settlers had already lit kerosene lamps and hung them on the sides of their wagons. Moths and other night insects were thick around the dancing flames.

"The colonists like their comforts," Quillian said disgustedly, "and no one can make them understand that half of those flying things bite."

The Morgen wagon was one of the few lit only by its cook fire. Jane was kneeling by the flames, frying something which smelled like venison. The light flickered against her face, showing eyes that were slightly reddened.

Dan nodded to her and she bent her head once, stiffly, continuing to busy herself.

From just outside the circle of firelight, Wil called, "Dan! Come and meet Reed Marman. We were just talking about you."

Dan walked over and shook hands with the pale blond man who was seated up against a wagon wheel beside Wil. Marman greeted him indolently, not bothering to wipe away the trace of anger that showed on his handsome face.

185

"We were having a little argument," Wil went on. "I want to stop and overhaul; we need an overhaul. But Reed's in a hurry."

"Nobody can tell when something will break," Marman said sharply. "Replace an axle today because it looks weak and tomorrow one that looked good will split down the middle. I know you've had a rough time, and I know the wagons are in worse shape than when we started. But we're also closer to the end of the trail."

"We're going into country that hasn't had any law since before the Spaniards came," Wil argued. "I want to circle away from the road and I don't want any of my wagons left behind like sitting ducks for guerrillas. You have a breakdown yourself almost every day, but you have experienced men to help. When something happens to one of my rigs, my colonists and their niggers stand around and wring their hands and wail and hope, but they don't help."

Quillian had lingered by the fire talking to Jane; he followed her, grinning, as she brought coffee to Marman and Dan.

Marman watched Jane closely as he took his cup. "I've explained to Wil that, if we must stop, my teamsters can do whatever is necessary to your wagons," he said. "But I don't want to stop."

Her gaze fell away from him. "Daddy," she said quietly, "I know you're right about the wagons, but Reed is right, too. The colonists are already quarrelsome and uncomfortable. If we delay, the wagons might hold up better, but I'm afraid the people will break down. I think we should go ahead."

Wil looked grim and bullheaded, a little angry at Jane as he threw up his hands. "T'en ve go!" He continued to sulk as Marman grinned broadly.

"I forgot to tell you, Kilbourne," he said, "we're glad to have you with us."

It occurred to Dan then that Reed had been threatening when he announced that his teamsters could overhaul the wagons; the implication had been that, if they had to stop and put the vehicles in shape, there was no necessity to hire Dan to keep them rolling. Jane had realized this and therefore had quickly taken Marman's side. Well, why not? She knew that Wil badly needed more help than she could give him, whether the wagons were doctored or not.

He was ashamed at his own thought, but the hurt of her betrayal cut more deeply whenever he looked at her and realized how much he had cared for her.

"Wil," he said, "if everything's settled, then I'll go."

"How about supper?" Wil asked.

"That's where I'm going, thanks. Good night, and I'll see you at daylight."

Mavis was dressed as though the flat plain of Mexico were really a Southern plantation, or the Menger Hotel in San Antonio. But Russell Todd, looking old and disheveled, was still wearing the brush jacket and levis in which he traveled. A gray stubble on his cheeks proclaimed that he had not shaved for several days. His voice, on the infrequent occasions when he spoke, was low and hesitant, and he appealed quickly to Mavis whenever there was need to reach even the smallest decision.

Supper was embroidered with white nappery and sterling silver. Dan felt an impatience bred of something more than just the desire to see Mavis alone and explain himself. Such finery out of a covered wagon seemed to smack of a charade where the mummers insisted on keeping up the masquerade long after the curtain had gone down.

"These pitiful things are all that's left," Mavis said, watching his eyes. "These and Peter, who doesn't have the courage to leave us, though he's free to do so."

"It's all very nice," Dan said.

"But foolish? I hope you don't think that, Dan. We're all doing it, as a reminder. Oh, I'll admit that some are only mocking themselves. They'll watch their fine things tarnish and crumble to dust and not realize that the same thing is

187

happening to them. But you mustn't think I'm one of them, Dan. I take strength from my finery. I look at it and I know that while the South has been burnt and crushed and the winds are scattering its ashes, it will draw itself back together; it will build itself up, and I will rise with it."

"Mexico seems a strange place to harbor such notions."

"Southerners have also scattered to Egypt, South America, wherever they can find refuge. But not all the ones who have fled have done so because they're afraid. Some are only searching for quick opportunity."

The meal continued and Dan's nerves grew taut. The warmth of the money in his belt—less than three hundred dollars now—plagued him with the thought that he was not, might never be, in a position to give Mavis the things that were important to her.

When they finished eating, Mavis said, "Dad, Dan and I are going for a walk. We'll be back soon, but don't wait up for us. You rest, now."

Russell Todd nodded his agreement and slumped back into his chair the instant she took Dan's arm.

"Don't you worry about Daddy," Mavis said as they started away. "He was once a great man—a very great man. He'll find himself again."

They were soon out of hearing of the camp, walking arm in arm along the bank of the creek. Water tinkled as it slid over the sharp rocks. The deep-throated croaks of the frogs melded with the sawing of katydids and the insistent chirp of the crickets. The stars cast a silvery light that was sometimes tinged with the golden flicker of the campfires behind them.

They found a grassy sward bordered by a semicircle of thorny mesquite. Dan stopped Mavis, put his hands on her smooth upper arms. Her lips gleamed and the stars reflected themselves in her eyes.

"I've got some things to explain," he said.

Despite his reluctance she pulled his head down and

kissed him; her lips clung, awakening memories of the night in Monterrey. He pushed her back.

"I've got to tell you why I left Shelby."

"It doesn't matter." Her breath came fast and her white teeth sparkled.

"It matters," he insisted, and told it as well as he could, talking rapidly, closely watching her face for a sign that the words disturbed her.

As though she had hardly listened, she brushed his lips, washing away the words. She put a pressure on the back of his neck. "Dan . . . in Monterrey you . . . woke me. I'm not the same any more."

"We'll be married soon—tomorrow if there's a preacher with us."

"Then whatever we do tonight won't matter, will it?" She began to sink down onto the grass, but he pulled her back to her feet.

"Yes, it does matter. It was a wrong that mustn't be repeated."

She pouted. "You're angry with me. And what happened . . . didn't mean anything to you."

"It brought me here to ask you to marry me—at least, it was one of the things that brought me." He began to shrug out of his coat. "I guess I do think we should sit for a minute." He spread the coat on the ground. "We need to talk about our future."

She smiled at his seriousness and sat primly, her skirts making a wide semicircle on the grass. He carefully seated himself beyond their radius.

"Now, then—I've got about three hundred U.S. dollars. Slightly less." He grinned a little. "I wouldn't have that if I hadn't played a few hands of poker in the Yankee army."

"I'm glad you're a gambler," she said. "Because I have something in mind—a way that we can make a lot of money. But we'll be gambling, maybe more than either of us has ever done before."

"I'm anxious to hear about it."

189

"Oh, not tonight. But—I will tell you about it, when the time is right."

He decided that she really didn't have a plan, but wanted to reassure him. "I was going to mention that we would have to start with a farm, and eventually begin to ranch."

"Dan, let's not talk about it tonight."

He stared at her for a long moment. "It's something that must be talked about."

"But not tonight. Can't we just sit?"

"I don't think we should. But there is one thing we can do. Now that I've explained what happened, and it doesn't matter to you, we can go back to camp and I'll speak to your father about our marriage."

"No! No, you mustn't. Not for the time being."

His eyes narrowed. "But why, if you mean it to happen?"

"Because . . . he's tired, very tired. He would worry. On the one hand he'd be afraid that we'll shuffle him aside, and on the other he'd worry that he'll become too dependent on us. But he won't be like that, Dan, when he's rested. And I do hope, now that you're here and everything is startin' to work out so well, you'll show a little patience."

Her accent was growing stronger and Dan grinned. She bounced up, elusive and gay and untouchable and more attractive than any other woman he had ever seen.

"Dan, I will try to keep you interested while we wait. In fact, I might just try to drive you out of your mind. But be careful; you never know when I might surrender. I do find you attractive. And Dan, I will need you to hold me from time to time. I'll need your courage."

She pulled him up, then snatched free. She kept teasingly beyond his grasp as they moved back along the creek bank.

"The reason we can't plan our future together," she said, "is because it will be filled with surprises. But they'll be delightful surprises, I promise you. I'll try to see to it that you're never sorry you came after me. And I expect before long you'll forget all about the unpleasantness you left behind you."

# 11

As the days wore on, blending into one another, the wagons passed through dry, sandy wastelands, and then climbed upward into verdant mountains where streams rushed and birds sang a perpetual song that in itself became a tiresome, monotonous trilling.

Dan remained polite and courteous to Wil and Jane, but reserved with both of them; he did not get in touch with them at all unless it was absolutely necessary. Jane, seemingly bewildered, tried once to smooth things between them, but his cool civility stopped her short. Thereafter she avoided him and he was grateful; her presence continued to remind him of the reason for his separation from the Brigade, and his resentment increased because he found himself drawn to her in some ways in spite of what she had done.

He thought often of the Brigade and sometimes mentally marked off its progress toward the Pacific.

But just as often he reminded himself that he had now embarked on a new life, and must make the most of it. Though Mavis kept insisting that she had an ideal solution to all their problems, he had come to discount that as no more than a hope on her part. Thinking in realistic terms, he knew that their life in the colony would be much the same as it would be for the other settlers—except that he had decided to ranch from the very beginning, and not farm at all; they would be painfully short of money, but at least it was a trade he knew. He hoped that in time Mavis would get used to it. Sometimes he concerned himself about it, just as he concerned himself with the fact that she still did not want him to speak to her father or in any way announce their marriage. But he still was sure that things would smooth out.

Fortunately, the opportunity to dwell at length on any given subject seldom came to him. In the best of times and under the most ideal conditions, wagon train work was neither pleasant nor easy; on this trip, in addition to the mistakes that came from inexperience, there were problems resulting from the peculiar sensitivities of the Southern "gentlemen." To his amazement, Dan found that a wagon's place in line had nothing to do with its speed, load or maneuverability. It was determined instead by its owner's rank in the government or army of the Confederacy.

The Negroes were as sensitive as their ex-masters. There were just certain things they did and all hell couldn't make a so-called house nigger put his shoulder against a stuck wagon or chop branches for lever poles.

Fortunately major breakdowns were rare, though common enough to be a constant source of worry.

Early one morning, as they lurched and braked their way down from the mountains toward a low, level valley, a wagon belonging to a portly colonel named Dutton skidded into a hole and the splintering of its wheel reached Dan's ear ten wagons back.

The rest of the wagons immediately began to pick a course around Dutton. It was a hard and fast rule of Marman's that the train was not to be held up for anybody or for any reason. A breakdown meant being left behind; if repairs could be made in time to catch up before evening, well and good. If not, the vehicle would have to be abandoned.

Dan gave orders for a spare wheel to be dropped off with Dutton, and thanked God for the uniformity of the army wagons as he raced ahead to get a jack from the Morgens.

Jane stopped and helped him get the jack up onto the sorrel without a word of comment. He hung onto it, thanked her civilly, and began the long climb back.

Most of the other wagons had already passed, leaving their cloud of dust. Dan's eyes teared as he wrestled the heavy jack under the axle and tried to base it on firm ground. A few passing teamsters grinned at him, reminding Dan that Marman had, after all, made one concession—his own wagons brought up the rear and thus the teamsters ate more dust than the colonists. Marman rode beside one of the teamsters and nodded politely as he went by. He made it a point to take no interest in anything that happened, as long as his own vehicles were not held up. At no time did he invite conversation, often walking away without answering if someone put a question to him.

Colonel Dutton watched Dan with interest and concern, but it had plainly not occurred to him to offer his help. After a few minutes he lost interest and went forward to sit in some sparse shade.

Mrs. Dutton came to stand in his place as Dan strove to drive the linchpin from the tough, sourgum hub. She moved closer by degrees, until she was beginning to crowd him.

"Mr. Kilbourne," she said finally, "you know, of course, that we're all dyin' to know what happened—why you left Shelby and came with us, that is. Are you and Mavis Todd goin' to get married?"

Dan put down his tools and straightened his back. He looked out across the valley, and then back at her. "If I take the time to satisfy your curiosity, you'll lose your wagon. But sit down, if you like, and I'll tell you all about it."

"Well, I—please, I didn't—" she moaned, and the colonel came thundering back to stand beside her.

193

"Now, see here, young man—you get to work and get that wheel on—as quickly as possible!"

"Colonel, as one civilian to another, I'm in no mood to take orders from someone who won't try to help himself."

The colonel's haughty manner dropped away and was replaced with uncertainty. He started to bluff, wrestled with his pride and judgment, knew he was beaten. He said pleadingly, "Look, Mr. Kilbourne, I don't want to lose my wagon. We couldn't stand it if we lost the few things we have left. Please—will you please hurry?"

"All right, I'll hurry—provided you keep this woman and her curiosity away from me."

The colonel, his fear still greater than his pride, hastily took his wife's arm and led her away. Tears had begun to course down her cheeks, making Dan ashamed and angry with himself. What the hell was getting to be the matter with him? Well, he defended, why the hell did people always want to pry into something that was none of their business?

He went back to work and a few seconds later Jane rode up to him.

"Dad took the wagon so I could come back," she said. "I wanted to see if I could help."

"No, I'll call the colonel in another minute, when I need help."

"Dan, I . . . I know things must have been bad—must still be bad for you . . . or you wouldn't be like this. Is there anything . . . anything at all that I could do?"

"No."

"Couldn't we talk about things, see if we can't clear up what is bothering you?"

"No, things are better the way they are. Colonel!" he called, "I'm getting ready to take off your wheel and I'll need help!" He dug into the tool box on the side of the wagon and found a heavy hammer. Bracing one hand against the iron tire, he took aim and began to swing away.

Tears stung Jane's eyes. "You've changed as much as—

Bill!" she accused. "I wish you hadn't even come with us!"

She swung onto her horse and he paused to watch her gallop away. For a fleeting moment her words caused him to see himself as he would have been if she had never mentioned his blue coat. The long line of wagons became a line of cavalry; he was riding alongside Maehler, and the mountains before them were not mountains at all, but the blue Pacific. The Brigade would start to swell its ranks now, and soon it would begin to fulfill its destiny. The sun shone brightly on the troops and they sat their horses pridefully because this day marked a significant change in the fortunes of the Confederacy.

But it was a sight that his eyes had not been intended to witness. The realization caused his vision to fade as abruptly as it had come; he saw mountains and drudging wagons again, and bent over the tire, resuming his steady, ringing pounding.

To Pop Maehler's way of thinking, the Iron Brigade's erratic course was just as apt to wind them all up in hell as anyplace else. Trouble had started to dog them two days out of Monterrey, while they were camped at the old Buena Vista battleground southwest of Saltillo. Maehler was rehashing all the gory details of that terrible battle and his companions were scoffing at his tale of the San Patricio regiment of American deserters when another fight with guerrillas erupted.

The *bandidos* were successfully fought off, but they continued to pick and snipe all along the road to Parras; and this hilly town, once gained, turned out to be no haven for the weary. The drunken French commander and Old Jo were preparing to fight a duel that would set off mass bloodshed when Marshal Jeanningros overtook them and put a stop to the foolishness. His arrival seemed like a stroke of luck until they found that he had come to relay fresh orders to Shelby. By command from the ranking French General, the march to the Pacific was no longer to be permitted; the Brigade must proceed instead to Mexico City.

They backtracked and turned south. When the month of July faded away they had covered a third of the long ride, but they were growing ragged, growing weary of the back country, weary of each other and of the persistent annoyance of the guerrillas. In this state of mind they reached the small town of Matehuala, held by the French but under bitter attack by Juaristas.

Maehler and Sherm watched from a hillside as Shelby's messengers made contact with the French. Sherm was aching for a fight, still seeking every living second to avenge Featherly's death.

As they sat their horses, legs cocked, Maehler said, "How you live through each day and wake up the next morning beats me. You got to get over these things, same as anybody else."

Sherm didn't bother to answer. He had busied himself taking in every detail of the town below, eying the roaring artillery of the Juaristas, figuring how he could best do the most damage in the quickest time.

Maehler followed his gaze. There was nothing to see, he thought to himself. The town was adobe, like all the rest of the towns, with barred windows, and pipes sticking out to drain water from the flat roofs into the narrow dirt streets. As for the Juaristas, hell, a man didn't have to look hard to find them; they were right down the hill, hundreds of them, in the open and busily firing every piece they had.

Maehler's eyes swept over the Brigade; they knew how to rest, he thought, when it was time to rest. They were carelessly sitting their horses and squatting in little groups on the ground as if they had just finished drill and expected any minute to be dismissed for the day.

Walcott was an exception. He sat his saddle as stiff and straight as he did on parade. He worried about the outfit more than most, Maehler knew. A few minutes ago he had spoken out loud what a lot of the others were thinking.

"The French haven't taken us in or put us out," he had said grimly. "But they'll have to decide one thing or the other if we keep fighting for them. This is our chance, right here today, to show them we're such God-damned good soldiers that they can't afford not to use us."

Maehler's eyes fell on Peal, who no longer was allowed to mess with him and Sherm since he had voted against Dan. Peal wanted to kill even worse than Sherm, and with Peal each death he caused was a personal thing, not complete until he had examined the torn guts of his victim.

The return of the messengers brought no noticeable stir, and even when the orders came to mount, the men on the ground got up, still talking, like somebody who was just leaving a card game long enough to take a pee. The chatter did not stop as they forked into hard saddles.

A minute passed, pistols were checked, and the bugle blared its message. A French bugle answered. The Brigade tore down the hillside and the French charged out from their small garrison.

A cannon was whirled to bear upward at the Brigade. It spoke and a great round ball cut a bloody path through the charging cavalry. Muskets swung up and popped and here and there saddles suddenly emptied.

Muskets were reloaded, ready to fire again, when the cavalry's pistols began to spit. Uniformed and cotton-clad Mexicans dropped. Comrades took their loaded guns, shot back. The horses bore down on them, trampled them. Some of the animals screamed, threw their riders. Men were pulled to the ground to be stabbed by dark bayonets.

Bill Morgen swept by Maehler, his reins held in bared teeth, his saber flashing in his good left hand. During the span of a battle, when Cogan couldn't help him, when nobody could help him, he was as much a man as anybody in the outfit.

The fight became a melee. The Mexicans, caught on two sides, tried to retreat, couldn't, and surged forward. Maehler's horse died on its feet. He plunged headlong, slammed

197

into the ground. Gravel tore his hide as he rolled and bounded up. Half-stunned, he looked for his hat. A rifle butt slashed at him and he ducked. He swung his empty pistol, drew the knife from his belt and moved inside to thrust the thick blade through a uniform coat. He wrenched the knife loose as the soldier crumpled.

The Mexicans sounded retreat, tried again to withdraw. They fired their cannon again at point-blank range and pulled them back. With so many revolvers emptied, with the French also trying to reload, they gradually were able to free themselves.

The fight was moving away from Maehler. He pressed caps into the nipples of his cylinder and fumbled for powder and lead. Sherm serenely squatted down beside him and began reloading three pistols of his own.

To their left a Mexican lying flat on his back involuntarily kicked and Peal, afoot, hastily approached him. Peal stood over him cautiously, watching his face. The beard seemed to widen as his lips spread. He bent over, cocking his pistol, holding its muzzle a bare inch from white cotton cloth. His finger began to tighten on the trigger.

An arm shot up and a blade flashed. The gun blasted, was covered with blood that gushed in a torrent from Peal's throat. Peal bleated, fell forward. His face was a mask of horror as he tore at his own flesh, trying to stop the great gushing spurts. He landed face to face with the Mexican soldier, rolled aside, kicked, was still, kicked again and was dead.

Maehler's stomach turned and he looked away. Sherm had not even noticed. Maehler got up, tore back into the fight afoot.

The range had grown, hand to hand struggles had practically ceased. The Mexicans were escaping, those who still lived, and the French were rushing forward to throw their arms around these strange mounted devils who had appeared from nowhere to save them.

Firing slowed. Smoke began to drift away. The wounded cried out for help, the dead lay twisted and still.

Walcott was not a man to kill for the hell of it, but beneath the grimness of his face was a hint of satisfaction. He rode over, looked down at Maehler, saw that he was all right.

"We fought good today," he announced. "Good enough to please an emperor. I just hope to God he takes notice."

Toward the middle of the afternoon, having eaten dust in the wake of the train for more than an hour, Dan finally caught up to it. The Dutton wagon was swaying perilously along with him; the colonel was driving the mules as though he were in a harness race. Dan had to hand it to the old boy—and to his wife, too—after they had once started to help him they had worked like Trojans. If they were any example then maybe, when the taste of defeat wasn't quite so strong in the mouths of all these fleeing Confederates, they could buckle down and make something of their colony.

He left the Duttons behind and rode the sorrel up alongside the Todd's front wagon. Russell was driving, rocking along, Dan was willing to bet, without a thought in his head. He was bent and gray, growing fat and apathetic and not seeming to care. He had long since knuckled under and needed constant guidance from Mavis. But then, Dan thought, he had been willing to dismiss Colonel Dutton this morning and the colonel had later showed that the spirit in him was not altogether dead.

Russell saw Dan and his face brightened some. "Hello, Dan. I was hoping you'd ride along. Haven't seen you all day."

"Was there something special you wanted?"

"No. It's just that I get a little lonesome sometimes. There always used to be so much to do . . . so many people to see. . . ."

"It will be that way again," Dan assured him. "Another

199

few days—two weeks at the most—and we'll be starting to settle. Meanwhile I'll visit with you later this afternoon, if I get the chance. Is Mavis in the other wagon?"

"Yes, she's taking her nap."

Dan fell back some and Peter, at the reins, said solemnly, "Hello, Marse Dan."

"Hello, Peter. Is Miss Mavis asleep?"

Mavis' head and shoulders came out. "Not when you come callin', Mr. Kilbourne."

Dan smiled. "There was something I've been thinking about. I've decided to ranch instead of farm. Would you like to talk about it for a minute?"

A little frown creased the pearl-smooth skin of her forehead. "Dan, I really wouldn't—not now. You know how hard it is to think with all this noise. Besides, I've told you I have something very special in mind. Can't it wait a little longer?"

Dan was annoyed and didn't feel like hiding it. "You're getting into the habit of putting everything off. You're never ready to talk about getting married—about any of it —though every woman on this train is anxious enough to discuss what we intend to do!"

"If all you wanted to do was ranch," she snapped back, "then you could have proposed to me in Texas and neither of us would be here now!"

She instantly looked contrite, even helpless as she touched the dark hair tumbling about her shoulders. "Dan, I'm sorry. I shouldn't have said that. And if you'll just let it go now, I promise to talk about all of it before this week is over—if you just won't mention it again for a day or two."

"I won't wait much longer," Dan said. "You'd better realize that." He reined away and started for the head of the column.

About midmorning on Wednesday, two days after Mavis' promise, the train entered a stretch of woods so

200

thick that tall trees made a narrow corridor of the road. It was pretty country, and cool—but a breakdown here would mean that all rearward wagons would have to wait for the one being repaired; it would be impossible to go around. Dan had a notion that Wil would be scouting up ahead and worrying some. He touched spurs to Cromwell.

Wil slowed his horse to let Dan catch up. He had regained several pounds, didn't seem to be as tired. "Everybody's rolling along good now, yah?"

"Yah," Dan said and smiled.

"We're in badt country here. Two or t'ree times already I haf trouble here."

"Why don't we forget politics and rearrange the wagons till we get beyond the woods?"

Wil shook his head, laughing a little to bolster his own spirits. "I wouldn't try it. I tell you, two days after we left San Antonio I could have told you why we lost the war."

Dan shrugged. "Well, I'd better go back along the line and tell everybody to keep closed up."

He was reining away when Wil said, "Dan! Look! By God, there's a man I'm glad to see!"

It was Esteban, in full uniform, coming through the trees on their right; as they watched, a detachment of at least fifty men came into view behind him. Half of them moved onto the road with him, the other half fell away, riding toward the rear of the wagons.

Esteban beamed. "Amigos!" He shook hands as if a year had passed since their last parting.

"I never look behind a bush that I don't expect to see you," Wil said, "and I'm usually right."

"This time," Manuel explained, "it is because a small band of guerrillas hovers nearby. Sixty or seventy men. We kill two birds—we guard you in the hope that they will come to us. If not, we will seek them out."

"Manuel, you beat me," Dan said. "You patrol this country as if you'd never heard of the French."

"I have told you," Manuel said, "they hold only the cities." His small face lit in a warm smile. "There is hope that even the cities will be lost to them soon. The Yankee General Sheridan hops up and down with rage on the other side of the Rio Bravo because Washington will not let him attack. So he does the next best thing—every night he puts guns out on the prairie and calls away his sentries. In the morning the guns are gone—and the Juarista armies are growing. Louis Napoleon worries about these things and one day he will wake up afraid and take his Frenchmen out of Mexico."

Dan might not have asked about Shelby, but Wil Morgen had a son to worry about. "Have you heard anything about Shelby's outfit? Anything about Bill?"

"Nothing about Bill," Esteban said. He motioned his soldiers on ahead as the wagons caught up to them. The three men moved off the road into the trees and let the train lumber past.

"What about Shelby?" Dan asked.

"He has caused much trouble, that one," Esteban said, shaking his head. "Aieee!"

"They fought again? Where?" Dan demanded.

"At Matehuala." Esteban clucked. "We had almost succeeded in driving out the French when the Brigade struck us from the rear. They were demons on horses. The love of battle was in their eyes as they charged into us with their pistols which shoot so many bullets without reloading. At the same time, by some signal, the French attacked out front. It was more than we could withstand."

"For your sake," Dan said, "I'm sorry." He thought a minute, frowning. "Matehuala—Matehuala is not near the west coast of Mexico. It's between Monterrey and Mexico City!"

"That is true. When Shelby reached Parras, his orders were changed. He goes now to Mexico City."

Dan felt the excitement mount in him. It must have

202

shown, for Esteban said, "You would still like to be with him."

The edge wore off. "No. My place is here."

"If you would join him only to fight Juaristas," Esteban smiled, "here are fifty of us. You are our friend, so we would even let you win a little bit."

Dan was in no mood for humor. "No. I've given you my reasons for wanting to be with him."

"Perhaps you have a chance—now that they go to Mexico City, where there will be other generals to talk for you."

Wil looked from one to the other. "You're talking about things that Dan hasn't mentioned to the rest of us," he said gently. "I'll leave you two to finish that conversation." He reined his horse back onto the road and started for the head of the column.

Esteban watched him go. "You . . . have not yet explained to them what happened in Monterrey?"

"No."

"Then you still have not asked Jane why she did it?"

"Why doesn't matter. She was the only one who knew, so she did it. I hope you won't say anything."

"It is not my business. But you are sure—now that there is a chance—that you will not go to Mexico City? Many of your people are there, more than in Monterrey, I think."

"No. I'll be staying here. Is . . . Governor Murrah in Mexico City, do you know?"

"I know. He is in Monterrey still. However, one of your Texas governors—Clarke—is there."

"It doesn't matter anyway. Manuel, I'd better ride along. I'll see you at supper tonight."

Manuel rode with him for a way, then spurred ahead to rejoin his men. Dan forced his eyes to check over several wagons, until he was even with the Todds. He waved at Russell, and dropped back to Mavis, who was seated outside for the moment.

"Mavis," he said, "tonight is the time for our talk. I won't put it off any longer than that."

203

She looked at him gravely. "All right, then. After supper we'll discuss everything."

He nodded and let her go past.

Dan ate with the Morgens because he knew Esteban would be there. The suave little Mexican, seemingly informed at all times about everything that went on in his country, chewed his beans and deer meat with gusto and said, "Tomorrow we will catch the guerrillas. They are no more than ten miles distant, camped at a small village. They think to fade away until we have gone, and then they intend to strike. There are many riches in these wagons, enough to make their eyes open wide."

Wil Morgen, seated close to the fire, sopped his plate with a soggy chunk of bread and said with a touch of worry, "And how will you catch them?"

"We will go away, as they expect. Then we will split into two groups and double back from two directions. As they approach we will meet them, attacking from two sides. We are better armed, better disciplined. It is sad, but necessary."

Jane got up from the shadows and lifted the coffeepot from the coals. "More coffee, Manuel? Dan?" She had the nature of an angel in spite of what she had done to Jim, Dan thought, else she could never have managed to keep on being so civil.

Manuel took more, but Dan said, "No, thank you."

They had visitors suddenly—Marman and Quillian. Dan had never been able to figure Marman, and he no longer tried. Marman's thoughts seemed always to be aloof and distant as though each thing he did now was of consequence only because it related to some future, hidden thing.

Quillian seemed as obvious as Marman seemed inscrutable, except for one puzzling fact—his eyes showed malice sometimes when he looked at Dan. The look of fury and hate he had shown that day back in San Antonio was not a mistake, as he claimed.

They both greeted Esteban, and Marman got coffee and moved to sit by him. Quillian, fancied up tonight with a string tie and a long frock coat—parted in front to call attention to his engraved belt buckle—immediately went to Jane. Dan thought that his eyes, illuminated by the campfire, were filled with suggestion as he smiled at her. Smiles came readily to him and made him look boyish in the way that was supposed to appeal to all women.

Jane was pretty, Dan thought, unbelievably pretty in comparison to that sun-reddened girl he had fought beside when the Indians attacked.

Marman was saying, "We've made good time. Not as good as I hoped for, but still good, and I won't forget the part you've played, Lieutenant."

"It is my duty. Of course, señor, we want good colonists —but beyond that it is a favor from *El Presidente* Juarez himself to Wil Morgen."

"Then I take it if my wagons—you know I'm carrying farm implements—if my wagons separated from the rest of the train and went ahead, you'd still protect only the colonists."

"Yes, that is all. We do not have unlimited men, and it would be better for us if you stayed with the others."

The firelight made Marman's fair face shine like polished white marble. He seemed strangely satisfied.

"Are you planning on leaving us?" Wil asked abruptly.

"No. Certainly not now. I might pull ahead when we're almost there if it seems safe enough. I could set things up for the rest of you."

"Then you would travel without protection," Esteban said.

"I think you should stay with us all the way," Jane objected. "It will make everyone feel much safer."

"Then perhaps I will. You know I respect your judgment. Lieutenant, with your soldiers scattered about, I

205

suppose it would be safe enough for Jane and me to take a short walk?"

"As long as you stay within the circle of the sentries, yes."

"Then, Jane, it seems I never get to talk to you—"

She had moved away from Quillian twice, and was now standing alone. "I'll throw something over my shoulders," she said, and walked toward her wagon.

Dan got up. "I think I'll be going. I'll see you all in the morning. Manuel, pleasant dreams, and good hunting tomorrow."

Esteban bid him good night and Dan headed for the Todd wagons, thinking of the way Jane had accepted Marman's invitation without hesitation. Well, why shouldn't she?

The Todds had finished eating and were sitting in folding chairs close to their front wagon while the Negro servant busily cleaned up after them. Russell spoke cordially enough, but Mavis said coldly, "I know we were to talk after supper, but we were still expecting you to eat with us. You've done that every other night since you've been with the train."

"I should have left word," Dan admitted.

"There," Mavis said sweetly, "and I shouldn't be picking a quarrel with you. I was only disappointed, I guess. Shall we go for a walk?"

"Yes, but it will have to be short. There are sentries all around us. Besides, there isn't much light tonight. The moon is almost down."

Mavis got up. "Good night, Dad." She took Dan's hand. "I really meant it when I said we shouldn't quarrel."

"I'm sorry, too," Dan said. "I guess I've been a little short the past few days."

"Then let's take a long walk and never mind the sentries. I want to be really alone with you."

They swung along till they were well away from the wagons.

"I think this is far enough," Dan said. "Esteban says the guerrillas are fairly close."

"Dan, don't be so practical," she chided gaily. "This is a special night for us. There's supposed to be a little waterfall just to the south of us. We can sit there."

"All right," he said, "if that's what you want."

They spoke to the sentry and moved southward. Dan stepped ahead, picking his way carefully through the knee-high brush and grass, with Mavis clinging to his hand.

They reached a tiny stream and followed it until they arrived at a thin, low falls. Mavis pulled him to one side, toward the black shadow of a thick-trunked tree; they sat down together and she put both hands behind his head and kissed him. A spray-laden breeze whispered softly; in the midst of this coolness her mouth was warm and stirring.

Dan gently broke the kiss. "Mavis, I want to know about that plan you keep mentioning."

"You've grown cold," she accused, pouting. "Lately—for several days now—you haven't even wanted to touch me."

"Mavis," he said quietly, "I'm impatient tonight."

"Will you be so impatient after we're married, then? Do I have so little to offer—"

He stiffened with a growing anger and she softened at once. She caressed his face and ran her fingertips down to the hair that grew high on his chest. "I know these days have been terrible for you," she said soothingly. "That's why I tried—why I was willin' to do all I could to make you gentle again. I'm still willin'—"

"I want to talk, nothing more."

"Then first of all you've got to promise never to tell anybody what I'm going to tell you. It's important."

"All right, I promise, but please get to it!"

"Dan, have patience. I know this might shock you, and you mustn't be shocked. That's why I'm taking so long. I . . . want to begin with Reed Marman. He . . . doesn't think like other people. He takes chances, builds plans so big that nobody else would ever dream they might work. But they do work more often than not—just as the plan he has now is working. His wagons . . . don't contain farm implements as he says. They're filled with guns."

Dan's first inclination was to scoff. "Why would he be hauling guns?"

"He's got a buyer for them. An ambitious man with his own private army, I'm told. Reed started this whole colony because of the guns, and for no other reason."

"But he does have title to the land?"

"Yes, he has that."

"Then at least the Morgens and all the others—you and your father—can go ahead with the colony?"

"Yes."

The great danger to the colonists was a thing he was just beginning to realize. "Mavis, how did you come to know all these things—from Marman?"

"No. From Ran Quillian. He had a scheme. The guns don't really belong to Reed. He sold them to the Confederacy, then stole them back. Quillian thinks that Reed has no more right to the money than anyone else. It's there for whoever can take it."

"It sounds like the way he would think."

"Dan, he's right! Whoever gets the money has an obligation to pay off the teamsters, and that's all! It belongs just as much to any one of us as it does to Reed. And you and I would use it more wisely, and for a better cause. Esteban told us that the Yankees are not being nearly as hard on Confederate government officials as we thought. Why, before long we could go back to Texas, or any place else you wanted, and we could buy a ranch and live as well as we did before the war. We'd be helping the whole country, and ourselves at the same time!"

The shock of what she expected of him was beginning to set in. The effect was as great as Mavis had predicted, but Dan managed to say calmly, "Then what would you have us do?"

"Let Reed deliver his guns and get paid. Then I could send for him, get him alone. We wouldn't even have to hurt him. We'd only be taking what's as much ours as his."

"And where does Quillian fit into this?"

"He doesn't."

"And suppose I hadn't left Shelby? Would he have figured into it then?"

"Dan, I . . . I don't know. He might have, back in the beginning. I've told you that I have to have money. I can't live by grubbing in the dirt like some people can."

He stood up, reached down and took both her arms, and jerked her to her feet. She winced from his hard grip.

"Dan, what are you doing?"

"Taking you back to camp." He started away, pulling her along.

"Dan, you—my legs are getting scratched. Dan, listen. Wait. We didn't settle anything!"

He stopped abruptly. "Not everything," he agreed grimly. "Where will the guns be delivered?"

"Near Mexico City. Reed is going to leave us in another day or two."

"Then there's no danger to the colonists from the guerrillas?"

"Of course not!"

He caught her wrist and began to pull her onward toward the camp. "Dan, wait—you've got to think about it."

He loosened his grip as they saw the sentry. "I've thought about it already. You've shown me what you were like and I'm grateful for it. You've freed me to go back to the Brigade."

She was walking rapidly alongside him rubbing her wrist. "Then . . . what's been between us means nothing?"

"It means as much as what has been between you and Quillian. Don't make me say more than that."

"But you don't realize what you're throwing away," she protested.

"I realize what I'm getting out from under, and it's a great relief."

She took a sharp, angry breath. "But at least you won't tell anyone what I've told you? You promised."

"I won't say anything, but not because I promised. It's because I'm afraid people would be hurt if I spoke. Esteban's men and the colonists. I don't know if the teamsters would fight for Marman, but I'm afraid they would."

They were nearing her wagon and her words were almost a whisper. "You're a weakling and a fool! You didn't have enough spirit to stand against the Yankees, nor enough to take from Marman. You'll have nothing in this world because you deserve nothing."

As he stopped, she saw the look in his face and drew back. "Mavis," he said softly, "I'm sorry I ever met you. And I feel dirty because I've touched you."

He turned and left her, his anger so strong that it nearly defied control. He thought again of telling Manuel, but shook his head to himself. One word could start a fight that would end in mass death. No, it was better to say nothing, particularly since Marman was leaving the colonists in another day or two and taking his danger with him.

A relief at being free of Mavis suddenly overtook him; gradually as she had revealed herself to him, he had found himself building excuses for all her mannerisms; but there was no longer a need for it. He breathed deeply and an air of excitement stirred in him as he walked toward his bedroll. Maybe Manuel was right; maybe if he saw Governor Clarke he could get him to talk to Shelby. He didn't know the Governor but that might not matter, since they were both Texans in a foreign land.

Wil and Jane crept into his mind, but he decided they did not need him any longer. Wil was well now, and on the last lap of his journey. Dan's thoughts, in chaotic

210

disorder, shot in all directions, touched again on Mavis and tossed her lightly aside.

He wondered what kind of reception the Brigade would get from Maximilian. With Shelby's persuasive powers brought to bear, his army could suddenly blossom into all that anybody had ever hoped for.

# 12

BY GOOD DAYLIGHT the wagons were checked and rolling. Dan found himself at the rear of Wil's portion of the train, and ahead of Marman's vehicles, which was just as well. Marman's very nature made it unnecessary for Dan to speak to him of his leaving. He could ride on out now, saying his few goodbyes as he went along.

He passed Mavis' wagon and was slowing to speak to Russell Todd when Quillian rode up to him.

"You're carrying your bedroll," Quillian observed.

"Yes."

"You leaving?"

"Yes."

"Well, I'm damned." He continued to keep his horse neck to neck with Cromwell, and Dan, though irritated, shrugged it off. Whatever he had to say to Russell could be public.

"I've stopped to say goodbye, Senator," he said. "I'm leaving you this morning."

"But I . . . I thought . . ." Russell stopped his protest, thinking better of it. "I wish you luck," he said.

"Thanks, and I wish you the same." Dan went on, and Quillian continued alongside him, riding annoyingly close. Dan greeted several of the other colonists, but did not slow until he reached the Morgen wagon.

Jane was driving and Dan would not have known what to say to her even without Quillian's presence. The hurt of her betrayal ran deeper than all of the unpleasantness it had brought about.

If he mentioned the blue uniform and all of the things that had happened after she had given him away to Bill and Cogan, what would she say? She could not deny it, since no one else had known about it. Would she at least apologize, then, and explain that she hadn't been able to stand the sight of Wil losing so much weight?

Looking at her slim figure perched on the wagon seat he was strongly tempted to bring it up, to drag the whole thing out into the open. But Quillian's unasked for presence beside him held him back. He started to ask the little dandy to move on, decided a discussion would only cause Jane discomfort and anguish, said a plain, "Good morning," and rode on.

They reached Wil and Dan explained quickly and simply that he was leaving the train to rejoin Shelby.

Wil was dismayed. "I thought we had you for the rest of the trip—that you would be one of our settlers." He considered and settled back in his saddle. "Maybe I've seen it coming, at that. You haven't been very happy here." He held out his hand. "I want to thank you for helping me get things in shape. I'm not as tired now, either. I'll make it the rest of the way easy enough, thanks to you."

"I didn't get to say goodbye to Jane," Dan said. "Will you say it for me?"

"No, I won't do that. It's easy to guess that there's trouble between you two, and you'll have to settle it yourselves. You can go back to the wagon and speak to her if you want to."

"I guess I want to," Dan said, "but I'll still leave it to you."

Esteban was waiting for them in the road. Dan finally

212

got away from Quillian far enough to talk to him privately.

"I thought you would go," Manuel said. "I was sure of it."

"There's one thing I want to tell you before I leave. Marman's wagons are definitely pulling away from the train within the next several days. As I understand it, the train will swing eastward a few miles this side of Mexico City. He'll leave about then, or before. I thought if you knew that it might help you plan to protect the others."

"I will remember," Esteban said gravely. "But after tomorrow I will have no soldiers. My men are needed elsewhere. That is why I told Marman that he could get no protection from us. I hoped that he would remain."

"Do you think there will be danger after he leaves?"

Manuel shrugged. "Danger is everywhere, for everyone. But I know of no armed bands of guerrillas so near the French forces."

"Then I'll say goodbye and get started."

"About four miles from here take a path which leads to the right," Manuel advised. "Six miles further you will come to a village. Wait there until other travelers come through, going to Mexico City. Otherwise, my friend, you will become one of the little white crosses."

"It will be hard to wait, but I'll do it."

Quillian could not stand to be away from them any longer. He caught up and by way of making conversation, said, "I was with Marman this morning until we rolled. I didn't see you talking to him."

"I didn't tell him I was leaving, if that's what you mean. I doubt if he much gives a damn if I go or stay."

Quillian laughed. "You're right about that. He wouldn't give a damn if I went, or you, or anybody else. Not unless it upset his own plans."

Dan waved at Esteban and turned away, realizing that the malice in Quillian's eyes had not been for Marman, in spite of his words. He still had it in for Dan Kilbourne, for no reason Dan could figure.

Reed Marman was on horseback when Quillian brought the news of Dan's leaving. He shrugged.

"We have only another few days. He won't be missed." He looked at Quillian sharply, knowing the little major's hatred for Dan. "You're sure he left of his own accord? If Esteban found him lying along the road somewhere—"

"I followed orders and left him alone," Quillian said darkly, "just like I did the last few days in San Antonio. But I still hobble sometimes when I step too hard. He damn near broke my leg that night. If I ever see him again, under different circumstances—"

"You have a wagon in danger of losing a wheel," Marman said coldly. "You can hear it squeak if you'll listen."

Quillian gave him a dark look and whirled his horse. He stuck spurs in deep and galloped back down the line.

Marman brushed away the dust he trailed, and swiveled in his saddle. The wagon was truly squeaking and needed attention, but his reason for wanting to be rid of Quillian came from seeing Mavis Todd riding toward him. She had not been on a horse for a week—since Kilbourne's arrival. Why on this particular day would she suddenly want to talk to him?

She greeted him with a smile. "Reed, I haven't seen you in days."

"But I have seen you—once or twice when you wouldn't have wanted to be seen."

She changed color, but said coolly, "We both know you're bluffing, but let it pass. I'm here to talk about the guns you're carrying."

The clatter and rumble of wagons and the rattle of pots rushed up to hammer Marman's ears. "Quillian! He couldn't keep his mouth shut!"

"There's someone else who knows," she went on evenly. "Kilbourne?"

She nodded. "Lieutenant Esteban's friend Kilbourne. He's probably a mile away by now, but he could still be caught."

"That God-damned Quillian!" Rage swelled his face. "I'll settle with him when it's time to pay him. But first I'll let him settle his score with Kilbourne. Wait for me while I get him." He started to spur his horse, then looked back at her. "Regardless of why you did it, you may have saved me a lot of trouble."

She smiled and said nothing; the taste of the defeat Dan had dealt her was bitter, but she still had no intention of grubbing out her life in a Mexican wilderness.

She watched Reed spur his mount into a gallop. Before they had left San Antonio she had briefly considered an alliance with him; she had discarded the idea because he was self-centered and ruthless, and far too strong to bend before her will.

But soon he would be rich and powerful, and if she managed things cleverly she could share his good fortune.

She saw Quillian nod to Reed's commands, then race his snip-nosed horse down the road. Reed reined back toward her and she smiled a welcome. She must convince him that she and Russell Todd could both be useful to him, now and in the future. After Reed got his money his first problem, she decided, would be to get the gold out of Mexico as quickly and safely as possible. The easiest method, if it could be arranged, would be to let the French transport it to Vera Cruz and see that it was safely loaded aboard ship.

Reed rode up to her and she said, "When Daddy and I were in Europe just before the war, I danced at Miramar with an Austrian archduke. He's the Emperor Maximilian now, and I have an idea he'll remember me."

About an hour after Dan left the wagons he came to the narrow trail Esteban had told him about. He angled onto the brush-choked path and let the sorrel pick its dainty way along the rock-strewn edge of a deep chasm. He wondered at the mighty cataclysm that had split the otherwise broad, rolling plain. It was nature at her mightiest, trying to make man seem puny by comparison; but man was not puny because he refused to disregard his own worth.

He heard hoofbeats behind him and turned away from the chasm, having to force his way into the brush. He crowded up behind a large mesquite and sat quietly in a leaning position that left him ready to stop Cromwell from nickering.

At first, peering through the ragged brush, he could make out only that the man was a Mexican civilian. The rider was dressed in black, with a black, flat-topped hat worn low over his eyes. And yet the snip-nosed horse seemed familiar.

It was Quillian. Dan let the sorrel walk back onto the path.

Quillian saw him and grinned, raising his right arm in salute as he slowed his horse. "Kilbourne!" he hailed. "I have a message for you!"

Dan walked Cromwell to meet him. When they halted, facing each other, Quillian was on high ground.

Dan said, "I wouldn't expect you to deliver a message."

"A favor to Miss Mavis," Quillian answered. His eyes narrowed as he stared down the road. "Christ! I've been tryin' to shoot one of those damned road runners ever since we left Texas!" He reached for his gun.

"Don't!" Dan said sharply. "You'll bring guerrillas like flies!"

Quillian did not pull the revolver but his hand remained on its polished butt. "Let 'em come," he said insistently. "We'll both be gone from here in a minute!"

The early morning sun was at his back, making it hard for Dan to see the little major's features clearly. The high ground also had its effect, causing Dan to look upward. The gun started to come out in spite of his warning, bringing a flash of alarm. That silhouette! It was the same that had stood over him in San Antonio as booted feet lashed at his side!

216

He slapped the gun aside and it went off at Cromwell's feet. He spurred Cromwell, grabbed Quillian's left arm. The sorrel charged up onto the high ground and Quillian was dragged from his saddle. Dan couldn't hold him, had to turn loose and keep going.

The major hit the ground rolling and Dan swung off the trail into the brush. A bullet nicked Cromwell's neck and brought blood. Another slammed past Dan's ear. Cromwell lowered his head and pitched, slammed himself against the hard trunk of a small tree. He reared and Dan tried to turn him back toward Quillian.

Dan's gun came out as the sorrel's forefeet hit the ground. Quillian had crawled into the brush. He fired, causing Cromwell to duck his head. Dan spurred the sorrel again and charged, blazing away at the black splotch of Quillian's clothes.

A shot came to meet him, missed. His own pistol clicked and he ducked low, thundering past. He covered forty yards, fifty, slowed and turned. He holstered the empty revolver, pulled his rifle. Quillian still sat facing the trail.

Cautiously, Dan guided the sorrel into the underbrush and waited.

Quillian did not move.

He might be dead. Or it might only be a trap. Dan climbed down, started edging his way through the brush, never taking his eyes off the major. He got behind him and still Quillian did not move.

He moved forward faster, dreading that an avalanche of guerrillas might come from nowhere to trap them both. The major's position remained unchanged.

Dan was virtually on top of him when he saw what had happened. Thick blood stained Quillian's back, had poured onto the top of a jagged stump. The bullet had entered his chest slamming him back against the stump, which had caught his jacket and held him. There were two more wounds, one in his face, and they were not pleasant to look at.

Dan swung around and headed quickly for the sorrel. Taking Quillian back to the wagons was out of the question.

He pulled himself up, whirled the sorrel and galloped down the path, wondering what had caused Quillian's hatred of him. But no matter how he puzzled at it, he could find no connection between the attack in San Antonio and this one; he knew only that the earlier attack had probably saved his life now because of his split-second recognition of the little major's silhouette.

Quillian had been a vain man while he lived. Dan wondered what he would think if he could know that his body was being left, unidentified, in a wilderness, to be plundered by guerrillas and picked over by vultures.

Late on the afternoon of the fourth day, Dan descended into the valley of Mexico in the company of a small party of Mexican merchants, their families and the escort they had hired to protect them.

To the merchants the city was home, and while they were properly glad to be back to it, its marvels were commonplace to them. To Dan it was something out of a fairy tale. He had thought Monterrey magnificent, but it was nothing when compared to Mexico City with its glittering cathedrals, orderly Plazas, fine homes and surfaced streets. He had heard older men, reminiscing about the Mexican War, speak of it in almost reverent tones, but he hadn't quite believed the wonders they had described until now.

Near the center of the town Dan bade the merchants goodbye and rode along the streets by himself in search of a suitable hotel that was clean but not expensive. As in Monterrey he attracted no particular attention from the average Mexican, Frenchman or *norteamericano*, because the city was used to the sight of its neighbors from north of the Rio Grande. Again, however, he was petitioned on all sides by beggars and peddlers to a degree that made passage down the street a slow and tortuous journey.

He began hailing each butternut-clad man he saw, asking always of Shelby, and sometimes about accommodations. Most had heard of Shelby, some were well acquainted with the Brigade's exploits, all whom he asked had advice about a place to stay. But none knew of the Brigade's present whereabouts.

He fought his way on through the serape- and *rebozo*-clad throngs, at last spotting two civilians who looked familiar. The men were standing near the door of a restaurant, talking to a well-dressed, mostachioed Mexican. He placed them, then, as members of a detachment that had ridden out of San Antonio with the Brigade, but had chosen its own path from Eagle Pass southward. He walked the sorrel up to them, frantically jogging his memory for names or titles.

He drew a blank, said, "Pardon, do you know if General Shelby and his men are in Mexico City yet—or when they might be expected?"

The taller of the two regarded him curiously. "Representatives of the Brigade arrived yesterday. The army will be here tomorrow."

"Then, do you happen to know where Governor Clarke is staying?"

The other man shrugged. "Ask at the Iturbide. If he is not there, someone will know where to reach him."

Dan breathed a fervent "Thanks," saluted, and had to restrain the sorrel because the animal felt his excitement.

He wanted badly to go to Clarke at once, but it was nearly dark now; he must find a place to stay, clean up and rest, marshal his arguments so that Clarke not only might mention him to Shelby, but would actually plead for him.

The blood coursed faster through him, and again he had to restrain the sorrel.

Here in Mexico City Shelby would come face to face with the Emperor, and the future of the Brigade would finally be determined. He meant to be a part of that future if he had to hold Governor Clarke at gun point in order to make him listen.

When the Brigade arrived the next morning it did not march triumphantly through the streets toward Maximilian's palace, as Dan had envisioned. Instead it rode in with a heavy escort of French troops and was guided inexorably toward permanent barracks which had been emptied especially for its arrival. Nevertheless the men rode with assurance and pride, as they had always done, and Dan felt his own stature shrink because he had to ride along behind them, well back out of the way, in the company of all the other sightseers.

He waited impatiently for the French troops to move on, then even more impatiently gave the Brigade time to settle some. When he could stand it no longer he rode up to the gate in the stone wall and spoke to the gray-clad guard, a youngish man with long hair and dark green eyes that looked out from a whiskery face.

Dan didn't recognize him, but the soldier said enthusiastically, "Kilbourne! Dan Kilbourne! I remember you. Saw you fight Cogan." His eyes were shining with admiration. "Sure wish you'd been able to stay with us."

"Thanks," Dan said uncomfortably. "Can I go in and talk with some of the boys?"

The guard looked contrite and said apologetically, "I'm sorry. I've got orders not to let anybody in but one or two Frenchies, and our own men. For the time being I can't even let anybody out."

"Oh? In that case, do you think Maehler could come here—to the gate?"

"Sure." The guard turned and surveyed the cobbled courtyard, then yelled, "Hey, Toby! You know Pop Maehler, the one who lawyered for Dan Kilbourne back in Monterrey? See if you can find him and send him out here, will you? He's wanted right away!"

"Ain't that Kilbourne with you?" Toby yelled.

"Yep! Now hurry!" the guard called back. Then, to Dan, "I bet he won't be a minute. Light down and have a chaw." He held out a plug of tobacco.

"Thanks," Dan said, refusing the plug. He got down, holding Cromwell's reins as Maehler came rushing across the courtyard, trailed by Toby.

"You old son of a gun," Maehler shouted. "I thought I'd never see you again!"

Dan wrung his hand. "You were damn near right! How's it going?"

Maehler shrugged. "We saw the sights, whupped a few Juaristas, and then rid down here to see the Emperor personally. Maybe that's progress."

"The Brigade didn't look any bigger."

"Smaller," Maehler agreed. "We lost men here and there. But I hear tell there's a number waitin' here to join up as soon as they know what ol' Maxl's goin' to do."

"Me included. I wanted to find out if anything had happened . . . that might change things."

"Nope. Not that I know of."

"How's Sherm?"

"Not too bad. Hell in a fight, but settlin' some. Peal's dead. Walcott's not as loud as he used to be, for some reason. Cogan's still just as big, and Bill Morgen is still ridin' his shoulders. Worse now, maybe. You got somethin' figgered?"

"I'm going to see Governor Clarke this morning. I'm hoping he'll put in a word with Shelby."

"He's the right man to see, I'll bet. Dan, I wouldn't want to foul you up again, but if there's somethin' I can do—you let me know."

"I will. And if they ever let you out of this fleabag, you'll find me at the Hotel Palacio." He grinned. "Don't let the name mislead you."

"By damn!" Maehler said. "You come back here soon's you see Clarke and tell me what happened!"

"Yeah," said the guard, who'd been listening openly with Toby, "an' if you find out what they're goin' to do with the rest of us, tell us that, too."

"I'll try," Dan promised. "But won't Shelby be seeing the Emperor today?"

Toby said, "Day after tomorrow. And damn it, it's a hard wait."

"Then I'll be on my way. Maybe by that time I'll be one of you again."

"I hope so," Maehler said fervently. "Damn it, I hope so."

Dan mounted. "Keep a place for me," he said. "I'll make it one way or another."

The clerk at the Iturbide was tall for a Mexican, and thin, with a sharp face and the jutting hawk nose of a Spaniard. His eyes superciliously swept over Dan's shabby gray uniform and shapeless slouch hat, and he stated in perfect, unaccented English that Governor Clarke was in his room and had left emphatic word that he wasn't to be disturbed. However, since some of the officers of the newly arrived Southern army were with him, a Lieutenant Randolph was taking messages. Perhaps he would do?

Randolph's room was on the second floor. Opening the door to Dan's knock, he blinked as though he had been napping.

"Why, Dan Kilbourne! What are you doin' here?" Once before he had opened a hotel door for Dan, and that had been the first step toward getting into Shelby's army back in San Antonio. The impression he left was still the same, too, Dan thought—an incredibly big man with prominent teeth and soft eyes.

"Lieutenant," Dan said, "if I'd looked the world over I couldn't bump into somebody I'd rather see."

Randolph invited him in. "Sorry I can't offer you a drink, but this is a sort of temporary job—just till the colonel comes out, as a matter of fact."

"You mean General Shelby, or one of the other colonels?"

Randolph grinned. "I nevah do seem to keep his rank straight, and that's a fact. But I mean Shelby."

Randolph sank onto the bed, but Dan remained standing. "Do you think I could arrange to see him—about getting back into the Brigade?"

"Uh-uh. He's got to plan for the day after tomorrow with ever' minute of his time and ever' thought in his head. It's too important to all of us right now."

"What do you think will happen to the outfit?"

"I'm worried the same as ever'body else. Scairt they'll want to break us up, put a few of us here, a few of us there. The only chance we've got is for Shelby to arouse Maximilian to the picture of the South's glory. You know the kind of talk I mean."

"I've got to see him, Lieutenant. It wouldn't take a minute."

"He wouldn't reverse your trial anyway, not without some potent arguments."

Dan sighed. "Then maybe I was on the right track after all. I came here to try to see Governor Clarke."

"That's not likely either."

"I've got to see him," Dan said harshly, "and you're in a position to talk to him. So I'm going to give you a choice. Either you give me your word that you'll do your best to set up an appointment for me as soon as possible, or I'll bust in this minute and hold the lot of them with my pistol till I've had my say."

"Why—you sound like you mean it!" Randolph had let his back sink onto the bed, but now he sat up. "You'd never get back in if you did that!"

"I'm not sure. Shelby got tough with Jeanningros, or we'd never have gotten past Monterrey."

Randolph fixed him with an uneasy eye. "I think you might wreck things for all of us, so I won't argue with you." He clucked. "I know the Governor has appointments today right up to midnight, but I'll give you my word that I'll try to arrange for you to see him at nine o'clock in the mornin'. And I can tell you one thing— at nine o'clock in the mornin' he's one tough hombre."

"So am I." Dan grinned. "And I thank you for your co-operation."

The last man Dan expected to see in the lobby of his shabby hotel was Mike Cogan. The big scarred soldier was trying to pace up and down in the cramped space and his presence was overwhelming the small Mexican clerk, who cowered behind his counter.

Dan could imagine no reason for his being here except to get even for losing the fight in Monterrey, and he automatically flexed his fists as he came in.

Cogan raised his palms. "Simmer down. It's not a fight I'm after, but some help." He looked worried and his breath was working fast through his whistling nose.

"You've come to a strange place for help," Dan said. "I don't owe you any favors."

"I know that. And I know you don't owe Bill anything either. But I thought maybe because of his sister and his father—I know you're friends."

"We were friends," Dan corrected, "until Jane told you and Bill that I served with the Federals!"

Cogan blinked in surprise. "I thought you would have that all straightened out; you went from us to the wagon train, didn't you?"

"Yes."

"Then—hell, you must have found out."

"Found out what?"

"That it was Mavis told us about the uniform."

"She didn't know. Only Jane knew."

"Hell," Cogan snorted. "You know women—they talk a lot. Jane let it slip one day when she was telling Mavis about you rescuing her. Mavis pretended not to hear and I doubt if Jane even knew what she did. You going to hold a slip of the tongue against a woman?"

Dan said slowly, "It's like a gun going off accidentally.

224

It kills just as dead." But he knew he was only making words to cover all the feelings inside him. If Jane hadn't meant to tell—hadn't even known when she did it—

"Come up to my room," he said. "We can sit down and talk."

His head was awhirl and shame burned him. He hadn't given Jane a shadow of a chance to explain, and she had tried to show again and again that it made a difference to her—maybe even that she loved him. The hurt she had dealt him was a mistake; he had struck back with a righteousness that came from considering his own feelings above anybody else's.

Cogan trailed him up the stairs like a big, gentle dog. Dan led him into the room and motioned him to a chair. He sat himself on the edge of his bed.

"What is it?" he asked. "What kind of help did you want?"

Cogan rubbed his face. "I don't know how to say it." His scars grew as purple as when he had been about to fight. His hands began to slap his thighs, like some big rooster who had awakened one morning to find his flock gone.

When he was able to summon up the words they came out with a rush. "You know how Bill is. I know it, too. He makes trouble and picks quarrels with everybody, knowing he's got me to back him up. And I keep doing it. You know how he saved my life—and you know how he's the only one who ever treats me like a human being; the rest can't seem to stand my being so big and ugly. But he's out of hand now. Every man in the outfit is beginning to hate him. He's kept getting worse till it's like a sickness. And I don't know what to do about it. I can't even talk to anybody in the outfit about it—how could I?"

"It's more than half your fault," Dan said. "Do you think he'd be like that if he didn't have you to back him up? You stand over him like a mother hen and an avenging angel all rolled into one, so he'll never get better."

Cogan glowered. "What the hell can I do? I can't expect him to fight with only one hand—when he lost the other one saving my life!"

"I don't think you're backing him because he lost his hand or saved your life, either one," Dan said. "It's because he's the only friend you've got, and you'd rather ruin him than lose him."

"What do you mean—ruin him?"

"If you didn't know what I meant, you wouldn't be here."

Cogan doubled his fists. "Damn you—don't think that just because you whipped me once you can say any damned thing you want to! You might not win the next time around."

"Why did you come to me, if you don't want to hear what I have to say?" Dan demanded.

Cogan's fists uncurled and he looked down at his feet. "I told you I couldn't talk to anybody in the outfit. They'd spread it all over camp." He hunched his shoulders. "I'll have to listen. Sooner or later, if Bill doesn't stop it, we're going to get thrown out and I think that'll break his heart."

"I still don't see why you came to me—why you didn't try to find your own answer."

"I couldn't find an answer. I . . . guess I figured you were smarter than me. I don't know how it all worked in my mind; maybe it's because you whipped me, or maybe it's because you know his father and sister. I don't know."

"But you don't really think I'm smart enough to listen to—not if it's going to hurt you. It goes back to what I said—you'd rather ruin him than lose him for a friend."

Cogan slumped. The wind seemed to whistle out of him and his mouth drooped at the corners. "I wouldn't want to lose him for a friend, but I'd do it—if I had to for his own good."

"Then the next time he picks a fight—one that's not apt to get him hurt too much—let him know you're not standing with him. Let him fight his own battle, even if it means a whipping. Maybe, by the time he gets over it, he'll even have sense enough to know why you did it, and thank you."

The thought horrified Cogan. "It would be a hard thing." His feet wouldn't stay still and he had to stand. "It would be the hardest thing I ever did."

"If you'd done it a long time ago," Dan replied, "things might have been different for me!"

"I guess so. Dan, would you do me a favor? Would you come out and have a drink with Bill and me tonight? There's a *cantina* called La Golondrina about a block north of the barracks. We spotted it when we were riding in today. If you were there—kind of to remind me—I know I'd be able to do like you said."

Dan shook his head. "I've got an appointment with Governor Clarke in the morning. I don't want red eyes or a big head."

"Hell," Cogan argued, shuffling his feet, "you can't go to sleep for a while anyway. Maybe it would do you good if you went out a little."

Dan sighed. He wished Cogan would leave; he had enough on his own mind right now without worrying about Cogan's problems. But the man was persistent. "What do you say, Dan?"

"I won't promise," Dan said finally. "But if I get too restless to sleep, I'll walk over that way. If you're still there, I'll buy you a beer."

"Good enough!" Cogan said eagerly. "Thanks. And . . . I'd like to shake your hand. I know it wasn't easy to out and say the things you did. And I'm sorry for the trouble I've caused you."

Dan stood up and shook his hand. "Maybe it won't matter in the long run. Maybe everything will work out tomorrow."

"I hope so," Cogan said. "If I get a chance to say anything in your favor, I will."

"I've had enough favors," Dan said. "This time I'm depending on myself."

Governor Clarke was as angry a man as Dan had ever met up with. "I'm seeing you this morning because that Lieutenant promised!" he thundered. "I understand you even threatened to come here with a pistol. Well, let me tell you something, young man, I've got a pistol, too, and I've used it before and I can use it again! Now say your piece and get out!"

The Governor's room, huge and luxuriously furnished, rang like a bell with the echoes of his voice, but Clarke did not seem satisfied. Oratory which had once helped sway the voters of Texas was not adequate to express even the surface of his anger now. Dan had not managed to get more than two steps beyond the door.

"I'll give you my pistol," he said, "if that will make you listen to me."

"I said for you to speak your piece."

"Well, I . . . was a member of General Shelby's cavalry. Through a sort of misunderstanding I had to leave the outfit. I would like to get back in."

"And you expect me to help you? Why should I?"

Dan said uncertainly, "Why, because we're both Texans, I guess. I can think of no other reason."

Clarke looked incredulous. "And suppose I don't?" he thundered.

"Why, I guess it didn't occur to me that you wouldn't."

Clarke looked even more incredulous. His mouth opened in astonishment. Then his lips began slowly to spread and his body shook with the beginnings of laughter. Sound began to pour from his mouth, began to fill the room, ringing more powerfully than his oration of a few minutes ago.

Dan stood petrified while the gales started slowly to subside, swelled up again, tapered off, leaving Clarke still shaking but breathless.

The Governor recovered, but his laughter was still near the surface, lightly controlled. He stroked his chin, beginning to strike an attitude of thoughtfulness.

"I suppose you wouldn't be a true Texan," he said finally, "if you didn't act like a wild bull at a tea party whenever you got into trouble. Come on in. I must admit I've heard something of your trial. We'll have a drink and a cigar and talk about it."

When Dan left Clarke, that part of him that wanted to be a soldier was elated, and at the same time humbled. Tomorrow morning, briefly, he could see Shelby—briefly because tomorrow afternoon Shelby would see Maximilian.

But even a minute, Clark assured him, was almost certain to be enough. He and Shelby had mutual respect for one another's judgment, and now that Clarke was convinced, Shelby was apt to snap his fingers and say that Dan was back in. Before noon he would have his things in the barracks and be listening to Maehler's tall tales. After that he could plan to do something about Jane.

As he stabled his horse and went into his own hotel, he felt a little like a man suffering from a hangover, but not objecting because of the good time he'd had last night.

Cogan was waiting for him again, with an expression that somehow combined a dark thunderstorm with the red fires of hell. His eyes were a mottled red and his puffed cheeks were wet with tears.

"You son of a bitch!" Cogan said. He doubled his fists and kept them churning. "I'm not going to fight you because it wouldn't help—not now!" He had to stop talking in order to breathe, because his nose, swollen till it spanned half his face, was clamped shut.

Dan was down to earth now, ill at ease and embarrassed because he was a witness to so much raw emotion. The small Mexican hotel manager was standing behind his counter transfixed.

"What the hell's the matter with you?" Dan demanded.

229

"You told me how to help Bill! I should have known—" He sobbed a little and tilted his head back to breathe. "I should have known you'd want to get even!"

"What are you talking about?"

"Don't act like you don't know!" Cogan roared. "Bill's dead and your friend killed him—and you know it as well as I do!" He sank into a woven mat chair next to the short counter. His head tilted back for air, then flopped forward into his big, hairy hands.

"So help me God," Dan said, "I don't know what you're talking about!"

Cogan raised his head and his bloodshot eyes glared into Dan's. "You said you'd come to the *cantina* last night! You said—don't back Bill the next time he starts an argument! Then you hired a greaser to stab him while I stood there with my hands in my pockets!" He sucked in great gulps of air through his mouth.

Dan said angrily, "I'm sorry Bill is dead, but I don't know what happened and I'm not responsible!"

"You did it and I know it!" Again Cogan gulped air through his mouth. "The Morgens know it, too. This morning that little Mexican lieutenant—Esteban—came to the barracks. He was sending a messenger to the wagons and he wanted to . . . send word how Bill was. I told him he was dead—that you had him killed! He'll be here in a little while and he'll have plenty to say!"

Dan sighed and rubbed the muscles of his neck. "All right," he said. "I'll see if I can straighten it out with Esteban. You'd better go back to your barracks and get some rest." To the clerk he said, "I'll have a visitor soon. I'll be waiting for him in my room."

He left Cogan still sitting and went upstairs.

He sat on his bed for a long time, seeing the hurt in Jane's blue eyes when she got the news of Bill's death. The hurt was double, the anguish on her face almost unbearable to look at because she thought highly of Dan Kilbourne, and believed he had caused it to happen.

A long time later he realized that he had found at least part of the answer to a question he had asked himself a long time ago. A man truly loved a woman when his concern for her feelings was so great that he did not think of himself except as he affected those feelings.

# 13

THE WEARING AFTERNOON was hot and oppressive. When Dan stood, he was weary; when he lay down his legs were so restless he couldn't keep still. He paced, settled, stirred, paced again. What the hell had ever gotten into Cogan?

He was lying, but not according to his own way of looking at things. Dan was convinced of that now. The big soldier actually believed that Dan had hired someone to knife Bill.

But why hadn't he had sense enough to spare Jane and Wil the added anguish that this notion would bring to them?

The afternoon dragged on and dark approached and Dan lit his lamp. Esteban arrived at last, and his feelings were evident when he ignored Dan's outstretched hand.

Dan dropped his arm. "Well, you may as well come in," he said wearily, "and we'll see if we can't straighten this out."

"I do not know what to believe," Esteban said. "On the one hand it is most difficult to think that you would do such a great wrong. But men do strange things under the burden of their troubles, and I know you have many. I know also of the great trouble Bill Morgen caused you."

At Dan's gesture he sat beside the small table that held the lamp. Dan had gotten a bottle of tequila and two glasses from the hotel clerk, but Manuel waved the drink away. "Perhaps it is not a friendly visit," he explained.

Dan shrugged. "All right. I guess I don't blame you. I know the story Cogan told you, because he told it to me. But the most important part of it isn't true. He asked for advice and I gave it and that's all I know."

"It was these two who caused you trouble with Shelby's army, was it not?"

"Yes, it was—more trouble than I like to remember."

"And there was nothing you wanted more than to stay in that army."

"That's also true."

"You were angry—very angry—when you left Monterrey. You were not polite to Jane, or to Wil when you arrived at the wagons. You said that you would marry Mavis Todd, but you left her also, driven by your desire to serve with Shelby. You have not yet managed to get back into the Brigade—and perhaps this has caused you to do things which you might not do at another time. An angry man will do things which make him sorry afterward, when it is too late."

Dan sank down onto the bed. "Damn it, Manuel, there's nothing I can say except that for Jane's sake I'd give anything if Cogan hadn't gotten everything twisted."

"You have forgiven her, then?"

"I'm the one who wants forgiveness," he said, "for the way I acted. Cogan says it was Mavis who told him about my blue coat. She found out about it accidentally."

"*Ay de mi!*" Esteban touched his forehead with his fingers, appearing to concentrate with all his being. "Why?" he asked finally. "Why would she do such a thing?"

"She had a scheme—something she wanted to do—and she wanted my help."

"You don't wish to tell me of this scheme?"

"No. It's better forgotten."

Manuel studied him intently. "And now Mavis Todd is in Mexico City," he said half to himself.

232

"Mavis? Here?"

"She and her father arrived this morning. They traveled with an escort hired by the Señor Marman." Esteban looked at Dan's tightly compressed mouth and sighed. "I think I will have that drink now."

"Then you believe me—about Bill?"

"I wish to believe you, so perhaps I do."

Dan got up and began to pour the liquor. "How do you think Jane will feel?"

"I think that she will believe that you have caused her brother to be killed."

"Would it help if I . . . dropped everything and went to her? Explained?"

"I do not think so. It is too soon. The hurt will be too strong."

"I'd like to do something to lessen that hurt, Manuel. I can't just ignore it." He stared off into space. "If I had come home from a Southern army and found Jane out on the prairie . . ."

He left the remark unfinished and Manuel said, "To change the past—that is the dream of many people." He touched the tequila to his lips. "Have you spoken with Shelby—with anyone?"

"With Clarke. I have an appointment with Shelby tomorrow morning, at the Hotel Iturbide."

"I will try to see you there—to tell you how Jane has received the news. My messenger left this morning, as you know, and the wagons at this moment are very near the city, though they will soon turn away from it."

"I'll appreciate hearing," Dan said. "I'm due at the hotel at ten. Manuel, I meant to ask you, how did you make out with the guerrillas on the day I left the train?"

"I am a military man," he said simply. "I had soldiers, the guerrillas were untrained. I do not like to kill my own people, but sometimes it is necessary."

"I'm glad you had such an easy time of it," Dan said. "I killed one guerrilla myself that day. His name was

233

Quillian, and he worked for Marman. He tried to waylay me."

Esteban looked surprised. "You had no personal troubles with him?"

"None. But he attacked me in Santone, too. I wish I knew why."

Thoughtfully, Esteban said, "His reason would be a good thing to know. Well . . . perhaps, one day." He shook hands, and added, "I will see you in the morning, when I have spoken to my messenger. Tonight I am . . . worried about many things I do not understand. But who knows? Tomorrow all could be clear."

Dan entered the Iturbide several minutes early and tried to settle himself in a lounge chair with a small newspaper published in English by an enterprising Southerner. But he was able to read only a few sentences before impatience caused him to put the paper aside.

As he came to his feet he saw Mavis walking toward him. Her pale green lawn dress was topped by a white leghorn hat tied under her chin with a matching green ribbon and her hands were sinuously drawing on white gloves.

Her dark eyes regarded him with an amusement tinged with malice, and anger boiled up in Dan. She had used him mercilessly, was responsible for his being here this morning instead of in the barracks with the rest of the Brigade—was largely responsible for the hurt he had dealt Jane. He had not known that he could think of a woman in the terms that he was thinking now of Mavis.

"Dan," she greeted with an edged calm, "I can't say I'm surprised to see you. When Raney Quillian didn't come back—"

"You sent him after me?" he asked harshly. "I've wondered."

She smiled suddenly. "I wouldn't want you to think that—or that Reed sent him, either. Reed and I are to be

234

married this week, and we wouldn't want some vengeful person to try and spoil our wedding."

"Then I take it the guns have been delivered, the money collected?"

"Delivery is tomorrow morning, but the money is ours already. My father collected it." She smiled again. "If that surprises you, he's absolutely honest and Reed knows it. Dan, have you thought about all the money you could have had—and regretted your decision?"

He shook his head fervently. "Mavis, do you think I could regret parting from the kind of woman who will marry a man she doesn't like in order to have what she wants?"

Her mouth turned down with an ugliness he had never seen before. "We all must compromise when we make mistakes. I made mine when I believed that because you had served with the Yankees. . . ." She let the thought go and recovered her composure. "Never mind. I will still have the fine things I want. And the money we are making here is not the end, but the beginning. You can think of that sometime when you're grubbing in the dirt."

Beyond her Dan suddenly saw Shelby entering the lobby. Mavis followed the direction of his glance and smiled. She said, "What you want out of life seems so paltry, I'm afraid I could never understand it." She turned and walked away, nodding at the General as she passed him. Her going had its effect on Dan because it emphasized that there was little he or anyone could do to prevent whatever wrongs she would plan for the future.

Shelby passingly paid her the deference due a beautiful woman, then turned his uncompromising eyes on Dan. He abruptly changed his course and came directly toward him.

As Dan stiffened, Shelby said, a little sharply, "You are Private Kilbourne."

"Yes, sir."

"I remember you, of course. You scouted under Sergeant

Walcott. I also remember something of your experience in Monterrey, although I had little time to look into it."

"I'm sure, if I explain, sir—"

"It has been explained."

When he didn't go on Dan felt a sinking in his chest.

"You have a heavy conscience," Shelby said. "So have many of us. I have ordered men executed with no more than a snap of my fingers. Do you think that I never remember it afterward?"

"At least that was in line of duty, sir."

Shelby's brows moved together, till his eyes seemed sharp and hawklike. Only his voice grew softer. "You know of the Kansas—Missouri border wars?"

"Yes, sir."

"Men, women and children murdered, homes burned and looted—"

"Yes, sir."

"I was one of those who took part," Shelby said gravely. "I was younger then, a little more sure that I knew what was right and what was wrong."

"Then, sir," Dan said just as gravely, "if you don't know how I feel, I could never make anyone know."

The crispness returned to Shelby. "I have other business with Governor Clarke. I trust that you won't need to see him for anything?"

"No, sir."

"Very well. I will inform him that the matter he mentioned to me has been attended to." He touched his beard. "You were with Sergeant Walcott before—you will report to him again and upon so doing will be considered to be a part of the Brigade."

It was almost impossible to remain at attention. Dan stammered, "Thank you," thought he saw a brief glint of humor in Shelby's eyes, and then it was gone.

"Now that you are one of us," Shelby said, "I'm sure you would like me to go about my business. All of our

236

futures are at stake, as you must know, and I have only a few hours now."

Dan grinned. "I wish you—all of us—luck, sir."

Shelby gave him a half-salute and turned about, starting briskly for the stairway. Dan stood numb, not fully believing; it had happened so quickly, so easily. . . . He looked about, but Mavis was gone now, and he was grateful. The anger she had left with him was overridden for the moment by an exhausting relief.

He saw Manuel, in the dress of a Mexican caballero, coming into the hotel and went to meet him. He gripped the lieutenant's hand, clapped his shoulder. "Manuel," he said, "I made it. I'm back in, the minute I report to Sergeant Walcott! It all happened so fast I can't quite believe it!"

"I am happy for you," Esteban said.

"Manuel, what's wrong? Did you hear from Jane—from the train?"

"Yes, I heard. The news I bring is not good. Jane believes the words that Cogan sent her. Why should she not?"

"Then she . . . she must feel awful about it."

"Yes. My messenger says she is sick from the things she thinks."

"Are you sure it wouldn't help if I went to her?"

"It would not help."

"What of Marman? Has he left the train yet? Mavis says she came here to make preparations to marry him."

"That I hear also, but there is more. Her father, the Senator, collected a sum of money this very morning—a large sum. From one of the banks. It has been transferred for safekeeping to the French authorities and arrangements have been made for them to transport it to Vera Cruz."

"And do you know who put up the money?"

"No, I do not know this." He said queerly, "For a man who is to be married here in the city, the Señor Marman takes a strange route. But many things are strange. Three days ago a Mexican arrived from nowhere to talk with

237

him. That afternoon the Todds left the train. Yesterday Marman's wagons moved ahead of the others."

"Ahead?" Dan asked. "But they were to turn away from the rest of the train!"

"No, they travel in the same direction, only faster."

Dan felt a weakness in his knees. "Manuel—Marman is carrying guns; bought—and paid for now—by a band of guerrillas. And if he delivers them along the same route the colonists are taking, they'll all be massacred! The guerrillas will lie in wait for them!"

Manuel's breathing was sharp. "You should have told me this! When did you discover about the guns?"

"Only a few days ago, and I couldn't tell you. I was afraid there would be a fight—afraid some of the colonists would be killed on the spot. But I was told that there would be no danger for them if I kept quiet." He started to move toward the door but Manuel held him.

"I wish you had told me," he said grimly.

"Maybe there's still time. There's got to be. According to Mavis we have till tomorrow morning before the guerrillas get the guns."

Manuel thought about it, his eyes narrowing as he quickly calculated. "Well, then," he said finally, "my soldiers will take care of everything."

Dan, his mind in a turmoil, hardly heard him. "How far are the wagons from the city—this minute?"

"This minute? Forty-five miles, I think. This morning they came closer. To within forty miles."

"Then we'll have to get started. We can't lose a minute!"

"I have told you, my friend. My soldiers will do everything. You will not be needed."

"Manuel, I love Jane, more than I thought it possible to love a woman. I'm going with you."

"You will not be needed," Esteban said insistently.

"You know I have to go and we can't waste time arguing."

"Dan, the colonists will not even know about the fight

238

until it is over. You can do nothing. Did you not tell me once that you were bound to serve with Shelby and his Brigade—because of the past?"

"Yes, I said that."

"Are you not still bound, then?"

"Yes, by the chains of my own conscience. If I could go to the outfit now, see this thing through, it would clear my mind."

"Tell me also, did you not love Jane when you were in San Antonio?"

"Maybe."

"But you did not go to her."

"If I had gone then, it would have been for myself, because I wanted to do it. Today it will be for her. Even if I'm no help at all she'll know that I cared enough to come to her. She'll begin to have some doubt about Cogan's story; her mind will be eased."

"I will tell her that you spoke of these things—what you were willing to give up for her."

As a protest started to form on Dan's lips, Manuel raised his hand. "Wait! Do not decide now." He waved both hands. "No. No. Do not decide now. Leaving the city I must ride by your barracks; there you can decide. By then you will realize that you can do nothing. And you will remember why you have left your own homeland and come to Mexico. Now! You are right about one thing. We must spend no more time with arguments. My horse is stabled with yours."

Dan tried to hurry Manuel as they pushed out into the sunny street, but the little Mexican imperturbably took his time, though he was not seemingly concerned when his black gelding jostled several people who impeded his progress. Nor did he seem concerned when their curses shrilled after him and they brandished fists and even an occasional knife.

"There is ample time," he assured Dan. "But still I have

arrangements to make. Minutes must not be wasted foolishly."

They began to fight their way across town in a series of hopeful spurts interspersed by maddening delays. Manuel's face remained bland through it all, until Dan finally began to believe that the lieutenant really did have everything under control. After all, he had seen the wagons through one crisis after another all the way across Mexico. Why couldn't he take care of things now?

"You might leave word with the French," Dan suggested. "I'm sure that under the circumstances they wouldn't clash with your soldiers. It might save some of your own men."

"Go to the French," Manuel said, "and you will go nowhere else today. They will ask questions. They will make you wait. They will take you to see higher ranking officers who will interrogate you as if the last officer had asked nothing. Then you will wait again. No, my friend, we will not bother the French. Besides, we do not need them."

"You're sure, Manuel, that you can take care of it?"

"I am sure."

The crowds grew thinner as they reached the wide *calle* over which the Brigade had marched into town only two days ago.

"It is to be a big day for all of us," Manuel said. "If your General Shelby convinces the Emperor, then my fight will grow harder each day, as your Brigade becomes bigger and bigger. If he does not convince him, many of your men will still join the French. Tell me, you said once that if your army crumbled to nothing while you were a part of it that your mind would be free, that you . . . would have done everything possible. Do you still feel like this?"

"Yes, I guess I do."

The iron-barred gate and the massive barracks loomed ahead. A sentry stood in his stone cubicle, watching their approach through the vertical oval opening in front of him. In the courtyard before the barracks a solid group of soldiers were loitering and they, too, looked up.

Manuel stopped his gelding. "Well, my friend, it is time to say goodbye. Perhaps, if Maximilian does not want Shelby, then you can come after me—to talk to Jane, to see what I have done with the guerrillas. In so little time—four hours, perhaps, or five—all that you felt you must do could be over and done with."

"And if Maximilian does listen to Shelby?"

"Then I will talk to Jane, as I have said. I will tell her what you were willing to do for her."

"She can't believe that I'm willing to do it unless I do it."

"That is not true. I will explain, believe me."

"Manuel, put yourself in Jane's place. If I go with you, she'll see things differently. Maybe she'd never really disbelieve Cogan, but there would have to be doubt."

"And suppose she still has no doubt?"

"She loved me—I'm sure of it—before this happened. Now—how could she trust herself to love anybody again? But if I come along she'll have to know that she was not altogether wrong."

"You hope this. But you have only to go inside and report to your sergeant and you know that all you have wanted will come about. Perhaps within the space of a few hours. You will not have another chance."

"I'll be sorry about that. But I'm coming with you."

"Then, if you are sure, we must start."

"I suppose it wouldn't be any help to have part of the Brigade come along?"

"On the contrary," Manuel said. "You alone can do little or nothing, as I have said. But to get many soldiers, without wasting more time . . ."

Dan rode closer to the sentry.

"I have something to say to all those men. I'm short on time, so I'll yell to them." He cupped his hands around his mouth.

"Men, I want to talk to you for a minute. You'll remember the wagon train that left San Antonio ahead of us—Marman's colony—we saw them again in Monterrey.

They're in trouble about forty-five or fifty miles north of us. We have information that a large band of guerrillas will attack them tomorrow and we need help."

The soldiers appeared sympathetic as they quickly began to talk to each other, but there was much head shaking among them. Maehler stood up and talked to them for a minute, then crossed toward Dan and Esteban, his footsteps clacking over the hard bricks until he drew even with the sentry.

"Dan," he said, "I'd do a lot for you. You know that. But we couldn't come even if we wanted to. The ways things are, we'd have to have permission from the French, and we don't even know what they're going to do with us. Most of the outfit wouldn't come anyway. Shelby's seeing the Emperor in a little while, and we've come too far and waited too long to find out where we stand. Hell, man, you see how it is."

"Yes," Dan said grudgingly, "I see."

"Then we must go," Esteban said sadly.

Dan nodded agreement and they started to rein away, but stopped at the rapid clatter of hoofs rounding the building. The rider was Cogan and somebody yelled, "Hey, my horse!" and Cogan yelled back, "Piss on you!"

He waved a hand at the guard to show that he didn't give a damn whether the man liked his leaving the barracks or didn't like it, and came on out into the street. The soldier whose horse it was started yelling some more and running across the courtyard, but the rest of the men shouted him down.

"Let him have the damned horse. You can take his!"

"I heard you talking and I grabbed the nearest saddled animal," Cogan explained. He was ignoring Dan, talking only to Esteban.

Dan was content to let the matter rest for a time as they started down the street. He was disappointed that a host of individual soldiers had not responded to his plea for help, but it was easy enough to see their side of it.

Cogan, his blouse only half-buttoned and his hair awry, asked Esteban to fill him in and his puffed face, already seeming to be frozen with a permanent bitterness, took on an even grimmer look when he learned of Marman's rifles. Knowing the loss the big soldier had suffered, and knowing that his love for Bill Morgen had brimmed over to include Jane and Wil, Dan felt a need to offer comfort.

"Esteban will have an army to meet the guerrillas," he said. "He assures me that they're in no real danger."

"But that is not true," Esteban said softly.

"Not true? But you said—"

"Amigo, I have told a lie. A bad one, perhaps. I have no army. As I told you only a few days past, our soldiers are needed elsewhere at this time."

"Then why the hell—!"

"What can one man do against so many guerrillas?" Esteban asked. "I will tell you—nothing. What can three do, for that matter? I am a military man. With soldiers I could stop them. But with one soldier—or even two—there is no chance."

Incredulously, harshly, Dan said, "Well then, why the hell were you going by yourself?"

"I must try," he said. "That is my duty. But I saw no reason to get you killed when you could not help. What can you alone do for Jane—for anyone?"

"Esteban, if ever I wanted to kill a man—!"

"But why? For trying to spare your life? For permitting you to go ahead with the thing which you held most dear? At least I thought that. Perhaps you thought it yourself."

Dan found himself unable to reason with Esteban, or to argue against the things he said. In his anger he turned on Cogan, who was trailing slightly behind them.

"Cogan, will you kick that bangtail in the ass and try to keep up? Because if you don't I'm coming back there and do it myself!"

# 14

SINCE DAYBREAK—two hours now—Jane had guided the lead wagon while her father scouted ahead. Much of that time, because of sharp hills and a twisting road that was little more than a trail, he had not even been in sight, but now he was dropping back, to change places with her, she supposed, although he would insist that she not roam as far ahead of the train as he had been doing.

During the last few days he had begun to grow tired again, but this morning she had noticed that a youthful sparkle seemed to be returning to his eyes. He was more than halfway glad that Marman had left them, she thought. For the first time it gave him a chance to be his old self, though there were problems connected with the train which would never be solved in the single week of travel remaining for them.

Wil stopped his dark bay gelding and let the rumbling wagon catch up to him. He continued to watch the train behind her for a moment, standing in his stirrups to try to see the long end of the crooked column. Then he swiveled his body and caused the bay to trot a few steps until he was alongside her. Instead of shouting to her, as she had expected, he clambered off the horse onto the wagon seat, though he made no move to take the reins.

"I do believe you're getting spry," Jane said.

"It's the worst thing you can say to a man," Wil answered at once. "Nobody ever calls a young man spry—only an old fool who moves about faster than people think he should."

She laughed and Wil patted her shoulder. She knew then that he had something disturbing on his mind, for though he was a man who often showed his affection in a thousand little ways, he seldom openly demonstrated it.

"I've been thinking," he said, "about all you've done for me on this trip—and what it's cost you. You're a pretty woman, Jane, but your hands are getting as hard as a man's, and you're growing as stubborn as a man when things don't go right."

"You mean I keep wrestling with a stubborn wagon instead of wringing my hands and crying?"

"Yes, I mean that, and more. I mean that I would like for you to be the lady you were back in Galveston."

"Maybe back in Galveston I would be."

His smile was filled with warmth and affection and the delight a child shows when he is about to spring a surprise. "You'll know the answer to that soon, because that's where you're going."

Jane's arms stiffened until the mules slowed and she had to urge them back to speed. The wagon lurched and settled back to its monotonous, swaying grind. "Have you made up your mind about the colony, then, before we even get there?"

"I guess I have," Wil admitted glumly. "Jane, I . . . I don't know what's the matter with me. I only know that whatever it is, I'm getting more restless instead of more settled as I get older. And now that Bill is . . . dead, I don't have as much reason for settling as I did."

Jane felt her lips compress. She tried to relax them, and relax her hands on the reins, knowing she must be presenting a grim picture. She knew that she had caught herself too late as words began tumbling hastily from Wil's turned down lips.

"I mean . . . you'll get married, have your own home. Jane, I don't always know how to say things, but I've never treated you right and you're all I have left and now I'm going to do the right thing. I'll stay with the colony for a while, until everything gets into order, but you're going back. You've got a right to a life of your own, and you can't find it here. We've got friends in Galveston, not the kind I left you with back on the farm, and you're going to them. I'd hoped for a while that everything would be all right, that you and—"

She had asked him more than once not to speak Dan's name to her. She wished that he would lose the habit of thinking about him! With Dan's jarring picture out of her own mind she took both reins in one hand and wiped her forehead with the other, trying hard to think. She knew that she was on Wil's conscience night and day, but she couldn't leave him. He needed her too much. It was nice to think of going back to Galveston, of trying to forget the old life and start a new one, but it was impossible. Her future was as solidly shaped for her as if it had been hewn in stone.

"I've got to say some things you won't like," Wil went on. "I'd rather lose a leg than hurt you, but I've got to tell you the truth for your own good. We used to hear back in the old country that there were two kinds of children— the ones who wouldn't bother with their parents after they got old and the ones who helped them until they couldn't do for themselves. I don't want you to be either kind, Jane. I just want you to live a nice, normal life."

She was a little hurt. "I guess you're right," she said. "Maybe I don't like all that you're telling me. I want to leave this life, but not simply because I'm interfering with what you want to do. You're the only family I have."

"I know that, but I mustn't lean on you so much. For my sake, and for yours."

Suddenly she felt a relief that left her limp. She really could go back, and without causing Wil any disservice. And there was no use pouting because he sounded as if he wanted to be rid of her; he had proved often enough that

246

he loved her, in spite of the fact that he was unable to settle down for her or anyone. The reins almost slipped from her fingers as she conjured up pictures of streets and stores and the thousand other things that a town meant. She didn't have to live in the midst of them all, but she needed to know that they were there and that she could go and be a part of them whenever she wanted.

She caught the reins again. "Daddy, there is something— I know you don't like some kinds of responsibility. But Reed, when he said goodbye, sounded very much like I'd never see him again. I think he's going to Mexico City, to Mavis, and won't ever be with our colony. If I'm right there'll be no one to run things except you."

"You're underestimating the older people again," Wil said. "Have you noticed lately how Colonel Dutton, for one, has been taking hold? Like a lot of others he's been afraid, but now he's getting to act like a man again. You— and everybody else young—have a way of looking at somebody and seeing a belly bulging over a belt and maybe some wrinkles and sacks under the eyes, and you think they're finished. But Colonel Dutton was a good fighter and a good leader. Everything looked different to him for a while because he had his wife with him, and he was afraid for her. Some of the others were the same way. But now they're beginning to find out that their wives are just as tough as they are. They can take care of themselves better than you think."

"If you're really sure about that," Jane said, "then I will go back. I won't say that I won't worry about you sometimes, but I'll know that you can take care of yourself better than I gave you credit for. There's one thing, though, that I want you to promise me: that you won't take a job like this again—one that's too much for you."

"I'll promise, if you'll make me a promise. I was afraid for a while that you might end up marrying Reed Marman, because you didn't have much else to choose from. Only three or four of the teamsters were really young enough and they didn't have sense enough to clean the manure off their boots. Don't take anybody for a husband until you know he's the one you've got to have. That's the promise I want. Don't settle down with somebody just because he's in front of you. I won't be with you and I wouldn't have sense enough to guide you if I was, I guess." He shook his head sadly. "Maybe I'm talking crazy. You can't be sure about anybody, can you? We both thought Dan"—he saw her stony look and continued resolutely, "—we both thought he would be perfect for you and he killed my son. Jane, do you think there's any chance that Cogan could have made some kind of mistake?"

"No," she said sharply. "I know that men can convince women of almost anything. I know that Dan could change the story of what happened and make it sound right, if he wanted to. But I wouldn't even let myself listen. Cogan would have no reason to lie about it, and I don't want to be taken in with a web of Dan's lies. I would always have doubts, even if I pretended to believe him. Now let's not think about it again. I want to enjoy the thought of going back to Galveston."

"What will you do to keep busy? If I know you, you'll have to do something."

"I guess I've thought about it more than I wanted to admit. I thought maybe I could work in a newspaper office."

They heard a commotion behind them. Wagons began to halt and somebody shouted. Wil said wearily, "A broken axle, probably, or a wheel has come off."

Jane sawed back on the reins and braked lightly. The wagon rocked to a stop and Wil reached for his horse, but Dan Kilbourne climbed onto it from the other side. Jane stared in wonder and surprise, and then the anger burned over her like a wave of red hot needles.

"Wil," Dan said, "my horse is exhausted. I'll have to

248

have yours." He seemed on the verge of exhaustion himself, but when she had recovered enough to put her thoughts in order she saw that his face was fiery and rock-hard.

Wil's mouth and eyes were set for his bitter protest when Manuel Esteban came up alongside Dan. The horse he rode belonged to one of the colonists.

"We have come," Esteban said quickly, "because guerrillas are about to attack your wagons. You must turn at once and travel in the direction of Mexico City. When you have started we will remain behind to try to give you time."

"There'll be no politics today," Dan cut in. "I want the fastest wagons in front and they must travel as fast as they can. The others will catch up whenever you are slowed by a hill or a creek. Those who think they might fall behind will have to leave their wagons and ride with someone else. You can't have more than an hour or so, and we can't hold the guerrillas long. There are only three of us."

Cogan charged up on a horse he had just finished saddling, tipped his hat to Jane and said a feeble hello, then listened to quick instructions from Dan. Wil had already climbed down and was searching for a suitable spot for the turning.

Esteban separated from the others and came over to her. "Dan is here because of you," he said.

"He can come or go. I don't care, and I won't listen to him or to you if you talk about him." Manuel followed alongside her as she moved the wagon forward in response to Wil's waving arms. "What will happen to Reed—to his teamsters?" she asked.

"Nothing. It is they who are responsible. Marman's wagons carried guns, and it is these that the guerrillas will use."

"Then, he—" She could hardly believe what she was hearing. "Will he come back to help us?"

249

"No. He and his teamsters will be gone before the guerrillas have the guns out of the wagons. You will have no help—except for the three of us. We will do what we can, but there is small chance. You must realize this and . . . be ready for what may happen."

He left her then to go to Dan, who with Cogan was forcing some of the protesting colonists to pull over and let some of the faster wagons pass, so that they would be ahead after the turning.

Jane reined the mules into the clearing. In spite of the quickness of it all she couldn't doubt that the threat of guerrillas was immediate and real. Hadn't Esteban been their guardian angel throughout the length of Mexico? But one minute she had been dreaming of returning to Galveston and the next she was fleeing for her life. The feeling of danger was just now beginning to seep through her.

Esteban's words penetrated fully: *You will have no help—except for the three of us.* She thought then that she would almost rather die than take help from Dan Kilbourne, but there were others to think of besides herself. She got the wagon turned full circle, and stopped as she reached the road again, sitting with nervous impatience while others filed past to begin their sweeping horseshoe.

Farther along the road Dan Kilbourne's harsh voice drowned out the shrill protests of a middle-aged woman. He put a quick stop to the argument by grabbing a mule's bit and forcefully guiding the crippled wagon to the side of the road.

When the road was cleared Dan helped the accusing woman and her glowering, bitter husband out of the tilted wagon and up into the next vehicle. The woman's bony fingers clung tightly to a small bag of her most prized possessions, and she railed shrilly against fate and God and Dan Kilbourne, but her politician husband, defeated and despairing, carried nothing and said nothing. His face was ashen and his movements were dazed as he stumbled across the wagon seat and virtually fell back into the bed.

The rest of the wagons passed, and then the cycle was complete and they started filing by again, headed in the opposite direction. Wil had climbed up beside Jane. Dan joined Esteban as he rode up, waving to them to stop.

"There is a place, perhaps ten miles from here," Esteban said, "where the road is narrow and the hills are broken on each side. There you must stop and prepare to fight. We will do our best to hold the guerrillas until you can get there. Who will be in charge of your . . . forces?"

"Colonel Dutton," Wil said promptly, and in answer to Dan's surprised stare, repeated firmly, "Colonel Dutton. He's in the seventh wagon back."

They were ready to pull away now and Dan wanted desperately to make his explanations to Jane, but her stony face said that she did not want to listen, and he could not have taken the time even if she had wanted to hear.

"Thank you for coming back to help us," she said in a hard, unfeeling voice.

There was nothing he could say; he touched his hat as the wagon began to move past. Esteban had already started back for Dutton's wagon. Dan spun Wil Morgen's bay and spurred after him.

Esteban was again explaining the terrain, but he could offer no optimism. "You have little chance to reach the place I speak of," he stated flatly, "but we will try to give you time. If you get there, the odds will still be great."

"We'll do our best," the colonel said quietly. "If we make it I'll post a force alongside the road and surprise them with a flank attack to try to separate them into two groups. Then we'll close in on the group closest to the wagons. After that we'll see."

The drivers behind them were shouting now and Esteban waved them on. Dan yelled after Mrs. Dutton, "I'm sorry for . . . that day," knowing she was bound to remem-

251

ber the time he'd threatened her with the loss of her wagon. He was not certain, but he thought that she smiled back at him. Exhausted as he was he felt a warm glow at seeing them take hold; at least they would try to fight, and sometimes that was more important than living.

Dust rolled out in waves on both sides of the wagons, billowing up also into the faces of the rear drivers as the lead vehicles began to gain speed. The last several drivers gave Dan hard, menacing looks because their position had been his doing, and he found a certain relief in their attitudes; hatred and bitterness both were to be preferred to despair.

Cogan dashed down the line and drew up to them as the end of the train went by. "What were you figuring on doing?" he demanded of Esteban. "Are we to tag along as rear guard?" The rumble of the wagons, the rattle of swinging tinware, the squeals of wheels against axles and the pounding of hoofs all combined to make him shout in a voice that reminded Dan of Sergeant Walcott.

Esteban held up his hand, waited another moment, then shook his head. He gestured at the wagon Dan had led off the road and beckoned for them to follow him.

The dust in their faces grew worse as the sounds finally began to diminish. Esteban coughed and cupped his hands like blinders to shield his eyes. He stopped at the wagon and dismounted, motioning for them to do the same. He indicated that the mules must be unhitched and slapped resoundingly and sent off into the woods. Cogan's thick fingers tore at the traces and Dan stood opposite him, on the precarious edges of a gully, working with him. The mules were freed, startled by flat slaps. They seemed astonished at their good fortune, then cut into the brush as though afraid the temporary insanity which had loosed them might reverse itself and bring them back.

Esteban blew his nose to clear it of the thick, swirling dirt. "Now," he said, "get into the wagon, take those things which appear most valuable and which can be carried across your saddle. Quickly, please."

"What the hell?" Cogan demanded indignantly. "Are we here to protect these people, or try to get a few gewgaws for ourselves?"

"Do what he says!" Dan snapped, and swung up, ducking under the canvas. Cogan came up behind him, but they both hesitated for the first moment. Snooping among personal things that did not belong to them, through the very heart of someone else's possessions, was a violation. The pitiful threadbare clothes and rickety trunks and battered boxes somehow made it worse.

Resolutely Dan unclasped the fasteners of the old trunk and pulled open the lid. He took a miniature cedar chest and several dresses from inside and handed them to Cogan, then moved over to a box and picked it up, smashing it open against the wagon bed. The box contained several items of scrolled silverware, all carefully wadded with newspaper. Dan handed it to Cogan also, began to break open other boxes as Cogan climbed back out of his way.

The other boxes contained tools, portraits, dishes, finely embroidered linens, a few items of silk, more silver. Dan did not look further, but took the silver and silk and made his way out from under the canvas.

Esteban helped him struggle down with his heavy load and told him to add it to Cogan's pile, already lying in the dust of the churned road.

"Now we must turn the wagon over, into the gully," he directed. "This will make it more difficult for them to get what is inside, and will therefore take longer."

"And the things we took?"

"Those we will drop from time to time, and thus keep the guerrillas from leaving the road. They must be made to take every winding until we lead them in the direction we wish them to travel."

Dan put the things down and got a firm grip on a sideboard. They began to rock the vehicle until, at Esteban's quick command, all three heaved with all their weight and strength. The wagon tilted further, rested on two wheels, and then toppled with a rending, sickening crash.

Esteban brushed his hands, studied the receding cloud of dust raised by the train, and slowly knelt to press his ear against the ground. The others waited until he said, "I am not sure, because the wagons make much noise. But it seems that I hear them."

"Then—you think the guerrillas will all be mounted?" Dan asked.

"It does not seem likely, but who can tell? We will not wait to examine them. That will come later, at a spot perhaps two miles from here, beyond the rushing creek we passed. We must hurry, I think. By now they are sure to have seen the dust traveling in the other direction, and they will come quickly."

Cogan mounted first and Dan handed several things up to him. He gave the small Esteban a lighter load. The remaining things he picked up and held cradled in one arm while he struggled to mount the bay, which for no reason he could figure had suddenly become skittish. He finally made it and they trotted down the road until their loads settled, then stepped up their pace to a slow gallop.

Dan became aware that birds were singing in the trees around them as if, with the departure of the wagons, the day had become normal and joyous again. A road runner darted in front of them and the bay shied, nearly unseating him. He clung on, and the road runner swerved and sprinted ahead, leading the way.

In a depression between two low hills a crippled wagon squatted in the center of the road, its axle broken. The mules were still hitched, but the wagon's occupants were gone, surely in one of the other wagons, Dan thought with relief, for there was room to pass here and several other vehicles had weaved around this one.

They stopped and unhitched the mules, but Esteban did not think it worthwhile to try to do more.

"They will learn a lesson from the other wagon," he pointed out, "and now that they have realized how much time is lost, they will merely put someone to guard this one, and the others will come on."

"Then why unhitch the mules?" Cogan asked. Dan was again struggling to hand him up his silver and the exhaustion of the long ride from Mexico City made it a precarious business.

"Perhaps some will be afoot," Esteban said. "We do not wish them to find transportation so readily."

Somehow Dan got up again and they rode on, lightening their loads from time to time, scattering the glittering treasure to slow their pursuers, and at the same time preparing themselves for the fording of the creek. The waters were shallow at the crossing, but fast. Cromwell, on his tired legs, had barely been able to make it earlier this morning. A sharp twinge of worry caused Dan to wonder how the sorrel was making out now. It was tied behind one of the wagons because Dan had thought that if somehow it could survive another few miles of travel, then at least it might not fall into cruel, unknown hands.

The bay he rode now was strong and fresh and pushed through the swirling waters without trouble. Esteban and Cogan came on behind Dan. They crossed and traveled another hundred yards and Esteban pointed to a thick screen of brush.

"It is here that we will wait for them," he announced, "and I do not think it will be a long wait. I am certain that I heard yells a short time ago—from the location of the first wagon."

"It doesn't look like the best place in the world to make a stand," Cogan objected.

"If we are lucky, it will not be our final stand. That will come later."

Cogan still had not spoken to Dan except when necessary, and neither of them had mentioned Bill's death. The trouble between them did not greatly seem to matter now, Dan thought. They had both been suddenly snatched from the uncertain future of Shelby's army and thrust into the path of guerrillas they had never even dreamed existed, ragged and hungry men, likely, who would slice and maim and torture and kill for the sake of glittering riches.

He rode into the brush, dropping the few items that he had not yet scattered before he climbed down.

"Dan, amigo," Esteban said, "I can this minute see them coming."

It was true, and at the rate they were rounding a bend in the road, they were only about three minutes away.

Dan took a rope from his saddle, cut off a short length, and securely tied the skittish bay to a tree trunk. When the time came to run he would slash the rope; in the meantime he wouldn't have to worry about the horse, except to keep it from nickering for the next minute.

"We will serve two purposes here," Esteban said. "If you will notice, not all of the guerrillas are mounted."

Dan studied them carefully before answering. They were a veritable swarm, like a cloud of gnats. Some wore black dress—tightly fitting costumes ornamented with countless buttons. These, predominantly, were riding the horses. The remainder, dressed for the most part in white cottons—some of which were broken by the diagonal slash of dark serapes—were riding mules, donkeys and shank's mare. Dan knew then that Esteban had been right to make certain that the mules were turned loose. The guerrillas afoot might be able to trot all day, and probably could, but they could not travel as fast as mounted men.

There were about a hundred of them, Dan saw with dismay. They hove up before the creek and the black-clad leader waited a few seconds for the men afoot to close up behind him. He addressed them in Spanish and Esteban, by cupping his ear, was able to pick up some of the words. He passed them on to Dan and Cogan.

"The ones with horses, with animals, will leave the others behind now," he said. "Though the leader knows that the wagons cannot go far, he does not wish them to stumble onto help. Therefore the mounted men will hurry now to catch them and the others will come as fast as they can."

The bay nickered and the Mexican leader spun his horse to face them. Cogan had a rifle and two revolvers ready, Dan his rifle and one revolver. Esteban had only a rifle, and Cogan handed him a pistol.

"I found two more in my saddlebags," he said. He eyed Dan. "We all had four to start with."

"I've got one more," Dan said. "My other two are in Mexico City."

Esteban took the pistol and looked at it doubtfully. "Alas, I am not so . . . accurate as you *norteamericanos* with one of these. Perhaps some of the guerrillas are, but not I. Much will depend on you now."

The Mexican guerrilla leader was splashing into the waters of the ford. "Let him pass," Esteban said, "and the two others behind him. They will be the biggest leaders. Kill the ones who follow them and try to make the others hesitate to enter the stream again. The leaders will charge us, and we will kill them up close."

"Why not stop all of them?" Cogan asked angrily.

"Because we must make certain of the leaders. Then we will run—not down the road, but at an angle away from the wagons, and because the leaders are dead and cannot stop them, the others will follow us for a time."

Even when Cogan agreed, he would argue because of the bitterness in his soul, Dan thought. The leaders splashed up onto the near bank, with several others close behind, and for some crazy reason Dan continued to think about Cogan. He knew suddenly what it was—Cogan was breathing silently. In the past he had always breathed to the accompaniment of a series of shrill whistles.

Dan squeezed off the trigger and a black-suited Mexican seemed to shrivel in the middle. He clutched a flat saddle horn while his horse took two more steps; his grip slackened then and he slid off into the rushing waters.

Esteban and Cogan were firing carefully; another guerrilla was off his horse and one was pushing back across the creek, nursing his shoulder and arm. His retreat was more effective than the death of the other two.

Dan got a new paper cartridge into his rifle and fired again. The unexpected attack was causing pandemonium. In spite of this, four men had crossed instead of the three they had counted on, and a fifth still remained in the stream, undecided, as the four charged ahead of him. Cogan placed a bullet in his middle and he collapsed.

The four bore down on them at top speed, riding straight up. Three held drawn pistols, clutched high as if they were to be plunged like swords into men who dared ambush them. The fourth fired a rifle, flung it away, drew his own pistol. Two more began to shoot and Cogan grunted with pain. Dirt splattered into Dan's face, but he continued to reload his rifle. The Mexicans at the creek would quickly have to be reminded that they must cross with caution, and that would require the rifle.

He put the long-barreled gun down and drew a bead on the rider to his right. There were two races of people, he thought, who, when their pride was aroused, would court death as though she were a beautiful lady. These were the Indians and the Spaniards, and the men about to fly into their faces were a mixture of both. He pulled the trigger and his man spun from the saddle and another sank in front of him. Dan left the other two to Esteban and Cogan and shot a cotton-clad guerrilla who had pushed his mule into the stream.

He realized then that someone had failed, and twisted his body aside to dodge flailing hoofs. He flung a shot upwards. A bullet tore into the Mexican's face and Dan turned and emptied the revolver at the creek.

He reloaded the rifle first because it was easier, then began the tedious job of charging the revolver. As his fingers labored he checked on Cogan and Esteban.

Esteban was working feverishly with his rifle, not even bothering with the pistol; it was empty and he had nothing with which to load it.

Cogan was also reloading, though his left hand was not functioning well. A bullet had ploughed into his arm and another had cut his cheek. Bullets continued to shower around them, singing off into the brush.

At the creek someone had assumed command. The new leader gave a shrill cry and pushed into the waters. The rest of the guerrillas came after him, a solid mass. Each of the three waiting men fired a quick shot with his rifle, and all tore for their horses. The remaining items from the first wagon were left now, for the guerrillas had hugged the road long enough. The time had come to pull them to one side.

Dan slashed his rope and got up into the saddle. He found time to think that his muscles responded slowly, but his exhaustion seemed to have vanished. Then he was onto the road and charging into the brush on the other side. Behind him Esteban's horse stumbled and Dan, seeing it over his shoulder, thought the animal had been hit. He pulled the bay up, spun it around, and emptied his revolver at the oncoming guerrillas. By then Esteban and Cogan were past, and he raced after them.

The country around them was overrun with shoulder-high brush. The land rose in front of them, and in one spot the heap of a sloping hill was seemingly braced by a clump of trees. They headed for the trees and bullets sang around them, but the screening cover of the brush and their twisting paths were enough to save them. Only one Mexican, on a sleek black horse, gained on them and Cogan, with a lucky snapshot, tumbled him from his saddle. The others came on, spurring hard to make up the ground they lost as the three men before them angled further off the road.

Someone among the guerrillas began to yell. For a time this had no effect, but gradually they began slowing. The yells grew louder, more insistent, until the pursuit had dropped well behind. Esteban also slowed, looking back at them.

"What is it?" Dan yelled.

"They will not be pulled further. They will let us go now and start for the wagons."

"Then we'd better try to get in front of them again."

"Yes, but we must go through the trees and around the hill on the other side, so they cannot see us."

"We'll kill the horses," Cogan yelled sourly.

"Once we get to the next place, my friend, we will not need the horses again. There we must make our big fight, as long as a breath is left in us. If we are lucky we can hold them an hour before the end comes."

His words registered on Dan, but made only a fleeting impression. It was no good thinking about death. It came soon enough to every man without the waste of worrying about it. It was no good thinking about Jane either—about things which could never come to pass, and above all it was no good thinking about her safety. He was doing all he could to insure the wagons a few precious minutes in order for them to reach the rough hills where they could make their stand, and he did not want to dwell on what would happen after that.

Riding as hard as the lathered bay could travel, covering the great half-circle that would lead them to their final stand, he wondered how General Shelby had fared with his long-awaited address to the Emperor Maximilian. His own need to pay his debt, the need he had fought so hard to fulfill, would not easily slip from his mind.

# 15

THEY CAME ONTO the wagon road again—three men so near exhaustion that the tension could no longer fire their bodies, and three horses so nearly dead it seemed doubtful they could make the final short climb toward the cleft in the jagged hills. Cogan's animal in particular was on its last legs, and Manuel sought to reassure the big soldier. He pointed to the cleft.

"It is there we will stand."

Cogan stared back at him incredulously. "What the hell's the matter with you?" he shouted. He pointed to his right. "It's not more than a half a mile around those hills. Maybe we can hold for a few minutes, but they'll send a detachment around and then hit us front and rear!"

"That is true," Esteban agreed.

Cogan shook his head in bewilderment and tried to coax his mount into maintaining its gallop. The animal stopped suddenly and balked, just short of the cleft. Cogan slapped it with the reins once, then grabbed his saddlebags and hit the ground running.

Down the slope of the road behind them the mounted guerrillas were sweeping onward. Cogan dropped the bags and grasped one of Dan's stirrups as the horse pounded up the incline.

The horse slowed, stopped, and Cogan hung on. Manuel reached him, bent over and pried at his fingers.

"We must get ready," he said gently. "They will go around only if they cannot come through."

Cogan turned loose and Dan persuaded the bay to take another few steps. He got down, reeling, prodded the bay onward, and sank behind a chest-sized rock. He rested his rifle against the rock, trying to catch his breath as his eyes took in the country around him.

To his right were bluffs and steep inclines topped by full-grown trees that bore no resemblance to the stunted bushes on the lower level. In front of him the road dropped, sloped gently for a hundred yards, leveled, and wound out of sight into the brush. To his left the hills were also rough, as though they had been thrust up suddenly in a burst of violent anger, and then had promptly been forgotten. But as Cogan had pointed out, a half-mile away the ridge stopped, and the plain beyond was level. This was not a good place to defend because they could be circled so easily, but Manuel had been right to choose it. They were physically able to go no further.

Manuel and Cogan were slumped on the ground on the other side of the narrow road; Cogan was attempting, with one shaky hand, to help Manuel reload the empty pistol he still carried.

"With all four pistols loaded," Cogan said, "that'll still leave about a dozen extra rounds. Maybe," he added hopefully, "we could fight here for a little while and then run again."

"I think not," Esteban said dolefully. "I do not wish to die either, my friend, but we are fighting for time—nothing else. Each minute we give the wagons is more than a minute, for they will continue to travel while the guerrillas are catching up."

"But you said yourself they wouldn't have much chance, even if they made it to the place you told them about!"

"That is true. But a small chance is better than no chance."

Cogan leveled his pistol and sighted through it. The guerrillas were still out of range. He looked over at Esteban. "Why the hell should those bastards go around when they can charge right through us?"

"That is the beauty of this place, amigo. They can charge through us, but it will cost them many men. We must teach them that. Then they will say, 'Why should we lose so many men, when it will take but a few minutes to circle the hills and attack from the rear?' So, you see, we have found a place to defend that is perfect—if we can hold back the first attack."

Cogan took a big breath and sighed. "I'm glad you didn't lead Shelby's outfit. We wouldn't have made it past Piedras Negras."

Esteban laughed. "Perhaps not. You—Dan, amigo, are you ready? The time has come."

Dan stared down at the guerrillas, pulling up now behind their chief. The bandit's head swiveled, as though judging the hills on either side of the road.

"Ready," Dan said. He thumbed back the hammer of his rifle and blinked, trying to clear the tired blur from his eyes. His body was one great ache. That was somehow more bearable, he thought, than all the little pains in his joints had been; but he wished he had more feel for the gun in his hands. A man shot by feel as much as by aim.

The guerrilla leader shouted up to them in Spanish and Esteban answered. The bandit laughed.

"What's so all-fired funny?" Cogan grumbled.

Esteban translated. "He said, 'Please let us through at once. We do not wish to kill you. If you surrender we will not harm you.' And I said, 'We believe you, and yet there is some doubt. Give us time to consider your offer—a day, perhaps.'"

Cogan grunted, squinched his eyes, and sighted along the pistol barrel. The guerrillas were spreading out across the road.

A yell, sharp and shrill, Indian-like, split the air. Sharp rowels dug into lather-flecked ribs and they surged upward.

Cogan's gun barked and one man fell. Another tumbled as Esteban fired. Dan took careful aim, shifting slightly to let his gun barrel swing in a short arc. He squeezed the trigger, then tried to will the bullet back into his gun; it was a clean miss.

The sheer weight of the *bandidos* was enough to carry them through the cleft if they were allowed to come close. They must lose men quickly and while they were still at a distance. But how could they be stopped, held?

Bullets sang around Dan and showered him with gravel. He thrust one revolver in his belt and cocked the other. He climbed to his feet, rounded the boulder that protected him, and began staggering down the hill. Manuel shouted something, but Dan stumbled on, hugging the bank to his right. He tripped, caught his balance, rushed on. A bullet burned across his leg. Would Maehler count it as a wound? he wondered. Another tore a jagged chunk from his left arm. He gained speed, rushed downward on wobbly legs, slipped and sank to his knees.

His pistol came up and roared. A bandit flew off his horse. The gun spoke again and again. The feel was back. The heavy recoil was good. He blasted and men tumbled. The charge slowed and guerrillas twisted their horses from the center of the road.

The empty gun slid from Dan's fingers. He dragged the other from his belt and fired. A man pulled up, yelled, turned his horse. He met others head on. Confusion began to spread.

Two guerrillas surged directly toward Dan, cutting at an angle across the road. He chopped one from his saddle. Ignoring the second he fired back at the main group.

The charging guerrilla bore down. Dan clicked his empty pistol at him. A musket blasted in his face. He felt no pain but the world grew too bright, took on many colors, turned dark. A great weight crushed his body and he rolled. A gun butt numbed his shoulder. He heard shouts from below. They were rallying, gathering to charge again.

His eyes could make out dark cloth. His fingers found a rock and smashed out. A groan showered his face with spit and he swung again.

The weight sank from him and he fumbled a shiny pistol from the black belt. His vision fought against the burn of the powder flash and he emptied the gun at the throng below.

"Dan! Dan!" He dimly heard Esteban's voice, shouting his name over and over again. He raised his head and looked up toward him.

"Dan! You must hurry back! Hurry! Hurry!"

He pushed away from the body, found one of his own empty pistols and began to crawl up the hill. Sharp rocks dug into his knees. The pain grew unbearable and forced him to his feet. He rocked, staggered on, risking a glance over his shoulders. The guerrillas had not rallied; they were drawing back.

"Dan! Dan! You must hurry!"

He saw Manuel clearly now, then Cogan. He bent his body forward to help his legs make the climb. His free hand dug into the dirt and he climbed upward like a wounded animal. He reached the boulder, sank against it, and slid onto the ground.

"—my friend," Esteban was saying, "it was a foolish thing. But magnificent. If they do not charge again it was worth any risk."

Dan's breath slowed and his head began to clear. He looked up; Cogan was watching him closely from his huddled position beyond Esteban.

"Dan," he said, "there's something I . . . want to tell you. You've got to . . . to try and understand."

"We have won!" Esteban interrupted excitedly. "We have won! Look, ten horsemen are starting around the hill! The others are settling to wait!"

"Won!" Cogan said bitterly. "Now they'll circle and . . . shoot you in the back . . . cut you up in little pieces!"

Dan had begun to reload. He was busily poking powder

into blackened cylinders when he realized Cogan was muttering on and on. "What the hell are you talking about?" he asked.

"The way Bill . . . got killed," Cogan answered. "But you wouldn't understand. Nobody would."

Dan placed the leaden balls on the cylinders and began to lever them down. "It won't make a lot of difference now," he said, "but if you want to talk about it—"

"You wouldn't have whipped me," Cogan said, "if it hadn't been for my nose."

Dan found himself grinning. "Under the circumstances I can afford for you to think that, if it makes you happy."

Cogan said furiously, "It's true, damn it! It's true!" His words became dull again. "It got busted when I was a little kid. Sometimes, on a hot day, I'd go out of my mind. Couldn't breathe at all."

"You're just about out of your head now," Dan said. "You'd better stop talking and rest."

"No. I've got to say it. We got into this fight, Bill and me. I . . . I didn't do like you said. I couldn't leave him. This Greas—" he looked at Esteban—"this Mexican—he pulled a knife when Bill touched his gun. One grabbed me. Another hit me in the nose. It—Dan, you don't know what it's like. For just one second, before it swelled, I could breathe. I . . . I never dreamed it could be so good. I couldn't stand for it to be hit again. I ran."

His eyes fell. "I came back but it was all over. I almost killed myself . . . then I thought . . . it was your work. You knew we'd be there. You hired somebody to do it. So it wasn't my fault, no matter what I'd done."

As he rocked his head forward into a big hand, a fusillade of shots broke out from below them and bullets sang off the rocks.

"Answer them, Dan," Esteban said. "One or two shots so they will know we are still here."

Dan levered down the last of the bullets and snapped a quick unaimed shot.

266

"Dan," Cogan said, "I brought you a letter and then forgot it. That first night. Been carrying it. A sackful of mail was shipped to Mexico City. Hit us just right."

Dan looked over at him, saw the letter in his fingers. Cogan clutched it tightly. Manuel saw his position, shook him. Cogan rolled over.

"He is dead," Manuel announced softly. "He was bleeding to death while he talked." His hand sketched the sign of the cross and he said softly, "Rest in peace, amigo." He gently took Cogan's gun.

"I wish I'd been a little easier on him a minute ago," Dan said. "He was right when he said I couldn't have whipped him except for his nose."

Manuel shrugged. "He does not care now."

"Manuel—the letter. Throw it."

Manuel fired once at the guerrillas, took the envelope and sailed it. Dan reached for it on the ground, tore it open. He read part of it, paused to shoot once, read on.

When he had come to the end he said, "It's from my sister. I gave her my ranch and she thanks me for it. She appreciates me thinking of the kids, she says. Gene—her husband—went to look at it right away. There wasn't any ranch, he said. The buildings were burned, the stock driven away. He says all the Indians left was ground, and that's cheap in Texas. He . . . doesn't want it." He said thoughtfully, "The Indians didn't range that far before the war."

Manuel said, "If I could comfort you . . . but I can say only that the land will not remain idle forever. Someone will have it, will use it."

Dan felt a touch of anger. "Someone like Reed Marman and Mavis? It could be. Manuel, do you think they'll make it? Will they get their money, go home—have everything the way they want it?"

"There is no doubt. You could not stop them now, even if you left this minute." He shook his head. "Ah, those two. I am only glad that they will be in your country and not mine."

There was an impatient stirring below and Manuel shot down at the *bandidos*.

"My friend, tell me, you worry about these things? You concern yourself with your ranch, with Marman, with Mavis Todd?"

"Yes, I guess I do."

"I, also, still concern myself," Manuel said. "It is a strange thing." He seemed to ponder the quirks of his own nature. "Once you asked me why I continue to fight, why I remain a soldier. I have thought about it."

"And the answer?"

"Not a very brilliant one. I do it for my poor, torn country. It deserves much and gets little. I must fight the French, guerrillas—whoever seeks to destroy the nation. Until we are united, or until I am dead and can fight no more."

He shot twice, idly.

"You, Dan. Does it matter now that you did not serve with Shelby?"

"Yes, it still matters."

"But . . . suppose it is over with now? Say that Maximilian did not wish to use the Iron Brigade."

"It still matters." The guerrillas were so far beyond pistol range that it was useless to aim at them. Dan took aim at a leaf about forty yards away and squeezed the trigger. The leaf fluttered wildly as it was torn from the tree and he felt a small satisfaction. "If I had rejoined them yesterday I would have stayed with them as long as they lasted. Ten years, if need be, or longer. At the same time, five minutes would have helped, if it were the last five minutes. Either way, I'd have done all I could."

Esteban nodded with understanding. "I have thought about that, too. It is a thing we all want—to wipe away the mistakes of the past with a single blow. But it is not so easy a thing. Most of us, we must keep the past, hold onto it, live with it. Because, if we spend today working for

268

yesterday, then tomorrow we must make up for today. It is a never-ending thing."

"You have been thinking a lot," Dan said. He strained his hearing. "Manuel, are they coming? I think I hear them."

Manuel cocked his head, listening. "No, I hear nothing. What will we do, amigo, when they come? Something foolish, perhaps? We could charge—die with much glory and give them something to remember. Many of the Brigade, I am sure, would do this."

Dan smiled. "I guess you're right about some of the others. But I never did go in for that kind of thing myself. I'd rather stick here. There's something I haven't wanted to think about, but I can't put it off any longer. Will Jane—all of them—have a chance now?"

"A chance," Manuel said with satisfaction. "They will make it to the place I spoke of."

"Are your guns all loaded? I know I hear them now."

"Not all, but enough." The hoofbeats began to pound louder and Manuel looked up along the road at their backs. He peered intently.

"No man who lives can have everything he wants," he said finally.

"What do you mean by that?"

"I think now that you will live, but you will never have your five minutes with Shelby."

Dan looked around, stared, and a lump swelled in his throat so quickly that it clamped his breath.

A detachment of cavalry—more than thirty men in gray uniforms—was riding steadily toward them. Maehler and Sergeant Walcott were in the lead. Directly behind them was Sherm—and Jane.

They rode over the high ground, in no particular hurry now, and stopped their horses to look down at Manuel and Dan.

"Well, you son of a bitch," Walcott said, "you got yourself into it, didn't you?" He touched his cap in Jane's direction. "Your pardon, ma'am. We picked her up," he added, "riding back here by herself. Damned if that wouldn't have been something! . . . Begging your pardon again."

"What happened?" Dan demanded. "Did Shelby send you? Or is it over with?"

"We'll go into that," Walcott said. "Are you resting, or trying to hold this road?"

Esteban got up. "Ten horsemen are coming around the hills. They are almost here, and do not know that you are with us. We must strike from ambush. And you, Sergeant,"—his black eyes twinkled—"please do not give the orders. We wish to surprise them and I have heard your voice."

Walcott grinned. "All right. You seem to have been doing pretty good. Tell us how you want it."

Esteban motioned for some of the men to take the horses over the brow of the hill. The others he ordered to fan out along the road, to use every depression, tree, bush, for concealment. He breathed his admiration as they began to move in a businesslike, professional way.

Jane surrendered her horse along with the others and walked gravely to Dan. He got up to face her.

"I remembered something," she said. "I remembered that I wouldn't be alive if it weren't for you. I thought maybe I'd find you lying along the road some place; I thought maybe I could help."

"Does Wil know you're here?" Dan asked. "He'll be worried."

"He thinks I'm at the rear of the train. I told him I would be when I borrowed the horse. But the soldiers passed them, only a mile or two from where they were going. He'll know I'm all right."

"We've got things to talk about."

Her eyes began to fill. "I said I wouldn't be caught in a web of your lies. Now I'll . . . I'll listen to anything you say."

270

He took her in his arms, held her for a m.. guided her to the safety of a boulder. He crouched a looking along the road. He saw no signs of the soldiers. The ambush was complete.

Stillness reigned, was broken by muffled hoofs. The horsemen appeared, riding cautiously forward. One dashed out in a quick semicircle to draw fire, but none came.

The rest of them came on, confident, certain. They rode within rifle range. Faces resolved themselves, individual expressions could be seen clearly. Men who did not fear death themselves were ready to mete it out with calm thoroughness.

"Fire!" Esteban shouted.

The volley broke out like the thunder of cannon. Nine of the men tumbled from their saddles, and the one, spared by some quirk, looked unbelieving. He had one instant to dwell on his surprise and then pistols spit at him and he seemed to draw together. His horse bolted, leaving him to fall lifeless.

Down below the hill the rest of the guerrillas were casually preparing to come forward. One yelled up and Esteban answered.

The guerrilla listened, thought, spun about to the others and talked rapidly.

"I told them it was done, over with," Esteban said. "But he knew my voice. They will continue to wait, to see what has happened."

The soldiers were coming out of concealment.

"All right!" Walcott roared. "Off your asses and come over here!"

Sherm was with the first little group that came to Dan.

"Sherm—what happened? What caused you to come?"

"Hell," he said, "we didn't have nothin' else to do, an' that's the straight of it." He sounded a lot like Maehler, who came up alongside him.

"Ol' Maxl, he told Shelby thanks," Maehler said, "but he don't want his beloved country torn to hell in a fight ally he began to realize that the train was preparing to move out. He heard a groan to his right and turned his head. Esteban was sitting up, rubbing the back of his neck and grimacing.

"I am one big ache," Manuel announced mournfully. "Only the smell of coffee makes me rise from my bed of pain."

Dan sat up gingerly and agreed with him. Then Jane brought them each a steaming cup of coffee and they forgot their muscles.

Jane's smile seemed to Dan like a special kind of daybreak.

"We're ready to pull out," she announced. "We let you sleep as long as we could." Her hand lingered on Dan's. "I love you," she whispered.

Esteban cleared his throat. "I will saddle the horses."

They watched him move away, carrying his coffee with him.

"I'm awful," Jane said. "They're saddled and I didn't tell him." She remained close to him until she could take his emptied cup. "We're all going straight to Mexico City," she said. "The soldiers were telling us last night that the Emperor thinks he'll grant land for a Southern city next to the main railroad. Shelby thinks he might settle there."

Dan got up and flexed himself. "I'd rather go back to Texas. The whole South, the West, all of it needs building and rebuilding. It will be a job," he answered.

She nodded gravely, put a few things away into the wagon, and they walked hand in hand to their horses.

"We're taking Cogan back to bury him alongside Bill," she said, misty-eyed. "I'm not sure why, exactly, but it will make all of us feel better."

The soldiers were already mounting, beginning to pull onto the road.

"In a way," she said, "I'm glad Maximilian turned them down—even glad about the colony. Now all of us can start

273

over again. Nobody can, really, until they admit they're beaten."

The wagons lurched into motion and the heavy rumble and clatter began. Wil Morgen's own wagon was bringing up the rear now, and he was checking the others onto the road.

He seemed pleased this morning. With the colonists settling so near a railroad, Dan thought, Wil wouldn't feel obligated to stay in Mexico more than a few weeks. For the first time since he had married he was free to come and go as he liked without a troubled conscience. He would probably show up at the ranch every few years to say hello and then drift away again whenever the wanderlust struck him.

Jane motioned for Dan to ride on ahead and he knew she wanted to talk to Wil, to reassure herself one last time that he didn't really need her any longer.

The wagons were beginning to stretch out as Dan pulled up alongside Colonel Dutton. An ex-Congressman named Williamson was riding with Dutton. He was a thin, wrinkled shell of a man who had lost his wagon somewhere along the road.

The colonel called to him. "We're having an argument, Kilbourne. Come and listen and tell us what you think."

Dan came closer.

"I say," the colonel explained, "that we can build us a town right here that will be just like home was before the war."

"And I say," Williamson cut in, "that you can't build a wall to fence out the rest of Mexico."

"I'm inclined to agree with Mr. Williamson," Dan said, "but I wish luck to both of you."

He waved and spurred up ahead to talk to Maehler. They hadn't really wanted an opinion—just a new audience.

Maehler was riding with Esteban, Sherm and Walcott.

"Pop," Dan said, pulling up to him, "what will all of you do?"

"Why, the outfit started to talk about it the minute we got the word. Lots will settle here with Shelby, farmin' an' such. Some'll ship out, goin' wherever the ships go. Some'll go back home, an' some are bound to be soldiers, no matter who they fight for. There's thirty-one of us here, an' we got thirty different opinions."

"Who's in agreement?"

"Me an' Sherm. We're shippin' out somewheres, don't much give a damn where. That French Marshal Bazaine told somebody he was goin' to give us each a few dollars to go on. We haven't got ours yet, but I reckon his word's good."

Walcott was not trying to join in the conversation, was not meeting anybody's eye.

"What about you, Sergeant?" Dan asked.

Some of the other soldiers were crowding up to them now and Walcott seemed strangely reluctant. He glanced over his shoulder at the men behind him.

"I'll tell you one thing," he bellowed. "Anybody who laughs will get butted in his God-damned belly!" He let this take effect. "I was cut out to be a soldier. I like soldiering. But I can't speak French or Spanish and I don't think I could learn. That doesn't leave me much choice. Maybe I'll go back to Missouri and after things settle some . . . well . . . how do you think I'd look in blue?"

"I think they could find something to fit you," Dan grinned.

"I'm goin' home an' to hell with any kind of uniform!" somebody said from behind them.

"Me, too!" another said emphatically.

"Hell," Maehler snorted, "you'll keep your uniform in a sandalwood box and brag about it, is what you mean."

Esteban said, "I, too, was cut out to be a soldier. I will take enlistments for all those who wish to join Juarez."

One of the soldiers expressed interest and Manuel promptly dropped back to talk to him.

"Dan," Maehler said, "the way I see it, we got into a kind of trap—this whole outfit. When Lee surrendered, his men was right there. The same with Johnston. At least lots of 'em were. But us in the West, hell, we didn't get bunched up and whipped there at the last like them others. We was supposed to go an' surrender ourselves, an' we just couldn't believe it was over."

"Maybe we were the lucky ones," Dan said. "We got it out of our systems."

Jane was galloping up to them and Maehler smiled at her and touched his hat.

"You can talk," he said. "She was what you wanted all along, an' you finally had sense enough to see it. Them others was lucky, too, the ones that sold the guns and got the money."

Esteban had come back to Dan's elbow.

"It is good to be rich," he agreed. "But they will gamble again and again. Perhaps one day . . ."

"You're only hopin'," Maehler said.

"Maybe. But I think Dan is the lucky one. And Jane." She was beside him now. "This is a glorious time of life for them," Manuel said. "Much lies ahead. They must fight Indians, *bandidos*, people like Marman and his so-beautiful wife. There will sometimes be sickness, and bad weather. There will be the birthing and rearing of children, and always much work." He smiled at Dan. "How I envy you, my friend, for the struggle which lies ahead of you, for the uncertainty you face!"

Dan grinned. "Manuel, I'm not sure if you believe all you're saying, or if you've been around Maehler so long you're beginning to spread lies like he does."

"Someday you will look back and know if I speak the truth. You will have new memories to replace the ones which are bad. You will remember with pride the moment you sat in front of Shelby's barracks and chose to help Jane instead of yourself."

"And I suppose from time to time," Dan said, "I'll wonder if I made the right choice."

"For that," Jane said, "you can just ride without my company." She spurred her horse forward, and Dan grinned and raced after her.

Let Esteban preach about the struggle ahead. It was real enough, but there would be lighter moments, too, and moments of tenderness and warmth, and these alone were worth all the rest.

# EPILOGUE

ALTHOUGH SHELBY'S ARMY was disbanded in August of 1865, Confederate immigration to Mexico continued to increase until the spring of 1866, when it was effectively stopped by General Sheridan.

In June of 1866, the colony of Carlota, where Shelby and a number of his men had settled, was destroyed by Juaristas, and the colonists were driven out.

Maximilian continued to support the Southerners. An attempt was made to start other colonies, one of which was Tuxpan, where Shelby again enacted a major role. This, too, failed, as the French withdrew and left it without protection.

Increasing numbers of the Confederates began to return to the United States. Although Captain Wirz, Commandant at Andersonville, was tried, condemned and hanged, war trials as such were not taking place; official Yankee vengeance was not being exacted. Even Jefferson Davis (with Horace Greeley on his bail bond) was released after a short imprisonment.

Shortly before the death of Maximilian, Shelby returned to Missouri, where he became a man of great influence. Years later his testimony was largely responsible for the acquittal of Frank James, who once had been a member of Shelby's Missouri Cavalry.

Shelby's latter years were spent in Kansas City, Missouri, where he served, until his death in 1897, as United States Marshal for Western Missouri.

A new concept
in a reference work
designed to help clear
up the two most
troublesome areas of
the English language

# Words
# Most Often
# Misspelled and
# Mispronounced

by RUTH GLEESON and JAMES COLVIN

GIANT CARDINAL EDITION GC • 613/60¢

If your bookseller does not have this
title, you may order it by sending
retail price, plus 10¢ for mailing
and handling to: MAIL SERVICE
DEPARTMENT, Pocket Books, Inc.,
1 West 39th Street, New York
18, N. Y. Please enclose
check or money order—
do not send cash.

PUBLISHED BY
POCKET BOOKS, INC. pb

"The best piece of comic literature in the last twenty years."—JACK PAAR

# A FUNNY THING HAPPENED TO ME ON MY WAY TO THE GRAVE

### the life story of a professional funnyman

by

PERMABOOK EDITION M • 5065/50¢

# JACK DOUGLAS

### author of

NEVER TRUST A NAKED BUS DRIVER—M • 4211/35¢
MY BROTHER WAS AN ONLY CHILD—M • 4170/35¢

If your bookseller does not have these titles, you may order them by sending retail price, plus 10¢ for postage and handling to: MAIL SERVICE DEPT., Pocket Books, Inc., 1 West 39th Street, New York 18, N.Y. Enclose check or money order—do not send cash.

PUBLISHED BY
POCKET BOOKS, INC.  pb